The THIRD Strand

BOOK II IN "THE OMEGA WATCHERS" SERIES - THE END HAS BEGUN

JANE E. WOODLEE HEDRICK

xulon
PRESS

ACKNOWLEDGEMENTS

Without the encouragement of my husband, Russell, this sequel would not have come to fruition. Many life circumstances crossed our paths the last two years causing the stops and restarts of creative writing. They were wonderful life events of family marriages and new grandchildren added; however, it made research and concentration very difficult. Russell was my biggest supporter in pressing forward and finishing the sequel I had started. Every day I thank my Heavenly Father for my wonderful soulmate who is not only my husband - but also my best friend.

A special thank you to my daughter-in-law Dreama Hedrick who has been with me every step of the way since the genesis of being an author. Her editing and honest feedback have been invaluable.

For technical and military dialogue, I thank Richard Everts who also has edited and advised me through writing both novels. His seemingly unlimited knowledge of technology astounds me. I am blessed to call him one of my dearest friends.

My first novel allowed me to reconnect after many years with Nathan Brotman, son of my dear friend the late Manny Brotman and step-son of Sandra Sheskin Brotman who inspired the name Sandee for my novel. Manny was a Jewish man who came to know Yeshua (Jesus) as his Messiah in the 1950's. He founded the Messianic Jewish Movement International and is considered a Father in the Messianic movement. He was one of the Godliest men I have ever known and the inspiration for my character the Professor. Nathan and I spent many hours discussing the more "edgy" topics of current events and their possible connection to bible prophecy.

We are truly of like mind on topics we love to study and research. Thank you, Nathan, for inspiring the title of this book and all your input.

For Hebraic edits on spelling and proper use of terminology I thank my Hebrew teacher, Tim Herron. Studying God's Word from the original language has opened a greater depth of understanding on so many levels.

After the creative writing and first edits, I had several dear friends willing to take their valuable time to read with fresh eyes and find areas that needed corrections. First, Mary Jo Dean offered valuable edits and honest advice, which was greatly needed and appreciated. When "The Third Strand" was in the final stages Linda Everts, Cornelia Stone and Douglas Woodlee were my test readers. Each of you were vital in the final critiquing. It truly "takes a village to raise a child". Thank you!

I thank my pastors, Michael Addison and Paula Farmer, for their encouragement and prayers on this journey as an author. To all readers of "The Omega Watchers" who have given me wonderful feedback for my first novel and encouraged me to continue with the sequel, I cannot express the depth of my gratitude.

ABOVE ALL, *Soli Deo Gloria, **TO GOD BE THE GLORY!***

INTRODUCTION

---•◆•◆•◆•---

"For then shall be great tribulation, such as was not since the beginning of the world to this time, no, nor ever shall be." Matthew 24:21 (KJV)

Matthew Chapter 24 is the prophetic 'outline' given by Jesus (Yeshua in Hebrew) to his disciples for end time events. All other prophetic scriptures relating to the time of the great tribulation fill in the details somewhere in this outline.

In Verse 3 Yeshua's disciples ask: *"Tell us," they said, "when will this happen, and what will be the sign of your coming and of the end of the age?"*

This is the question that has challenged the minds of bible scholars for 2000 years.

Those who diligently study eschatology all have their opinions on the timelines of end time prophecy. Varying hypotheses exist of how these events will come to fulfillment (when, where, how...), all with seemingly valid Bible references for a good argument.

After decades of study and research, I still do not assume to know all the answers. What I do know is prophecy *will* be fulfilled. We already see many prophetic events taking place on the world stage. I believe the most important prophecy is the rebirth of Israel as a nation, marking the *"generation that will not pass away until all these things be fulfilled"* (*Matthew 24:34*). If I am correct the events in this book, the final seven years foretold by Daniel the Prophet, will soon start to unfold revealing the prophetic truths.

'The Third Strand' is a fiction novel. It does not take the position of predicting how events will actually play out. However, the prophecies in this book will in some form become reality as the False Prophet and the Antichrist take their position fulfilling Revelation 13. Readers, we are truly approaching the end of days and the Second Coming of Yeshua Ha Mashiach (Jesus the Messiah) to set up His Kingdom and rule and reign upon the earth.

My prayer is this novel will challenge each reader to follow the prophetic signs and, above all, be ready to meet The Lord. "We know not the day nor the hour."

Contact: janeehedrick@hotmail.com
Facebook: The Omega Watchers – Jane E. Woodlee Hedrick, Author
Blog: http://janeehedrick.blogspot.com/

CHAPTER 1

Gabriella's eyes flew open. Everything was a blur as she struggled to focus. The voices she heard while sleeping were ringing loud and clear in her head. She could hear her father crying, "I was wrong, Gabi, I was wrong about everything." Mingled with his voice was Caleb's: "Wake up, Gabi, I don't want to leave you. Please wake up before it's too late."

She sat straight up in the bed and screamed, "Caleb!"

The Israeli police officer assigned to protect the now-missing mysterious research team came running into Gabriella's room with panic in his eyes. "You're awake, Gabriella. Thank heaven you're awake!" She could see the fear on his face and knew immediately there was much to be afraid of.

"Oh, my God!" Her entire body was shaking. She could not hold back the panic riveting her as she surveyed the room. "They are gone. They are *all* gone. I must be dreaming. I have to be dreaming."

Gabriella's crystal blue eyes penetrated the officer's soul. He cautiously sat down on the side of her bed, trying desperately to conceal his own panic. Struggling to find the police demeanor needed, he made a fruitless effort to calm the situation. All that he could muster was a facade of being in control. "What do you mean, all gone?"

She just shook her head as tears flowed and her body vibrated in agony.

He took her trembling hand. "Do you mean the team? Do you know where they've gone?" He was making every effort to not lose self-control.

Gabriella could not control her emotions enough to speak. Then, struggling to take deep breaths between sobs, she looked around the unfamiliar room. The tranquil green walls had no windows, and pictures that hung there were now lying on the floor. The rustic wood furniture anchored the room with a feeling of home, but it felt like a vacated home. Books were scattered on the stone floor next to the corner table. The rocking chair that recently held Gabriella's beloved Caleb now sat empty and motionless next to her bedside. Next to the nightstand was a lamp that had fallen on the floor. She noticed a stack of papers in perfect order on the bedside table, miraculously unmoved.

Gabriella took a deep breath and exhaled her next words: There was an earthquake, wasn't there?" The officer nodded, affirming what she already knew. "I could hear things that were happening even though I couldn't respond." She continued to tremble but was gaining a meager measure of self-control.

"Help me up, please." He took both hands and pulled her to a seated position on the edge of the bed. Gabriella's head was dizzy from days of lying in bed in what the policer officer thought was a coma. Her legs felt weak, but she sensed an unfamiliar strength begin to flow.

Still in a daze, she gazed at the stack of papers on the nightstand. Reaching for the one on top, an ill-boding reality was engulfing her. With the first page, her eyes widened and the color drained from her face. "It's all true. It wasn't a dream...it's all true." She looked up at the officer, a virtual stranger to her, with pleading eyes to tell her it was not so. "My father was alive, wasn't he? He was right here in this very room."

His eyes told her all she needed to know. He barely nodded his head in affirmation.

Gabriella clutched the papers to her chest in horrid disbelief and allowed the tears to flow like a river. She did not know this man, but she did not care if he witnessed her raw agony. She no longer cared what anyone thought.

"But he's gone with all the rest?" Her voice was barely audible as her mind grappled to process the truth. After twelve years of believing her father was dead, he had been beside Gabriella, within reach, but she was unable to touch him.

Officer Harris knew this police assignment had gone far beyond the norm. With his mind spinning in every direction trying to find some reasonable explanation for the team's disappearance, the officer wanted and needed to maintain a professional composure.

As Officer Harris sat in the bedside chair, watching her clutch the papers as if clinging to life itself, he knew he had to be strong in spite of the collapsing world around them. He was assigned to protect her team, and although there was no reasonable explanation to their disappearance, he was determined to solve the mystery.

Gabriella looked up at him and the sorrow in her eyes wrenched his heart. He fought back tears of compassion. He kept his jaw firm so as not to reveal any weakness.

"The letters are from your father." He spoke with a kind voice. "He said they would give you detailed instructions on the days ahead. I wasn't sure what he meant, but he said the letters would explain everything."

She quickly thumbed through the stack. It was just as expected. Gabriella had heard her father's voice while she was sleeping telling her he would leave instructions of what to do, what not to do, and how to survive the worst days that will ever come upon the earth.

"If only for a moment I could have seen him, touched him, and told him how much I love him." The words echoed in her mind with an empty resolve.

She rocked back and forth, remembering the final words of her father vibrating clear in her soul: "I was wrong, Gabi! I was wrong about everything! What seemed to be truth was all a lie and I was caught up in the great deception. Use the truth discovered in your project to reveal the identity of the evil one that will declare himself to be the Messiah."

"I will, daddy, I will." She whispered under her breath, determined to complete the mission Professor Brotman had begun.

Her father's final words solidified her determination. *"Perhaps you were chosen for such a time as this."*

She looked at the young officer. Several times he ran his hands through his black hair in a nervous gesture. Obviously, he was at a total loss of what to say or do and was trying to contain his own apprehensions in an effort to not alarm her.

"Where are we? What day is it? How long was I..." she paused not sure how to explain to this stranger her paranormal journey. "Please tell me everything that happened after..." Gabriella took a deep frustrated breath. Would he even believe her? How do you tell someone you have traveled through time and that you have seen the portals to both heaven and hell? He would never believe that Satan himself had lured her to the brink of external destruction before her soul was caught in untime, a vacuum where time does not exist. Had she not lived it, she would not have believed it herself.

"I'll fill you in on all the details, but first you need to eat something." He got up from the chair and left the room. "I'll be right back. Will you be okay for a few minutes?"

Gabriella nodded her head and watched him leave. Collapsing backwards on the bed and struggling to prop her head against the wooden headboard, she continued to clutch her father's handwritten letters. Looking around the room, she could not believe that only minutes ago, everyone she loved was gathered around her bed, praying she would awaken.

Gabriella had heard their voices as her soul slowly returned to her body. She had tried to reach to them, but not a single muscle could be forced to move. The sting of tears burned again in her eyes remembering Caleb calling to the others that she was crying, happily believing and declaring she was still with them. Then the earth started to shake and in an instant, they were all gone. Everyone she loved had vanished in the twinkling of an eye.

Officer Harris returned with a tray of cereal and juice. "Try to eat something," he commented gently, setting the tray in her lap. He sat down in the chair beside her. "I don't know if you remember me. We briefly met when we all arrived at the lodge. It was shortly after that..." He was not sure how to finish the sentence regarding her comatose state.

"Thank you for the food," she replied, although she had no appetite. "And, yes, I do remember you. I believe you work with Detective Richards." She stirred the oatmeal and took small bites, gazing into the air, seeing nothing. With agony of soul, she was reliving every moment before and after her awakening.

The officer sat motionless and silent allowing her time to mentally process all that had happened. He also was reliving his assignment in an effort to bring sanity to the current situation. All efforts were failing.

After a few minutes, Gabriella set the tray to the side. She looked at his kind face and admitted her fear. "For the first time in my life, I have no idea what I'm going to do. I feel totally lost." Her blue eyes stared ahead, seeing nothing.

He held up his hand in a gesture of knowing the next step. He left the room again, returning with a book in his hand. She immediately recognized Professor Brotman's research journal for The Omega Watchers Project.

With wide-eyed anticipation, she exclaimed, "Does it have the Professor's final translation of the ancient writings? We worked on that project for years. I wasn't sure if we would ever see it come to fruition."

In spite of the anxiety and uncertainty of the circumstances, the officer smiled. His dark brown eyes gleamed as he spoke the words she was longing to hear, "Yes, Gabriella, your project was completed."

She handed him the food tray in exchange for the journal. "Do you know what it says? Were you there when the translation was finally read?"

"Yes, I was." He sat back down beside her. "However, I won't even pretend to understand what's going on or what any of it means. It's all new to me but there is no doubt it's all very real." An expression of deep regret spread across his face. "If only I had listened to Caleb." He dropped his head into his hands and muttered under his breath again, "Caleb tried to tell me."

Just hearing the love of her life's name sent a stab through her heart. "Caleb" Gabriella whispered. "The only man I ever loved is gone." Pain filled her face, as she remembered how she had pushed him away. "He truly loved me and I allowed my pride and refusal to see the truth separate us. I wouldn't listen to any of them. It's too late for us now." She looked with penetrating eyes into the sorrowful eyes of the officer. "Do you realize that? It is too late for us!" Her words rang with a veracity that cut through the body, soul, and spirit.

The raw truth was beginning to completely set in. Gabriella had awakened from her astral sleep with the full stark knowledge the end had begun. The great tribulation, the final seven years, the rise of the anti-Messiah, the outpouring of God's wrath...they were entering into the end of days and there was nothing they could do now to escape.

Satan and his fallen angels were about to be released upon the earth. The great deception had begun.

"I want to go back to sleep," Gabriella stammered. "I want to wake up again and be with those I love...but I know it's too late."

CHAPTER 2 -

Gabriella struggled to sit up on the side of the bed. Officer Harris held her arm as she attempted to steady herself.

Beyond her bedroom door was the sound of a TV reporter broadcasting breaking news. It was the same tone of voice she had heard as she was awakening. The reporter's trepidation was obvious as he gave the reports.

He continued to update the listening public: "The shofars that sounded all around Jerusalem, at the last trump of Rosh Hashanah, are now silent. The sun has gone down over the City of David. At this present time, there are no sounds of explosions or new attacks. A few brave souls are venturing out of their bunkers to assess the damage to their homes and communities. We are continuing to receive reports from around the world of mass devastation in all countries and of millions of people who have simply vanished. We are waiting for an official statement from the United Nations, which has called world leaders to an emergency session. Unconfirmed sources tell us this historic meeting is being held at the Vatican. This is totally unprecedented!" His voice momentarily went silent as he struggled to compose himself. With an anxious voice, he muttered, "The world will never be the same."

Gabriella thought about Caleb's parents in Germany. Did they survive? They were going to be her new family. They were welcoming her as the daughter they never had. Were they gone too? Was there anyone left who cared about her? The soulful pain was sickening as she accepted the fact that nothing would ever be normal again.

She held the side of the night stand for balance and attempted to stand. Office Harris continued to hold her arm while she took small, measured steps towards the living room.

"Where are we?" Her voice was filled with apprehension as she managed to negotiate the distance to the sea-blue sofa where she collapsed to survey her surroundings.

"We're safe here, Gabriella," he assured her. "Your father built this bunker as a secure hiding place in the event anyone discovered his true identity."

"His true identity?" Her eyes left observing the room to look straight at the young officer. Her stare demanded answers. "Tell me everything. Don't leave out a single detail, Officer."

Officer Harris sat down next to her, muted the television, and began to slowly explain. He was concerned how she would mentally adjust to the news.

"First of all, please call me Chris. Is it okay if I call you Gabi?" She nodded her head, observing the man that sat next to her. He was obviously physically strong and a good police officer or he would not have been assigned to protect their research team. His words seemed genuinely caring and tender compared to his <u>tenacious</u> face. "Gabi, do you remember why I'm here?"

She nodded as he continued, "I had no idea the multitude of twists and turns this assignment would take. It was just another mundane assignment, or so I thought. I quickly realized, however, there was something very different about this group of people I was protecting. It was out of the ordinary and it took me a little while to get my head wrapped around what was really going on."

Gabriella could see he had been deeply affected by the events of the last few days as she verified his words. "Yes, you are absolutely right, Chris. The Professor had been working on a secret project for many years, even before I joined his research team over ten years ago. He was one of the translators of the Dead Sea Scrolls. Did you know that?"

"Yes, Dr. Brotman told me that when the final translations were being read. He must have been an amazing man."

Gabriella felt tears sting her eyes as Chris referred to the Professor in the past tense. "Amazing doesn't even begin to describe him. He was one of the top linguists in the world and his translations of the Dead Sea

Scrolls opened a prophetic door that he was never able to walk away from. It consumed him." Her voice echoed the pain of loss welling inside her.

Chris's face filled with both perplexity and sincere interest.

Gabriella continued, "A large portion of the Dead Sea Scrolls was from the Book of Enoch, which many do not consider an authentic book since it isn't in the canonized bible. In his translations; however, Dr. Brotman discovered an ancient prophecy from Enoch that gave a timeline for the end of days. The Professor was convinced the end of time, as we know it, was quickly approaching. He truly wanted to warn the world that a great deception was coming before it was too late. That was what the project was all about." She sighed deeply as tears cascaded over her cheeks. Breathlessly, she whispered, "Apparently, time ran out."

Her words sent a new wave of reality through Chris as he responded. "I could tell as soon as I got here there was urgency in whatever was going on. I tried not to pry, but just listen and ascertain all that I could. There was an air of mystery about the entire assignment. Detective Richards wouldn't give me any details...just said that I was assigned to protect your team while you were in hiding here at the lodge."

Gabriella reflected on the days before the vanishings. "I guess you know I was in complete rebellion to what they believed about the project. They tried to tell me, warn me; but, no, not me! I thought I was so much smarter than they were. I had the answers. I had the real truth, so I believed. I tried to keep Caleb from believing them, too. I tried to suck him into my paranormal deception. But, he wasn't deceived like I was." Her voice faded in deep regret.

"Yeah, Caleb tried to tell me, too," Chris stated grimly. "I didn't listen either."

Gabriella pushed her long blonde hair away from her eyes and hopelessly tried to compose herself as she continued her confession. "I opened myself to the world of the paranormal. At first I thought I was just having fanciful dreams, but then I realized it was much more. For a while it was all so beautiful and it was *very* real. While sleeping, my soul would leave my body. I traveled with a beautiful spirit guide, through the universe, where he taught me the mysteries of life. He convinced me there really was no death of the soul and spirit. He convinced me I could know all truth...he called it the Akashic Knowledge, the eternal knowledge of all that exists." She looked at Chris to see if he thought her crazy.

"Wow," he whispered. "I've heard of such experiences but I thought it was just the stuff of movies and paranormal quacks. So, that's what your father kept referring to. What I thought was a coma was some sort of supernatural sleep? You were actually in another dimension of time?"

Gabriella stared into the air, remembering every detail vividly. "It is where time doesn't even exist. In the spirit world, it's referred to as untime. It's what many people believe as eternity, but it can also be another dimension existing along with ours."

She turned to face Chris and her countenance changed dramatically. Her eyes were blazing. "It is real. It is very real and there is no escaping it. When we leave these human bodies, there are only two destinations. It's every person's decision where they will be forever. My spirit guide tried to convince me that wasn't so, that we were all gods and there was no Divine Creator. All we had to do was release the godhood inside us and we would become one with the universe, enter an alternate dimension of untime and live in perfect peace forever."

She hesitated, realizing how ridiculous it all sounded, but Chris encouraged her to continue.

Her voice was gaining strength as she recounted her tormenting experience: My spirit guide convinced me everyone had supernatural powers within, but had not been taught how to tap into their inner godhood. He told me I was chosen by the Ascended Master to bring that truth to the world." A sarcastic half laugh escaped her mouth, realizing she actually believed him. "It was all a deceiving lie, Chris. The Professor called it the end time great deception. I can't believe I fell for it." Her voice quivered, admitting she had fallen for the entire lie...hook, line and sinker.

He had no words to respond to her emotional turbulence. He just took her hand and encouraged her to continue. "Can you tell me the rest, Gabi? How did you find the truth?"

Her voice was tender in reflection. "It was the prayers of those who loved me. They rescued me from the convergence - the point of no return." Again, her eyes gazed into space as she relived her miraculous deliverance. "I could hear their prayers even in the dark dimension of untime. It was a multitude of prayers that became sharp, glistening swords raining down between me and total destruction. Death was drawing me into everlasting darkness. The swords became a protective wall delivering me from Abaddon, the prince of evil. The horrid fear that had captured me transformed into peace as I was drawn back into my body. The next thing I knew was the voices of those I loved, praying around my bed...even the voice of my, I thought, dead father."

Chris was amazed at her words, and yet he did not doubt a single one of them. He had seen too much in the last few days not to believe there was something far beyond man's short time on this earth.

Gabriella looked towards the TV. The sound was muted but 'breaking news' kept running across the screen. She knew there would be at least seven more years of constant breaking news, the last seven years of earthly time which the Professor Brotman called The Great Tribulation. It would be news worse than anyone could even imagine. It will be the worst days that will ever be upon the earth.

CHAPTER 3

G abriella and Chris sat quietly, reflecting on their lost opportunities and trying to wrap their minds around the circumstances by which they were captured.

"Now we both must face the horrible days ahead because we wouldn't believe, Chris." She took a deep breath, jarred by reality, and looked him straight in the eyes. "I've told you what was happening while I was asleep. Now tell me what was going on in the world around me."

Chris took her hand for a moment and squeezed it gently. Then he got up and began to pace the floor trying to remember every detail. In his police officer countenance and voice, he related the facts. "The Professor had finished the translation and he wanted all of the team to join him for the reading. He sent Caleb up to your bedroom to let you know it was time. Caleb found you lying on the floor. I remember well, he thought you were dead and he was in a state of panic. He said there had been several times you had stopped breathing in the past couple of weeks." He stopped and looked at Gabriella for confirmation.

"Yes," she admitted. "I had no idea what was happening. For no reason, I would just stop breathing. The episodes started at the same time I began to astral travel."

"Well, this time we all thought you were dead." Chris stated with guarded emotion. "The Professor checked you for a pulse and Sandee immediately called a doctor. Within minutes, and too short of time for a doctor to arrive, a man appeared that I didn't even know was on the premises. I thought he was a Hasidic Jew. He had the typical apparel, beard, et cetera."

"A Hasidic Jew?" Gabriella gasped. "It was such a man that appeared to me several times after I came back from our last cave exploration, where we found the ancient writing."

Chris nodded as he continued: "I was about to stop him from going upstairs since I had no idea who he was, but Sandee just pushed me away and they ran up to your bedroom. I had to know who he was to report back to Detective Richards. So, naturally I followed them. I stood at the door and watched it all unfold."

"What do you mean?" Gabriella was pressing. "Who was he? I have to know if he was the man I called the Prophet that appeared to me. He warned me that I was in danger and

I must be careful of the deceptions. He told me I was chosen. Tell me, Chris, who was this man?" She was at the point of begging when the mystery was finally unveiled to her.

"That man, the Hasidic Jew, was your father." Chris had dreaded this moment, fearing the emotional effects of the truth.

"What? That *can't* be." Gabriella knew Chris was totally mistaken.

His voice was firm but compassionate. "It was all a façade to protect you. He's been living here in Israel incognito, providing for and watching over you this entire time."

Her head was spinning and she felt sick to her stomach. As the surreal truth settled in her mind and heart, she felt she was going to pass out. Chris caught her as she slumped over.

It took several minutes to grasp the incredible revelation. In a voice so low Chris struggled to hear, she whispered, "Not only was he still alive, but I was actually with him when he came to me at the coffee shop in Haifa? I talked to him and didn't even know who he was?" Her voice became stronger as her reasoning was rejecting the truth. "How can that be? No, you're mistaken, Chris. You must have misunderstood. This can't be true."

Chris briefly took her hand in comfort. "He was very convincing, Gabi. The disguise was perfect and he spoke with a deep Israeli accent that camouflaged his voice completely. You thought he was dead. How could you have known?"

Gabriella tried to recall every detail of the encounter she had with him. "I do remember there was something about his eyes that felt so familiar." Slowly the bizarre truth was sinking in to her mind. "Now I understand. I also understand why I wanted so badly to see him again. Subconsciously

I must have known." Her words faded with sorrow beyond words. "I lost my only chance to be in my father's arms one more time." She could not restrain the tears any longer.

"You were in his arms, Gabi. He held you for hours and hours, praying for you. He would talk to you with endless words of love and affection. He so regretted the deception, but he felt it was the only way to protect you."

"Protect me from what? What are you talking about?" Her eyes demanded the absolute truth, holding nothing back.

Chris released her hand and got up from the couch. He once again began his police officer pace, back and forth across the stone floor, as he relayed the details. "You will probably find this part hard to believe, Gabi. Apparently, this project the Professor and your team have been working on had to have some deep pockets to finance it all these years. Your father was the person that did that."

"What do you mean? Even if my father was alive, he didn't have that kind of money. He was just a college professor. They don't make much money at all, especially not that kind of money."

"Your father apparently made some very, *very* good investments in the electronics stock market before the big explosion of technology. He said he used the life insurance money from your mother's death for the investment. Before he faked his death, he had in his will all the income would go into a trust fund. His attorney became the Executor and was advised to make monthly deposits for you, provide funds for the project, and transfer all remaining money to an Israeli bank account in the name of Eli Sheskin, which was the new identity of your father."

"Jim Tomaw was his attorney. I knew him well and was aware he was trustee; but, he knew about this? I can't believe he never said a word."

Chris shook his head. "Apparently, his attorney didn't know the truth. He thought your father really died. He just carried out the stipulations of the will. Only the funeral director and the Professor knew the truth."

She just shook her head in disbelief. "All this time and I never knew. Surely there could have been some way of him letting me know."

"Someone killed your mother because of their research. Right?"

Gabriella nodded her head. "What's that have to do with all of this?"

"After your mother was killed your father did all his research in secret. For a while he was left alone. With the new discovery, whatever that was, he knew the two of you were in great danger. It had to appear that he was out of the picture, you knew nothing, and the research project was dead. It was the only way he could protect you." Chris apparently was still confused. "I have no idea what he was talking about, but whatever he discovered was major and someone was going to make sure no one found out about it. He said it was all in the journal he left you."

"It was." She stated sadly. "He left me his research papers and told me to make sure I finished reading everything before I jumped to any conclusions. Again, I didn't listen. He was researching extraterrestrial life and its existence in the world of the paranormal. That's how I was captured by it. His journal writings opened my mind to the astral mysteries and I let it consume me. If I had read the entire journal and his letters to me, as he instructed, I would have known the truth."

She shook her head in anguish and her long blonde hair swayed from side to side. "Now I'm left alone, because of my stubbornness. I never listened to anyone. I did exactly as I pleased. Now where am I? I'm facing the end without anyone who loves me or even cares what happens to me."

"Well, at least you're not totally alone. Seems we are in this together." Chris stated emphatically, squeezing her hand in reassurance.

Her head stopped shaking and she gazed around the room, observing what was now her home. "My father built this bunker to hide in and instead it's become *my* place of safety. Now I understand how he could afford it." Then it dawned on her. "The lodge...he built that, too? So, that's why the team would come here for retreats."

Chris smiled remembering her father's words. "I had some time to talk to your father, Gabe, while we were secluded here in the bunker. He said it was a way he could be close to you and know you were all right. He would often watch you from a distance, disguised as a gardener or maintenance man, and you had no idea. He said it gave him great comfort just being close to you."

"Of course, now I understand! He and Professor Brotman were in this together from the start. Everything makes sense now." She laid back in the sofa and rested her head against the soft cushion. So many realities were dawning simultaneously. "That's what the Professor was going to tell me when he thought he was dying."

She squeezed her eyes trying focus on her new actuality. "My father was the Hasidic Jew that appeared to me. He was near me the entire twelve years. He owned this lodge. My father financed the project." Gabriella was shaking her head as all the pieces begin to fit together. "He and the Professor were working together the entire time and made sure I was part of the research." The puzzle was now complete.

She sat straight up, dropped her face into her hands and again shook her head from side to side, blonde curls bouncing with each movement. "If only I could have talked to him, everything would be different now."

She attempted to stand, but was too weak from both emotional and physical exhaustion. She collapsed back onto the sofa.

After a few moments of silence, she began to enumerate what happened just before her awakening. She closed her eyes, reliving the last moments. "Just before the earthquake, I was beginning to hear the sounds around me. I heard the words of my father and Caleb. I thought my father's voice was coming from the spirit world of untime and Caleb's from the natural world. I didn't realize they were both actually together in the room with me." She took a deep breath and slowly exhaled, keeping her eyes closed. For a moment, there was silence. Then she whispered, "It's comforting to know my dad got to know my Caleb."

She was remembering the last moments before the team's disappearance. "I also heard the voices mingled together of the Professor, Sandee, KJ, Aaron, and Faith. As I was awakening, I could hear them all. I knew beyond a doubt they really did love me and I had been a total fool. I could have gone with them and been with them forever."

She looked straight at Chris and shared from the depth of her soul. "There is an eternal life beyond this existence on earth. I have seen it. I will never doubt it again."

"We both have been fools," Chris stated emphatically. He dropped his head to conceal his agony.

Gabriella could feel warm tears rolling across her cheeks, remembering all the chances she had. Her words were barely a whisper. "We both could have gone, Chris." She echoed her words in a mere whisper, "We both could have gone."

There was a long silence as each reflected on the decisions they had made and the future they now faced, knowing there was no escape. They individually collected their thoughts and tried desperately to decide what their next steps should be.

"Chris, would you bring me the Professor's journal? After all these years of research and exploration, I must know what was discovered." Gabriella's mind was racing with the possibilities of what prophetic mysteries might be in the ancient words Dr. Brotman translated. The Professor was positive it would be a message for the end of days, the days in which she and Chris now were entering.

Chris retrieved the journal and placed it in her hands. She turned to the back of the book and found the Professor's final entries for The Omega Watchers Project. With a quivering voice, she began to read out loud:

Journal Note: The following was translated from the clay tablets given to me by the Prophet.

In the day of the great judgment, a day of terror and affliction as never seen by man, the fallen Watchers will be released from the chambers of the abyss. My two witnesses will return to proclaim truth against them. I will give power unto my two witnesses, and they shall prophesy a thousand two hundred and sixty days; and when they shall have finished their testimony, the beast that ascends out of the bottomless pit shall make war against them, and shall overcome them, and kill them. Their dead bodies shall lie in the street of the great city for three days and a half day.

Journal Note: The following was translated from the scroll given to Gabriella by the true Prophet.

They that dwell upon the earth shall rejoice for they will hate the voice of the prophets. After three days and a half day my Spirit will enter the dead bodies of my prophets and they will rise and ascend to heaven. The world will watch and be amazed. I will then send a great earthquake and I will shake the earth as it has never been shaken. The people will tremble in fear and the beast with his mark will arise and work wonders to deceive the nations. When you see Israel surrounded by her enemies and the man of false peace signs a covenant with my chosen ones, the day of the great tribulation has begun.'

Journal Note: The following was translated from the lava cave wall discovered by my research team.

"Here lies a gateway to the Grigori (Watchers), who turned aside from the Lord, 200 myriads. And who went down as prisoners in the bottomless pit, imprisoned in great darkness until the time of the great tribulation when they will be released to align with their prince Satanail before their eternal judgment."

Gabriella finished the translation and sat silently mulling over the ancient words.

"It is a true prophecy, Chris. The others are gone, just like they said it would happen. This must be true too. The Professor made a final note that connects his translations with the Bible. *II Peter 2:4 – "God did not spare **the angels who sinned**, but threw them into hell and locked them up in chains in utter darkness, to be kept **until the judgment...**"*

Chris was trying to grasp the meaning of the prophecies. "There were angels that sinned? God chained them in hell until the end of days? We are in the great judgment and the fallen angels are about to be released...now!" He took a deep breath and exhaled with a voice of anguish. "God help us!"

"You're exactly right...God help us!" Gabriella agreed with a trembling voice. "What we have to realize is that the fallen angels will not come as evil ones. They will come as deceiving angels of light, led by Satanail himself. I've already seen it. It will all look good, sound good, and be so convincingly mystifying that most of the earth will follow what the Bible calls the great deception. The Professor used to tell us only the elect would not be deceived, those who knew the truth. I used to laugh at him, thinking he was caught up in his unrealistic, religious credence. I'm not laughing anymore. Now, I know the truth!"

Chris got up and paced the stone floor. His police officer mentality was telling him to be prepared, be alert, and do not be caught off guard. Get ready for the inevitable.

"Gabi, we have to learn as much as we can about what's going to happen in these next seven years. We've got to be prepared."

Gabriella knew exactly where they had to start. "Would you get me the stack of papers on my nightstand?" she asked. Chris immediately retrieved the letters penned by her father and laid them on the coffee table in front of her. On the top was her father's journal with a note in his familiar handwriting, 'Finish reading this first.'

She motioned for Chris to sit down beside her. "My mind was awakening even before my body could move. I could hear my father talking to me. He told me he had written down everything I would need to know to face the days ahead...everything to do and not do, to make sure we are reunited at the end. His letters will be our guidebook."

She picked up his journal and stated, "First, I will finish reading this."

Gabriella turned the worn pages to the last entry written just before he faked his death.

My dearest daughter,

This will be my last journal entry and it is a personal letter to you. I want you to understand the sum of all that I have researched and the conclusions I have made.

I have made the most difficult decision of my life. I know it will break your heart, but it will also allow you to live a normal life. I will no longer have to fear losing you as I lost your mother. Someday you will read this letter and understand why I made the decisions I have and, hopefully, you will not hate me for what I have done.

I have decided (for your protection) to fake my death. Bob Donald, the funeral director, will be assisting me. He and one other person will be the only people on the face of this earth that know. I will assume a new identity. I have made sure you will be well provided for to continue your education and begin a new life.

I mentioned in my last letter I had been collaborating with a scientist on the implant. His name is Dr. Manny Brotman. He will be the only other person that knows I am faking my death and he will be assisting me to arrange for your future and safety. I believe he will become a trusted friend to you, also.

It was not until I met him the veracity of my research began to unveil. I completely understand now why the ones behind killing your mother have tried to stop me from revealing this information.

Dr. Brotman has proven to me through ancient Hebrew writings what I thought to be extraterrestrial beings were actually demonic spirits of deception. There is so much depth to this, but Manny will explain everything to you when the time is right. After all these years of hiding my research, I want you to understand both my discoveries and why I had no choice but to fake my death.

When I began making entries into this journal, DNA had only recently been discovered. Scientists were far from understanding the complex nature of the double helix strands and were convinced it could not be altered. As more research was done it became apparent some changes could be made; but what Dr. Brotman and I discovered about DNA totally changes the future of mankind. The human genome can not only be altered by the implant your mother and I discovered, a third strand can be added to the DNA helix! The third strand brings cellular and molecular changes to the body. The body begins to transform and becomes mentally and physically healthy, youthful, all physical imperfections start to disappear and the human body becomes resistant to disease and aging. The body will no longer die. Satan told Eve 'you shall not surely die'. The deceiving lie in the beginning will also be in the end.

This will be the 'wonder' of the Antichrist. The masses will be deceived and line up to receive the miraculous fountain of youth. This device will genetically modify God's creation and it will be as it was in the days of Noah. Once they have sworn their allegiance to him and taken his implant (mark), they will become unredeemable...lost for eternity.

Now you know the total truth; what I discovered and why I had to disappear from your life. It was the only way to protect you.

I know I leave you in good hands with Dr. Brotman. He will be my liaison to you. You won't know it, but I will be watching over you from a distance. It will break my heart to stay away, but it is for your safety. If it is ever known I am still alive or you have my research documents, your life will again be in danger.

I pray you will find it in your heart to forgive me. I also pray someday you will find the love your mother and I shared. Above all, I pray you find Yeshua as Messiah and Lord of your life.

You were always the best part of me. I love you, my princess,

Dad

Gabriella got down on her knees next to the coffee table, where her father's precious instructions for the final days awaited. Chris was not sure what was going on. He sat silently in anticipation.

"In Caleb I did find the love my mother and father had, then through my stubbornness I lost him. I won't be stubborn again. There's still hope for us, Chris. The only hope is to accept Yeshua, Jesus as our Messiah. Let's do this together and ask Him to protect and guide us through the days ahead. It seems for some reason we have been divinely put together."

He knelt beside her and a supernatural peace saturated the room. In spite of the horrendous years facing them, there was still hope for eternity.

Gabriella again felt 'The Presence' and this time she knew from where it came.

CHAPTER 4

Gabriella and Chris sat silently in the midst of The Presence. Neither of them wanted to disturb the atmosphere of total peace. Both instinctively knew they would be given the strength to face the days ahead, whatever they held.

Finally, Gabriella broke the silence. "The mercies of God endure forever to those that will call upon His name. The Professor often quoted that." She gazed into the air, remembering his words and regretting she did not heed them sooner.

Chris picked up the Professor's Bible which had fallen from the table during the earthquake. It lay next to the chair where the Professor sat while reading the long-awaited translations of the ancient prophecies. His pipe and cherry tobacco lay there awaiting his return. It would never be.

Chris gently placed the precious Bible back in its proper place, handling it with the respect so rightly deserved. He watched Gabriella as she stared into the air, seemingly in a world of her own. He was acutely aware she was struggling to deal with the uncertainty of her life. He did not intrude upon her personal solitude, allowing her all the time she needed to process her emotions. In silence, Chris continued to pick up items that had fallen from the shelves, rearranging and bringing order back to the room.

Gabriella looked at the doors lining the side and back of the bunker. She knew it would be agonizing, but she had to confront the obvious. Behind each door would be the personal belongings of the people she loved that were no longer with her. She walked to the doorway of each room and looked inside. It was immediately obvious who would have been occupying the room by the contents.

The second door, the one directly next to her bedroom, was her father's room. The large black box still filled with the research papers sat in the floor next to the outer wall. She started in and then retreated. The emotional upheaval was just too much, the wound too fresh. "I will come back later," she whispered to herself.

At the final door, her heart skipped a beat. There was Caleb's backpack and sunglasses on his bed. She crossed the threshold and sat down, lovingly caressing the familiar bag. Her mind retreated to the many explorations they made. This backpack was always with him as they traveled through airports and to their final destinations. The last time she saw it was upon their return from Saudi Arabia, the place she first met Arcturus... the nemesis of her soul.

She unzipped the bag. On top was Caleb's favorite blue shirt. She pulled it out and wrapped it around her, holding the sleeves next to her face. His cologne packed in his bag had scented his shirt. The aroma released memories that poured like water. For a moment, she could feel his strong arms embracing her once again.

She sat entranced, visualizing his blond hair that would toss in the wind and hang down in his eyes - his beautiful blue eyes that sparkled every time they would see her and the look of love that he allowed to finally show through after years of being camouflaged due to her own stubborn denial.

"Why was I so stubborn?" She asked in remorse. "We could have had so many wonderful years together, but it's too late." Reality once again captured her and the mental pictures faded.

She regained her composure and with Caleb's shirt still around her shoulders she rejoined Chris.

"Do I have personal items here, Chris? I'd like to take a shower."

"Everything you brought from your apartment is in the drawers in your bedroom. The bathroom and the closet are well stocked with all the personal items you could possibly need." He was well aware of the shirt she was holding around her, but he made no comment. In the close quarters of the bunker, he would allow her as much privacy as possible.

"Thanks," she muttered, disappearing into her bedroom.

Chris could not get out of his mind the words of Gabriella's father. How could such a device exist? Could Gabe be mistaken? Whatever he found, someone wanted to make sure he was stopped from revealing it.

Chris was consumed with the possibility of a third strand of DNA and the effects on the human body.

To give himself a mental break, he turned up the volume on the TV while Gabriella gathered the items she needed. Closing the bathroom door behind her she assured him, "I won't be long. I know time is not on our side." She left Chris to his private thoughts and reports of the world in chaos as reported by Channel 2.

Turning his attention back to the latest news, the updates continued with ominous overtones. Chris studied the reporter's face as he narrowed his dark eyebrows and made his best effort to hold his facial muscles firm. Chris knew even a seasoned reporter could not help but be affected by all the tragedy being reported. As a police officer, he was well trained in body language and facial expressions. It was obvious the reporter was making every effort to stay calm and poised while reading the chilling news being reported from around the world.

"The news is breaking faster than I can report." The reporter's voice was slightly quivering. "I am going to read to you this report, raw and unedited, as it comes across my screen." He took a deep breath and continued, "A nuclear tipped ballistic missile was launched from a Russian freighter just off the eastern shore of the United States, and it detonated in the atmosphere over mid-America. The blast generated an enormous electromagnetic pulse that has taken down America's entire electrical grid system, essentially throwing the country back to the mid-19th century. America's electrical grids were not only outdated, but unprotected. It is estimated it will take decades to get electricity fully restored." He took a deep breath and swallowed as he forced out the next words. "Experts project over ninety percent of the American population will not survive the first year." The reporter motioned for the producer to go to a break. He did not want all of Israel to see tears streaming down his face.

Gabriella emerged, looking refreshed with her hair pulled up in a ponytail and a look of determination on her face. She took one look at Chris and stopped dead in her tracks. "What is it? What's happened?" She did not expect any good news but she was not prepared for what she was about to hear.

Chris motioned for her to sit down and he repeated the latest news about America. "Also, Gabi, while you were in a coma there was a massive earthquake on the New Madrid fault line. The news reported it just before we secluded ourselves in the bunker. That quake had already brought the United States mainland to a standstill and it appears Russia took that opportunity to finish America off, permanently."

Her face turned white as she felt fear trying to steal the peace she had just received. "My homeland destroyed?" Her mind could not even imagine the glory of America gone forever.

"You know what this means, don't you, Gabi?" Chris's voice was becoming louder as he envisioned the coming days. "Without help from America there is no hope for Israel. We are doomed! We can't fight the entire world alone and expect to win."

Gabriella stated solemnly, "The Professor told me this would happen."

Chris had a look of total confusion. "What are you talking about? What did he tell you?"

Gabriella got up and walked to the table where the Professor's Bible lay. She picked it up and held it close to her heart. "This, Chris, is what I'm talking about. The prophecies in this book tell it all. Professor Brotman studied it his whole life. He knew what was coming for Israel and the entire world. I heard, but I wouldn't believe."

She took the Bible back to the couch and laid it next to her father's letters. "These two together will be our roadmap through the next seven years. According to what the Professor told me from the ancient prophecy of Psalms 83, the nations around Israel will join together in an attempt to completely destroy her but they will fail."

"That happened just before everyone vanished." Chris interjected. "Most of us here at the lodge stood outside and watched the fighter jets coming from Syria. They were the ones that initiated the war. The international news falsely reported Israel bombed Damascus first to destroy the nuclear weapons stored there before Syria used them on Israel. Apparently, weapons of mass destruction were secretly brought to Syria from Iraq before the U.S. invasion in 2003. That's the reason there were no WMDs found in Iraq afterwards."

Gabriella was speechless. It was exactly as the Professor had told her. She sat silently as Chris continued.

"All the nations around Israel believed Israel attacked first, considered it an act of war and joined together to completely destroy us. Amazingly, the Israeli Military not only held them off, but was able to defeat the coalition."

"It's amazing to us." Gabriella responded. "But not to those who study the ancient prophets. It happened exactly as they foretold and, according to the Professor, Israel will survive all wars. Israel will never be destroyed again. He said the ancient prophets declared it and that made it so."

Chris shook his head in disbelief. "I have lived my entire life in Israel and never studied the Torah or the prophets. I had no idea any of this was coming."

"Most people don't have a clue. I feel I have to let people know, but I have no idea where or how to start." Gabriella mused.

Chris paced the floor. "My police training keeps telling me to get prepared. Don't be caught off guard. Be ready to defend, but I have no idea what to do to get ready. I don't even know if we can get out of this bunker."

Gabriella had not even considered that possibility. "Do you mean we could be stuck here? No way out?"

"I don't know. When I realized everyone was gone, I looked to see if the bunker door was open. I thought just maybe during the earthquake they tried to get outside. It wasn't open and when I saw you were still here, I didn't even check it. I knew Caleb would not have left without you. The bunker door was the last thing on my mind."

Chris sat back down with a thump as reality hit him again. "They had all just disappeared and I knew then..."

He could not finish the sentence. Instead he jumped back up and climbed the steps to the only way out. He turned the lock and pushed on the door. It was jammed so he pushed harder. With one last, strong push, the door slightly opened. He froze when he heard faint voices in the distance. Gabriella was following him and he put his finger over his lips warning her to be silent.

They heard a few words but most were too muffled to understand. A deep, unfamiliar voice was approaching the kitchen area. The bunker door opened into the pantry, which created a barrier between them and the kitchen. The pantry door leading into the kitchen was securely shut so he knew they could not be seen. He opened the bunker door just enough to hear the conversation.

The voice continued: "There's no one here. The house is deserted. We've searched every inch of this place. There's no sign anyone has been here for a while. There's no food in the pantry, no supplies...nothing. There are ashes in the fireplace but those could have been there for a long time. Who knows? The cottage behind here is vacant, too."

"I was sure this is where they would come. The whole lot of them." A coarse voice responded. "I just knew it. If they were part of the ones that vanished, their personal belongings would still be here. Signs of recent activity in the lodge would be obvious, too. *Or*, maybe someone planned it this way." The strong voice paused obviously considering that possibility. "He's a sly fox, that one." A deep cough followed his words.

Chris briefly shut the door long enough to make sure it was sound-proof. There was dead silence when the bunker door was closed, as if a mute button had been hit. There were no sounds to be heard above them and that meant no one could hear them below. He immediately reopened the door enough to continue to hear the conversation.

There was a strange cigarette odor filtering through into the pantry. After another deep cough, he cleared his throat and continued. "We'll keep a surveillance of the lodge and grounds. We don't want anything obvious, though. It should appear as though it remains his safe hideaway."

The deep cough was heard again. Gabriella knew she would never forget that sound or the stranger's arrogant voice that gruffly continued. "We thought taking out his wife would shut him up. Then we thought he was dead. Now, of all times, he shows back up under the assumed name of Eli Sheskin, and we can thank his pretty little daughter for helping us find him." He laughed at his own humor. The laugh ended in the irritating hacking cough. "We'll make sure neither he nor his daughter ever says a word about the implant." As the two men were leaving the kitchen of the lodge, Chris and Gabriella barely could hear the coarse voice's fading words, "I would have bet my life Brotman wouldn't have survived."

Chris instinctively put his hand over Gabriella's mouth. He knew she would be gasping with shock. He barely caught her before the sound escaped.

The deep voice was fading away, but they could still hear, "We're too close now to let anyone upset the worldwide apple cart. Ugo is not going to be happy when he has to report to the 33rds that Gabe has slipped through our fingers...again." The voices completely disappeared with the sounds of doors closing behind them.

Slowly pulling the bunker door shut, Chris locked it back in place. He and Gabriella descended the wooden stairs without saying a word.

CHAPTER 5

"I can't believe it!" Gabriella exclaimed. "These people killed my mother and tried to kill the Professor. They knew my father wasn't dead and they believe I know about his research...which I do." She went back to the couch and collapsed as the truth gripped her mind. "Who is Ugo? Who are the 33rds? Do you have any idea, Chris?"

Chris was assessing what had just transpired. "I wish I knew, Gabi, especially about the big man they referred to. Ugo sounds familiar, but I can't place him. He must be the one calling all the shots. These guys are no amateurs, that I'm sure of."

Gabriella's panic was gradually subsiding and was replaced by intense determination to know the truth. "Well, any suggestions on what to do now, Mr. Police Officer?"

"If I were at headquarters I might could get some information." Chris ran his hand through his hair, trying to decide what the next step should be. "I need to get back there as soon as possible."

"But you can't leave, Chris. That man said he would have someone watching the house."

"I know," he reluctantly admitted. "Let me think." He began pacing back and forth, eyes squinted and arms folded. "Since they think no one is here, there can't be any movement of any kind seen around the house. Cell reception is impossible down here so I can't contact Detective Richards and I don't even know....," Chris stopped. His arms fell to each side and he took a deep breath, not wanting to admit the distinct possibility. He muttered under his breath, "I don't know if he's dead or alive after all the bombings. The news said Haifa was hit several times."

Gabriella felt the same anxiety, wondering if Caleb's parents were still alive. She whispered a prayer of hope.

Chris began pacing the floor again, trying to ascertain a plan of action. "I can't imagine your father not having a back-up plan for escape, Gabi. He seemed to plan for every possible scenario and being trapped in this bunker without a way out just doesn't sound like his reasoning."

Gabriella knew Chris was right, but she had no answers for him.

In frustration, he continued, "There's got to be a way." Once again, he ran his hand through his thick black hair. His dark brown eyes were full of confusion. His olive skin was flushed from the vexation of the circumstances that captured them.

"Isn't it amazing how fast everything in your life can change?" She asked him. "Just a few days ago you were totally in control, living what you thought was the good life, and today it's all gone. Why are people so stupid as to live in their normalcy bias thinking things will always be the same? I want to just scream from the mountain tops, Wake up, you idiots!"

Chris knew exactly what she meant.

"There is one thing we can do." She spoke with a voice on a mission. "We can read the instructions my father has left. Knowing my father, he has given me detail by detail what to be prepared for."

"Do you think that's possible?" Chris asked, narrowing his eyebrows in doubt.

Gabriella replied with certainty. "The Professor always told me Yahweh, from the beginning of time, knew every event that would take place until the end of days. The ancient prophets recorded it for the generations to come."

She went straight to the couch, picked up the letter on the top of the pile, perched on the side and was ready to begin. She motioned for Chris to join her. As he sat down beside her, a stab of emotional pain cut through Gabriella's heart. This was exactly what she and Caleb had been doing only days prior. Side by side they had read through her father's journal, written before he had faked his death.

In a bizarre twist of circumstances, a strange man was now joining her. Side by side, she and Chris read through the new letters written by her father as he sat by her bedside praying for her awakening. These letters would give her instructions on how to survive the years ahead.

She fought back the tears and pushed the memories of the past from her mind. Hesitantly, she picked up the letter on top, preparing herself for a poignant roller coaster of emotions.

My dearest daughter,

Once again, I am writing a letter that I hope you will never have to read. If you are, that means Yeshua has come for the believers and you have been left behind. It is with that assumption that I am leaving instructions for the days to come. It rips my heart into pieces to pen these words.

As I sit at your bedside watching you sleep, you cannot imagine the pain I feel not being able to hear your voice or look into your eyes. Utter turmoil reels within my soul, knowing you are captured somewhere between time and untime. I've tried to reach you with my love but you have not returned to us. I am still praying you will come back, before it's too late.

Caleb is here with me. He refuses to leave. He also is writing you letters, should he be gone when you awaken. I know you doubted his love and thought he had betrayed you. Please, my precious one, do not ever doubt that he loved you uncon-ditionally. Let the knowledge of knowing you were greatly loved by us all help strengthen you through the days and years ahead. Carry our love with you and do not give in to the deceptions that are coming; but most importantly, let the love of Almighty Yahweh and his Son Yeshua be what carries you, guides you, and protects you.

Gabriella looked toward her bedroom door where the letters from Caleb awaited her. Instinctively, Chris understood her thoughts and waited until she was ready to resume reading. She took a deep breath, slowly exhaled and continued:

Officer Harris may still be with you. He was given the opportunity to believe, but he did not. If he is, at least you are not alone. I pray both of you come to the knowledge of The Truth and can support each other in the days that lie ahead.

The last trumpet is about to sound in Jerusalem at the temple mount. It will bring to a close The Feast of Trumpets, the season of the Messiah's coming. It will be at the last trump, the harpazo, the catching away of the Bride of Yeshua, that we shall go to be with our Lord.

If you are reading this letter, you already know the truth. What the Professor and your friends have tried to tell you, has taken place. You will be facing the worst years in the history of this planet. I know you are strong, my daughter, and you can endure with Yahweh's help. You must endure until the end and you still can be saved! Please follow my instructions closely.

I write this with a trembling hand. My agony cuts to the depth of my being and it grieves me beyond words that I can do nothing more for you. This bunker has provisions to last for many years. I thought it would be for me, but instead it may be for you. In the storage room you will find both non-perishable food and personal items. The water comes from an underground artesian well and the electricity is generated by solar power with a windmill back-up. You should not be without any necessity.

Of utmost importance! There is a hidden escape behind the back-pantry wall. Reach behind the shelf on the top right corner. You will feel a lever. By pulling it forward, the pantry wall will open to a tunnel leading out well beyond the lodge grounds to a secluded area. This was an alternate way to escape in the event my true identity was ever discovered.

When you exit the end of the tunnel, you will find a concrete building well hidden by a thick grove of juniper trees. It cannot easily be seen from the air. In it you will find a Jeep filled with gas and ready to go. It is the vehicle I personally used and I kept it in perfect running condition. There are also containers of additional gasoline stored there. The keys to both the building and the Jeep are hanging directly beside the lever that opens the passageway.

I pray with all my heart for Yahweh's protection upon you. It is up to you now if we will be together again. Remember, do not be deceived by the signs and wonders you will soon see and do not take the implant of the evil leader that will arise and will seduce the people of earth into his alluring, satanic trap.

Lastly, when I visited you in Haifa at the coffee shop, appearing to be a Hasidic Jew, I told you that you were chosen. It was just before you were given the box with my journal and research. My plan was for you to read it all and come to the true knowledge of the great deception. I knew it would be dangerous for you to have access to this world-changing information, but time was running out. I had to take the chance before it was too late. Now the truth is in your hands and there are dangerous people that will stop at nothing to insure the implants are not revealed until their planned time. I was not able to discover who these evil people are, but I know for sure they will not let anything upset their plans for world domination.

The sum of the matter is this: Anyone that understands the truth of the implants, refuses to take them and will not worship the false Messiah can still be saved. You know the truth now! Perhaps, Gabriella, you are chosen as Queen Esther was chosen...for such a time as this.

I love you, my little princess,
Dad

With tears in her eyes she held the paper to her chest. "I can't get out of my mind the last words I spoke to Caleb and my team were in anger." She covered her face with her hands, sobbing from the depth of her being.

Chris did not know how to comfort her, so he simply sat silently as she vented her sorrow.

While Gabriella was fighting to regain self-control, Chris' mind was racing with the knowledge that Gabe *had* planned for every scenario. He had built an escape route from the bunker; plus, a car was waiting.

He kept wondering how these unknown men discovered Gabe was still alive and who was this person Ugo? "Too little, too late for them," Chris thought to himself. "They'll never find Gabe now." He wanted to laugh in the face of the sarcastic man he had heard in the lodge upstairs, but laughter choked in his throat when he remembered Gabriella was also their target.

He took a long look at Gabriella. She looked vulnerable and innocent, but he already detected a strong, independent woman beneath the soft exterior. He knew, whoever these villains were, they would not stop until they found her. Apparently, Ugo was their contact person and above him was the 'big man'. Whoever these men were, Chris was determined to carry out his mission. He was assigned to protect the entire team. Gabriella was the only one left and he would complete his assignment.

He watched her as sorrowful emotions from the loss of those she loved flowed through her. Her teary eyes were sparkling in the lamp light and her long, blonde ponytail fell across the side of her face as she hung her head in misery. Chris was amazed at the passion that had so quickly birthed in him to protect her. It was more than assignment now and he wanted to wrap his arms around her and protect her from all harm. He never had a sister, but he imagined this is what a brotherly love would feel like. Instead he just sat quietly, hoping his mere presence would be a comfort.

Suddenly, Gabriella laid her father's letter back on the table with a thump. She got up from the couch and went to the kitchen. Her countenance changed and a look of determination spread across her face. He did not know her well enough to realize this was how she dealt with conflict. She could file her emotions deep into her soul to deal with later and rise to face whatever challenge faced her. Her painful past had created an ability within her to separate her agony of soul from the mission at hand.

She opened the cabinets and then looked back at Chris. "We do have coffee, don't we? I know my dad. He would have plenty of coffee on hand."

Chris looked surprised at her sudden metamorphosis, but then he had no idea just how tenacious this woman could be when she made up her mind.

"Upper cabinet, lower shelf," he replied, waiting to see what was coming next.

"Enough time spent feeling sorry for myself." She kept talking while she made the coffee. Soon the caramel coffee aroma filled the room as it brewed. "I created these circumstances and now I will face them." She looked at Chris with certainty, "With the help of an Israeli Police Officer and with the good Lord above. That's quite a combination, don't you think?"

Chris could not help but chuckle, realizing she considered Yahweh and himself a team. However, he knew The Lord did not need him but he certainly would need the help of The Almighty in the days ahead.

Gabriella brought a tray of coffee to the table and sat it next to the stack of letters and the Professor's bible. "Let's start reading. I just hope we can keep TV reception to know what's going on in the world around us." As confident as she sounded, he still detected undertones of apprehension.

She picked up the next letter and looked at Chris. "Are you ready?"

He nodded his head and the journey through the end of days began.

CHAPTER 6

G abriella picked up the first letter of instruction from her father. She sat on the edge of the couch with Chris by her side. She took a deep breath and attempted to disguise the dread in her voice as she began to read:

Dear Gabriella,

I am writing this with the assumption the harpazo, or 'catching away' has taken place. I am going to walk you, step by step, through the next seven years. The ancient prophets and the Book of Revelation prophetically outline what will come upon the earth. As you see these events unfold, you will be certain in your heart of hearts that the Word of Yahweh is true and without question.

My heart breaks that you must endure these things; however, I trust you have now accepted the spiritual truth of the end of days and Yeshua is your Lord and Savior. When He becomes your strength, there is nothing that can defeat you.

Before our disappearance, the prophetic war of Psalms 83 had started. We saw the beginning. Israel will not only survive but will actually enlarge her borders. I am sure the world will be in amazement of the military power shown by this small nation. Neither the world powers nor Israel will realize (yet) it was

Yahweh that directed what will be Israel's unbelievable victory. Every nation will hate 'the apple of God's eye' even more after this current war, and a much larger war will quickly be on the horizon.

Israel's victory in the Psalms 83 War will be so amazing the world will fear them for a brief time. Due to this fear, Israel will have a deceptive interlude of peace and safety; however, only for a short span will she enjoy her victory. In all countries, a greater hatred for Israel will quickly escalate. The Jews have always been hated and anti-Semitism was already growing at an exponential rate even before this war, but it will explode after Israel conquers the nations that surround her. Persecution of God's chosen people will become so horrible, they will come to Israel from all over the world for safe haven and survival.

Very quickly all of these things will take place to set the stage for the war foretold in Ezekiel 38. The False Messiah will take his place to bring supposed peace and a New World Order from the reigning chaos. He is preparing now to make his appearance. Keep your eyes on Rome and the Vatican. I believe this 'man of sin, son of perdition' will be introduced through the most respected spiritual man on the planet, The Pope. I have left you a copy of the Prophecy of St. Malachy to help you understand why.

Take time to absorb, study, and understand what I have written before you go to the next letter. Follow my instructions to you step by step.

I love you, my princess, and I pray God's hand of protection upon you and upon Officer Harris. I feel certain he is there with you and will help protect you.

Until we are together in the New Jerusalem,
Dad

There were no tears in Gabriella's eyes, only a look of total determination. Chris was amazed at her resilience and felt honored her father trusted her in his care.

"Let's read this prophecy of The Pope first, Chris." Gabriella picked up the paper attached to the first letter. "Then we'll go from there."

Chris watched as her anticipation and trepidation of the days ahead grew stronger. Her voice had lost its quivering edge as she began to read the prophecy. "It says at the top of the page, Prophecy of the Popes written by St. Malachy in 1139AD."

"Who was St. Malachy?" He asked. "Never heard of him."

Gabriella quickly scanned the document and looked up at Chris. "It says he was an Irish archbishop, canonized as a saint in 1190AD. Seems he predicted there would be 112 more popes from his day until the day of the great judgment. He also wrote something about each pope to identify them when they were elected. His prophecies have been totally accurate with every Pope."

She reread her dad's notes to be certain she was stating it correctly. "Number 112 will be the final Pope before The Black Pope. Many, including the Catholic Church, believe the final pope will be the False Prophet prophesied in Revelation 13."

"What number is the current Pope?" Chris waited in anticipation.

Gabriella took a deep breath and answered as she exhaled. "He is 113, The Black Pope."

Chris could not help but gasp. "This St. Malachy person was accurate in his description of every Pope? Every single one of them?"

"This states his prophecy was officially sanctioned which means it is a true prophecy." She replied. "Apparently, a select few of the Roman Catholic Church declares them a forgery, but most believe the prophecy to be real."

Gabriella looked at an additional paper attached to her father's letter. There was a note at the top with an asterisk for importance.

*Gabriella, many try to discount the prophecy of St. Malachy. I believe it to be true. Time will verify its authenticity and there are many other prophecies canonized by the church that speak of 'The Evil Pope', also called 'The Black Pope', who will deceive the faithful by working miracles and

wonders through Satanic powers. He will compromise the Roman Catholic doctrine; multitudes will follow him and accept the new world religion. The final seven years will begin under his papacy.

"This is the final personal note from my father," she said, leaning towards Chris. "*Watch for these events to take place. Beware of the man that makes evil appear to be good and good to be evil. He is a ravenous wolf in sheep's clothing.*"

Gabriella looked up from the papal prophecy and waited for Chris's reaction.

Chris seemed at a loss for words. He stared at the television that was on, but the sound still muted. It was obvious he was lost in his perplexing thoughts. He took the paper from Gabriella and reread it silently, slowly trying to process the extraordinary information.

Finally, he spoke, "This is all pretty amazing. We can't deny the fact your dad, Dr. Brotman, and the others just vanished just like they said would happen, and they've left these instructions for us to follow. Even before we read this, the news was already reporting the Pope is meeting with the UN to help in the peace process. Is that coincidence?"

"I don't think so," she grimly stated. "The Professor continuously told us the word 'coincidence' did not appear in Yahweh's perfect language of Hebrew. Everything is divinely designed with no happenstance. No, I don't believe it's a coincidence. I believe it's proof my dad was correct."

Gabriella glanced toward the television and the breaking news caught her attention. She grabbed Chris's arm. "Look!"

Chris read the large, red letters running across the bottom of the screen: 'Breaking News, Israel's war victory astounds the nations'. Continuously it ran, over and over, as the reporter gave an update on the news pouring in.

The voice on the screen, previously filled with undertones of doom and gloom, was now penetrated with excitement. "This is Michael Adelson reporting from Channel 2 in Haifa. An amazing turn of events has taken place. The Russian fleet in the Mediterranean Sea has turned away and headed back out to sea, fleeing the coasts of Israel. We have a live report now from the Lieutenant General of the Israeli Defense Forces."

The TV screen blinked and went black for a moment. Then the face of the General appeared. He cleared his throat and addressed the Nation of Israel in a tone of confidence and certainty. "Today Israel has shown the world we will not be destroyed. We have tried to live in peace with our neighboring countries and the world community. We have given up land and made every effort to come to reasonable solutions for peace. We did not choose war. We did not want war; *but* we were prepared if war came. It was thrust upon us when Syria made the first attack three days ago hitting Jerusalem, Tel Aviv, and Haifa simultaneously in their first bombings. A coalition had been formed of all countries that surround us, with the intent of concurrent attacks that would not stop until we were destroyed. We had the right, as any nation does, to defend our country no matter what measures had to be taken."

The General paused briefly, looking at his notes before continuing: "This war was different from the localized wars we have fought with Hamas in Gaza or Hezbollah in Lebanon. This war was intended by our enemies to completely wipe us off the map. For Israel to survive and continue to exist as a nation, we counterattacked. Our only choice was to destroy our enemies before they destroyed us. Damascus was our first target.

"For decades, Damascus has been the command and control center of all terrorist activity in the region. Also, we were fully aware that weapons of mass destruction were shipped from Iraq before the U.S. invasion and stored underground near Damascus. Many of these weapons were nuclear and we could not allow them to be used against us. We had to be preemptive. To assure complete success we deployed three nuclear devices. Two nuclear tipped bunker buster bombs were detonated underground at the WMD stockpiles north and east of the city. The underground detonations ruptured the casings of the nuclear WMD's spreading highly radioactive unexploded fissionable material into the atmosphere. The third bomb was a 4-megaton surface detonated two-stage thermonuclear device. The surface detonation of the thermonuclear weapon while not being as effective as an airburst in destroying structures over a large area, did aid in distributing the enormous amount of radioactive material contained in the WMD's over hundreds of square kilometers around the city rendering it uninhabitable for many decades.

"We could not wait for further attacks that could have debilitated our defense systems and we could not wait for the approval of the United Nations. The survival of Israel was at stake. We simultaneously hit Iran's nuclear enrichment and manufacturing facilities using nuclear tipped, penetrator bombs developed in secret by the IDF. They had not been officially tested prior to our attack on Iran, but they proved to be a complete success. Additionally, all Iranian military headquarters, weapons arsenals, and key personnel were also neutralized. Iran is no longer a threat to the security of Israel.

"There were multitudes of terrorist groups embedded in Gaza, Lebanon, Syria, Jordan, Saudi Arabia, and Egypt. To counter and eliminate the enemy's threat to our existence, neutron bombs were simultaneously and successfully deployed. The exception is Gaza, which surrendered and their residents will be relocated by Israeli Defense Forces. Miraculously, the winds have blown strong and constant since the nuclear attacks, carrying the radioactive fall-out towards the east and away from Israel.

"For our security, Israel has taken possession of the enemies' land. We were on the verge of complete annihilation and our military had no choice but to use any weapons needed to insure our survival. Our new Iron Beam System successfully destroyed the short-range rockets coming from Lebanon and Syria. The Iron Dome continued to be a major defense. The turning factor of the war was technology heretofore not used and that technology had been reserved for the Samson Option. Our secret weapons have produced total victory for the Nation of Israel. Alone we have conquered."

Again, the General paused, allowing a moment for viewers to process what he had announced before continuing: "Israel has prevailed against our attackers. The world community now knows we are both capable and willing to defend our right to exist. We are fully aware that our decision to launch the first nuclear and neutron attack will be condemned by all nations; however, for the first time since Israel became a nation in 1948 we will dwell in peace and safety.

"One last word," the General continued, this time with sadness in his face and voice. "Many have been affected by the recent vanishings. I have no answer now but I vow to you we are committed to finding the truth. This has not just affected Israel, but seemingly every nation on the planet. There have been reports of varying possibilities but until we have more information we cannot verify anything. Any substantiated news will be reported immediately."

The General turned from the news cameras and walked away as reporters shouted questions he deliberately ignored. Chris and Gabriella watched as Adelson fought back tears of joy. "You heard it from our Chief of Staff. Victory is ours! When there seemed to be no hope of survival, Israel not only survived but we have informed the nations we are here to stay and we have enlarged our borders."

In a voice steeped in compassion he continued, "There is great sorrow in the mystery of the vanishings, and it is the prayer of all of Israel these souls to be found safe."

As the news spread around Israel that the war was over and Israel was victorious, Israelis began to stream from their bunkers and places of safety. Soon everyone knew Israel had expanded her borders to encompass the surrounding nations. It was a mixture of great joy and great sorrow...joy for victory and sorrow for the vanished.

News cameras on location in Jerusalem, Tel Aviv, and Haifa showed shofars of victory being blown across the cities. Mixed with the scenes of rejoicing, numerous people searching the war-battered streets were desperately trying to find missing loved ones. Rabbis were gathered on the temple mount raising their hands to Adonai, praising him for victory over the enemies, while others were praying for Adonai to reveal the location of those that had vanished. It was like nothing the land of Israel had ever experienced.

Gabriella swallowed hard. The prophecy from her father's first letter had already been fulfilled. "It's already begun, Chris, just as the prophets wrote. We know the peace and safety will be short lived and we know where the vanished have gone."

He simply nodded his head. There was no way to deny the obvious truth.

CHAPTER 7

I t was 10:00 PM Israeli Standard Time. Gabriella could feel both mental and physical exhaustion sweeping over her. Chris was preparing a late evening meal, allowing her time to emotionally process the events of the day. She fought back the tears, longing to feel Caleb's arms around her just one more time. Mixed with that sentiment was the knowledge her father had held her in his arms again, after all the years of believing he was dead. It was almost more than her aching soul could endure.

Regret again flooded through Gabriella. Echoing over and over in the depth of her soul were the words, "I could have gone with them". She leaned her head on the back of the couch and closed her eyes. She could hear Caleb's voice as clearly as if he were in the room. "I love you, Gabi. Please wake up. Please wake up." Try as she may to prevent it, tears escaped the corners of her eyes.

Chris watched her from the kitchen. He saw the agony in her face and wished he could comfort her; instead he whispered a prayer. Talking to an unseen God was new to him, yet it felt so natural. With each word he uttered, peace slowly and surely filled him.

Chris brought a tray of soup and sandwiches to the coffee table. Gabriella quickly wiped her eyes and sat up, positioning herself to make room for Chris to join her.

"Before we eat I would like to say a blessing." Gabriella said. "The Professor never ate any meal until he blessed the food. We always joined hands as he prayed. Although it meant nothing to me spiritually then, I respected his faith and joined in the prayer."

Chris nodded his head. "Sure, go ahead."

Gabriella reached for his hand and spontaneously Chris's hand closed around hers. *"BA-RUCH A-TAH A-DO-NOI ELO-HAI-NU ME-LECH HA-O-LAM HA-MO-TZI LE-CHEM MIN HA-A-RETZ.* Blessed are You, Lord our God, King of the Universe, Who brings forth bread from the earth. Amen."

"Amen." Chris echoed.

Gabriella released Chris's hand and noticed a tear escaping from the corner of his eye. She looked towards the television, pretending not to notice. This strong police officer truly had a sensitive heart. She smiled, for the first time since her awakening, as she turned the sound up to hear the latest news.

Michael Adelson was still reporting breaking news. "He has to be exhausted", Gabriella commented. "He's been on the air since before I woke up."

Chris looked at her with a strange, questioning stare.

She admitted to him, "I could hear the sounds around me. I kept trying desperately to reach to someone, but I couldn't. I couldn't move. I couldn't speak. I could only hear. It was as though I was dreaming and yet wide awake, too. I can't explain it."

"I understand, Gabi. In our police training, we are told that hearing is the last sense to leave the body when a person is dying and often is the only sense that stays awake when the body is in a comatose state. I guess that's true in astral sleep, also. I've never encountered that one before."

Breaking News captured their attention. A strange map they had never seen before covered the screen. Beneath the map were the words 'The New Expanded State of Israel'.

"What is that?" Chris exclaimed in total confusion.

"I have no idea." Gabriella answered, laying her sandwich down to focus fully on the report.

Adelson's voice gave the answer to their question. "The map you are seeing on the screen shows the expanded borders of Israel, after our unbelievable war victory. Rabbis are saying this is the geographical area called The Promised Land, which Yahweh gave to Abraham and his descendants." Genesis 15 from the Torah appeared on the TV screen as Adelson gave the report. Obvious excitement infused his voice.

Gabriella picked up the Professor's Bible and turned to Genesis. "This is Genesis 15:18-21," she stated as she began:

*"On that day the L*ORD *made a covenant with Abram and said, 'To your descendants I give this land, from the Wadi of Egypt to the great river, the Euphrates; the land of the Kenites, Kenizzites, Kadmonies, Hittites, Perizzites, Repha ites, Amorites, Canaanites, Girgashites and Jebusites.'"*

"I have no idea where those places are", Chris admitted.

"I'm not totally sure either, but in our cave explorations we covered a lot of areas and some of those ancient names are familiar." She turned to the maps in the back of the Bible and began to compare ancient lands with contemporary countries. She then compared them to the map on the TV.

After closely making the differentiations, she was convinced and stated as a matter of fact, "The land God gave to Israel included everything from the Nile River in Egypt to Lebanon, south to north; and everything from the Mediterranean Sea to the Euphrates River, west to east. It's all of the land modern Israel currently possesses, *plus,* all of the land of the Palestinians, the West Bank and Gaza, all of Jordan, and some of Egypt, most of Saudi Arabia, Syria, and Iraq." She looked at Chris in amazement.

"It's exactly what your father said, Gabi! After the Psalms 83 War, Israel would expand her borders and possess the land of the Abrahamic Covenant." He found it hard to believe his own words. "You know what this means, don't you? He also said Jews everywhere in the world are going to be hated and persecuted like never before because of this. Israel may be feared as a nation for our military power, but individual Jews will become targets no matter where they live outside of Israel. They will have no choice but to make Aliyah and come home."

Gabriella knew he was right. "The Professor said in the end of days all the descendants of the Twelve Tribes of Israel would be forced to come home. The ancient prophets wrote Yahweh will draw them from the north, south, east, and west."

She sat silently in contemplation before continuing. "I wonder what we should do in the days ahead. Just hide and hope to survive? Or, is there a greater plan since I may be the only person outside that evil group that knows about the implant?"

"I think it's time you explain to me about this implant. I need to fully understand what's going on."

Gabriella turned to face him. She had no doubt Chris could be trusted and he needed all the facts. "This is how it began. The research my father was involved in for decades was about extraterrestrial existence. There was a time when he was convinced that ET's existed and communicated with people on earth that possessed high vibrational frequencies. These people could be used by the aliens as test subjects to set the implant base line parameters."

She paused to see if he was going to laugh at her. If he found it humorous, he gave no sign, so she continued, "I won't go into all the details, but my parents discovered these human test subjects had an implant under their skin. The implants seemed to be altering the DNA of the victims, which at the time was thought to be impossible."

She kept watching for signs of disbelief from Chris, but none showed so she went on with her story, "A few years ago, Dr. Ventura from Italy announced DNA can be altered by using a combination of magnetic field frequencies, but my parents had discovered this was already being done even before I was even born. However, they truly believed it was a superior extraterrestrial race performing DNA modifications. My parents realized this discovery could literally change the world. Imagine no more sickness, no more aging, even no more death. And that was just part of the amazing affects it would have on mankind."

"I definitely see their thinking on that," Chris commented, totally captured by the information.

"My father had a meeting with some high U.S. government officials. Dad revealed the magnitude of what they had discovered. These men said they would contact him." She paused remembering what the contact was. "They contacted him all right. Their contact was blowing up my father's truck and trying to kill my parents."

She had to take a moment to compose herself before continuing. Chris sat silently and waited. "Normally, our whole family would have been in the truck that morning, but it was just my mom. I was only five years old. Everything changed after that."

"That was the end of it? Your dad just dropped it?" Chris leaned towards Gabriella hanging on her every word.

Her voice gained intensity. "No. By far that wasn't the end of it. He kept researching and discovering more and more, but he didn't tell anyone. He wasn't willing to put my life in danger. The whole time I was growing up, I had no idea of any of this. Not until a few weeks ago, when Sandee gave me the box that contained all of my father's research notes. Since then it has been like a horror movie that has no ending."

Chris kept pressing. "What else did he discover? What led him to faking his own death?"

"My father discovered the government already knew about the implants. In fact, they had developed numerous modern inventions from the technology gleaned from, what they think, were alien aircrafts that crashed at Roswell in the 1940s. Among them were nuclear power, hydrogen bombs, microchips, integrated circuits, laser beams, and...the implants. Gradually these discoveries were introduced to society as modern inventions and became part of our everyday existence. Society never realized it was from what the government thought was alien technology. The implant has been withheld and for good reason." She leaned back in the couch, taking a moment to organize her thoughts.

"And...? Don't leave me hanging, Gabi. What do you mean?"

She took a long breath and sat upright again. "It's really hard to explain. At first, my father was totally convinced, just like the government, the technology all came from the extraterrestrials that crashed at Roswell. However, he and my mother had pictures they had taken in a cave here in Israel before I was born. The cave drawings looked like alien aircraft with beings in them, ascending and descending over a large mountain. The top of the mountain appeared to be some type of inter-dimensional portal for the aircraft to pass through. It all tied into their extraterrestrial theories. There were ancient writings on the cave wall and my mother took close up pictures in hopes of getting the writing translated, but they could find no one who recognized the language."

"I think I know where you're going with the next part of this." Chris said. "He found out about the Professor and his worldwide status as a linguist?"

"Yes, the Professor is...," she hesitated, "was brilliant." Referring to him in the past tense made shivers run up and down her spine. "I had no idea until today when I finally read my father's last journal entry the Professor was the scientist dad wrote about in his journal. It all makes perfect sense. I understand now why I was offered the scholarship, so good I couldn't refuse it, to the University of Haifa. It was dad's plan to connect me with Dr. Brotman. I studied and worked with him for over twelve years and had no idea he and my father had planned it all. I feel like I'm living a dream. None of this seems real."

She forced herself to continue, "My father wrote in his journal he had contacted a scientist, which I know now was Dr. Brotman, about translating the writing found in the cave. Apparently, it was a divine appointment. The Professor had found timelines that revealed when the end of days would come and my father had discovered the implant the false Messiah will use. I'm sure it wasn't easy for the Professor to convince my dad the implant did not come from an extraterrestrial civilization, but instead from deceiving demonic beings appearing as ETs." A slight chuckle was evident under her breath as she tried to imagine that heated exchange of knowledge. "Together they could have changed the world, Chris."

She briefly paused, imagining her father and the Professor brainstorming on the world of the paranormal. She sighed, wishing she could have been part of it all. "You know the rest. The last translations of the ancient language were completed just before the vanishing. Those translations confirmed what they believed to be true...but it was too late."

Chris was getting a clearer picture of the mysterious research. "I think I'm beginning to understand some of this, but there's one thing still confusing me. There apparently is some nation developing all this modern technology so why have they not used the implant to help people and just leave your father alone? They're already using the RFID technology, which is a form of what you're describing."

"They have a plan to introduce this implant at just the right time and it's not any single nation doing this. My father said there is a group of powerful people from many nations planning a one world government and one world economy and they will have a leader who will deceive all the world into one religion."

"I can't see that ever happening!" Chris exclaimed, almost laughing. "Especially the Muslims...no way!"

"That's where the implant becomes the vital factor. It will be gradually introduced by this group of powerful people and then become the tool of the Antichrist when he takes his position as the new world leader. Can't you just imagine how people will want what the implant will give them? It's the proverbial fountain of youth. All they have do is worship the new world leader."

"I'm sure I would have fallen for the deception hook, line, and sinker had I not met you" Chris admitted.

"Most of the world will not even think twice about taking the implant. If they refuse the implant they won't be able to buy or sell anything. No food, no medications, no place to live...nothing. They will literally be hiding or running for their lives. Many will become martyrs for their faith." Gabriella's voice was solemn. "No one was to know this was being developed, and especially where the technology actually came from." She took a deep breath. "If they think there is the slightest chance I have my father's discovery, they will not give up until they find and eliminate me."

Chris was well aware of the danger she was in, but he would not allow his concern to show. "I'm still trying to understand how the demonic world works in all this. I didn't believe demons were real."

She was not sure how Chris was going to react to her answer. "It was difficult for me to understand, too. It took my own experience of living it to finally make me realize the truth. The extraterrestrials, the UFO's, all the paranormal experiences are real, Chris. They are very real and people every day are being sucked into it. What they do not realize is it's all a façade, a deception from the demonic realm."

Again Gabriella hesitated, wondering if he would think she had now gone off the deep end. "All of the paranormal world is demonic spirits, entering our dimension of time, capturing the minds and souls of people wanting supernatural experiences. They are appearing in many different forms: some appear as extraterrestrials, some appear as angels of light, others as spirits of the dead, and the list goes on. These spirits of darkness have great mystical powers and superhuman knowledge. The information brought from extraterrestrials, or any other form of paranormal appearances, is really coming from powerful evil spirits ruled by Satan. They are shape-shifters that can appear as anything they wish to be, and then simply disappear through parallel dimensions."

Gabriella leaned forward in her seat to look directly at Chris. "It is through evil deceptions and powers the false messiah will soon rule the world. He will work wonders and miracles through Satan's powers. The implant will be his mark, his tool of deception that will cause people to worship him. That is the Antichrist's ultimate goal, to be worshiped as God! He will have an evil spiritual army working with him. The project we worked on with the Professor revealed there is an evil force about to be released upon the earth again. They are the fallen angels."

"What? Are you kidding me, Gabi?" Gabriella wondered if she had shared more information than Chris was prepared to digest.

She shook her head. "I'm very serious! According to the Book of Jude, they chose to leave their heavenly estate and have been chained in the abyss until the end of days. They will be released when the false messiah takes his position on earth and then all hell will break loose."

Chris was trying to process the volumes of information she was unloading. "This does sound like a horror movie," he stated solemnly. "And you really believe all of this?"

She turned away and looked towards the TV without seeing it. Her mind was racing with thoughts of what was soon coming. "I didn't want to believe it. I wanted to believe everything was good and nothing would ever change. I wanted to go on with my life, get married, have children. But it doesn't matter what we want. Prophecy is being fulfilled and nothing can change what's about to happen." She turned abruptly back to face Chris. "We can't change the world events but we can let people know what's coming. One thing for sure though, we can't do it from here. We either sit here and wait, or we get up and do something."

As a police officer, Chris knew to avoid confrontation if at all possible. To stay in the bunker would make the most sense. Gabriella would be safe there. No one knew they were at the lodge except Detective Richards, if he was even still alive. However, even he did not know about the bunker.

"I don't think I like where you're going with this, Gabi. It's not the same world anymore." His voice softened with his next words. "I'm not concerned about myself, but I am concerned about you. You're in a safe place here."

Her voice became slightly agitated. "Yes, in a safe place, but accomplishing nothing. It seems to be perfectly safe out in the streets of Israel, at least for now. We have a mission, Chris. I'm beginning to understand why my father said I was chosen. I have to use the knowledge I've been given as a weapon against the evil that's coming. What's the worst that can happen? I die? That just means I'm with those I love that much faster. Right?" Her voice softened. "Caleb is there…" She could not finish the sentence, the words longingly lingering on her lips as the pain of lost love penetrated her eyes.

Gabriella got up from the couch. "I'm exhausted. I'm going to bed." Then suddenly she sat back down as fear filled her face.

"What is it, Gabi?"

For a few minutes, she would not answer. "I'm afraid to go to sleep", she confessed. "You have no idea the tormenting experiences I've had during my sleep since I returned from Saudi Arabia." Dread completely saturated her countenance as she desperately tried to keep from emotionally collapsing.

"I do know some of it," he assured her. "It was impossible to not hear conversations in this bunker. I heard Caleb talking about it."

"During my supernatural sleep, I could hear Caleb praying for me. He kept repeating verses from Psalms 91. Then I heard the voices of all those who love me praying in unison. Their prayers sounded like beautiful music, nothing like I've heard before. Satan himself had come to destroy me; but their prayers became spiritual swords that separated me from Satan and he could not breach the wall of protection."

Chris picked up the Professor's Bible that Gabriella had just read from and searched for Psalms 91. "The Professor has this underlined, Gabi. I'll read it to you."

"Whoever dwells in the shelter of the Most High
*   will rest in the shadow of the Almighty.*
² I will say of the LORD, "He is my refuge and my fortress,
*   my God, in whom I trust."*
³ Surely he will save you
*   from the fowler's snare*
*   and from the deadly pestilence.*
⁴ He will cover you with his feathers,
*   and under his wings you will find refuge;*
*   his faithfulness will be your shield and rampart.*
⁵ You will not fear the terror of night."

Gabriella smiled as she heard the familiar words and fear vanished from her mind and soul. "I will not fear the terror of night," she repeated.

Chris continued to stare at the words from the Psalm and Gabriella was not sure if he was talking to her or himself when he repeated verse two. "*I will say of the Lord, He is my refuge and my fortress, my God, in whom I trust.*"

He looked up at Gabriella. "We're going to need those promises in the days ahead."

She nodded in agreement as she got up again to go to bed. "Thank you, Chris, for reading to me. I feel better." She leaned over and gave him a kiss on the cheek. "Thank you for everything."

She entered her bedroom and closed the door behind her. Changing into her pajamas, she kept hearing the words echoing in her mind. "You are my refuge and my fortress. In you I trust, Oh Lord."

She picked up the letters that Caleb had written then laid them back on the night stand. "I can't do this now," she whispered, totally exhausted.

She switched the lamp off and pulled the cotton sheets around her chin. A dim nightlight glowed on the wall. Silence filled the room as she closed her eyes. She whispered as her eyes closed, "I will not fear the terror by night."

Peace filled the room and Gabriella went into a deep sleep. All through the night she continued to hear the voices of both Caleb and her father continually begging her to wake up before it was too late. She tried to respond, to reach to them.

The wall of time and untime separated them.

CHAPTER 8

The voices disappeared as Gabriella awakened to reality. Before her feet touched the cool stone floor, she silently thanked God there were no more bedeviling night visits, only the voices of the ones she loved and she would always welcome those dreams. Quietly, she exited her bedroom while Chris was still sleeping. She wanted to tour the bunker in solitude, allowing her mind to envision her father moving from room to room. She was amazed at every detail that was considered in the event of an emergency. Overwhelmed, she returned to the kitchen and tried to process all that had happened, while she prepared breakfast. Shortly, Chris joined her.

"Morning, sleepy head." Gabriella glanced up as Chris ran his hand through his ruffled, thick hair in a futile effort to smooth it. It was immediately obvious he had little sleep. "Breakfast is almost ready," she said as if she had not noticed his countenance.

"I'll have a quick shower first and be good to go." He disappeared and left her to continue preparations. Shortly he reappeared. "Can I help?" He asked as Gabriella placed a platter of pancakes on a tray.

"That was perfect timing to be no help," she sarcastically commented as she motioned for him to carry the already prepared tray of food to the coffee table. Chris set it in front of the TV where the news reports continued from around the world. He settled on the couch watching the updates.

Gabriella joined him carrying their coffee. "My father did a great job stocking food and supplies. I've been looking through the stock room and found the button that will open the passageway outside. Let's check it out after we eat."

"Sounds like a plan to me." Chris agreed, anxious to see the light of day again. "How did you sleep last night? I checked on you a couple of times and you looked completely peaceful."

"I really was. It was the best night's sleep I can remember in a very long time." She did not mention dreaming of her loved one's voices. That was a private matter. She took a long sip of hot coffee, longing to hear those voices in the world of reality.

They watched the news while they ate. It was pretty much as the night before. Israel's expanded borders trumped everything else currently making news. 'Breaking News' would continually stream across the bottom reporting other major worldwide events, but in Israel nothing else took priority over the nation's magnificent victory.

Reports were coming in from the city of Jerusalem, showing Israelis cleaning their streets and yards from the numerous bombs that exploded during the three-day war. From the pictures, it looked like a futile effort; however, Jews are a very stubborn people. They were singing and rejoicing as they worked, determined to rebuild all that was lost. In the distance, heavy construction equipment could be seen already coming to remove the rubble and begin the rebuilding process. Not a moment was being wasted.

Excitement was evident in every face the camera panned. One voice of a Hasidic Jew shouted to the camera: "We are now the nation Adonai promised our father Abraham. We cannot be defeated! Our enemies have been destroyed and we can now live in peace and safety. Yahweh be praised!" In unison, all the voices within hearing distance echoed his words. *"Adonai be praised! Adonai be praised!"*

"Let's see what's going on in the rest of the world," Chris said changing the TV channel to international news. "I'm sure the rest of the world is seeing our victory very differently." He was correct. The Worldwide Intelligence Network was depicting a very distorted view of the last few days.

An attractive reporter was verbally painting an anti-Israel picture. "I am in Vatican City, reporting on the crucial changes on our planet. We are not living in the same world we knew just a few days ago. The nation of Israel initiated what they have termed The Samson Option. It took only three days for Israel to initiate the first nuclear and neutron war on our planet and conquer all of the nations which surround her."

The reporter delayed her next words to allow the full impact of her information to penetrate the minds of the viewers. "The nations surrounding Israel were all attacked simultaneously with no time or opportunity for defense. Damascus was the first city hit and destroyed by nuclear bombs. Damascus is now totally uninhabitable and will remain so for decades, perhaps centuries, due to the nuclear contamination. That strike was immediately followed by neutron bomb attacks on cities and military bases in Lebanon, Syria, Jordan, Saudi Arabia, Egypt, and Iraq. Simultaneously, Iran's nuclear reactors were demolished by Israel's use of kinetic orbital strikes. The damage is beyond human description and millions upon millions, mostly Muslims, have been murdered by the Israeli military forces."

Chris gasped. "That's not true. It's not, Gabi. You were in a coma, but the rest of us stood outside this lodge and watched the Syrian jets flying southwest over Israel. Then we heard bombs exploding. It was after those first attacks Israel counter-attacked. They did *not* initiate this war. No matter what happens in the Middle East, Israel always gets the blame." Chris's voice was filled with exasperation.

Gabriella briefly took his hand, squeezed and released it. "I know. I've lived here for twelve years and I'm fully aware of the truth, but the world only sees the media bias."

The female reporter continued her spew of hatred: "A few pictures taken by helicopters have come in, revealing the destruction in many of these nations." The scenes began to flash across the screen with the names of Israel's surrounding nations displayed at the top. "At this point cameramen cannot report from the ground. The video is being transmitted by drones, which does allow us a visual of the devastation Israel has created. The exact chemical composition contained in the bombs they used has not yet been determined. We will give updated reports as they become available." Then with a look of obvious contempt in her eyes and venom in her voice, she stated, "As the death toll continues to rise, we lay the blame directly at the feet of Israel."

The reporter's voice went silent as the cameras began to zoom in on the complete desolation. The pictures were almost too gruesome to watch. Cities had been turned into piles of rubble. There was no sign of life anywhere in the pictures being aired. How easy it would have been to hate Israel if you did not know the truth, *and* the biased news media made sure you did not.

Chris was getting more agitated with each report. "You know the media is showing this to intentionally turn everyone in the world against Israel. It creates sympathy for our enemies, the nations who had every intention of wiping Israel off the face of the earth. Definitely, they would have done just that if Israel had not been prepared to be proactive."

Gabriella allowed Chris the time to vent before she somberly replied, "This is just the beginning, you know."

The reporter allowed several minutes of silence for the pictures to continue to display over and over. The horrendous images, no doubt, were sinking deep into the minds of viewers around the world who still had the capability of receiving television transmissions. The full intent was for all nations to believe Israel had initiated the devastation and for the scenes to create a global hatred for the Jewish people.

The camera again focused in on the female reporter as she spoke: "This is a sad day for the world. We have all feared the time nuclear war would be waged. We have dreaded the heinous aftermath. We are now fully aware of Israel's military capabilities and her intent to conquer and expand. Any country that possesses nuclear weapons now knows if retaliation is launched against Israel, be ready for their own country to potentially be destroyed. Is that a price any nation is willing to pay?"

Chris got up and took their breakfast tray to the kitchen. It was obvious he was filled with frustration. Returning, he voiced that agitation. "Why couldn't the world see we just wanted to be left alone? We were a small nation and all we wanted was to live in peace and to have a home for the Jews to come to and live in safety. We have never initiated a war, but we always get the blame when another nation attacks us. Everything is always *our* fault."

He sat back down with a thump. "Well, one thing is for sure; no one would dare touch us if they want their nation to continue to exist. Maybe Israel ought to just take them all out and rule the world."

Gabriella tried to calm him, but the more he talked the more agitated he became. "Settle down, Chris. Apparently, this is the way it's supposed to be. Prophecy is in motion and it can't be stopped. There will be another war soon, so Israel's peace and safety is going to be short lived."

Chris got up and extended his hand to help Gabriella up from the couch. "Let's find our way out of here." Just as he was going to turn the TV off, the screen again caught their full attention. Behind the female reporter were masses of people beginning to gather at Vatican Square. They were praying to The Holy Mother for answers and guidance.

The reporter waived her hand, bringing the viewer's attention to the multitudes congregating who were filled with hope The Infallible Pope would have answers for their grieving hearts.

Raising her voice to be heard over the roaring crowd, she ended her segment: "Thousands upon thousands of people have come to The Vatican looking for answers in a world of chaos. The Roman Catholic Church believes the infallible Holy Father and his spiritual guidance will lead them through the dark, uncertain days ahead." The camera slowly panned the mourning faces of those gathered in The Vatican courtyard and then focused back to the reporter. "We all pray for peace. This is Katja Lody reporting from Vatican City in Rome." With those words, she disappeared from the screen and the central news desk resumed reporting.

"They will replay and replay those horrible scenes throughout the coming days," Chris projected. "They want to make sure everyone that still has TV or internet reception will believe Israel is to blame for everything. I can't even begin to imagine the hatred for the Jews that will explode from this."

"Just as my father wrote," Gabi reminded him. "From every direction, Yahweh's chosen people will be forced to come back to the safety of Israel, their homeland."

"I need a break." Chris spoke with a somewhat less irritation in his voice. "Let's see where your father's way of escape takes us."

Chris led the way to the storage room and Gabriella followed him. As they entered, she was again taken aback by the forethought of her father. "I have heard of doomsday preppers and even watched a few of those ridiculous TV programs, or so I thought. I would never have dreamed in a million years my father was one of them, but I am so glad he was." In spite of all the infelicitous circumstances of their lives, she was still able to manage a forced smile.

The storage room was the size of a two-car garage. Shelves lined the walls all the way around the room, filled from top to bottom. Along three of the walls were huge buckets of survival foods. On the fourth wall were survival necessities: paper supplies, personal items, batteries, flashlights, medical supplies, emergency radio, and numerous other boxes labeled with the items contained. In the middle of the room were stacked boxes that were unmarked. It appeared they had just been recently stored and not yet labeled. What caught her attention was the one huge box that was marked 'guns and ammunition'.

"Unbelievable." Chris muttered. "Just unbelievable." Your father truly was prepared for every scenario." Chris's police instinct took him immediately to evaluate the box containing the weapons. He quickly opened and briefly surveyed the contents. "Wow," was his reaction.

"I don't like guns," was Gabriella's response.

Chris turned to face her. "This was one of my big concerns, not having the protection we might need. No concerns now. You may change your mind about guns before this is over."

"I've never shot a gun and don't want to." Her voice was defiant.

"We may be doing a lot of things we don't *want* to do in the coming years." He retorted back. His voice slightly softened with compassion as apprehension filled her blue eyes. "Gabi, everything in our lives has changed, absolutely everything. We'll have to figure this out day by day as we go. Now, show me where that opening is to the tunnel."

While Chris found flashlights and tested them, Gabriella walked to the back wall and reached as high as she could. She felt the button and looked at Chris. "It's right here." Pushing it, she stepped out of the way as a four-foot-wide shelf filled with paper supplies opened backwards, revealing a passageway. Gabriella focused her flashlight in the darkness before them. She gasped in disbelief. "Oh, my, I can't believe this." Her eyes grew wide in amazement.

She looked at Chris with sheer delight. "Do you know what this is, Chris?" Her voice was shivering in excitement as she stepped from the storage room.

He peered into the darkness not sure what he was seeing. Gabriella instantly knew.

"This is a lava cavern. Dad built his bunker in a cavern with an exit into a lava tunnel, leading to the outside. Brilliant, absolutely brilliant!" Gabriella felt totally at home in this underworld since caving had been the crux of her life. "I'm sure he purposely had the lodge built right over the cavern. Can you believe this?"

"I never cease to be amazed at that man." Chris stated, cautiously stepping into the darkness. He shined his light to survey the height and width and get acclimated to his new environment. "I'd say this is approximately twelve feet high and twenty feet wide. Looks like it narrows as we go out."

"That's normal for caves," she informed him. "You will have small passageways that open to larger caverns of all sizes. Sometimes you come to a dead end, which is apparently what dad wanted this to appear to be. I still can't believe this!" Her voice was filled with excitement for the first time since her awakening. It was obvious she was totally at home in this subterranean world.

"The way of our escape is a cave, literally at my door." She chuckled and the echoes rang through the rock corridor. Thoughts of Caleb were invading her mind. For twelve years of cave exploration, he had been by her side in every subterraneous journey.

"Caleb would have loved this," she whispered to herself.

Chris pretended not to hear, but there was a sting in his heart, sympathizing with her pain. He turned their attention back to the cave. "Look at this," he said pointing his flashlight back towards the opened bunker door. He pushed the button that closed the door. On the cave side it was an artificial lava rock, very light weight for moving. Any possible explorer would think it was simply the end of the cavern.

"He truly thought every detail out perfectly. Simply amazing," she admitted as she surveyed the artificial wall.

"Are you up to this, Gabi, after all you've been through?"

"Really, I feel fine. Seems like it was all just a dream. Even now I feel like I'm dreaming. Nothing feels real." A brief look of sorrow crossed her face and then quickly disappeared. "I've gone miles into black caves, climbed over massive rocks, and dropped into lava tunnels all over the world. I won't give you the exhaustive run down, but this is a breeze."

Together they started the half-mile journey through the underground passageway. The tunnel floor was mostly flat and created an easy exit. The archeologist in Gabriella took over as she kept moving her light around the tunnel as they exited, surveying for any interesting details. Nothing appeared unusual. It was not the sort of cave that would draw exploring enthusiasts, which she was sure was her father's plan. Shortly, daylight became visible as they neared the opening of the cave.

Before they exited, Gabriella turned back toward the cavern and yelled, "We'll be back!" Her voice echoed over and over as the sound reverberated along the lava walls through the darkness of the tunnel.

"What was that all about?" Chris asked, surprised at her outburst.

She slightly blushed in embarrassment. "It's what my mother did when she left the cave here in Israel where they found the ancient writing. She thought they would someday return."

"If this is too hard for you, Gabi, you don't have to talk about it."

"No I want to," she assured him. "Now I'm here in the same area they were in, the very area I was conceived, and I believe it's for a reason. I've got to find out who murdered her."

"I promise I'll do everything possible to help you." Chris put his arm around her shoulder in comfort. Briefly, she leaned against him for moral support.

Gabriella's somber mood changed to one of apprehension as she stepped into the sunlight for the first time in several days. Her eyes immediately darted in every direction for signs of movement. She noticed Chris also was visually searching the area. Nothing was moving except the trees in the mountain breezes.

The cave exited into a totally secluded place, just as her father wrote. Both stood for several minutes basking in the sunlight and each inhaled the fresh mountain air.

Gabriella glanced back at the opening. "I should have known my father would include a cave in his doomsday scenario, if at all possible. Caving was the biggest part of our life together." A beautiful smile graced her face as the wonderful childhood memories replaced her sadness.

"You'll have to share some of your cave adventures with me sometime. I've never had the time or opportunity to try it for myself. I always thought it'd be interesting though."

"Interesting doesn't begin to describe it, Chris. It is more like magical, intriguing...soul capturing. The underground mysteries are beyond what the mind can imagine. Caves tell us stories of ancient life. They open a world of the unknowns and surround us with new mysteries. I would often try to imagine who drew the cave art. What were they like? What messages were they trying to send to the future?"

He watched her expression totally change when she began to describe the majestic beauty of the thing she loved most in life.

Gabriella focused back on the task at hand. Her attention was immediately drawn to a block building about one hundred yards away. It was built in a thick grove of juniper trees that camouflaged its existence from the air. A narrow path led from the mouth of the cave to the place where her father had stored the Jeep.

"There, Chris." She pointed to the building her father had described in his letter. They started down the rough, rocky trail, Chris leading the way.

"I wonder how many times my dad walked this path? I can almost imagine him, dressed in his disguise as a Hasidic Jew, leaving the bunker and taking these very same steps to come to Haifa. Apparently, he would watch me when I would be on campus or at the local coffee shop and all the while, I thought he was dead." The last few words were barely whispered.

Her countenance quickly changed as she caught a glimpse in the distance of a beautiful volcanic lake with the majestic backdrop of Mt. Hermon. The sunlight appeared to be caressing the snowcapped mountains, reflecting in the sparkling waters.

Gabriella's breath caught as memories of The Omega Watchers Project came flooding back into her mind. She pointed to the apex of the mountain range. "That's Mt. Hermon. It was the central point of the entire research project, Chris. According to the Book of Enoch, that was the supernatural portal of entry for the fallen angels." She stood still for a moment enraptured by the beauty. "Can you imagine such a magnificent place being a gateway for evil?"

Her eyes fixated on the resplendent mountain that loomed in the distance. The sun was directly over the top of the mountain, casting a hypnotizing illumination across the rippling waters. The limbs of the juniper trees swayed melodically in the mountain breezes, as if to a symphony only nature could hear. The birds were singing in perfect harmony on this crisp, fall day. It seemed all was well with the world...reality said differently. Her thoughts returned to Caleb and her desire to share this magnificent place with him, only to remind herself it would never be again.

Her voice was peaceful when she finally spoke. "In this perfect place, it's impossible to believe the world is in total chaos and the catastrophic end just a few years away. None of this feels real." She reached over and took Chris's hand for comfort. It surprised even her that she was so comfortable with this man she had just met. He closed his hand around hers and said nothing. Their friendship felt natural for both, knowing they must lean on each other in the days ahead.

Chris led the way towards the block building through the maze of juniper trees. There they found the rough road that led to the garage size metal door. He inserted the key retrieved from the storage room wall and the lock clicked open. Pulling open the door allowed the natural light to filter in and reveal the Jeep safely stored. The wall was lined with gas cans. Chris checked each can to make sure they were full. He got in the Jeep, inserted the key and started the engine.

"Perfect," he said, turning the engine back off and exiting the vehicle. "We are all set when I need to leave."

"Where are you going?" Gabriella asked as apprehension of being alone captured her.

"I need to contact headquarters and find out if Detective Richards survived the attacks. If he did, you know he'll come back for us. That could put him and us in danger."

Gabriella nodded her head in agreement as Chris continued: "Plus, from the police station I can do some checking, try to get some information on our visitors. The name Ugo sounds very familiar to me for some reason. Since Detective Richards had already started checking your background, trying to find who had sent your father's research notes, he may have some clues. Richards has no idea the case of the mystery box has been solved, but he may have discovered something that will give us a solid lead on who Ugo or our visitors are."

"I'm going with you," she stated unequivocally. "When are we going?"

"I'm not sure *we* are going," Chris answered with consternation in his voice. "You would be safer staying put in the bunker."

"Oh, no," she argued. "You are not leaving me here alone. What if someone, somewhere, knows about the bunker?"

"We'll discuss that later." He knew he was fighting a losing battle. "It may not be safe to go back to Haifa just yet, but I do need to reach Detective Richards. His appearing at the lodge could be detrimental to us all." Chris pulled his cell phone from his pocket, hoping maybe... "Darn it, no signal. Let's drive a bit and see if we can get reception."

She agreed as she headed for the Jeep and climbed in. Chris joined her and started the engine. He checked the gas gauge and it registered full. All gauge levels were normal. He put it in gear and pulled out of the secluded building, following the rough trail made by Gabriella's father for his ventures from the lodge.

Chris would not speak the concerns flooding his mind. He knew there was a possibility the lodge was being watched. What if they were watching the end of this trail? What if these men or their cohorts were waiting at the end? He instinctively felt his side to reaffirm his pistol was in its place.

Slowly they descended around the mountain on what appeared to be a hunter's trail. Gabriella kept trying to get a phone signal but there was none. After about half an hour they came to a main road intersection. Across the road was a sign with an arrow pointing in the direction of the mountain. The sign read 'Hermon Ski Lodge'.

"Now I know where we are," Gabriella exclaimed. "If you turn left it takes us back up the mountain past the gated entrance of the lodge. Beyond that is the entrance to the ski resort."

Chris looked in all directions. He saw no signs of anyone watching for them. Everything was perfectly normal, even tranquil. The only movement was the limbs of trees continuing to sway in the mountain breezes.

He hesitated for a moment, trying to decide which would be the safest direction to try to find phone signal. He looked at Gabriella and raised his eyebrows, then immediately made the decision. "I'm sure they would have a signal at the ski resort. Let's head that way. Let me know when we get reception." He handed her his cell phone and slowly pulled the Jeep off the trail onto the black top road. He proceeded north, constantly checking the rear-view mirror to make sure they were not being followed.

Gabriella continued to monitor the phone. She glanced up as they neared the gated entrance to her father's mountain lodge. Just before the entrance to the lodge there was a graveled road exiting to the right of the main road. "Look, Chris, there's a black vehicle parked under that thicket of trees up the driveway. Do you see it? It's just sitting there facing toward the gate to the lodge."

In a commanding voice, he instructed: "Get down in the seat, Gabi." She immediately bent down so it would appear only one person was in the Jeep. Chris did not glance toward the parked vehicle, but turned his face in the opposite direction until they were past the lodge entrance and safely out of sight. He continued to check the rear-view mirror to make sure they were not being followed.

"Okay, you can get up now." The relief in his voice was obvious.

Gabriella exhaled a long breath as she sat back up in her seat.

Chris continued checking the mirror. "We're clear. There's nothing behind us. That was just a precaution. I doubt there was any real threat."

Slowly Gabriella relaxed once again and continued to check the phone. A few miles later, as they neared the ski resort entrance, the phone connected. "Okay, we've got it."

Chris pulled off the winding mountain road at the first opportunity. He called Detective Richards' cell number and anxiously waited. One ring, two rings, three...and then voice mail. Frustrated he turned the phone off. "Well, we still don't know anything. I'm not taking the chance of leaving a message. If I can't reach him by cell, I'll have to make a trip back into the city soon."

"I'm going with you. No arguments." Gabriella shot him a determined look that said 'you will not change my mind'.

"I won't even try," he responded. He already knew she was a strong-willed woman and he would have to learn to live with it.

She noticed Chris' countenance suddenly changed with his last glance in the rear-view mirror. He slightly accelerated the Jeep and continued to watch behind them.

"What is it?" She knew something was not right as he took a sharp turn faster than was safe. Instinctively she put her head back down out of sight. Chris quickly pulled off onto a mountain trail, obscure from the main road. Within seconds they could see the black vehicle appear from around the curve. It sped past them, totally unaware of their location.

Gabriella looked at Chris and his face told her all she needed to know.

CHAPTER 9

hris exited the side road and headed east in the direction of the black SUV, through the northeast section of Mount Hermon. The road turned and twisted around the mountain terrain as Chris hurried to catch up with the vehicle that had passed them. Gabriella held to the seat as she swayed back and forth. Her body tensed with foreboding, remembering the attempt to murder Professor Brotman on a similar mountain road.

"Why are you following them?" Her eyes were pleading with him to turn around.

"I need that license plate number." Chris accelerated even more in his attempt to catch up, swerving around the curves and speeding up on the straighter stretches of pavement. Gabriella's window was down and she could feel the crisp air blowing in her face as the vehicle went faster and faster. They came to an intersection in the road and Chris skidded to a stop. It was obvious he had lost them.

He glanced at Gabriella realizing his hot pursuit had totally unnerved her. "Are you all right?"

She managed a nod, but her face told him otherwise.

"I'm sorry, Gabi. The police officer in me took over. I wasn't thinking about what it would do to you."

Chris pulled off at the first available trail and parked the Jeep far enough off the road to be out of sight. He turned the motor off, allowing Gabriella time for her fears to settle. They both sat quietly with their windows down, listening to the mountain sounds. The tranquil rushing creek flowing over rocks and down the mountainside soothed her anxiety. She closed her eyes and listened to the rustling melody of tree limbs as they blew in the mountain breezes. It was a pseudo peace which made it seem all was well with the world; however, they both knew that was far from the actual truth.

Chris realized despite her strong will and independent spirit, Gabriella was really feeling vulnerable and uncertain. She had her hands clenched in her lap and her back upright. Her blond ponytail had blown loose in the wind and was hanging down around her face. She turned away, trying to conceal her apprehensions. She did not fool him, not for a second. She needed him and he decided then and there, without a doubt, he would protect her through whatever the coming years presented. He would protect her with his life, if needed. He had no idea how prophetic his thoughts were.

They sat quietly for a while, allowing nature to minister a measure of equanimity to their minds and bodies. When Gabriella turned to look at Chris, he knew self-control had regained its hold on her.

"Isn't it weird there's no traffic, Gabi? We've only seen the one vehicle since we got on the main road."

"Not just weird, its plain eerie." She observed. "I've been this way many times and in all different seasons. There's always traffic. Just ahead is Shebaa Farms and the southern portion of Mt. Hermon's natural reserve. There would be lots of tourists traveling if life was normal."

Chris nodded in agreement. "Is there phone reception here?"

Gabriella checked and shook her head. "Nope, sorry."

Chris started the engine, turned the Jeep and slowly approached the main road again.

They both noticed a military vehicle approaching. The driver stared at them as he passed on by.

"I bet he thinks we are crazy to be out here. Maybe we are." Gabriella admitted.

"According to the news, the war is definitely over, at least for now. People will start venturing out again." Chris shot her a smile, assuring her he would not put her in danger again.

"Let's drive closer to Shebaa Farms and try again for reception." Chris started the engine and pulled back onto the main road. Gabriella sat quietly watching the beautiful mountain sceneries.

The higher altitude became rocky terrain more than lush vegetation. Breathtaking, early fall blooming crocus hermoneus were majestically displayed along the roadside. The branches cascaded over the rocky cliffs, hanging in clusters of limbs exhibiting a large array of delicate lilac flowers. The limbs swayed in the mountain winds, giving life to the rugged limestone formations.

"Our team spent a lot of time driving through these mountain areas when we came to the lodge for a retreat. We all loved the outdoors and it was a welcome break from the caves. Sometimes the Professor would join us and interject both the historical and religious significance of this area."

She pointed towards the right. "Over in that direction is Neve Ativ. It's a small settlement of Israelis who built their community in alpine style around the ski lodge. It gives them the opportunity of capitalizing on the tourists that come here, especially during the ski season. It's too far off the main road to really tell how enchanting it is, but you can see in the distance the chalets and ski slopes."

Chris slowed the Jeep to take a better look at the landscape.

"Breathtaking, isn't it?" She asked as reality registered back in her mind. "Just a few days ago, this whole area was considered occupied territory and illegal settlements by the international communities. Now the world knows Israel not only owns all the Golan Heights but also owns all the land and nations around them, just as God promised to Abraham and his descendants. In fact, we aren't too far from Har Habetarim, where the rabbis believe Yahweh made His blood covenant with Abraham."

Chris found that bizarre. "Odd that on the very day the news is breaking that Israel has expanded her borders to the land of the Abrahamic Covenant, we are where the covenant was made. You said there is no such thing as coincidence so is this some kind of sign?"

Gabriella looked at Chris to see if he was serious or joking. His face showed no amusement. "I guess we'll see soon enough," she replied in contemplation.

"I have lived in Israel all of my life, Gabi. I'm thirty-four years old and have never been to this area. I've been skiing, but just up to the resort and back down. I didn't take time to study the history of this area, religious or otherwise. My loss, I think now."

Gabriella saw a sign ahead. "There's Highway 98. If we go north, it will take us to Har Habetarim. It's close to the Lebanese IDF check-point on the Israeli side. There's a constant dispute on who owns Mount Habetarim." She paused. "At least there was a dispute until a few days ago. The Muslims and the Israelis both wanted control, both being descendants of Abraham."

"Since we are this close, I want to see this place for myself," Chris said, turning on the highway leading to the sacred place. Something deep inside him was stirring that he never felt before. He was a descendent of Abraham. That reality and all that it meant had never fully registered with him. This land was promised to Israel and now they had taken full control. His Hebraic lineage was beginning to root in his spirit. It was exhilarating to realize he was the son of the Almighty Creator who controlled both heaven and earth. Something inside of him wanted to shout for joy, but his dignified police officer countenance managed to remain in control.

He pulled into the large parking lot marked 'visitors'. The empty lot was another blatant reminder of the dubious circumstances surrounding them. Exiting the Jeep, they both were watching for any signs of moving vehicles, especially a black Suburban. Feeling the area was safe, they walked the short distance to the entrance of the rocky trail. The incline led to a stone monument, erected to memorialize the place Yahweh met with Abraham. This place marked the spot the Abrahamic Covenant was sealed.

Gabriella's voice was soft and reverent, "When Yahweh makes a covenant with man, He never changes. From that day and forever The Promised Land belongs to Israel."

They walked side by side not saying a word until they reached the top. This holy place, surrounded by a large grove of kermes oaks, was steeped with tranquility. Some of the trees were at least twenty feet in circumference and over two-stories high.

Gabriella sat down on a bench beneath the tree closest to the shrine and motioned for Chris to join her, while she continued with her history lesson. "The Professor was continuously teaching my team from the Torah and even though Caleb and I didn't really believe it, at that time, we still respectfully listened. Professor Brotman had a way of captivating you with his stories and I truly learned a lot. He told us the spiritual significance of the kermes oak trees."

"These are spiritual trees?" Chris asked, captivated by their beauty.

"No, silly, these trees contribute to the spiritual life of Israel. There are kermes worms that feed from these trees. They are also called crimson worms or *tola'at shani* in Hebrew. You've heard of them?"

Chris nodded his head, wondering where she was going with her story.

"Well, those worms get their red color feeding from the kermes oak trees. In the Bible, when it describes the priestly garments, the crimson wool dye came from the kermes worms. It's extremely expensive and was only used for priests and kings. Because these kermes oaks have spiritual value, they are referred to as sacred oaks or oaks of righteousness. Not only do these very trees produce a dye needed for holy garments, they also witnessed the Abrahamic Covenant. In this place, God gave Abraham's descendants the land they have finally possessed in the last few days. It is Israel's land no matter what anyone says. It is The Promised Land."

Chris stood up and did a complete turn ingesting the panoramic beauty of the surroundings. To the north, one could see Lebanon. To the west across the Golan Heights was Syria. To the south was Israel, and in the far distance to the east was a glimpse of the Mediterranean Sea. "Yahweh actually came down to this very place and met with Abraham." His voice was filled with awe as he lingered in the wonder of the holy ground.

"This truly is a sacred place, Chris. Every time I've been here there were so many tourists it was impossible to feel the spiritual tranquility. Now we are the only people here, and it seems Yahweh is making a covenant directly with us."

They stood in silence soaking in the serenity of the atmosphere, both trying to imagine Abraham being in that very place making an eternal covenant with the Divine Creator. They had just witnessed the Abrahamic Covenant come to fruition with the prophecy of the Psalms 83 War being fulfilled. The Promised Land at last belonged to Israel.

Reluctantly, they left the magnificent grove of sacred oaks and began the fall afternoon journey back down the steep, rocky path to their Jeep.

"There's something else about the kermes worms the Professor told us", Gabriella continued her exposé as they walked. "The Catholic Church, soon after its formation, started making scarlet robes. Their dye was also made from the kermes worms. These robes have been worn by the Cardinals down through the centuries. The Professor thought the Catholic Church was trying to replace the Jewish Temple and the Levite Priests." She stopped and turned to face Chris. "Have you heard of The Book of Revelation?"

"That's in the Christian Bible, isn't it? It tells of a coming world apocalypse or something like that? I used to laugh at it...but I'm not laughing now." Chris' last words were spoken with grave conviction.

Gabriella was trying to remember exactly what the Professor had said. "I think I have this right. The Professor said in one of the chapters, I think it was in Chapter 17, there was a woman dressed in purple and scarlet riding on a dragon. He said the crimson and purple robe represented the Catholic Church and the Pope. The dragon was Satan. Think about this, Chris, my father said to watch the Vatican and the Pope. It seems to me something major is about to happen in The Catholic Church or with The Pope, maybe both."

Chris just shook his head as they continued down the rocky trail. "This is all so weird. It's like an apocalyptic movie, but instead I'm actually living it."

They had reached the end of the path to the parking lot where the Jeep awaited them. It remained the only car in sight. Chris opened the door for Gabriella and helped her in. He took one last look toward the kermes oaks at the top of the hill before climbing in behind the wheel. He was amazed at how all the details were tying together.

"Ready?" He asked starting the engine and backing out to begin the mountain drive back to the bunker. Gabriella continued to check for phone signal as they drove. When they turned back on the main highway reception resumed. Again, Chris attempted to call Detective Richards with a dead end at voicemail. Again, he left no message.

"If he can check his calls, at least he'll see I'm trying to reach him. I'll try one more time before we lose signal again."

Gabriella wondered if Chris did not have a family he needed to call. Surely, there was someone he wanted to check on. She did not want to be too personal, so she decided to wait until he brought the subject up.

It was as though he could already read her expressions. He knew she was questioning something. "Ok, Gabi, let's have it. I know there's something you want to ask me. What is it?"

"Maybe I shouldn't. I really don't know you, Chris."

"I guess you'll have to get to know me. We're stuck together, like it or not. Now what is it?" He glanced toward her with his eyes silently demanding she answer him.

She took a deep breath trying to find the right words. She did not want to offend him. "Don't you have someone or some family you need to check on? You haven't mentioned anyone."

His face grew solemn and for a few moments it was obvious he was struggling with his answer. He continued to drive with his eyes focused on the winding road as he answered, "My parents came from Great Britain to Israel not long after they married. The Muslim population in Western Europe was beginning to grow slowly but surely around them and they could see what you might call the writing on the wall. They wanted to raise a family some place that would be safe."

"So, they made Aliyah to Israel?" Gabriella interjected. "That's what the Professor did too, but then almost every family in Israel has come from some other country. What happened to your grandparents and other relatives?"

"My grandparents had passed away. There was nothing holding them there. I was born in Israel so I never knew the few distant relatives I had still living in Western Europe. When my parents first moved to Israel, they lived on a kibbutz and that's where I was born. They had hoped to have a large family, but complications during my birth prevented that from happening. Both my mother and I almost died during delivery."

He tried to lighten the mood. "Good news is, we both survived." His voice was filled with jesting.

"Obviously, you did." She pushed his shoulder in a playful gesture.

"I had a wonderful childhood and no child was ever loved more than I was. I think sometimes they loved me more than normal, knowing there was no hope for another child. Anyway, before I started school, we moved to Tel Aviv. My father joined the police force there. I guess that's when my love for law enforcement was born. He would come home telling his wonderful stories of how he saved fair ladies in distress. He was quite the comedian. My mother never worked. She dedicated her entire life to me. Everything she did was to create a home, a life, and happiness for me and my father. She was so worried when I turned thirty and didn't have a wife and family of my own. To her it was the only thing in this world that really mattered. I kept telling her when I found the right woman, I would know it. Until then I would just save women in distress, like my father did." He winked at Gabriella implying that was exactly his mission with her.

The wink sent a stab through her heart, remembering how Caleb always winked when he was teasing her. She quickly pushed his memory to the side. The pain was too deep. "Are they still in Tel Aviv?" Gabriella saw his expression quickly change again when she asked.

"I don't know. I think probably not." He muttered.

"Why wouldn't you? You've got to try to contact them," Gabriella insisted.

"There's more to the story, Gabi. About a year ago, my parents invited me for a special dinner. I drove down from Haifa not sure what the special occasion was and really expecting they would have invited some woman they wanted me to meet."

"Was there a woman?" Gabriella asked, slightly teasing.

"No woman. I was really shocked at the reason they asked me to come. I had been working in Haifa for over five years and wasn't familiar with their social life and things they were personally doing. The times I would see them, they seemed happier and had a peace I couldn't explain. Something was different, but I didn't question. Just figured it was because my father had retired and they were enjoying their golden years. However, that night at dinner I was told about the transformation."

Gabriella turned sideways in her seat so she could fully watch Chris recount his story. She leaned a little forward, her body language telling him she wanted to hear every word.

He kept his eyes focused on the road as he explained. "It's really hard for me to share this, Gabi, especially in light of current events. I'm ashamed at my reaction, and the fact I've hardly seen them this past year. Anyway, that night my mother had a wonderful meal prepared and afterwards she cleared the table and brought the coffee tray. Everything seemed normal. Then my father started by telling me they had gone back to their Hebraic roots. I wasn't even sure what that meant, except maybe they had started going to synagogue. Like I told you, we never went when I was growing up."

Gabriella detected a slight quiver in his voice as he continued: "Father explained to me after he retired he began to think about facing the end of life. He questioned if there was more to this existence? Was there a God? He began his search for answers by reading Torah and the prophets, more as historical writings; but then the desire came to understand more of the spiritual history of our nation and learn about the God of Israel. They joined a small group that met in homes and they all studied together. The group was a Messianic group. They believed the Messiah of Israel had already come and been rejected. The more they shared, well, I thought they were going off the deep end and losing their hold on reality. What's more, I told them so. I couldn't believe at their age they would fall for such foolishness. Even though I was not a religious Jew, I knew the rabbis did *not* believe the Messiah had already come. I wouldn't listen to their nonsense and immediately left."

"I can imagine your parents were very upset."

"Oh, yes. Not angry, but concerned when I would not listen to their, what I thought, were tall tales of ancient fables. I refused to speak to them again about it. The few times I saw them, I made it perfectly clear that religion would not be discussed. I had in my mind if there was a loving God he would not allow the suffering we see in this world. He would not send good people to a burning hell just because they didn't blindly serve a God they couldn't see."

"You know now, don't you? We both know now how stupid we were." Gabriella replied softly.

"Yes, I know now." Chris' voice was filled with regret. "I think I really knew when Caleb tried to talk to me and gave me another chance. I have no doubt it was my parent's prayers being answered when Caleb shared the truth of The Messiah with me. I was given one last chance before it was too late. I wanted time to think about it, you know, weigh it out. I needed to figure things out in my head...but I was one day too late." The last sentence kept painfully ringing in his mind, over and over.

Gabriella knew now why he would not call his parents. "You believe they're gone, don't you? Gone in the vanishings?"

"Gabi, I know they are. I feel it in my gut. I'm sure if they were still here, they would be ringing my cell phone constantly to make sure I was alive and well. There's nothing from them."

They both were silent for a moment. "You know, Chris, we will see them again. I'm holding on to that with everything in me," Gabriella reached over and took his hand. "...if we will endure until the end."

Chris squeezed her hand and then put both hands back on the steering wheel as they approached the long curve that circled in front of the gated entrance to the lodge. This time there was no suspicious car parked beneath the trees across the road.

Gabriella longingly gazed at the iron gates as they slowly drove by. She desperately wished the team was arriving from Haifa one more time for a restful retreat. "It will never be again," she whispered under her breath.

Within a minute, they were past the entrance and had one steeper curve before they were back at the hunter's trail that would take them to the cave entrance. Chris pulled far enough off the main road to be out of sight of any passing traffic, even though there was no traffic to speak of.

"Phone signal, Chris!" Gabriella exclaimed as though she had won the lottery. "Just one bar, but maybe it will connect." Chris tried one last time to reach Detective Richards. Still there was no answer. He laid the phone down with a sigh.

"We'll have to start thinking about a trip to Haifa soon. This can't wait."

Gabriella nodded her head in agreement. "I'm ready when you are. I want to see how much of Haifa is left after the attacks. I know I can't go back to my apartment, but I can't help but wonder if it's still there."

"Is there anyone you want to call, Gabi?" He asked, handing her the phone.

"No, Chris. Everyone I love is gone. There would only be Caleb's parents and I have no idea how to reach them in Germany."

Chris reached over and with a fist gently nudged her chin. "Guess it's just you and me, kid." She could not help but smile with his feeble attempt at a Humphrey Bogart impersonation.

Silently, they drove back up the rough trail to the grove of juniper trees and parked the Jeep in the block building. They had only been gone a few hours, but now they both felt they had long been friends. They exited the Jeep and Chris locked the building door. Side by side they retraced the rocky path to the lava cave.

Reentering, they turned on their flashlights and silently backtracked through the dark passageway. Once inside, the bunker door closed behind them secluding them into safety. Both were wondering what the most current breaking news would bring. Both also knew, it would not be good.

CHAPTER 10

———•◆•———

hris prepared a late lunch while Gabriella took time to freshen
up. He brought the tray to the coffee table in front of the TV.
Shortly, she joined him.

"What's new?" Gabriella asked, as Michael Adelson was still reporting.

Adelson's voice was filled with sorrow. "We can now confirm the earlier reports regarding the destruction in Jerusalem. This is the saddest day
for all Israelis since the rebirth of our nation. We are going live now to
the temple site."

The sad face of an Israeli reporter appeared on the screen. "This is
Sarah Jacobs reporting from the Temple Mount in Jerusalem." Her black
hair was blowing in the wind and she continually pushed it out of her eyes
struggling to hold back tears. The reporter's voice was quivering in spite
of every effort to maintain self-control. "The heart of every Jew has been
pierced. The symbol of our faith, our history, our future, and our country
has been destroyed."

The cameraman panned the area where thousands of Israelis filled the
Temple Mount praying and crying out to Yahweh. The reporter struggled
to continue: "Rabbis and devout Jewish men from all over Jerusalem are
gathering at the Temple Mount to mourn this great loss and pray for the
coming of the Messiah."

The camera zoomed in on one of the rabbis. He was dressed in the
traditional black suit, with a white shirt and black tie. He was holding
his prayer shawl tightly over his head as it tossed in the wind. The tallit
covered his head, but the black brimmed hat was still obvious underneath.
His sidelocks hung down his cheeks and swung back and forth across his

long gray beard as he continually rocked with groans and moans no man could understand. Tears flooded from his eyes and pervaded his beard. He appeared glued in the direction of the Temple Mount taking no notice of the camera.

The voice of the reporter was silent as the camera went from one area to another. The pictures all depicted the same scenes of Israelis mourning. Faces were filled with sorrow and eyes full of tears. Groups of men were gathering in huddles, hugging and weeping in unison. The Temple Mount continued to fill with lamenters and the sounds of grieving grew louder.

The reporter took a deep breath as the camera zoomed back to her. "Fellow Israelis, what you cannot see on your television screen is the Wailing Wall. It was completely demolished by our enemies. Not one stone of the Western Wall of our ancient temple still stands upon another. The initial strike in the three-day war was to demolish our only holy place, the symbol that promised our Messiah would come. It was an edict that Israel and our religion would be destroyed; however, Israel was victorious and we will rebuild!"

The mourners closest to the reporter heard her words and began to chant, "We will rebuild, we will rebuild!" As the words reverberated through the masses, a wave of voices one after another could be heard chanting: "We will rebuild, we will rebuild!" The continuous, strong winds carried the words as the declaration resounded throughout the entire Temple Mount. "We will rebuild!"

The cameraman again focused on the crowds, capturing the excitement. He allowed their shouts of determination to air to all of Israel. The noise became so loud the reporter could hardly be heard.

She held her microphone near the mouth of a nearby rabbi. "Do you have any words for our listeners? The rabbi raised his voice struggling to be heard over the surrounding pandemonium, "Our mourning will be turned to joy. Our ashes into beauty. We will build our holy temple and our Messiah will come."

The reporter motioned for a cut and almost instantly Michael Adelson was facing the camera again.

Adelson's gloomy expression prior to the segment at the Temple Mount now was filled with hope. The camera panned the news room to the faces normally behind the cameras. They, too, had been infected with the optimism as they saw the lamenters' cries turn to shouts of victory.

Excitement and expectation now glowed from Adelson's face. "Never has there been a day like today in the modern history of Israel. I don't know whether to laugh or to cry. Amid our nation's mayhem, a spirit of hope is emerging."

Gabriella and Chris rarely had seen such raw emotion from a news reporter, but this day it seemed appropriate. They sat silently, contemplating the unexpected news. Gabriella picked up the Professor's Bible and began to turn the pages. "I know it's here somewhere in the 24th Chapter of Matthew. The Professor quoted this many times. Oh, yes, here it is. *Truly I tell you, not one stone here will be left on another.* The Wailing Wall was the only wall still standing of the Jewish Temple. This was prophesied by Yeshua and He said it would be another sign of the end."

Chris was confused and Gabriella understood why. Had it not been for twelve years of listening to the Professor's biblical exhortations, she would have no idea either.

"This is the way Professor Brotman explained it to us. Just after Yeshua told the disciples the temple would be destroyed, they came to Him in private and asked what the signs would be of His return at the end of days. They are listed one by one in this chapter."

"And what just happened to the Wailing Wall is one of the prophecies?" Chris was struggling to understand.

"That was the first one in Matthew 24. He prophesied the Jewish Temple that stood in the day he lived would be destroyed, not one stone would be left standing on another. In 70 AD, the Romans destroyed the temple, but the prophecy wasn't complete, the Western Wall did not fall. It became the Wailing Wall, the holy symbol of hope for Israel that one day the temple would be rebuilt. The Western Wall had to come down, too, for the prophecy to be totally fulfilled. Now that has happened the countdown to the end has begun."

"What about the new temple, Gabi? I know the rabbis plan to rebuild, but will there be time? Why would they if everything is ending in just a few years?"

"The Temple Institute in Jerusalem has everything ready. You would not believe what they've already done. They've made the temple vessels, the priests' garments, everything. They have the blueprints already drawn and even the stones cut, ready to transport to the temple mount. They believe it will only take about three years or so to build it. The descendants of the Levite Priesthood have been training to perform the temple ceremonies. They believe they must rebuild the temple for the Messiah to appear. They just don't understand the false Messiah will appear first."

"I just wish somehow my parents could know I've found the truth they found." Chris spoke in a voice of deep regret.

Gabriella covered his large, strong hand with hers. "I think they do know, Chris. I truly believe our loved ones know." He turned his hand to fully embrace hers. With a gentle squeeze, he nodded his head and got up to remove the lunch tray.

Gabriella marked the chapter and laid the Bible down to listen to Adelson's continued reports. A Rabbi was now seated beside him in the station's newsroom.

Adelson started the interview. "I have Rabbi Zimmerman on the set to discuss the impact on the religious community with this latest news regarding the destruction of the Wailing Wall. Welcome, Rabbi."

"Thank you, Michael. I am excited and honored to be discussing both the destruction of our sacred Wailing Wall and The Promised Land of Israel. I must add, we are praying for those that have lost loved ones in the vanishings. That is a very strange thing."

Adelson nodded in agreement. "It certainly is strange. There have been varying explanations, but nothing substantiated. We will keep on top of any reports here at Channel 2. Today, let's start with the new territory you just referred to. You believe in the Torah that Adonai promised this new expanded State of Israel?" Adelson waited for his response.

The Rabbi did not mince words. "I knew from the sacred writings, from the pure Word of the One and only Holy God that someday Israel would possess The Promised Land. The defeat of our surrounding enemies, those who would destroy us, was directed by the Divine Hand of Yahweh. He promised to our father, Abraham, this land would one day belong to his descendants. Today is the day." The Rabbi's eyes gleamed in sheer joy. "This means our Messiah is soon to come and we are to prepare the way for Him."

"Just how will you prepare, Rabbi?" Adelson again paused for him to answer.

"We will rebuild our temple on the Temple Mount in Jerusalem, according to the instructions of the prophet Ezekiel. When it is finished, The Anointed One will appear. From Jerusalem, our Messiah will rule and reign forever, not only over Israel, but over all nations. He will bring peace to the earth and there will be no more pain or sorrow. This is the promise of Yahweh."

"And you think the destruction of the Wailing Wall is your sign it is time to rebuild the temple?" Adelson asked.

The Rabbi's voice was firm and certain. "When the first explosion in the three-day war was intentionally planned to destroy the sacred wall of the ancient temple, it was a defiant fist in the face of our God. Our enemies intended to follow with simultaneous attacks to wipe us off the face of the earth. Instead destruction turned upon them and fire rained down from heaven upon those that would destroy Israel. It was the fire of nuclear and neutron bombs. Yahweh's vengeance was released upon our enemies and now they cease to exist. Those nations possessed our land, the land promised to Abraham almost 4000 years ago, and it has been returned to the rightful owner."

"Do you have *any* sympathy for the millions who have died, Rabbi? Do you have any remorse for the innocent victims who had nothing to do with waging the war?"

The Rabbi's voice remained poised. "Did they have sympathy for the millions of innocent Israelis they have murdered and were still planning to murder? Was there any sympathy for the Jewish bloodshed and the inhuman suffering at the hands of Hitler or Stalin? For thousands of years we have been hated for no reason, except for the fact we are Jews. No, I have no sympathy. I have no remorse. If it's Israeli blood, no one cares. The secular media looks the other way. *But*, if it is the blood of any other peoples, then the media cries out for revenge against us. Israel was only protecting their right to exist."

Rabbi Zimmerman looked directly into the camera with his next words. "Our enemies not only attacked our sacred wall, they attacked our Holy God! Israel has prepared for this day knowing it would eventually come. We have prevailed and we will rebuild. We will rebuild our Holy Temple as a sign to the world our Messiah is soon to come and we can never be defeated." Defiance blazed from the eyes of the rabbi as his words became verbal daggers hurled to the world.

The camera focused back on Adelson. "Thank you, Rabbi Zimmerman, for a very enlightening interview. If the IDF had not been prepared for the preemptive strikes, you and I would not be here talking today. Israel would no longer exist." Adelson reached a hand of friendship to the Rabbi as the segment ended.

Chris was pondering the international effects of the Rabbi's words. "How do you think the world will react, Gabi, when this Rabbi's interview is picked up by the international station? WIN TV will definitely air the controversial comments. Israelis will agree with the rabbi, but the world opinion is going to be very different. When they replay over and over his statement of no sympathy for innocent people, no Jew will be safe anywhere but in Israel. Oh, this could be really bad for Jews living outside of our nation."

Gabriella got up from the couch, poised as if ready to make a speech. "What I see is the whole world is being orchestrated per the words of the ancient prophets. Yahweh knew what would happen in the end and he told the prophets to write it down and make it known for those who would hear. Yes, the world will react with extreme and violent hatred toward the Jews. As a result, Jews all over the world will come home to Israel, just as the prophets said they would. It's another sign the end is near."

CHAPTER 11

W ith a heaviness of heart and mind, Gabriella succumbed to physical weariness. "I'm going to bed. It's been a long day. Sleep well, Chris. Good night."

Chris watched her cross the floor in front of him. "Good night, Gabi." He silently prayed her sleep would be restful, with no haunting dreams.

She changed and crawled into the comfortable bed, sinking into the soft mattress. Propping her head upon two feather pillows, she once again read from Psalms 91. After finishing the chapter, she felt the overwhelming peace that was becoming familiar to her. She picked up the stack of letters Caleb had written before the vanishings. These she would not read with Chris. Caleb's letters were personal and private. She would treasure every one of them in the days, weeks, and years stretching before her.

The letters were neatly folded and numbered in the sequence he wanted them read. She unfolded the first one and the engagement ring Caleb had given her fell out. She relived the enchanting moment he put it on her finger. Then quickly her thoughts were replaced with a sob of agony as she remembered throwing it at him in anger. She never had a kind word for him from that time until he vanished. Tears of regret cascaded down her cheeks.

She placed the ring back on her finger, vowing she would never take it off again. Then with trembling hands she began to read. Just the sight of his handwriting took her breath away. She knew it as well as she knew her own. From the first day they met as freshmen in college, they had constantly been together. They had studied together, worked together, and explored together. All the time she would never allow herself to admit she was in love with him. Not until time had run out. She swallowed hard and began to read:

> *My dearest Gabi,*
>
> *I have never written a love letter to anyone and I don't know how eloquent this will be, but know it is truly from the heart. I am compelled to leave with you the surety that I have loved you from the moment we met and I always will. I know in the last few days, before you entered astral sleep, you felt I had betrayed you. You doubted my love. You had just allowed yourself to open your heart to me and then almost immediately you felt I had intentionally turned against you. I tried to tell you then and I also tried to reach you while you were sleeping. I sat at your bedside and prayed that somehow you would hear me.*

Gabi reached for a tissue to wipe her eyes and to allow a moment for his words to digest. She whispered in the silence of the room, "I'm sorry, Caleb. I did hear you. I tried desperately to reach to you. I couldn't wake up and now it's too late." She forced herself to focus back on the letter and continued to read through the blur of her tears.

> *These past few days I have relived over and over the night I gave you my grandmother's ring and asked you to marry me. I have never felt such joy. My parents were ecstatic with the news they finally were going to have a daughter. Life seemed to be complete with you by my side. How quickly that changed.*
>
> *It was that same night the Professor's car brakes were cut and he was almost killed; in fact, it was a miracle he survived. Even the doctors said it was a miracle. We both felt the Holy Presence that came into the room when our research team prayed for him. It was a peace that passed all understanding and from that moment on I wanted that Presence every day of my life. I tried to talk to you about it, but you only*

pushed me away. When I finally surrendered and took the step of faith, I knew beyond a shadow of a doubt I had found the One True God. All the years we searched for spiritual truth it was standing right in front of us in the form of Dr. Brotman, Sandee, Aaron, and Faith. They tried to tell us, but we refused to believe.

While I was discovering Yeshua as my Messiah, you were discovering the world of the paranormal. It has taken you completely away from me. I don't understand how astral sleep works, but as I watch you lying there, I realize your body is there, but the woman I love is not. The strongholds of the dark side hold you some place in time that I cannot reach.

Aaron told me to read Psalms 91 and Psalms 23 for guidance. I have read them over and over and there were times I felt as though I was in a war and swords were flying around me in a dimension I could not see. I am sure my prayers were reaching you and protecting you, even though you gave no sign. I hold to the promise that prayer changes things.

I continue to pray for your awakening before it's too late.

All my love,
Caleb

"I understand now," she whispered once again to the empty room. "Oh, how I wish I could do it all over." The tears trickled down her face as she read the letter over and over until finally she closed her eyes in sleep. All through the night she could hear Caleb's voice pleading with her to wake up. At one point, she dreamed his strong arms wrapped around her and held her against his chest. He was whispering over and over in her ear, "I love you, Gabi." When she opened her eyes again it was morning. Caleb's letter lay on her chest, stained with tears. She held her left hand up and gazed at the antique ring that graced her hand. The symbol of the love she had, she lost, and she would never have again.

Gabriella forced herself out of bed and slowly dressed, repeating the words of Caleb's letter over and over in her mind. Desperately, she wanted to gaze into his blue eyes filled with love just one more time.

She straightened her back and squared her shoulders trying to give the appearance of self-control before she opened her bedroom door. Chris had made coffee and was already watching the continuing news reports. He looked up and immediately noticed the redness around her eyes and the sorrow in her face.

"Morning, Gabi. Sleep well?" He said nothing about her appearance. If she wanted to talk, he would listen. If not, he would respect her privacy.

She muttered a few incoherent words as she continued past him to the bathroom. Shortly, he heard the shower running and later the hair dryer. He kept his eyes on the breaking news and waited for her to return.

Soon she emerged, poured her coffee and joined him on the couch. "Anything new this morning?" she asked, settling in beside him.

Immediately, he noticed the antique ring that she had not worn previously; however, he made no comment. "Well, it's just like we thought. WIN TV has picked up the Israeli news broadcast from yesterday and already there are uproars and protests demanding Israel pay for their war crimes. They are constantly replaying the words of the rabbi stating he reflects the sentiment of all of Israel having no sympathy for the innocent dead."

"If you think about it, Chris, just that line alone sounds very condemning. When it's played with the rest of the interview, then you understand he is justified in his convictions. Naturally, the news is going to edit that part out."

Chris immediately agreed: "Without a doubt, bias against Israel has now turned to all out hatred. The UN is having a special meeting on what the appropriate response to Israel's attacks should be. The spokesman said no individual nation would attempt to militarily respond for fear of nuclear retaliation. World leaders are hoping for a diplomatic solution. That solution would include Israel giving up their newly expanded borders and I don't see that happening. Controlling all that area is a buffer zone that helps guarantee peace and safety. They won't need walls of separation against the Palestinians any longer."

Gabriella thought for a moment as she sipped her morning coffee. "Isn't that what the prophet Ezekiel said? Israel will be dwelling in peace and safety when sudden destruction comes? No longer would there be any walls? More pieces of the puzzle are falling together, don't you think?" She mentally was trying to place the pieces in their proper prophetic order.

The familiar words 'Breaking News' again rolled across the WIN newscast. "We have important breaking news. We're going now to our international headquarters in Rome for a special report."

The stern face of a man dressed in a black suit, white shirt, and black tie appeared on the screen. Microphones surrounded him as reporters were pressing in. Two men, one on each side of the director, pressed the media a safe distance backwards. They positioned themselves at his side as they stood guard.

The director began in a solemn voice: "Good morning. I am Ugo Strozza, Director of International Intelligence and Investigation."

Gabriella and Chris looked at each other in shock. "Could he be the Ugo the men were talking about, Chris?" They both focused back on the TV so as not to miss a single word of his speech.

"For several days, we have been working closely with the delegates of the UN to find answers and solutions to the horrific events that have taken place across our planet. There are two I will now address."

He glanced at his notes and continued: "Israel has initiated preemptively the first full scale nuclear and neutron war on planet earth. We cannot even estimate at this time how many lives have been lost. With sudden and totally unexpected attacks, Israel has destroyed the governments and military of all surrounding nations, and virtually wiped out their citizen populations. In these attacks, Israel also used secretly developed weapons. Weapons no other nations were aware existed. They have been developing these weapons for years, waiting for the strategically consummate opportunity to attack. They accomplished their mission in only three days. The Prime Minister of Israel has declared the Expanded State of Israel, claiming possession of all the lands bordering her."

The reporters began to simultaneously chatter asking questions about the war. Strozza held up his hand and the voices silenced. "The world is also dealing with an international mystery. Across our planet millions of people are missing. We cannot establish an age, nationality, gender, or ethnic connection of why certain people vanished. It seems there were no specific targets. With that in mind, we have looked at several scenarios of possibility. At this juncture, I cannot give a definitive answer. Almost all families worldwide are affected in some way. We will continue our investigations and will immediately report any facts. Thank you."

Ugo Strozza left the platform and ignored the questions being hurled by the media. He looked neither to the right nor left as the men that stood beside him during his speech now protected him on each side as he exited the room.

The cameraman focused on the back of the exiting director until he disappeared. The cameras then centered on the pretty Italian reporter as she began a summation of his report. "We now have confirmation Israel did in fact initiate the Middle East War. Before her enemies could prepare to defend their countries and their people, they were wiped out. Israel may have exercised her military muscle and expanded her borders, but she will stand alone in the community of nations. Although we received no news from Ugo Strozza on those that have vanished, there are unsubstantiated reports that Israel knows more about the disappearances than they are willing to admit. More news as it develops. This is Katja Lody reporting."

Chris's face was red from anger. His voice was deep with emotion. "I cannot believe this! They are blaming Israel for the entire war. Not one word regarding the Western Wall being destroyed by Syria in the very first attack of the war. All of our major cities had been hit before we even fired the first time. How can they just stand there and lie to the world? It makes me just want to..." He stopped before he totally lost control.

"It's always this way, Chris. The media consistently lies about Israel, and people just believe what they hear. They never question or try to discover the truth for themselves."

His anger was not to be soothed. "This time it's gone beyond slanting the news. It's outright lies. We used to have a few countries standing with us, but no more. America was all that was left and now she is destroyed. Our nation stands alone...totally alone."

Gabriella was remembering the words of the Professor, "In the end of days *all* nations will gather against Israel."

CHAPTER 12

I mmediately after the International Intelligence Director announced to the world Israel had waged a nuclear war against her border nations, the anti-Semitism exploded. News reports were being broadcast from around the world and being picked up by both the Israeli and international news.

The prophetic signs Gabriella's father left her were already being fulfilled just as he said. Next on his checklist of signs to watch were Jews being persecuted and killed around the world, forcing all that could escape to return to Israel. It had begun.

"We have major breaking news." Adelson's voice was filled with expectation. "The Prime Minister of Israel is going to address the current persecution of the Jews living outside of Israel. We go now to Jerusalem, where he has been assessing the damage at the Temple Mount."

The Prime Minister was the most respected man in all of Israel and now feared by the world. There was no arrogance in his face as he stood to face the cameras. In fact, it was a countenance of humility but with overtones of complete control.

He stepped closer to the multitude of microphones and began with a voice of compassion. "It is with sadness and great concern that we watch the attacks against the Jewish people living among the nations. I have received reports from around the world of our people being murdered in the streets, in the synagogues, and even being attacked in their homes. The nations fear the military might of Israel, so they attack our innocent people who live among them as a source of revenge against us."

The Prime Minister reached to the man beside him for a document he held. Holding it up in the air he waved it in a sign of victory before he continued: "I hold in my hand a declaration of Exodus II - The Return." His voice became excited as he read the document. "To all who are of the seed of Abraham through his sons Isaac and Jacob, we call you to return to the land of your fathers. Come out of the nations to The Promised Land. Come from the north, the south, the east, and the west. Israel is your home and we welcome you with open arms."

There was a roar of rejoicing from the crowd gathered at the Temple Mount. The Prime Minister waited until he could be heard over the excitement. "We not only welcome our people, we are prepared to help them settle in homes and begin a new life of peace and safety. Come! Come now to the Expanded State of Israel, The Covenant Land, and be part of the new settlements in our expanded territory."

The roar of excitement drowned out the Prime Minister's voice. He waited patiently until the excitement calmed enough for him to continue. "We are currently organizing an evacuation plan for The Return. We will send all Israeli passenger jets to international airports for free and safe passage back to Israel. We call upon the civilized nations of the world to allow those who are Israelis by blood to make Aliyah. We are prepared to take all measures necessary to assure this evacuation plan succeeds."

Again, the crowd roared around him and the chants of 'We will rebuild' echoed throughout the Temple Mount. The Prime Minister held up his hand to continue his announcements and the crowd respectfully grew silent.

"I can confirm over recent days America has become completely desolate with its power grids being destroyed nationwide and the massive earthquake on the New Madrid fault literally splitting the nation in two. We have over six million of our fellow Jews that live in that one country alone. I sadly realize we cannot rescue them all but we will make every effort to reach as many as possible. I will continue to give updates on Exodus II - The Return as we go forward in the days ahead."

The Prime Minister made one last statement to the media. "We also continue to investigate the simultaneous vanishings here in Israel and around the world. It appears we are being blamed for that as well since it occurred at the same time as our three-day war. I assure you we had nothing to do with this mysterious event, although world sentiment does not agree. However, we will not stop our efforts to solve this enigma. Thank you." The camera panned the roaring crowd as the Prime Minister exited the scene.

Chris quickly turned the channel to WIN TV, in Rome to see if they were carrying the Prime Minister's address. As expected, they had immediately picked up the feed and Katja Lody was preparing to make her personal assessment of the speech. She was still on location at The Vatican. The camera panned Vatican Square as the crowd was chanting: "Death to the Jews, death to the Jews". Obviously, the media had succeeded in brainwashing their audiences into believing Israel had initiated the war. Only those living in Israel knew the absolute truth.

The reporter's face was grim as she addressed the world. "If you have just tuned in, there is breaking news. The Prime Minister of Israel has sent a message to all Jews around the world to come to Israel to live in safety. This new operation has been named Exodus II – The Return, and it is already in the early stages of being initiated. From the reports I am receiving from various news agencies, the only place Jews *will* be safe is in Israel. After Ugo Strozza confirmed Israel initiated the three-day war, outraged citizens from all nations have banded together to send a message to the Prime Minister of their anger of Israeli dominance."

The camera briefly panned and zoomed in on the more agitated protestors and then quickly returned to Katja Lody. "The Russians have sent an especially clear message as outraged citizens have burned Jewish homes and synagogues around their nation. The President of Russia has done nothing to control the attacks; however, it has been reported he will allow a thirty-day window for all Jews to leave his country. He believes they have brought a curse upon their nation. In fact, the entire world is blaming Israel and the Jewish people for the devastation that has occurred." The reporter had a sardonic smile on her face making it obvious she was in total agreement. "It is believed all nations will follow Russia's lead in allowing the Jews to leave to avoid martial law in their countries due to the extreme anti-Semitism. Nations also want to avoid possible retaliation from Israel if they refuse to do so."

She pointed to The Vatican behind her. "As I am reporting live, behind me in the private chambers of The Vatican, The Holy Father is meeting with delegates of the UN. His religious guidance has been requested to assist in creating a new world order from this international chaos. I will continue to update you as reports are made available. This is Katja Lody reporting." The reporter disappeared from the camera and was replaced by angry mobs chanting behind her. "Death to Israel, Death to the Jews!"

Chris only had one word to say: "Wow."

Gabriella sat stunned at the news report. "It's happening so fast, Chris, and it's just as my father said it would be. In the forefront of world events Israel has expanded her territory to take in all the land promised to Abraham, the Jews are coming home, Russia is taking a world lead, and The Pope is becoming the UN's religious counselor. According to my father's notes, after the Jews come home the war prophesied in Ezekiel 38 will take place and Russia will be the leader of the coalition of nations. No doubt the President of Russia will immediately start negotiations and..."

Chris finished her prophetic sentence: "And when Israel is dwelling in peace and safety, sudden destruction will come."

She pondered the ancient prophecies of the return of the House of Jacob: "Extreme anti-Semitism may be the fault of the media, but would all the Jews be forced back to Israel otherwise? These reporters don't even realize they're puppets in Yahweh's prophetic plan. Professor Brotman told us someday all the descendants of the sons of Jacob would come home. I didn't see any way that would happen. Jews had it too good in many of the countries, especially in the U.S. Why would they ever leave? Well, I understand now what he meant when he said Yahweh would put a hook in their mouth and pull them back to Israel. That's exactly what He's done."

"Think about it, Gabi. Where will millions of Jews live? How will they survive in Israel with no jobs, no income, nothing?"

She had her response ready: "I have been thinking about it. Israel has just multiplied several times over the size of her territory. There are entire nations to expand into. One of the Israeli reporters was talking about this earlier while you were in the shower. The neutron bombs were detonated at such a high altitude it maximized the destruction of organic matter, but left the infrastructure; and since neutron bombs leave very little radiation, it quickly clears."

She paused attempting to paint a picture in Chris' mind of what the aftermath would be and the new homeland for the returning Jews. "Entire nations will be virtually empty and ready to occupy. I know there will be some obstacles to work through; clean-up, food supplies, farming, etc. but I'm sure the Prime Minister thought through all that before he announced

The Return. The Professor would often remind us of when Israel came out of Egypt. He said there would be a second exodus at the time of the end. What Yahweh did for Israel during the first exodus, He would do again when they return from all the nations at the end of days."

Chris squinted his eyes in amazement. "That's why the Prime Minister called this Exodus II."

"Exactly. Exodus II – The Return." Gabriella repeated as she picked up the Bible and was thumbing through the pages. "Here it is. It's from Deuteronomy 6 - *When the* LORD *your God brings you into the land he swore to your fathers, to Abraham, Isaac and Jacob, to give you—a land with large, flourishing cities you did not build, houses filled with all kinds of good things you did not provide, wells you did not dig, and vineyards and olive groves you did not plant—then when you eat and are satisfied do not forget the Lord who brought you out.*"

"Hatred for Israel is gonna explode," Chris stated as a matter of fact, already seeing the writing on the wall.

Gabriella was thinking even further ahead. "Do you realize the wealth of Israel will become the envy of the world? Israel already controls the vast majority of the oil in the world with the recent discovery of the Leviathan Reservoir off the coast of Haifa. With the expanded borders, Israel will be the richest nation on the face of the earth."

"Even more reason to hate us," he responded dryly. "That alone could bring an invasion of nations against us."

"It's amazing how the Professor's words keep coming back to me." Gabriella was staring into space. "I can almost hear his voice commenting on everything we're discussing. He was sure wealth would be the main reason for the Gog and Magog War; they would be coming to take the riches of Israel. Until recently Israel had no riches. Now she's swimming in black gold."

"How long do you think we have before the Russian coalition forms and invades?" Chris asked.

"I suppose nobody knows for sure. It would have to be long enough for the Jews to come home and start resettling the expanded land. Russia only gave them thirty days to get out and probably the other nations will follow their lead. Once they get here, who knows?"

Chris was mulling in his mind the possible scenarios. "We've got a lot to do. We don't know how much that war will affect our ability to be mobile or for how long. I think tomorrow we should go to Haifa. I have to know if Detective Richards is still alive. He and Detective Harold are the only links between you and me, and our location."

"I remember him," Gabriella replied. "He was the other officer that came with you and Detective Richards to hide us at the lodge. Do you know him very well?"

Chris shook his head. "We hadn't worked together before but he's been on the force for quite a while. Actually, longer than I have. Detective Richards wouldn't have brought him if he wasn't completely trustworthy."

"I hope so, but one good thing is neither of them knew about the bunker. Even if someone discovers the lodge, we are still safe in here. Right?"

"Absolutely," Chris assured her. "No one in the lodge would ever find this bunker the way your father built it. That man knew what he was doing." He paused and teasingly added, "Not like his daughter at all."

"Very funny," she retorted, swinging her long, curly hair back over her shoulders in an act of defiance. Her blue eyes flashed a challenge daring him to prove it.

"You win," he appeased her. "I think you're probably *just* like him."

"And don't you forget it," she jestingly glared at him.

"I'm sure you'll remind me," Chris said sarcastically making an effort to have the last word. Gabriella was not about to let that happen.

She ran her fingers through his thick black hair and laughed. "Get smart with me, wise guy, and you might just wake up bald one morning."

"Just you try it, little missy! You better think twice if you treasure those long, golden locks of yours."

"Huh, you think I'm afraid of you, big guy?" Her eyes teasingly pierced his.

"Be afraid, be very afraid." He stared into her eyes without blinking.

Gabriella picked up a pillow and started to throw it at him. Instead, she just dropped it and plopped into the couch. Her expression instantly transformed. The teasing expression changed to guilt.

Chris sat down in the chair across from her. "What is it, Gabi? Talk to me."

Tears formed in her eyes. "What's wrong with me? How can I be joking when I've just lost everyone I love? Not to mention the world around me is falling apart." An expression of remorse instantly replaced the smile on her face.

His voice was gentle and caressing. "Gabi, think of where they are. That's nothing to be sad about. I know you miss them, but would your father want you to grieve? I barely met the man, but it was obvious to me he loved you with all of his heart. Caleb loved you too. They both would want you to glean any joy you could from the dire circumstances we're in."

"I know you're right, Chris. It's just so hard," she replied with a quivering voice. "After I lost my father I built walls around my heart. I was afraid to fall in love and take the chance of losing someone else. For years I worked with Caleb, exploring and researching. We were together constantly and I struggled with my feelings for him. I kept telling him, and myself, we were just best friends. I gave him no indication it was anything more. I knew how he felt about me and would often see the hurt in his eyes when I emotionally pushed him away. I was too stubborn and too afraid to admit I truly loved him."

Chris made no comment, allowing her time to grieve.

Gabriella sat silent for a few minutes. She was thankful she was not left totally alone.

When the tears subsided, she sat up straight. "Thank you for listening. It helps to talk about it. I'm trying my best to deal with the loss. I can't blame anyone but myself. All this emotional agony was brought on by my own stubbornness, and I realize it...but it's too late."

Chris had never experienced the kind of love she and Caleb had. There had never been a woman he would wait for even for a few minutes, especially not years. "I can't tell you I understand, because I've never really been in love, Gabi. I'm willing to listen, though, anytime you need to talk. Don't be too stubborn again. If you need anything from me, I'm here for you."

"Thank you. I know you mean that. I was always Miss Independent, thinking I needed no one." She paused and looked down at the antique ring on her left hand. The future should have been filled with promise. Instead she had very little future left. "I never want to be alone again."

"You won't be," he vowed to her. "We'll get through this together."

CHAPTER 13

Gabriella had prepared an evening meal. Over dinner, she and Chris discussed the details of their return to Haifa.

Chris, like most police officers, had his pocket notepad ready to jot down details. "We'll leave around eight. It's a three-hour drive back to the city under normal circumstances. We'll take the main route through the Hula Valley. I really don't know what to expect on road conditions after the bombings but we'll just have to adjust accordingly. I have no idea if the police station sustained any damage either. In fact, Gabi, I just don't know what to expect, period. If I can get to the station, the main thing is to find out about Detective Richards. I also want to run the license plate on your father's Jeep to see what comes up. Could be dangerous if it's in the name of Eli Sheskin, since it's known now that was your father's assumed name."

"What if it is registered under Eli Sheskin?" She asked. "Will it be safe to drive it?"

"There are a lot of *ifs* right now. We'll just have to deal with them one *if* at a time." His face was very stern and professional. He obviously was very good at his job and when he was in work mode, there was no jesting. It gave her a sense of safety.

He continued with his plan of action. "No one at the station knew what my assignment was when I left, except Richards and Harold. The other officers just knew I was on an assignment indefinitely. I don't want any one there to know about you...no one. I'm taking no unnecessary chances."

A cold chill ran up and down Gabriella's spine. His words brought back memories of the years after her mother was murdered and constantly being followed. She wanted Chris to understand all the circumstances creating their current situation.

She took a deep breath before beginning. "I'm going to open my heart to you, Chris. In our circumstances, there is no reason to have secrets or hold emotions inside." She took another deep breath and let her past agony spill out. "After my mother was murdered, my father and I moved every year from one university to another and several times our homes were broken into. I constantly felt a fear someone would break in while we were home and I only felt safe when my father was in my sight. I didn't know until the last few weeks why we were targeted. Now I'm thirty years old and the same people, whoever they are, are still looking for my father's research papers. I know it's more important to these people now, more than ever before, that his discoveries do not resurface and fall into the wrong hands after all these years of obscurity."

Chris was intently watching Gabriella's face. He knew after fourteen years on the police force when true fear was in a victim's eyes.

He reached up and gently took her chin and turned her face, forcing her to look directly in his eyes. "I said I would take no unnecessary chances, Gabi. You don't have anything to worry about. Okay? Do you trust me?"

"Okay," she barely whispered. She reached up and briefly covered his hand with hers. "I do trust you."

Chris took a deep breath and steadied his voice. "Now that's settled, I think we both need to get some sleep. Tomorrow, I'm sure, will prove to be a very enlightening day." Chris got up and stretched. His muscular arms reached to Gabriella to help her from the couch.

"I'm going to sit here a while longer. I'll see you in the morning." She waved her hand for him to go on to bed.

"Good night, Gabi, sleep well." And he silently prayed she would.

Gabriella watched him walk away. When his bedroom door closed behind him, she quietly got up and went into the bedroom that belonged to her father. She had avoided his room, knowing the emotions would be overwhelming. The first step in was difficult but it was immediately followed by a peace. On the floor and next to his bed sat the black box that contained his research, the very thing putting them all in danger. She sat on the side of the bed and ran her hand across the box remembering the hours she and Caleb spent going through each page.

She looked around the room imagining her father sleeping in the bed, planning his trips into Haifa, and sitting at his desk arranging every detail to make sure she was safe and provided for. She got up and crossed the floor to the closet, pulling open the door. There were several black suits and white shirts like those worn by the Hasidic Jews that he used for his disguise. The rest were everyday casual clothes he would have worn around the lodge. She took one of the flannel shirts from the hanger and wrapped it around her. It was the closest thing she would feel to being in his arms again.

On the floor were numerous framed pictures that had fallen from the dresser during the earthquake. She picked them up one by one and each of them was of her. Some included pictures of them together. The most special of them all was a picture of her with both her mother and father when she was five years old. It was the last one taken before her mother's murder. When she was growing up it always sat on her father's desk no matter where they lived. These were his precious reminders of the life he had lived before assuming a secret identity. Gabriella fought back tears as she carefully placed the pictures back on the dresser.

She opened the dresser drawers one by one and it was just as she expected. Everything was carefully folded in a precise pattern and arranged by color. She picked up the wooden lamp that had fallen off the nightstand and set it back in place. Opening the door to the nightstand, she found a large metal box. Inside was cash, bank account information, property deed, stock certificates, personal documents, and several cell phones.

She imagined the phones were purchased in different names so they could not be traced. "Those could come in handy", she thought to herself. She took the cash and laid the box on the bed, deciding she would go through the other contents later.

She opened the second door in his bedroom assuming it would lead to his personal bathroom. She immediately stopped and gasped. "Oh, Wow!"

She took several minutes to survey the room then ran to Chris's room and banged on the door. "Are you awake, Chris? Chris, wake up."

Instinctively he grabbed his pistol and ran to his door. "What's wrong? What is it?"

"Sorry to wake you, but you've got to see this." She took his hand, quickly leading him into her father's bedroom and to the mysterious door. She pointed inside. "Look."

One glance and he stopped dead in his tracks. "Imagine that," he whispered, his eyes not believing what they beheld. "I've seen every kind of advanced security system and this is top of the line."

"Do you understand this?" Gabriella asked, trying to make sense of the multiple screens and equipment that surrounded the room.

Chris began to survey each piece of equipment. "This is an enhanced CCTV system. You can see and perhaps hear, and talk with any would-be intruders. It can probably connect directly to a police station, though I doubt this did." He motioned for Gabriella to come next to him. "All the rooms in the lodge and even the cottage behind the lodge appear to have hidden cameras monitoring them twenty-four hours a day. The grounds outside are monitored in every direction with cameras, and the electronic grid map on the wall indicates he also used motion detectors. From this room, nothing can move on the entire lodge property without activating motion detectors. He must have feared his past would eventually catch up with him."

"This had nothing to do with fear." Tears began to fill Gabriella's eyes as the full meaning impacted her. "Do you realize, Chris, when I was here for retreats, which was often, he could watch me and I never knew it. He could have recorded every step I made and watch it over and over, like a home movie. He would have seen the project being discussed, the laughter we all shared, the meals the team shared together even the games we sometimes played and all the time watching from a distance...never being a part of my life. That's how he knew that Caleb and I were in love. He watched us. I know he saw it even though I hadn't admitted it to myself." A single tear slowly drifted down her face. "He knew if he was hidden down here, we would never suspect a thing."

Chris instinctively knew her father had a double meaning to the security system but was not about to burst Gabriella's emotional bubble. He was convinced she was right. However, it was obvious with the supply of guns and ammunition and the tunnel escape with the hidden car, Gabe knew the possibility was always with him that eventually someone would know Edward Gabe Russell did not really die.

"If we had known this was here a couple of days ago, we could have seen and heard the men upstairs and even recorded them and their voices. I sure hate we lost that opportunity." Chris was running his hand through his thick hair, which Gabriella had come to understand as his gesture of frustration.

"At least if they come back, we'll be ready." She replied softly trying to sooth his irritation.

"That may well be the case," he replied, continuing to survey each part of the security system.

"I'm sure, Gabi, being able to see you was his foremost purpose and intent of heart." His voice was tender as he put his arm around her shoulders in comfort. "But he was also ready just in case the truth ever came out. Seems to me he wanted to make sure he stayed around to be your guardian angel." He gave her shoulders a gentle squeeze before dropping his arms to survey the system more closely.

She nodded her head, fully understanding. "Isn't it quite the dichotomy these people hunting him thought my father wasn't anywhere on the face of the earth these last twelve years, and he really was? Now they believe he's alive and well on planet earth and he's gone. They will never find him. You have to laugh at the irony of it all." However, neither was laughing knowing now Gabriella was also on their hit list.

Chris moved to the control board that monitored the cameras and began to study the various components. "This has a built-in computer system too."

Chris sat down and turned on the computer, "Just as I thought. It requires a password."

Gabriella leaned across his shoulder. "Try Princess5," she instructed him.

He typed the password in and the system activated. "How did you know that, Gabi?" His voice was filled with excitement.

A smile graced her face. "That became his password for everything after my mother passed away. They always called me their little princess and I was five when she died."

"Fortunate for us he was a creature of habit." Chris murmured as he tested the system. "I'm going to try the internet." He clicked the Google icon and the familiar sound of the connection was heard. "I got it! Can you believe this? For now, we are connected to the world, or at least parts of it."

Gabriella wrapped her arms around his shoulders from behind and gave him a bear hug. "We're part of civilization again, Chris."

"Yes, we are." He replied in amazement. "Yes, we are. I think I'll do some research for a while. Maybe I can find out about road conditions and the damage in Haifa. Go on to bed and get some rest. I'm too wound up to try to sleep now."

Gabriella gave him a pat on the head and turned to leave. "I'll leave you to your work and I'll do mine. I'm going to read more of dad's letters. We can discuss both our findings in the morning while we drive back to Haifa."

"Night, Gabi," he murmured, concentrating on the screens around him. "It will take quite a bit of time spent in this room to figure out all the components. One thing is for sure, if anyone else comes around here we'll be ready to get them on candid cameras."

Gabriella watched him, admiring his capabilities. There was no doubt she was in a safe place and in safe hands, at least for now. "See you in the morning," she replied and left the security room. She retrieved her father's letters from the coffee table and retreated to her bedroom. She closed the door behind her, laid the letters on the nightstand, and changed into her light blue pajamas. The soft, caressing fabric was soothing and relaxing to her body; however, the uncertainties of the day ahead were spinning in her head making it impossible for her mind to rest. She settled into her bed propping pillows behind her head and picked up the next letter from the neatly stacked pile. Taking a deep breath, the journey into the future continued:

Dearest Daughter,

If my eschatology is correct, you have already seen Israel deploy the 'Samson Option'; the use of nuclear and neutron weapons resulting in a quick war between Israel and her surrounding nations. Israel's borders will have been enlarged to possess the land of The Abrahamic Covenant, The Promised Land. The nations will have seen the military power of Israel and at this juncture fear her power to retaliate if any further attacks are waged.

I have already warned you to watch The Vatican. I believe the seated Pope will play a large diplomatic role in the final events of the world. He personally will introduce the Man of Sin, the Antichrist, and call for all religions to come together as one to bring peace among all nations. The stage is now quickly being set for the final seven years. The interim events between the harpazo, the rapture of the believers of Yeshua, and the countdown of the final seven years will happen rapidly.

The world will be in turmoil over the multi-millions that have died in the war. The nations will also be in distress over the multi-millions more that have mysteriously disappeared. They will struggle to explain and, most likely, will believe Israel knows what has happened or was responsible for it all. Anti-Semitism will explode and Jews will flee to Zion from around the world.

As the nations are trying to settle into a new normal, with Israel as the powerhouse of both oil richness and military dominance, an alliance is quickly forming behind the political scenes. Russia, Iran, Turkey, Libya, Ethiopia, and Western Europe, with many other smaller Islamic nations, will secretly form a coalition preparing to simultaneously attack and destroy Israel before she has a chance to retaliate. Their purpose is to possess her wealth and destroy all military capabilities. Believe me, Israel will never be destroyed! Read the details of how Yahweh will intervene in Ezekiel 38 and 39 and miraculously win the war.

The devastation from this war will be so immense it will seem there is no hope for mankind. The stage is now set for the False Prophet and Antichrist to take their positions to bring peace and a 'new world order'.

Gabriella, I pray you have supernatural wisdom and understanding of the years ahead. I pray for divine protection.

Above all, I pray I will see you again on the eternal side of this earthly life.

As I write this, I am watching you sleep. You seem to be at perfect peace, but I wonder where your mind and soul are. What are you battling?

Deep in my spirit I sense Yahweh has chosen you for such a time as this. I desire more than anything that you awaken before it's too late but if not, a position of destiny awaits you. Psalms 68:11 is a prophecy of the end of days. "The Lord announces it, and the women who proclaim it are mighty". The way will not be easy, but The Lord is with you!

I love you,
Dad

Gabriella longed to understand how she was a woman of destiny. "How am I chosen; for what?" She whispered her heart's prayer in the silence of the night. "I am willing. I submit to you, Heavenly Father. Show me the way."

She laid his letter in her lap, remembering the astral travels beginning in such arcane beauty and ending in inconceivable horror. She was fully aware had it not been for the prayers of her loved ones, she would have converged with the powers of darkness and been lost forever. She was only one step away from entering eternal darkness, when the sound of many voices cried out for her deliverance. The words of Psalms 91 being prayed over her created supernatural swords of protection around her. She now understood the power of prayer.

She reached for her father's bible and turned to the marked page and read again the words that protected her from the snare of the evil one.

Psalms 91
Whoever dwells in the shelter of the Most High
  will rest in the shadow of the Almighty.
I will say of the LORD, "He is my refuge and my fortress,
  my God, in whom I trust."

Surely he will save you
  from the fowler's snare
  and from the deadly pestilence.
He will cover you with his feathers,
  and under his wings you will find refuge;
  his faithfulness will be your shield and rampart.
You will not fear the terror of night".

The now familiar Presence erased the turmoil from her mind and she fell into a restful sleep. All through the night she heard the gentle voice of her father. "I love you, my princess. Please wake up."

Her father's Bible lay upon her chest creating a shield of protection. She had no idea how badly she would need that protection the following day.

CHAPTER 14

———◆•◆———

G abriella awakened early the next morning. Her father's letter and Bible still lay on her chest exactly as they were when she fell asleep. The sound of his voice from her dreams still resonated in her ears. "Wake up, Gabriella." She held his letter close to her heart not wanting to let go. He felt so near to her.

She knew she had to prepare emotionally for the trip to Haifa. She was dreading what the day might unveil. Gathering her personal items, as limited as they were, she slipped quietly to the bathroom trying not awaken Chris. She brushed and pulled her hair into her usual ponytail. She dressed in jeans and sweater, perfect for the early fall temperatures.

Reentering the living area, she saw Chris was already up, dressed and making coffee. She took a deep breath, savoring the aroma. "Caramel coffee, my favorite."

Chris poured her coffee. "Here you go." He handed her the cup.

Memories flooded through Gabriella. So many times, she and Caleb would sip coffee together and discuss their explorations. "Caleb and I loved this coffee," she casually commented, sipping from the hot liquid. "We would often sit on the balcony of my condo over Haifa Bay and watch the mariners coming and going out to sea. Caramel coffee was part of our routine." She closed her eyes and tried to envision the scenery they loved and shared together.

"It was on that balcony he proposed to me. He gave me his grandmother's engagement ring and it was the happiest day of my life." She paused looking at the ring on her hand. Chris thought she had finished her walk down memory lane when she abruptly continued her verbal journey.

"A few days later I threw the ring at him, thinking he had betrayed me. He tried to warn me I was being captured by the paranormal experiences. They all tried to warn me. I was too stubborn to even listen to his explanation. I thought I was the one who had found the truth." Her voice faded as she rued the choices she had made.

Chris knew she was voicing her memories and not really sharing her heart with him so he said nothing. He sat down on the wooden bar stool next to the counter and allowed her to vent. He did not ask how the ring returned to her finger.

Gabriella sat down across from Chris and continued her reminiscing. "On that same balcony, Caleb, Aaron, Faith, and I spent long hours discussing The Omega Watchers project. I never really bought into the whole prophetic timelines belief, but I loved the Professor like a father. I was willing to do anything I could to help him, all the time believing he would finally see there was no validity in it. He believed it to be absolute truth and in the end, he was right."

Briefly she looked up at Chris. "I was an absolute fool."

Chris still sat quietly listening. He knew she needed to deal with her emotions before she could face the days ahead. He had seen this many times over with criminals who needed to confess to their crimes to feel ease from their shame and guilt.

Gabriella again began to stare into the air and verbally relived her final cave exploration that brought the entire project to completion. "The day we were in the cave in Saudi Arabia, something changed. The local Bedouins warned us of the ancient myth that the cave of Tartarus was in the area we were exploring, the place of the fallen evil ones. It was in that cave we discovered a seemingly bottomless pit. I came very close to falling in, and if it hadn't been for Caleb, I would have. I know it sounds weird, but the pit was drawing me...pulling me towards the abyss. I tried to stop, but I couldn't. Caleb grabbed me just in time and pulled me back."

She stopped and looked Chris directly in the face. He recognized the pleading in her eyes, begging him to understand. She again turned her head away from him, staring into the air, seeing nothing, and remembering. "Everything changed that day. I felt a presence leave the cave with me. It haunted me all through the night. The next day I met Arcturus in the transport from our hotel to the airport. He was mesmerizing. He was the most mysterious, most beautiful man I had ever seen. When he looked at me I felt like I was melting. After I returned to Haifa, he began to come to me in my dreams and that was the beginning of the paranormal captivity I entered. It almost captured me forever." Remembering the threshold of the convergence, she stopped. It was still too fresh in her mind to vocalize.

She got up from the stool in an obvious gesture she would share no more. "Okay, Chris, let's get to the business at hand. What time are we leaving for Haifa?"

He did not push for any more information, but he certainly was curious about Arcturus. He followed her lead, leaving the finite details of her paranormal experience for a later time. Instead he began to map the day ahead of them. "We'll have breakfast and then head out. I have a better idea now, after having Google access, where the greatest damage is and what routes to take into Haifa. We'll discuss the specifics as we drive."

Together they prepared breakfast. Gabriella said the Hebrew blessing before they ate. Now the words burned with passion in her soul every time she spoke them. She understood what the Professor meant...it was a matter of the heart.

Within an hour, they were leaving the bunker and retracing their steps through the lava tunnel. Gabriella had taken some of the money from her father's box in his bedroom. Any purchases would be cash only.

They exited the end of the cave into another beautiful morning. Mt. Hermon's majestic peak was illuminated by the glimmering morning sun. She waited while Chris unlocked the storage building and drove the Jeep out. Climbing in the passenger seat, they were soon on their way down the rugged path to the main road. Neither said a word as Chris concentrated on the mountain terrain.

As they neared the main road, Chris' eyes were searching in every direction for any signs of parked cars or human movement. Nothing was evident as he pulled on the main road and drove down the mountainside.

He finally broke the silence. "Still no real traffic flow. Makes me wonder what the real impact of the war has been on this area. Here in the mountains you would never know anything happened from the look of things."

Gabriella nodded her head and rolled the window down to enjoy the fresh air. A hint of fall colors was creeping into the trees. The sounds of rushing streams could be heard along the roadside. She tried to focus on the soothing early autumn sounds and scenes.

Instead, the thoughts of Arcturus were tormenting her.

Chris could read her body language like reading a book. It was what he was trained to do. Her entire countenance changed when she mentioned Arcturus. He tried to draw her into their task at hand and release her mind from the agonies of her past.

"Here's the plan, Gabi. I have mapped out a route through the Hula Valley. From some of the pictures I saw on Google Earth last night, it looked like some of the main road sustained damage from rocket fire. Shouldn't be hard to get around it though. When we get to Haifa we will head straight for the police station. There was a lot of damage in the city, but it appears the station was not hit. It may be difficult to maneuver through the debris so we'll have to adjust accordingly once we get there. What happens at the station will set the rest of the day's plans. Are you up to this?"

"Yes, I am." She replied. "By the way, what did you learn about the security system after I went to bed?"

"A whole lot. It has many more features than I imagined. First, the CCTV cameras each have a built-in motion detector and two-way voice capabilities instead of just being able to hear what is being said in each room; in other words, a selective room-by-room intercom system. The motion detectors activate the grid map of the buildings and grounds and the recorder camera surveying that particular grid. Also, there is a system capable of deploying a gas fog anywhere in the lodge. The fogs appear to consist of various chemicals that can be varied in strength from benign to 'you shouldn't have come here'! Believe me, he was ready in case anyone unwanted showed up. I haven't tested the fogging system yet because I'm not sure which chemicals do what. That will take some time and gas masks to determine.

"Lastly, I discovered the computer operates on high speed land lines so as long as the phone lines are operating we will have internet capabilities. Another interesting thing is your dad employed the use of multiple worldwide proxy servers to conceal the computers IP address making it almost impossible to trace the location of his computer."

"He certainly thought of everything." The technical information was more than she could comprehend and she was thankful it was Chris' forte.

She continued to stare out the window trying, without success, to erase Arcturus from her thoughts. When they arrived at the bottom of the mountain she finally spoke. "I can't believe it's only been a week since we started up this mountain with the team. We had no idea how long we would be there. I didn't know my father was still alive. I didn't know the lodge belonged to him. I certainly didn't know a few days later everyone would all be gone and I would be left alone."

Chris reached over and patted her hand. "You're not alone, Gabi."

She briefly looked at him and tried to force a smile. "You are the only ray of sunshine in this dark existence." Immediately, she turned her head back towards the window.

"I'm more than that, you know. Seems now I'm not only a ray of sunshine but your protector, your roommate, your confidant, your friend, and anything else you need me to be." He put both hands back on the wheel focusing on the road ahead.

She would not look at him. There was a slight tremor in her voice when she responded: "I do feel safe with you and I know I haven't said it enough but thank you for everything."

As they reached the bottom of the mountain the scenery began to change. Cars were abandoned along the roadside. Some had crashed into trees and houses, with no obvious endeavor to move them out of the way. Some homes were boarded up and appeared deserted while others seemed to be flourishing with activity. Apparently, families were gathering in one location comforting one another after the horrific world events. Few cars were traveling the once extremely busy highway. There was a feeling of despondency hanging heavily in the atmosphere.

They continued the drive through the lush, fertile valley filled with enchanting vineyards and fall vegetation. Hula Lake was the temporary home to hundreds of migrating birds passing through during the autumn and spring. Amid the chaos, it was a picture of pure serenity with rippling waters sparkling in the morning sunshine. Nothing of the natural beauty gave evidence the world all around them was in total mayhem.

Gabriella finally began a conversation, reminiscing again of days gone by. "The Professor said when he and his mother first moved to Israel in the early 1950s, this whole valley was marshland. The new state began a project to drain the swamps to increase the area for settlements and agriculture. They designed it to leave the Hula Lake as a nature reserve where the fauna and flora, the ingenious plants and wildlife characteristic of the area could remain. I am always captured by the beauty when I come through here. You would never know there is a maelstrom taking place elsewhere on the planet."

Chris continued her train of thought: "This whole nation was nothing but wasteland when Israel declared their statehood in 1948. It has gone from wasteland to a prosperous, fertile nation with the multitude of kibbutzim which developed the land. Now we possess all the territory of The Abrahamic Covenant and we are the most powerful nation on the face of the earth. Amazing, truly amazing."

Gabriella nodded her head and gazed at the beauty of the passing vineyards and fruit groves. "Every time we would drive through this valley the Professor would quote from Isaiah the prophet: *The wilderness and the solitary place shall be glad for them; and the desert shall rejoice, and blossom as the rose.*"

They both knew the beautiful scenery was about to take a drastic change as they neared Haifa. Chris slowed the vehicle. "Just ahead is where Highway 90 took a rocket hit. We'll probably have to detour. I think we can take Route 886 around the damage."

Gabriella straightened in her seat and looked ahead. There were no detour signs, but it was obvious obstacles were ahead. "There it is," Gabriella was pointing to the next turn. Chris exited and turned southwest towards Haifa.

Gabriella looked back to the northeast where she could now get a panoramic view of Mt. Hermon looming behind them. She took a deep breath as her eyes drank in the beauty.

"Breathtaking, isn't it?" Chris responded.

"It certainly is. I just can't wrap my mind around the fact something so beautiful was the portal of entry for something so evil." Gabriella knew it was time Chris fully understood the nature of The Omega Watchers project.

"What are you talking about?" He glanced over to see if she was serious.

"Chris, you came in at the very end of the project. You were there when they read the final prophecies concerning the end of days. However, what you haven't heard was the beginning. The two tie the project together."

"Go on," he urged her, wanting to totally understand.

"I'm sure you're familiar with Noah's flood?"

"Of course," he answered. "I may not have been religious growing up, but everyone knows that mythical story."

"I used to think it was part of mythology, too. Every culture has their version of a worldwide flood, so I didn't take Noah's flood as anything different. Not until near the end of the project."

Chris looked at her questioningly and then turned his eyes back to the road. Gabriella shifted in her seat to face him. "You're going to get the abbreviated version, but you'll understand the gist of it. You and I are new to this but I've had twelve years of being with people who have always believed every word in the Bible. Caleb and I were the only two on our team that had no spiritual background of any kind. We heard the Bible quoted over and over throughout the years, but we both were looking for something with hard core proof. Our scientific viewpoint was you have to prove it. Believing through faith didn't cut it for either of us."

Chris nodded in agreement. "I felt the same way. Even when my parents became believers, they couldn't convince me. They had no proof. I thought the religion stuff was just messing with their aging minds."

"Exactly," she agreed. "However, out of respect Caleb and I would listen to their conversations, their prayers, their biblical dissertations, and all the time believing none of it. It wasn't until the last exploration, the one I told you about this morning, everything changed for both of us. Now I know the truth. I can look back and see how it all fits together."

"How does Mt. Hermon play into all of this?" Chris asked, glancing towards her.

"That's where the story begins. When the Professor was translating the Dead Sea Scrolls, a large portion of them was from the Book of Enoch, which most people don't even read anymore...Christian or Jew. These scrolls had been hidden by the rabbis in the Qumran caves, to protect them from destruction thousands of years prior. They were found by a sheepherder in the late 1940's. Professor Brotman believed Yahweh had the scrolls safely hidden to be found when Israel once again was back in their homeland. The scrolls were to instruct Yahweh's people to study and understand the Book of Enoch which gave a clear picture of the days of Noah. Yeshua said at the time of the end it would be just like it was in Noah's day."

Gabriella could tell from his expression he was confused. "I know this is a little overwhelming, but here it is in a nutshell. In the days of Jared, who was the great, great, grandfather of Noah, a world-changing event took place. In Genesis six it says the Sons of God, who were the holy watchers, saw the beautiful women of earth and chose to leave their heavenly estate and take them as wives. The children they bore were half human and half fallen angels, the Nephilim; or many Bible translations call them giants. They were mighty with supernatural strength and great knowledge. The Book of Enoch goes into a lot more detail but these angels chose to leave heaven and enter the dimension of time. Their portal of entry to the human realm was on top of Mt. Hermon."

"Are you kidding me?" One glance and he knew she was not kidding, not at all.

"That was my reaction, too, when I first heard it. There's a lot more I won't go into now, but bottom line is these fallen angels and their offspring were unredeemable. The two hundred original fallen angels are chained in the abyss until the time of the end when they will be released for a short time before their final judgment. When Yeshua said as it was in the days of Noah, he didn't just mean a vile, sexual society. He meant the fallen angels would be released from the abyss and again they, along with their leader Lucifer, will deceive people into a lie that will make humans unredeemable...lost for eternity. It is called the mark of the beast."

"And your father believes the implant he discovered will be used for just that purpose?" Chris was beginning to pull the fragmented information into a clearer picture.

"Precisely," she confirmed, leaning back in her seat. "Apparently, he discovered way too much since the same people are still searching for him after all these years. What was it the man in the lodge said? Something like they were too close now to let one man, meaning my father, upset the worldwide apple cart?"

"Your father definitely knew too much. I've got some ideas on how to research these guys, if I can get access to the computers at the station."

They were nearing the Mediterranean coast line and the junction of Highway 4. Haifa was now only an hour away. The civilian traffic was still very scarce although military vehicles were in abundance monitoring the highway. Wreckers were slowly and methodically removing abandoned vehicles, clearing the freeway.

"There wasn't any highway damage between here and Haifa so we should be able to move quickly down the coast." Chris accelerated the speed to the legal limit.

Gabriella leaned back in her seat and watched the scenery. The waves splashing on the coast and the seagulls soaring across the water crests gave the illusion nothing had changed. The sea breezes were whipping through the Jeep's opened windows and she could feel the mist on her face. It was impossible to control the flood of memories rolling through her, just as it is impossible to control the waves rolling upon the waters. They both were endless. Playing over and over in her mind was one question. Who was trying to find her father...and her?

Chris did not push for conversation. They both knew the plan for the day. He realized she needed time to emotionally adjust for the return to Haifa after losing everyone she loved. He was dealing with his own sentiments and did not know what to expect at police headquarters. In addition, Chris did not know who to trust.

Nearing the city, they drove by the Haifa International Airport. Gabriella and her team had flown in and out of the airport innumerable times. Caleb was always with her carrying her luggage, protecting her, and assisting in whatever she needed. She sighed deeply knowing life would never be the same.

Several airplanes had crashed near the airport complex. Airport crews were attempting to extinguish the smoke from the remaining smoldering aircrafts and remove the piles of metal. Gabriella wondered how many lives had been lost during the war. How many were ready to meet their judgment?

"Looks like the military has taken over the airport." Chris commented, glancing back and forth between the road and the airport structures. "Feels really weird. Look over there, Gabi. That terminal has been completely demolished!"

Gabriella did not say a word. She just nodded, feeling a grave sense of foreboding.

They were almost to the city limits and both were fully aware nothing would be the same as when they left. They exited Highway 4, turning on Nathan Elbza Street. Shortly they arrived at Haifa Police Headquarters. In front of them stood the building, all fourteen floors still intact and undamaged.

"The best I could tell from Google Earth, the greatest damage is more city-center and south towards Old Haifa where the largest saturation of Hasidic Jews lived. I didn't want to tell you this, Gabi, but it's close to the area where we picked you up at your condo to bring your team to the lodge."

"Could you tell if my building took a direct hit?" Her voice quivered as she struggled with the thought of her home being destroyed.

His voice softened in solicitude. "No, I couldn't tell for sure. There was a lot of damage in the area and I don't think we could even drive close enough to know for sure."

Gabriella tried to visualize her home of the last twelve years gone. She had brought very little with her from America. Everything in that condo reflected her new life in Israel; her new friends, her education, her research, and her only love.

She straightened her shoulders, determined to be strong as she replied: "It doesn't matter. It's just stuff. I couldn't go back there anyway; in case the building is being watched."

"Gabi, nothing can take your memories. You're right, the rest is just stuff and stuff isn't going to matter at all in the days ahead. Hold on to the words and thoughts of those you loved."

She was touched again by the softer side of this strong police officer. His words were comforting and she added her new words of wisdom: "We must both hold on to our new faith, believing our Heavenly Father is with us."

Her blue eyes sparkled through the tears falling upon her sea-blue sweater. He took her hand and gently squeezed. "Amen, Gabi."

They had reached police headquarters. He pulled into the parking lot designated for personnel only. Chris showed his badge to the attending guard who promptly opened the gate. The lot was filled with military vehicles.

"This is really strange. I wonder what's going on." Chris observed, camouflaging his apprehensions.

"Maybe we should pray for protection, Chris." She took both of his hands and softly spoke. "This is new to both of us but my friends would just talk as if Yahweh was a friend sitting next to you. Apparently, it's not any magical formula or certain words we have to say. We just say what we feel and God hears our heart."

Chris's prayer was simple. It was not for himself. His prayer was for Gabriella's safety who was putting her trust in both him and God.

She squeezed his hands before releasing them. "Now that wasn't so bad, was it? Now what?" She asked. "Do I stay here and wait?"

"No way," he answered, opening his door and going around the Jeep to open hers. "No way I'm leaving you alone. No one here knows anything about you outside of Detectives Richards and Harold. To the people here at the station you're going to be my girlfriend, like it or not."

His strong arms pulled her from her seat and briefly hugged her in assurance everything would be fine. "Are you ready?"

She nodded and forced a smile. Neither knew what to expect but it certainly was not what would soon follow.

CHAPTER 15

Chris took Gabriella's hand as they approached the double glass doors entering police headquarters. A sign posted on the door advised citizens to contact their local police station to report missing people. Above it in bold red letters was another sign stating: "Authorized Personnel Only. Doors will remain locked at all times."

Chris looked at Gabriella with an expression of perplexity. "Very odd."

He rang the buzzer and a voice came on the intercom. "Identify yourself please."

In a firm, confident voice Chris stated, "This is Officer Christopher Harris." Immediately, the buzzer sounded and the door unlocked.

Entering the main lobby, only one officer sat behind the reception desk. His dark eyes were focused on the computer screen in front of him. He looked up as the two approached.

"Chris! We've all been worried about you, man. Glad to see you're okay." The officer came around the desk and slapped Chris on the back. "Who's this?" He asked looking at Gabriella.

Chris gave no indication anything was amiss. "This is my girlfriend Gabi. Gabi, this is Peter." Chris put his arm around her shoulder in support as she reached to shake Peter's hand, forcing a convincing smile. Peter's questioning eyes pierced hers. She did not flinch.

"Girlfriend, huh? Been keeping secrets, big guy." Peter slapped him once again on the back and returned to his seat. "Glad to see there's still a little normality in this crazy world around us. Gives a man a little hope for the future."

"Not used to this place being so quiet." Chris changed the subject looking around the large empty lobby.

"Everything's changed since the war. We lost several officers." Peter paused to steady his sorrowful voice. "Not sure if it was by rocket attacks or the vanishings. Naturally, the military has called up all reserves and everyone's on high alert just trying to deal with the aftermath of the last week. Some of the IDF have taken over offices here in the building, coordinating efforts with local authorities. There's also been a steady stream of big wigs from Europe coming and going, meeting with the military heads. That's why we keep the doors locked and only authorized personnel can pass through those doors." He pointed to the multiple elevators that had access to all fourteen floors.

"Where's all the officers' cars?" Chris asked him. "The parking lot's full of military vehicles."

"Except for a few upstairs coordinating with national security everyone else is out working the havoc. Where've you been, Chris? Richards just said you had been on assignment before the war and he hadn't heard from you since. We were beginning to think the worst."

"Is Detective Richards alright? Is he here?" Chris avoided addressing the assignment comment and cut through the chase.

"He's in his office. He's been dealing with a lot of the international coordination. There've been quite the array of characters coming in and out of his office since the war. I'm not sure what's going on and he's not talking. Never saw any of them before."

Instantly, Chris knew something was not right. "Peter, I'm going to leave Gabi out here with you while I talk to Richards. I don't want the guys upstairs asking any questions; you know how they are."

"Sure, no problem. I'll take good care of her and no one will know she's with you. I'm sure your fellow officers would love to give you a heckling. Everything's been so grim around here, they'd enjoy a little teasing." Peter chuckled and motioned Chris on to the elevators.

Chris led Gabriella to a chair in the corner facing out the window and handed her a magazine. He gave her a long hug so he could whisper in her ear. "Stay turned toward the window and if anyone comes through the lobby keep your face covered with the magazine. You'll be safe here with Peter but I prefer no one get a good look at you."

Gabriella wrapped her arms around him, not for a show of affection for Peter's sake, but for the safety she felt. "I'll be back as soon as I can," he assured her.

She dropped her arms and let him go, watching him disappear behind the closing elevator door. She stared out the window, silently praying he would be safe.

Peter refocused on the computer screen. Briefly he looked up. "If you need anything, Gabi, just let me know."

"Thank you," she answered, opening the magazine and facing away from Peter's desk.

She tried to occupy her mind but it was a lost cause. She laid the magazine back in her lap when she heard the outside intercom buzz and Peter's voice request, "Identify yourself, please."

A deep voice with heavy Italian accent answered. "This is Russo and Moretti. We have an appointment with Detective Richards." The buzzer sounded and Gabriella heard the doors open.

She did not dare turn and look. Instead, she dropped her head as though she was reading and unaware of their entrance. She heard their footsteps approaching Peter's desk. He instructed them to wait while he confirmed the appointment with the detective.

"Detective Richards, your twelve o'clock appointment is here." There was a brief pause before Peter replied to the detective. "Okay, sure thing."

She heard the click of the receiver. "He'll be with you in just a few minutes, gentlemen."

She could hear the men mutter something unintelligible and took seats to wait. She kept her head completely turned from them. They were talking in low, muted voices and she was unable to understand their conversation; however, their voices inflected a serious nature. The more she listened, the more familiar the voices sounded. One of the men had a deep cough. Every few sentences he would stop and clear his throat. Then the smell! One had lit a cigarette and it was the same repulsive aroma that came from the kitchen at the lodge when they heard the intruders. The voices, the cough, and the smell came together to confirm these were the very same men.

Gabriella struggled to remain calm, mentally asking herself: "What's the chance the same two men at the lodge would be sitting here in this room waiting to see Detective Richards, exactly at the same time we are here?" Her whole body begin to tremble. "I've got to get a grip. Stay hidden," her mind was telling her. Yet at the same time she knew what she had to do. "I must see their faces. I have to know who these men are."

She turned her face just enough to get a glimpse out of the corner of her eye. Their backs were to her so she turned a little more for a better view. All she could tell was two medium built men in black suits. One was bald and the other had thick, light brown hair. The man on the left shifted in his chair towards her direction and she slowly turned her head away with no obvious quick moves.

She dropped her head back down pulling the paper from her lap closer to her face. She leaned slightly in their direction in hopes of hearing their conversation but their voices were too muffled. She was determined to attempt one more look when Peter's phone rang.

"Okay, I'll send them on up." He hung up the phone and addressed the two men. "Detective Richards can see you now."

Gabriella kept her face turned away as they passed behind her approaching the elevator. She heard one sentence clearly. "Ugo is expecting that information today." Cold chills moved up and down her spine as stark reality dawned crystal clear. These were the same men! Their footsteps stopped and silence filled the air. She clutched the magazine continuing to stare at the page but seeing nothing. One of the men walked directly past her chair and to the window. His jacket brushed the side of her arm.

"Excuse me," he said politely, looking down at her.

She kept her head down and simply nodded. She dared not say a word lest they recognized her voice. They had been keeping her under surveillance for only God knew how long. He continued to the window and briefly stared out. She noticed he had a slight limp when he walked. On his right hand was a gaudy diamond ring that flashed as it caught the sunlight filtering through the window. Over his shoulder, he addressed his companion. "I'm sure he'll meet us here soon. We'll go on up." He passed her once again and she could feel his stare. She held her breath and did not move a muscle. Waves of fear were creeping up and down her entire being. She was finally able to breathe when she heard the elevator door open and then momentarily close behind them.

She took a deep breath and looked around the room locating the Ladies restroom. When she had the strength to stand she stood up and stretched as if nothing was wrong. She composed her posture and walked confidently to the restroom saying nothing. Once inside she locked the door and collapsed in the floor.

"Oh, God. Oh, God," she repeated over and over futility trying to relieve the panic. She took deep breaths and exhaled slowly regulating her breathing. She looked at her watch. Chris had been upstairs for over an hour. "He won't know who those men are," she whispered in a panic. "Do they have any idea who Chris is? Are they here looking for him?" Terror gripped her at the very thought of losing him and facing the end of days alone.

She wrapped her arms around her knees and rocked back and forth. She knew Peter would suspect something was wrong if she stayed indefinitely in the restroom but she could not take a chance of those men seeing her or the unknown man yet to arrive.

"Dear God, what do I do?" She continued to rock back and forth, back and forth, clenching her knees and praying for some reasonable solution. A knock on the door froze her motion.

"Gabi, are you in there?" At the sound of Chris's voice, relief inundated her. Jumping up, she rushed to the door. Before flinging it wide open, she realized she had to compose herself. Peter could not suspect a thing.

She drew a deep breath and slowly exhaled in attempt to control her quivering voice. "I'll be right out, Chris."

Momentarily, she opened the door, glancing around the room. It was empty except for Peter who was still working on his computer. She sighed in relief and took Chris's hand whispering, "Let's get out of here...*now.*"

He held her hand tightly and led her towards the exit. "See you later, Peter," he called back as they exited. Peter waved not looking up. "Take care, man."

Coming towards the door was a man who looked very familiar to Gabriella; however she could not place who he was. She looked down at the sidewalk as they passed, avoiding any eye contact. As she and Chris turned the corner to the parking lot she glanced back and he was entering the police station. He had to be the man the other two were waiting for.

"Did you know that man that just passed us?" She asked Chris still struggling to compose herself. "He just went into the station."

He shook his head. It was obvious his mind was elsewhere. "Something was very different about Detective Richards. I'm trying to figure out what's going on." He focused his attention back to Gabriella. "Why were you so anxious to leave? Was Peter giving you a hard time about being my supposed girlfriend?"

She waited until they got back to the Jeep to answer. Safely inside with doors locked, she turned to face Chris. Her heart was racing again as she remembered how close the strange men were to her.

"Chris, did you see two men go into Detective Richards' office a few minutes ago? I heard Peter tell Richards his twelve o'clock appointment was waiting." She watched his face intently.

"I passed them briefly as I was leaving his office. Why?" He could see the trepidation in her eyes.

"I am almost positive they are the same two men who were in the lodge a couple of days ago. In fact, I'm sure of it." Her voice was edging on hysteria.

Chris took her hand. "Settle down, Gabi, and explain how you know." He did not start the Jeep engine but instead turned to fully face her.

She recounted the previous events in the police lobby. "When they passed by me I heard them mention the name Ugo. That's the same name they used as being the person they reported to. That's when I knew why the voices, the deep cough, and the cigarette smell were so familiar. They are one and the same! Why would they be meeting with Detective Richards?" Her eyes were pleading for an explanation.

Revelation dawned on Chris. "Of course!" His mind was piecing together the mysterious conversation he just had with the detective.

"Of course, what?" Gabriella pressed him. "What, Chris?"

"Let's get out of here and go somewhere we can talk away from the station. Give me a few minutes to think this completely through and then I'll explain. I want to try to get to my apartment. It's only a few blocks from here."

As he backed out of the parking space he heard Gabriella gasp. "Look, Chris."

He hit the brakes and immediately saw her concern. A black Suburban was parked only a few vehicles down from where the Jeep had been. Chris backed further down and stopped where he could see the license plate. Quickly he pulled out his note pad, wrote the number down and immediately exited the parking lot.

"It could be a coincidence, you know." He glanced at Gabi knowing she would not believe a word of it.

She shot him a look that needed no explanation. He also knew the chances were great it was the same Suburban following them the day before on the mountain.

Chris sped the Jeep up and wasted no time driving to the apartment. It had been his home for the past five years and circumstances told him it would never be again.

All along the city streets were pictures of missing people taped to the windows of closed buildings. Family members were silently pleading for someone, anyone, to call them if their loved ones had been seen. Numerous people were walking up and down the sidewalks, giving out flyers with pictures and contact information of the vanished. Gabriella wanted to scream out the window. "They're gone and never coming back!" Instead she sat silent in empathy with their pain.

Within minutes they were pulling into an apartment complex. The buildings were concrete and stucco and appeared to be fairly new structures. Chris' apartment was on the first floor and he pulled to the rear entrance allowing privacy from the main street. The back-door entrance led to a galley kitchen, which led to the living area in the front section of the apartment.

"You're safe here." He assured her. "I want to pack some of my personal items before we head back to the mountain. Then we'll talk. I'd offer you something to drink but I cleared everything out not knowing how long I'd be on assignment."

"I'm fine," she replied as he disappeared behind his bedroom door.

Gabriella looked around the apartment. It reflected everything masculine. A weight bench was in the corner, police journals were lying on the coffee table, and a big screen television was mounted to the wall across from his leather couch. Over his desk was a bookshelf filled with framed certificates of awards from the police department. On his desk, strategically placed next to his computer screen, was one lone picture, apparently of his mother and father.

She walked over and looked closer. The couple appeared to be in their sixties and looked so happy. She held the picture closer to her face as if the framed couple could hear her. "Caleb and I were going to grow old together just like you," she whispered to the smiling couple. "We were going to have a family and live happily ever after just like in the fairy tales." Her voice was tainted with mourning as she placed the picture back in its place. "Sure, we were," she retorted in agony of soul. "Fairy tales are just that...make believe and they never come true."

She turned to sit back down and was face to face with Chris. She blushed, realizing he had heard every word. She stuttered trying to come up with an explanation for her mythical dreams. "Caleb told me he was my Prince Charming and would take me to a land far, far away where we would live happily ever after. Well, seems he went without me." She crossed the floor and dropped into the couch. "But then that was my fault, wasn't it?" She could not get away from the reality of the decision she had made. "My choice was not make believe. It was very real. Just wrong."

She pulled her thoughts back to the present and took a deep breath, then slowly exhaled in an effort for self-control. She patted the cushion next to her on the couch. "Sit down, Chris, and tell me what happened with Detective Richards."

He joined her on the leather couch and leaned his head back allowing his intuitive thoughts to form his assessment. "Needless to say, Richards was surprised to see me and his words were guarded, almost pre-calculated. He told me he had called the house phone at the lodge and no one answered. Then he sent someone up to the lodge to look for us and no one was there. They reported the entire grounds had been thoroughly checked."

He paused for a moment. "If we had known about the security system then we may have seen the men he sent and trusted them enough to expose our hideaway. That definitely would have been detrimental. Richards thought we all may have vanished like so many others. I told him we are the only ones left; the others did vanish. I wasn't sure how much to tell him. Normally it would have been everything with nothing held back but something just didn't feel right."

"Really?" She questioned. "I felt like I could completely trust Detective Richards."

"Me, too, Gabi, but something was different about him and it wasn't just the stress of what's happened this past week. I've worked with him long enough to see how he handles pressure. I also know when he's holding information back. He was watching his words very carefully. I decided I wasn't giving him any information about the bunker and I never mentioned your father. When we first arrived at the lodge only the Professor and Sandee knew your father was still alive. There's no way Richards could have known. He was still trying to find out where the mystery box containing your father's research came from. He did want to know where we were when they came to the lodge to get us and how we got back to Haifa."

"What did you tell him?"

"Something inside was warning me not to tell him about the escape tunnel or the hidden Jeep. I didn't lie to him; I just didn't tell the whole truth. I told him there was a car in one of the storage buildings there at the lodge."

"What did he say?"

"He wanted to know where you were. When I told him you were out in the lobby he got a very strange look. It really concerned me. Now that you've told me the two men coming to see Richards were the same ones at the lodge his actions make more sense. He knows something, Gabi. Whoever these people are, they've got to Richards. I'm not convinced he's in cahoots with them because he wants me to stay on assignment protecting you, but they've definitely got to him."

Relief flooded through Gabriella knowing Chris was instructed to stay with her, but she clarified the original assignment. "It was really the Professor the police were protecting when we were hidden at the lodge. The rest of the team was more of a precaution." She mentally relived the night someone attempted to murder Dr. Brotman before refocusing on the present. "I thought Detective Richards would tell you to come back to the station, your assignment was over. I didn't know what I was going to do if he did." She was holding back the tears that formed at the thought of being alone.

He took her hand and gently turned her face to look him directly in the eyes. "Gabi, listen to me. Assignment or no assignment, I am with you for the duration. I will *not* leave you. Do you understand me? I will not leave you." His voice was stern, but compassionate. His eyes were determined, but caring. His hand was firm, yet tender.

She forced a smile and nodded.

Chris got up and began pacing back and forth, thinking out loud. "Detective Richards must know there is still danger for you or he wouldn't keep me on an official assignment, but if he's being influenced by this Ugo fellow the less Richards knows about us the better. From this point on I am not looking at my job from an assignment standpoint. This is a survival mission."

He continued to pace, brainstorming their strategic plans. "He says we'll be safe going back to the lodge. If you remember Detective Harold and I brought a truckload of supplies when we took your team up there so Richards knows we would have enough food and necessities to last for a while. I didn't tell him about the men at the lodge a couple of days back. I just went along with his plan and told him we would go back this afternoon. Now we have the surveillance system, we can both watch and record 24/7 and know when and who comes around."

Gabriella was anxious to get back to the safety of the bunker. "If he knows what these men are up to, Chris, do you think he knows my father was still alive? Detective Richards read some of my father's journal when we were trying to determine why someone tried to kill the Professor. He knows bits and pieces and maybe these guys have filled in the blanks for him." She hesitated to voice her next words. "Could this be a set-up?"

He entered his bedroom to get his luggage. He knew if she saw his face she would know that was his grave concern; and if he could not trust Detective Richards then he would trust no one. Without a doubt, the world had become a different place. It was evident everywhere they turned.

CHAPTER 16

———— ••◆•• ————

Gabriella laid her head back on Chris' couch reliving the events in the lobby at police headquarters. She would never forget the names Russo and Moretti. She was branding every detail in her mind for future reference: the voices, the deep cough, the distinct cigarette smell, the limp, and the gaudy diamond ring the baldheaded man wore on his right hand. Even though she had not seen their faces she would be prepared to recognize them in any future encounters.

Chris finished packing the items in his bedroom. One final bag was packed with his computer. Gabriella noticed he took a flash drive from his shirt pocket and stored it in the zippered bag. He took the picture of his parents from its resting place on his desk, lovingly wrapped it with a towel for protection, and laid it on top of the computer. Zipping the bag, he turned to face her.

"I'm ready when you are." He crossed the floor to the couch and extended his hands to help her up. She reached to him and felt the strength of his arms pulling her upwards. She was once again amazed at how she could so completely trust someone she had only come to know a few days prior.

As they exited the apartment together, Chris laid his cell phone on the kitchen counter, turned out the light and locked the door. Gabriella knew if anyone traced his phone it would lead to a dead end.

As they pulled out of the parking lot Chris glanced in the rear-view mirror for one last look at his apartment. He knew he would never be returning. With that glance, he saw the black Suburban pull in behind his apartment and two men approach his back door. He gave no indication to Gabriella as they drove away but it was now confirmed; the enemy was looking for him also.

As they drove the streets through northern Haifa, thoughts were rolling in Chris' head. Were the two men looking just for him or did they now know Gabriella was with him? She had no idea of the encounter they narrowly missed and was somewhat relaxed watching the business district as they drove out of the city. Some businesses were reopening. Most still sat dark and empty as proprietors were struggling with the aftermath of current events. An eerie aura hung in the air.

As Gabriella watched the city scenery, Chris kept watching his rear view. He tried to conceal his apprehensions. "Anything you need before we go back to the bunker?"

She answered him with a shake of the head. She truly longed to go to her apartment or at least drive by to see if it still stood after the bombings but she knew it was too risky.

Instead she focused on the drive ahead of them. The early fall day next to the Mediterranean Sea was warm compared to the brisk mountain air at the lodge. Gabriella longed to enjoy the beauty of the outdoors while she had the chance. "I would love to stop by the sea for a few minutes. There's something about the sound of the waves and the mist in my face that clears my mind." Her face lightened at the thought and then quickly changed back to a somber expression. "You know we won't have many more days like this, Chris, maybe no more at all."

"Sure, no problem." He turned on Derech Allenby Street and headed towards Mount Carmel's coastline. Driving northwest, they passed a sign that read 'Elijah's Cave – 1600 meters'. Chris could hear Gabriella catch her breath. "What's wrong, Gabi?"

Memories of the meeting with Professor Brotman shortly after the team's return from Saudi Arabia came rushing back. She took a moment to collect her thoughts and recall the events he had shared with the team before she tried to relay them to Chris.

She turned in her seat to face him so she could see his reaction. "Just a few weeks ago, the Professor was telling my team about Elijah's Cave and the connection with the UFO crash on Shikmona Beach. Have you heard about that crash?"

Chris nodded his head. "Yeah, I've heard about it. I was just a kid when that happened and was living in Tel Aviv. Why?"

She was trying to recall as closely as possible the details shared by the Professor. At the time she did not take it seriously, not until she read her father's journal account of extraterrestrial existence. "The Professor told us in September of 1987 there was an unidentified craft that crashed on the beach. The disc shaped aircraft burned into the sands and the remains proved to be nothing known to man on this planet. There was also a burned image in the sand of a pilot facing a control board. It's considered by UFOlogists to be absolute proof of extraterrestrial existence; and, there was another crash a year later and another two years after that, all on Shikmona Beach."

"Really? I didn't know that." Chris was evidently captivated by the story.

"These crashes were very close to Elijah's cave. It was at the very same place of the biblical account of the prophet Elijah calling down fire from heaven defeating the false prophets of Baal. Inside the cave where Elijah lived are still ancient drawings, thousands of years old, and the spitting image of the craft that burned into the Shikmona Beach sands. The Professor believed these spaceships were actually demonic spirits entering our dimension of time, and it was a sign of the end of days and the return to the days of Noah. After the 1987 crash, there was a flurry of UFO incidents all over Israel. Some strange things happened and were officially documented by the Israeli Government. The Professor believed this was a sign the fallen angels were soon to be released out of the abyss."

Chris glanced at her in amazement. Then he slowed the vehicle as they approached the entrance to Elijah's Cave. "Do you want to go in?"

She hesitantly nodded. "As long as I've lived in Haifa and as many caves as I've explored, I've never been in Elijah's cave."

Chris turned towards the entrance of the Stella Maris Monastery on the lower slopes of Mount Carmel. The parking lot was filled and he had to circle several times before he found an empty slot.

"I wonder why so many people are here," he observed. "You would think they'd be home trying to get life back to normal after the war."

"It does seem odd," Gabriella commented. Neither understood the immense spiritual importance of the ancient structure.

As they approached The Monastery of Our Lady of Mount Carmel Church it was so awe-inspiring it caught Gabriella by total surprise. They stopped and simply gazed allowing the serenity and beauty to enfold them. The thick stone walls had few openings and those were covered by bars.

The structure was built in the shape of a cross and stood majestically at the base of the Carmel Mountains looking out to the Mediterranean Sea.

A Carmelite monk was positioned at the bottom of the steps giving informational pamphlets to all who entered. Gabriella stood quietly for a moment and quickly read the information, then shared it with Chris. "Stella Maris means Star by the Sea. This monastery is the center of the Carmelite Holy Order for the entire world and dates back to 1761. The church was heavily damaged by Napoleon's 1799 campaign. The sick and wounded soldiers were taken into the monastery and cared for by the Friars. When Napoleon retreated, the Turks killed everyone in the monastery including the Friars." Gabriella paused for a moment allowing the historic information to process.

"That's so sad." She spoke with a soft voice filled with compassion.

Near the entrance of the monastery was a six-foot pyramid graced at the apex by a metal cross. Gabriella continued to read the historical facts: "This pyramid is a memorial to the French soldiers who died here after Napoleon's retreat."

They walked closer to read the inscription. Chris read out loud the words engraved, "How are the mighty fallen in battle. King David's lamentation over Saul and Jonathan."

They climbed the stone steps to the main monastery entrance and crossed the threshold feeling they had stepped back in time. In the room to the right of the entryway was a charming nativity scene, displaying in a rich cedar wood, the Holy Family. To the left was a museum with artifacts from the Byzantine church that once stood at the same site centuries before.

"I can't believe I've never visited here." Gabriella mused. The magnificent structure of Italian marble was so brightly and vividly patterned it appeared as though it had been painted by a master artisan, just as the colorful paintings on the church dome had been. The circular dome scenes depicted episodes from both the Old and New Testaments. The most dramatic, and taking the center position, was the scene of Elijah swept up in a chariot of fire. Around the dome were captivating pictures of David with his harp, the prophet Isaiah, the holy family and the four evangelists, Matthew, Mark, Luke and John. Latin inscriptions of biblical verses were written around the roofed dome.

Above the altar, carved from cedar of Lebanon, stood the statue of the Holy Virgin Mary holding Jesus on her knees. Under the statue a brass plate was engraved, "Our Mistress of Carmel". Embossments dedicated to Carmelite figures were hoisted on all four corners of the central hall. At the western wall of the church was a large organ that was played in religious ceremonies and special concerts. Underneath the altar of worship were stairs leading to a quarried cave, the Cave of Elijah.

Chris and Gabriella reverently walked down the marble aisle towards the main altar passing between the parishioner benches that lined both sides of the massive room. The benches were filled with mourners crying to The Holy Mother, Queen of Heaven for help in their distress of war and lost loved ones.

They crossed the center of the mosaic walkway which displayed a ten-foot marble circle containing an eight-pointed star, the symbol of the Carmelite Order. Beneath the altar, steps led down to Elijah's Cave. This was the place believed to be where Elijah, the Patron Saint of the Carmelite Order, lived. Numerous prayer candles burned on the altar above the cave, each representing a Carmelite community in another country.

"Look, Chris, they are praying for Americans, too." Gabriella pointed to a candle on the upper left. It was noted to be in remembrance of those in the United States. An ache stabbed through her heart as she thought of her homeland and the devastation America had experienced. She paused for a moment and silently prayed for her beloved country. Chris stood by her side in reverence.

Descending the stone stairway leading to Elijah's cave, they saw another solemn faced Carmelite monk standing at the bottom warning all visitors to respect the holy atmosphere they were entering.

The circular roof cavern was filled with additional sojourners seeking peace for their anguished souls. Muted cries could be heard coming from the altar at the far end of the cave. More wooden benches lined both sides of the cave aisle. They, too, were filled with the praying broken-hearted souls.

Gabriella walked to the outer right aisle next to the wall that led to the altar at the front of the Grotto of Elijah. Displayed there was a large statue, engraved with the words *Eliyahu HaNavi*, Elijah the Prophet.

She motioned for Chris to follow her as she moved slowly, surveying the limestone wall covered with ancient, indigenous drawings.

She stopped half way down the aisle and held her breath, pointing to the drawing on the wall. There was no doubt it was the ancient spacecraft the Professor had told her about. The disc shaped object drawn was surrounded by flames of fire.

Gabriella whispered to Chris, "Do you think this is the chariot of fire Elijah was taken up into the heavens in or the fire that came down from heaven on the altars of Baal?" She contemplated for a minute then answered her own question. "Maybe both," she whispered. "One being real and the other a demonic counterfeit."

Chris shrugged his shoulders in confusion. "Strange," was his only whispered answer.

They continued down the wall to the front. There was no room to kneel and pray amongst the gathered grievers so they stood next to the wall and bowed their heads for a time of silent reflection and individual communion with the God of the Universe. The title given to an individual's faith of Catholic, Jew, Christian, or whatever, did not matter to the group gathered. There was a common grief and uncertainty that bound all their spirits together.

Gabriella closed her eyes and tried to imagine the Prophet Elijah living in this very place and hearing the voice of Yahweh. She thought back to the Passover Seders the Professor would preside over which were held at the lodge each spring. She thought of the Seder as a beautiful, religious ceremony and respectfully attended; however, she put no spiritual or prophetic value in the annual event. Forefront in her memory, at that moment in the cave, was the part of the Seder where a place was always set at the table for the Prophet Elijah. A cup of wine was placed at his special seat and the door left open for his welcomed entry to the home. The Professor would proclaim each year, "Elijah will one day come heralding the return of the Messiah."

Gabriella opened her eyes and gazed at the statue. To the left, she saw the figure of a man standing in the corner dressed very much like the image of Elijah. She first thought it was another statue. The light was dim and she squinted her eyes trying to see him more clearly. As the image came into focus, the man was dressed in a long, ashen-colored robe tied around the waist with a braided rope. A tunic overlay in dark brown hung to his knees. His head was bald and his face was mostly covered by a long, gray beard. He was staring straight at her. She tried to look away but her eyes remained fixed on him. He lifted his arm and pointed straight towards her. A kneeling monk rose to his feet from the altar and passed between them. With her eyes still glued to the corner, he was no longer there after the monk passed by. She looked in both directions but the strange old man was not to be seen.

Chris looked at her and then in the direction in which she was staring. His eyes were questioning but he did not want to intrude upon the silent reverence of the sacred altar. He took her hand and led her back down the aisle, up the stone steps to the main level and across the marble floor exiting the monastery.

"What is it, Gabi?" He asked as soon as they were outside. His eyes penetrated hers and she could not deny what she saw.

"I saw a strange man standing in the corner by Elijah's altar. He was staring at me, Chris. Then in an instant, he just disappeared."

"What did he look like? Could you tell?" The police officer instantly took over. "Which way did he go?"

She hesitated, feeling he would think her delusional. "He was dressed the same as the statute of the Prophet Elijah over the altar, only this man was *real*. He just vanished into thin air."

Chris led her to a bench close to the pyramid. "Stay right here. I'll be right back." He disappeared back inside the church.

Gabriella sat down as instructed and tried to rationalize the encounter. She closed her eyes and envisioned the man again. He did not frighten her, not at all. In fact, she felt a sense of peace from his penetrating eyes. She was about to go back to the cave in hopes of seeing him once again when Chris rejoined her.

"Well, that didn't go as I thought it would," he admitted. "I thought they might have someone that dressed as the Prophet Elijah, perhaps giving drama exhibits or such. I questioned one of the monks and he was very definite they did no such thing."

"The man didn't frighten me, Chris. The light was dim but I could see his face. There was something peaceful about his eyes. If he had been in the clothing of a Hasidic Jew, instead of the robe, he would have looked exactly like..." She stopped as realization dawned on her.

"Who, Gabi? Who would he have looked like?"

She knew this would take some explaining for Chris to understand. She took a deep breath and exhaled. "The Prophet".

"The Prophet?" He echoed.

He sat back down on the bench beside her as she explained. "Just before the Professor's attempted murder, a man appeared to me and gave me an ancient scroll. This same man had also appeared to the Professor years ago, and he gave him two stone tablets with ancient writings. The two together, along with what we found in the cave in Saudi Arabia, gave us the message the Professor finished just before the vanishings. You were privileged to hear the very first complete reading with the rest of the team while I was still sleeping."

"And who is this so-called Prophet with the ancient messages?" Chris questioned.

Gabriella could not believe she was speaking the words out loud. "The Prophet Elijah." She paused to process the revelation. "He has returned for the end of days just as the Professor's prophecy translation said he would. He is one of the two witnesses that God sends to warn the world of the final judgment."

Chris sat stunned. He knew she was not being melodramatic. She really believed what she was saying. "I don't mean this to be insulting but why did he come to you with a prophetic scroll? You didn't even believe then."

"I don't know, Chris. Maybe because he was trying to convince me as an answer to the many prayers the others prayed. Maybe because my father and the Professor had discovered the implant that will ultimately, and in some form, become the infamous 666. Maybe because I *have* been chosen for some special purpose for such a time as this, as my father said. I don't have any idea what's going on. None of it makes any sense to me." Her voice was quivering, while her mind was spinning with a deluge of emotions.

"Let's take a walk, Gabi. I have a lot of questions."

They got up and silently walked the couple hundred yards to Shikmona Beach. They passed the Stella Maris lighthouse and soon were on the warm sands. They pulled off their shoes and rolled up their pants legs. Still silent, they walked to the water's edge and allowed the gentle waves to caress their feet.

Throughout the afternoon, they walked along the seaside watching the gentle waves. Chris' eyes would often scan the lighthouse area making sure the two men had not found them. Gabriella was totally unaware of his trepidations.

He asked more questions about The Omega Watchers Project in any effort to understand better both Gabriella's life before they met and the prophecies soon to be fulfilled. They shared childhood stories and memories from the past before the team came to the lodge, where everything changed. Without the necessity of words, they both knew from this point on their individual lives were now entwined to one.

CHAPTER 17

The sun was descending into the Mediterranean Sea. The brilliant colors gradually evanesced into the blue, rolling waters. Chris and Gabriella sat on the shore watching the sun completely fade. The sky darkened and the sea breezes cooled giving a foreboding aura as they individually processed the events of the day.

"Time to head back up the mountain?" Chris asked.

Reluctantly, she agreed. The fresh air and tranquil sea had been exactly what she needed to calm her soul. They retraced their steps across the sand, past the lighthouse, and to the Jeep. Only a few cars still awaited passengers in the Stella Maris parking lot.

After helping Gabriella in, Chris joined her to begin the drive. Pulling out, he turned toward Highway 4 that would lead them north up the coast. They had barely exited the parking lot when Chris noticed a black Suburban pulling out of the lot behind them. He slightly sped up and so did the vehicle to their rear. He sped up again with the following vehicle following suit. He did not want to alarm Gabriella. On the side of caution, he slowed the Jeep hoping the vehicle would pass. Instead the vehicle behind pulled onto a side road. Gabriella noticed the speed reduction and looked at him questioningly.

"I thought someone might be following us, but the car turned off on a side street. Nothing to worry about." Chris kept glancing into the rearview mirror. He knew something was not right. Within a few minutes, he again noticed the same vehicle behind them maintaining the same speed as he was. He slightly accelerated allowing more distance between the two vehicles. He gained some leeway but the vehicle continued close behind. Gabriella was totally unaware of Chris' suspicions.

"I'm going to pull off at the next gas station and fill up." His voice was poised and she suspected nothing.

She nodded her head and took out some of the cash she had taken from her father's bedroom. "Don't use any electronic payments when we stop. Use this," Gabriella insisted. "I found it in my father's room and I know it was for emergencies. I'm sure he would consider this an emergency." She looked at him with a half jesting smile. He did not like taking the money but knew the wisdom in conducting only cash transactions.

She laid her head back and closed her eyes reliving the encounter with The Prophet. In her mind's eye, she could still see his kind face and a feeling of peace freshly flowed through her. "Why did he point directly at me?" She silently asked herself.

Chris broke her concentration. "There's a station just ahead." He did not turn on a signal but instead waited until their Jeep was directly at the exit making a right turn too quick for the Suburban to follow. He watched the vehicle behind abruptly hit their brakes but it was too late to maneuver the exit.

When he pulled to the gas pump Gabriella got out and stretched, totally unaware of any possible danger. "I'm going to the restroom," she muttered.

Chris kept his eyes on her while filling the tank. He could see her head across the aisle tops and then she disappeared into the ladies' room. He cut off the pump and went in to pay glancing in all direction for any potential followers.

When he approached the counter to pay Gabriella was at the coffee bar. Chris was about to join her when two men in black suits approaching her from behind. One was bald and one had light brown hair just as she had described the men in the police lobby earlier that day. He halted suddenly, stepping behind an aisle display where he could see them between the shelf openings. Gabriella was totally unaware they were approaching and Chris did not want to alarm her or the other shoppers. He immediately went into police mode placing his hand on the gun under his shirt ready to draw.

The two men moved closer and it appeared one would go to each side of Gabriella. They were only a few feet away when the door to the men's restroom opened and a Hasidic Jew came out and joined Gabriella at the coffee bar. Both men hesitated then backed a few feet away apparently waiting for clear access to her. The Hasidic Jew leaned over and said something to her. She looped her arm through his without hesitation and the man led her across the market floor and out the front door.

Chris kept his eyes on the two men. They exited the back entrance and disappeared. He quickly followed Gabriella and the strange man out the front with his hand on his gun should the men circle to the front of the station.

Waiting for passing cars to clear, Chris crossed the lot to the waiting Jeep looking for Gabriella and the stranger. He found her inside the vehicle with the doors locked. She was staring straight ahead as if in a trance. He glanced in all directions, unlocked the driver's door, and got in beside her quickly locking it back.

"How did you get in, Gabi? I locked the doors before I went inside. Who was that man?" Chris did not breathe a word about the two men that were closing in on her at the coffee bar.

At the sound of his voice she blinked her eyes and looked around her in confusion. She blinked hard again trying to focus on her surroundings. "How did I get here?"

"You don't remember?" Chris's voice was edged with confusion.

"The last thing I remember was standing at the coffee bar trying to decide what to order."

She turned to face him with an exacting gaze. "What just happened?"

"I wish I knew." Chris was struggling with how much he should tell her. Neither did he know how to explain what he just witnessed.

She continued to press him. "Tell me what happened, please." Then the possibility hit her. In a trembling voice, she voiced her worst fears. "I'm slipping back into the paranormal world."

He knew then he could hold the facts back. Something beyond anything he had ever observed had just occurred, but it definitely was not occult and she had to know the truth. As he recounted the phenomenon Gabriella's eyes widened in disbelief.

"You actually saw that happen?" She would never doubt his word but it was more than her mind could fathom. "You saw the Hasidic Jew speak to me and I willingly just went with him?" She closed her eyes allowing her mind to process his words and tried unsuccessfully to recall just one little detail. Her mind was completely blank. The coffee bar was the last thing she could remember. "How could you be sure the two men were after me?"

Chris' voice was firm and definite as he responded: "I can read body language. That gives me keen information but it goes far beyond that. Somehow, I can instinctively tell what a person's next actions are going to be. My police chief used to tell me I had a gift for assessing the unknown like nothing he had ever seen. That's the reason he put me on special assignments instead of patrol and the very reason I was assigned to your team at the lodge. Detective Richards knew this was potentially very dangerous."

Chris abruptly started the Jeep, watching for signs of a following vehicle as they pulled from the gas pumps. Nothing seemed amiss. He merged back on Highway 4 and accelerated, anxious to return to the bunker where she would be safe. He continued to watch for any signs of followers but his police intuitiveness was at rest now.

They retraced their morning's journey up the coast and east through the Hula Valley. Night had settled upon the peaceful views of the landscape and only the road ahead could be seen. They hardly spoke. Each was reflecting on the evolution of the day's events. Neither could wrap their minds around the unexplainable supernatural occurrences.

As they neared the lodge area Chris slowed the Jeep and exited onto the now familiar hunter's path leading back to the cave entrance. The night drive made the path more challenging and he fully concentrated on the terrain as they ascended the mountainside. He took one last look in the rear-view mirror to be certain no vehicles followed. Only darkness greeted his eyes. Soon they were back to the tunnel and reentering the bunker. The door closed behind them locking them into safety.

Shortly, Gabriella was in her bed. She hoped the voices of Caleb and her father would be heard again. However, as her eyes closed in sleep, a new night journey began. One Arcturus had no control over.

CHAPTER 18

Gabriella snuggled into her bed and attempted to sleep. She would doze and then awaken rehearsing over and over the day's occurrences. Finally, she fell into a REM sleep. It was impossible for her to ascertain if she was dreaming or physically transported when her new journey began.

Whether in the body or out of the body, she instantly stood at the altar in Elijah's Cave. The Prophet, clothed in the ashen colored robe and dark tunic, appeared in the cave wall. There was no passageway. He simply emerged from the stone. His face was kind and his eyes full of wisdom. She felt no fear.

He reached towards her and laid his right hand upon her head. His words echoed throughout the cave. "Daughter of Israel, you are chosen from among the tribes to proclaim The Truth."

Her legs weakened and she dropped to her knees with her face bowed before the holy altar. The Prophet held in his hand a vial of oil. He lifted the vessel over her head and began to slowly pour. The warm oil cascaded through her hair, down her face mingling with the pouring tears, across her shoulders and flowing to her feet. The liquid warmth saturated not only the outside of her body but virtually penetrated her soul and spirit.

Forcing breath from her lungs, she lifted her head and addressed the one who anointed her. "I do not understand, Prophet. I'm not born from the House of Israel."

A discerning gaze pierced her as he extended his arms. She put her hands in his, feeling a charge of electricity flow through her body. His anointing hands closed around hers and lifted her up. Her feet did not touch the floor. She stood suspended in mid-air. "Daughter of Zebulon, you are now sealed by the Blood of the Lamb. Understanding will come." He released her hand and with his eyes still penetrating her soul, he faded into the limestone wall.

Blackness filled the cave. The image was gone. She blinked, trying to focus her eyes in the darkness, and was instantly back in her bed.

Gabriella sat straight up inspecting the room, acclimating herself back to reality. Nothing was changed. The room was exactly the same. "It must have been a dream," she determined, "but it felt so real." She touched her head and she felt oil mingled in her hair. "It was real," she whispered, still feeling the warm oil saturating her body, soul, and spirit.

She sat up on the side of the bed and quickly wrote down every word The Prophet had spoken. "What did The Prophet mean when he said I am sealed?" Her mind went back to the mysterious man who supernaturally rescued her at the gas station. "Could there be a connection between the two encounters?" she asked herself but with no answers forthcoming.

The speculations rolled over and over through her mind, akin to the endless waves of the sea, never reaching a conclusion. From mental exhaustion Gabriella finally drifted into a restless sleep. The voice of her father echoed through the night. "I was wrong, my princess, I was so wrong. Please wake up." Hours later the smell of coffee awakened her. As her eyes opened she ran her hand through her hair. The oil remained as a sign of the night's encounter with The Prophet.

She quickly dressed and joined Chris, anxious to share her night journey. Over their morning coffee Gabriella poured out every detail. He listened intently with no interruptions. She had him feel the oil in her hair, proof of her extraordinary night visit. She ended the dissertation with her uncertainty and confusion. "What do you think it means, Chris?"

For several minutes, he said nothing. He arose from the sofa and started his contemplative pacing but then abruptly stopped. He turned to face Gabriella. "Rule of thumb for solving a case is thorough investigation. Yesterday we encountered both the enemy and the protector. I will investigate the first and you take the latter." Chris's voice was filled with certainty he had devised a plan. "Obviously, mine will be in the physical realm and yours will be spiritual."

Chris went to his computer bag and pulled a flash drive from the zippered pocket. "I downloaded some files while I was at police headquarters.

I'm pretty sure there'll be information on Ugo, Ruzzo, and Moretti somewhere in the information. I'll start there."

Gabriella went to the table where the letters from her father were stacked. "Until now I've been afraid of what his letters would reveal," she admitted. "When The Prophet poured the oil over me last night it washed away all apprehension. I'm ready now." She settled on the couch with a pencil in hand to make her personal notes. "We'll compare our findings at lunch."

Chris worked from the security room researching the flash drive files and monitoring cameras for any unwanted visitors. Gabriella read her father's letters giving prophetic instruction for the coming years. Periodically, Chris would walk to the kitchen and observe her expressions which seem to transmute from sorrow to joy, perplexity to revelation. A myriad of emotions flowed through them equally in their individual quests for understanding.

At lunch time, Chris closed his computer and rejoined her, hesitant to share the information he had uncovered. He was aware Gabriella had found peace and he did not want to immediately strip it away.

Gabriella reluctantly laid the letters to the side with a heavy sigh. "So much information and so little time," she commented referring to her father's letters. One look at Chris's face told her his news was not good. "What is it?"

He crossed the stone floor that separated them and joined Gabriella on the couch. "I've solved the Ugo mystery." Chris's eyes reflected it was an ominous revelation.

Her eyebrows rose in question and she clenched her hands together. "Well?"

His demeanor immediately altered and became very official. His voice was firm and certain. "Peter told us Haifa's police headquarters is being used by both military and international liaisons. Seems the International Intelligence and Investigation Agency deems it necessary to have an office in all the major cities in Israel, since our nation is now the world military and financial powerhouse. They are not just using Haifa's but all the police headquarters in every city for their offices to coordinate with the ongoing investigations of the vanishings. Also, as the official document read, to assist in coordinating a universal peace agreement and New World Order. Ugo Strozza is personally heading the NWO project."

"*Ugo Strozza?*" Gabriella exclaimed. "The IIIA Director? That's who sent the two men to find my father?" Her last words faded as veracity dawned. "Dad was right. He first thought it was the U.S. Government trying to stop the implant from being exposed. Then he believed it was much larger, it was an international plot."

Chris paused, hesitant to share the personal connection. "You're exactly right, Gabi. Seems Ruzzo and Moretti are his right-hand men assigned specifically to the finding of one Edward Gabe Russell, alias Eli Sheskin. The indictment stated your father possesses illegally obtained information that jeopardizes world safety and the implementation of the New World Order." He did not tell her they were also looking for his daughter, Gabriella Russell, who is believed to be an accomplice.

"All three of those men were meeting with Detective Richards yesterday. For the head of the IIIA to be present at that meeting...well, let's just say it doesn't get any bigger than that." Gabriella's voice was quivering. "And Detective Richards has to know!"

Chris nodded in agreement. "That explains his unusual behavior. He was sending me body language signals without saying anything just in case our conversation was being recorded. I'm also convinced that's why he didn't answer my calls."

"Detective Richards knows now my father was still alive when we came to the lodge and Ugo and his thugs all think he still is."

Chris' strong demeanor faded and foreboding filled his face. "They believe if they can get to you, they can get to the information they want." He stopped short of voicing the fact they would do anything necessary to complete their mission.

"Do you think they recognized me in the police lobby yesterday?"

"He may not have been sure at first. Probably confirmed it, though, when he saw me coming out of Richards's office. Since they have access to all the police records now, they would know I was assigned to protect your team. You can be sure they've carefully studied our pictures, our profiles, and know exactly who they're looking for. Now they know the license number of the Jeep and it's registered to Eli Sheskin; however, I have a slight decoy."

The luggage he brought from his apartment lay on the floor by the pantry door. He had not yet unpacked. He went over and unzipped the larger bag pulling out an oblong box. Rejoining Gabriella, he opened the end and pulled out a stack of license plates. "When we do undercover work, we often use alias license plates. I've accumulated a nice collection under various alias names. It would take quite a while to run all of these down. Also, I brought an array of disguises I've used through the years. I could get close to my suspects without being identified. 'Always be prepared' is my motto."

A nervous giggle escaped Gabriella. Not one of humor, but of apprehension. Chris knew it was time to change the subject. "Let's have lunch and you can tell me about your father's letters."

She attempted to put the trio of adversaries out of her mind and refocus on the instructions left by her father. She helped Chris with lunch preparations. They ate at the kitchen bar where Gabriella did a quick review of what they already knew was coming and then shared the immediate sequential events.

"We know Israel will have a very short span of peace and world dominance. It will quickly end with the Russian-led Gog and Magog War. Israel gives herself credit for winning the Psalms 83 War which the world has termed the Three Day War, but Yahweh will reveal himself supernaturally in Israel's victory of the next war. The aftermath of the Gog and Magog war and the devastation it causes will have a worldwide impact. It will be the turning point of the nations to a one world government, economy, and religion. Every nation will unite together against Israel."

Chris was continually amazed at how the ancient prophets were so exact in their future predictions. "Did your father say how long between wars?"

"No, he just said a short time. There is no way of knowing, but in the horrible aftermath of that war the False Prophet will be the one to introduce and spiritually sanction the new world leader. With signs and wonders together they will lure the nations into this new earth-wide government and into taking the implant." She looked up at Chris with questioning eyes and he nodded that he understood.

She continued: "According to the Book of Daniel, this evil world leader will make a seven-year peace covenant with Israel, confirm the Abrahamic Covenant, and allow them to keep the land gained in the Three Day War. The major stipulation of this peace treaty is Israel will be allowed to rebuild their Holy Temple with no interference from any nation."

She could see unbelief saturating Chris's eyes. "That one is difficult to swallow, Gabi, especially with all the hatred spewing at us from every country."

She stated matter of fact: "They *will* rebuild, that is certain, but three and one half years after the covenant is confirmed the evil world leader who is the Antichrist, Satan incarnate, will enter the rebuilt temple and declare himself as the true God and mandate everyone must worship him and take his mark. The implant my dad discovered in some form will be used as his mark. The final three and one half years will be evil like the earth has never experienced before."

She paused for a moment before her last comment. "Yahweh is preparing a spiritual army that will preach His truth and save a multitude from the coming great deception. However, most of those who believe and refuse to worship the Antichrist and receive his mark, the implant, will be martyred." She paused allowing Chris time to digest the information.

He sat quietly trying to process the magnitude of these revelations. In all of his years on the police force, he never imagined encountering any scenario like this.

"Chris, the ancient prophets warned what would happen at the end of days and it will begin immediately after this next war."

Gabriella picked up the letter and read the words of explanation penned by her father. *"Yahweh will send two messengers to preach in the streets of Jerusalem. He will also choose 12,000 from each of the 12 tribes of Israel to expose the Antichrist and proclaim the True Messiah to his chosen people."*

Chris was perplexed. "But, Gabi, many of those tribes are lost. No one knows who or where they are."

"They are not lost to Yahweh," she exclaimed before reading the last sentence of her father's letter: *"Yahweh's messenger will anoint and seal the chosen ones."* She laid the letter on the counter waiting for Chris to connect the prophetic dots.

She could see the color drain from his face as comprehension fully dawned. He stared at her at a loss for words.

"Could it be, Chris? Could I be from a lost tribe? The Prophet called me Daughter of Zebulon. Is this why he said I was chosen? It's never made any sense...until now." She spoke the possibility but the truth seemed illusory. "Surely this cannot be true." Her ending words were barely audible.

Chris was desperately trying to assimilate the obvious. In the past, the prophetic seemed fanciful to him, without true substance. It was polar opposite of all police training, but now he had no doubt it was all bona fide. What did this mean for Gabriella? What would it mean for the two of them?

Suddenly, the formidable final seven years morphed into a new divine assignment.

CHAPTER 19

Something deep within Gabriella was now driving her to wholly comprehend the prophecies written in her father's letters. She carefully compared each with the biblical references. Each inspired word was being supernaturally encrypted on the tablets of her heart.

With a hunger to understand the ancient prophecies, she devoured every word. Driven by a force beyond her control, spiritual knowledge was being systemically filed into her spirit to be released at the appointed time. Knowledge she would need for The Chosen calling.

Chris gave her the privacy needed to concentrate. He secluded himself in the security room to review more files from headquarters and to monitor the cameras around and in the lodge. He knew Ruzzo and Moretti had not followed them up the mountain, probably because they already knew he and Gabriella would return there. He thoroughly expected the two men would wait a couple of days before returning, hoping to lure their prey into a false sense of security.

His mind kept replaying the recent experiences and the appearance of The Prophet when Gabriella was in danger. There was not a doubt in his mind a supernatural encounter had taken place. He was an eyewitness.

He laid his head back on the leather chair facing the cameras and closed his eyes in prayer. "I don't understand any of this. I have no doubt, Father, You have placed me here. I know this was not a coincidence. Please help me understand your purpose and plans for me in the end of days."

Exhaustion suddenly washed over him. Passing through the living area he told Gabriella he was going to bed. She barely nodded her head, totally engrossed in her reading.

Restless, he tried to sleep, but sleep evaded him. He tossed and turned in a conundrum of emotions. His memory was a panoramic view of the day's phenomenon, playing over and over. After several hours, finally, sleep captured him. He seldom dreamed but this night a prophetic vision would be an answer to his prayer.

As he drifted into a slumber, he found himself walking through a heavy mist of fog. His instincts told him something was very wrong. He intuitively knew Gabriella was in trouble. He called her name and could hear her faint voice crying out in the distance. He followed the sound, continuing to call for her as he inched closer through the ill-omened obscurity. He could feel her presence even though his eyes could not pierce the dark, misty cloud engulfing them.

"No, I will not!" Her voice screamed just ahead of him. He pressed harder through the hazy unknown. The fog slightly cleared allowing a blurred view of her image. Panic struck him. Gabriella was on the ground with her hands tied behind her back. Clothed in a glistening white robe, her head was bent over. Her blonde hair was obscuring her face as an apocalyptic image dressed in all black grabbed her hair. He jerked her head backward allowing her face to become visible. Chris was awe-struck by the peace in her countenance. She emanated no fear at all. With a sickle sword in his hand the dark image positioned it over her throat ready to strike.

"Deny Jesus or die! Deny him!" The screaming voice of the man in black echoed over and over through the misty haze, *"deny him...deny him... deny him..."*

Gabriella's voice resounded loud and clear, echoing in return, "I will not! *I will not...I will not...I will not..."*

The scene began to move in slow motion and Chris not only saw but felt each movement. The evil image tightened his hold on her hair again jerking her head further back. The sickle was moving inch by inch toward her neck, edging closer and closer to her throat. Chris ran through the cloudy mist lunging towards the attacker grabbing his arm and pushing the blade away from Gabriella's head. The slow motion continued as the man in black swung the sickle towards Chris losing his balance, then falling forward on the penetrating blade. The weapon intended for Gabriella's beheading pierced through the chest of the evil man as he collapsed. The assailant was dead.

The scene returned to normal movement as Chris pulled Gabriella to her feet, untying the binding ropes and freeing her hands. She was not shaking and her face expressed no terror. There was a glow radiating from her that illuminated the foggy cloud that engulfed them.

From the shadowy mist an angel in gleaming white garments emerged holding a golden vial in his right hand. His eyes penetrated Chris's soul and his voice sounded like thunder as he proclaimed, "You are chosen and anointed to be a divine protector."

Chris fell to his knees and bowed in the holy atmosphere that surrounded the heavenly being. The holy messenger approached Chris and poured oil from the golden vial. The warm liquid ran across Chris's head and down his shoulders. It washed away all apprehension of the coming days. A sublime peace flowed through him. He now understood why Gabriella had no fear.

Chris remained kneeling in The Presence with his hands raised worshipping Yahweh, the Almighty God and Creator of all things. When Chris finally looked up the angel was fading back into the mist.

Gabriella stood beside him clutching his hand and pulling him to his feet. "We have both been chosen for such a time as this." Her voice reverberated in the light immersing them.

Chris bowed his head and remained immersed in The Presence as the dream faded and a restful sleep overshadowed him.

When he awakened the next morning, the dream remained vivid in his mind and for a moment he questioned the reality of the night vision. He sat on the side of his bed and ran his fingers across his forehead and through his hair in contemplation. All doubt vanished as he felt the residue of oil that remained upon his head. He knew he had been visited by a Heavenly Messenger.

His purpose for the final days of time was now crystal clear. Yahweh had divinely brought Gabriella, one of The Chosen, into his life to protect; and he would protect her with every fiber of his being.

With an inner passion like nothing he had ever experienced, he exited his bedroom to share his dream with Gabriella. He found her asleep on the couch. Her father's letter, which she was reading before she had fallen asleep, was still lying on her chest. Her long hair framed her tranquil face, the same tranquil face he saw in his night vision. He picked up a blanket and laid it across her.

"I will protect you until my dying breath, Gabriella." He prophetically whispered and quietly withdrew.

CHAPTER 20

Late morning, the smell of Gabriella's favorite coffee awakened her. She sat on the side of the couch and pulled on her fluffy blue house slippers. She pushed her tangled hair back from her face and stretched. Forcing herself to get up she joined Chris in the kitchen area. "Morning," she muttered in a half audible voice. He knew that was the best he would get until the caffeine worked its magic.

"Morning, sleeping beauty," he replied, carrying the coffee tray to the couch. "Sleep well?"

"What little I did sleep. I slept on the couch and didn't go to my bed until sometime this morning," she said through a yawn.

He knew she was neither fully awake nor ready for deep conversation so he clicked on the television for current news updates. He anxiously awaited the opportunity to share his profound night vision.

Michael Adelson was continuing to give all the latest news. "Does that man ever sleep?" She muttered, blowing the hot liquid before taking another sip.

Adelson was interviewing their religious correspondent, Rabbi Zimmerman. Zimmerman was clothed in a black linen robe, traditional of a rabbi's garments during the High Holy Days. His gray sidelocks hung over each ear beneath his black rimmed glasses and black hat. He was anxiously waiting to give his religious perspective on the latest news regarding The Return.

The news reporter began: "This is Michael Adelson coming to you from the Channel 2 newsroom in Haifa. I have with me again today Rabbi

153

Zimmerman who will shed some new light on the spiritual significance of the Prime Minister's announcement of The Return."

Adelson turned to face the Rabbi. "Rabbi Zimmerman, Israel's Prime Minister announced a few days ago this unimaginable effort to allow and assist Jews all over the world to come to the expanded State of Israel. What is your spiritual opinion of these amazing events?"

The Rabbi cleared his throat trying to control his excitement. "Michael, as you know, we are amid the High Holy Days, the Days of Awe, leading us to Yom Ha'kippurim, the Day of Atonement. That is the appointed day each year when Yahweh determines the blessings of His people for the coming year, based on our contrite hearts and repentant spirits. Jews all over the world, since the days of Moses, consecrate the High Holy Days to a time of prayer and soul searching. This time frame is strangely coinciding with the vanishings and we are crying out to God for understanding and guidance." A smile crossed his face as he continued: "In the midst of much agony and sorrow of soul there is reason to rejoice. The sons and daughters of Zion are returning from all four corners of the earth just as the prophets proclaimed." There was an exhilaration in his entire countenance as he heralded the words to the world.

"It is an exciting time in Israel," Adelson agreed. Immediately, the reporter's face grew more solemn. "Do you believe the extreme anti-Semitism developing from the Three Day War is responsible for the large number of Jews coming to Israel?"

The Rabbi partially agreed. "Yes, but it is not just anti-Semitism that drives the children of Israel to their spiritual and physical homeland. Many feel the supernatural tug of their hearts to come to the land of their fathers: Abraham, Isaac, and Jacob. They don't really understand why they feel so compelled, but the ancient prophets told us this day would come."

The Rabbi turned the pages of his Tanakh to the writings of Ezekiel: "Ezekiel, Chapter 37 foretold the dispersion of Israel's people to all the nations as judgment for their disobedience to God. It happened exactly as prophesied, but in verse twelve we find a restoration in the days just before our Messiah comes to establish his earthly kingdom. I will read it for our viewers: *Therefore, prophesy and say to them: This is what the Sovereign LORD says: My people, I am going to open graves and bring you up from them; I will bring you back to the land of Israel. Then you, my people, will know that I am the LORD, when I open your graves and bring you up from the nations. I will put my Spirit in you and you will live, and I will settle you in your own land. Then you will know that I the LORD have spoken, and I have done it, declares the LORD your God."*

Zimmerman smiled with certainty. "This is only one of the many ancient prophecies of The Return."

"Very interesting, Rabbi. We certainly appreciate your religious perspective on this fluid situation. Our station is receiving reports of thousands upon thousands who are preparing to leave nations around the world and come to Israel. An Aliyah Processing Center is being established in Tel Aviv which will help those returning to integrate into their homeland. I believe these current numbers are just the proverbial tip of the immigration iceberg."

"It is indeed exciting times," the Rabbi reiterated. "The House of Israel is returning and our Messiah will soon come to establish His Kingdom."

Anxious to share with Gabriella his dream, Chris had his hand on the control ready to mute the television. At that precise moment, she leaned forward engrossed in Adelson's next words which directly impacted her.

Adelson turned to a news producer behind the glass wall and asked, "Do we have the documentary ready?" The man nodded.

"Rabbi, I want to show the audience a very interesting video. Long before the Three Day War, many descendants of the ten lost tribes of Israel were being identified. Their connections to the lost tribes have mainly been through the cultures sects of people maintained after the diaspora. However, they are now being verified through DNA. Start the video, please."

The camera left the two men. The TV screen began showing the processes of determining the authenticity of Israeli blood, the Y chromosome being the first major factor. There were clips of various peoples only recently determined as being from the ten lost tribes. The Lembas and Morranos were first featured in the documentary.

The next segment sent cold chills up and down Gabriella's spine. The picture of a traditional American Cherokee Indian appeared. There were arrows pointing to different parts of his face. One arrow noted his high cheek bones and another, his nose. These were common Jewish features. Another arrow pointed to the braid on the forehead that was exact to *tefillin shel rosh*, worn by Jewish men during prayers. The arrow then moved to the braided hair hanging over the ears of the Cherokee men in the design of sidelocks which was worn by all Orthodox Jews and customary since the days of the Old Testament.

The documentary showed the garments worn by the Cherokee which were also similar to the Jewish Orthodox: the fringed clothing akin to the fringed *tallit* shawl, the braided belt with fringes very similar to the *tzitzit*, and leather sandals tied with thongs exactly as worn for thousands of years by Israeli ancestry. The last picture of the Cherokee Indian showed him playing a six-holed flute. The narrator stated it was the same design as was played in the temple of Solomon and an instrument native only to Israelis.

The video ended with a summation of further evidence that the Cherokee Indians are descendants of one of the lost tribes. The masculine voice stated: "Besides the obvious features and clothing of the Cherokee, there are additional evidences indisputably tied to the descendants of the House of Israel: Cherokee are monotheistic, the phonetics of their ancient language is very similar to Hebrew, and they live by the letter of the Torah's Ten Commandments."

A picture of a rock appeared on the screen with ancient writing obviously of Hebrew origin. The narrator continued: "This picture is an inscribed stone in a burial mound about ten miles south of Newark, New Jersey in the United States. The stone dates to pre-BCE and is inscribed on all sides with a condensed version of the Ten Commandments or Decalogue written in a peculiar form of post-Exilic square Hebrew letters. There is an image of a robed and bearded figure on the front. He is identified as Moses in the letters fanning over his head. The ten northern tribes of Israel, exiled by Sennacherib 772 BCE into Assyria, later migrated in all directions from the Middle East. Some sojourned through Europe establishing communities in various areas; others continued westward eventually crossing the northern Atlantic and first arriving in Newfoundland. Over hundreds of years they gradually settled from northeast America down the east coast and across the land to the west."

The camera zoomed in on the stone writing as the documentary continued: "This writing pre-dates by many centuries the founding of America and can only be explained by settlers with Judeo beliefs, the descendants of the lost tribes of Israel. The genetic evidence concludes that some American Indians are from the tribe of Gad; however, using DNA testing we believe the Cherokee Indians descended from the tribe of Zebulon."

Gabriella dropped her coffee cup onto the table in shock splashing the warm liquid onto the wood top.

"Oh, my God!" She exclaimed. "It's true, Chris. The Prophet called me the daughter of Zebulon. I had no earthly idea my Cherokee ancestry was linked to an ancient lost tribe of Israel. Everything is making sense now!"

Chris was wiping up the spilled coffee and trying to process the amazing revelation. He muted the sound to draw Gabriella's attention to his words. "I have another piece to your puzzle." His face was serious and she allowed him her full attention.

Chris sat down beside her on the couch looking directly into her eyes. "I almost never dream, Gabi. When I do, it has never been detail by detail like the one I had last night." He expected expressions of fear as he explained his night vision especially when he shared about the evil assailant. To his surprise, peace was the only emotion she displayed. The identical peace he had seen on her face in his dream.

She took his hand and smiled. Her big blue eyes sparkled as she shared her heart. "That just confirms the peace I already feel. I know our God has put us together for His purpose, in this time and in this place. I have no doubt of that. I've been reading about what will happen to The Chosen during the coming years. As horrible as it will be, I know God will not leave us nor forsake us. It was *not* just happenstance you were appointed to protect our team. Yahweh was setting up a divine encounter and all for His purpose."

She released his hand and picked up the Bible, turning to the Book of Revelation 6:9. She read: "*When he opened the fifth seal, I saw under the altar the souls of those who had been slain because of the word of God and the testimony they had maintained.*"

She looked straight into Chris's eyes. "Those are the souls of The Chosen."

The night vision of the apocalyptic man poised to behead Gabriella flooded his mind. "No!" The exclamation escaped Chris's mouth before he could halt the word. His face was turning red from gripping perturbation and his police mentality proclaimed: "No, Gabi, I will be with you every step you take. I refuse to let anything happen to you."

For a moment, Gabriella detected a look in Chris's eyes much like those Caleb would often portray in potentially dangerous cave explorations. It was the determination to protect no matter what the cost.

157

She laid the precious book back on her lap and again took Chris's hand. "Our callings and our destinies are sealed. We will follow the instructions of The Prophet, wherever that leads."

CHAPTER 21

———•◆•◆•———

The High Holy Days were coming to a close. The Levitical Priests from the Temple Institute were preparing for the Day of Atonement and calling the nation of Israel to observe the twenty-five hour fast as required by the Torah instructions.

Rabbi Zimmerman had now become a regular commentator on Channel 2 News, bringing the spiritual significance of the events taking place throughout the new expanded nation. The rabbi sat with folded hands next to Michael Adelson on the news set, patiently waiting for the interview to begin.

As the camera zoomed in on the Rabbi's face, there was a glimmer of tears in his eyes. "This is a day like no other, Michael. For the first time in 2000 years we are not only celebrating the Day of Atonement in the land of the Abrahamic Covenant, we are dwelling in peace and safety *and* we are preparing to rebuild our holy temple! There are simply no words to express my joy." The Rabbi did not try to hold back the tears of joy flowing from his eyes.

"Rabbi, for those who may not understand, please explain to our viewers from your spiritual perspective what that means." Adelson leaned towards the Rabbi with body language speaking loud and clear that he wanted to truly understand for himself, too.

Wiping his eyes, the Rabbi began his exhortation. "According to the instructions of The Book of Moses, the Torah, the Day of Atonement is the holiest day on Yahweh's calendar of appointments with man. Every year on the Day of Atonement, we are to refrain from work and all earthly pleasures. We are instructed to fast and repent of our sins so we might be forgiven and sealed by Adonai's protection for the coming year."

The Rabbi picked up a prayer book as he continued: "The Day of Atonement, in Hebrew *Yom Kippurim*, ends with the blowing of the Shofar. This is the trumpet that heralds the coming of the Messiah. An ancient prayer in a Jewish Day of Atonement liturgy reads:

Our righteous Messiah has departed from us,
We are horror-stricken, and have none to justify us.
Our iniquities and the yoke of our transgressions
He carries who is wounded because of our transgressions
He bears on His shoulder the burden of our sins.
To find pardon for all our iniquities.
By His stripes, we shall be healed -
O Eternal One, it is time that you should create Him anew!

The Rabbi laid the book on the news desk and looked directly into the camera. "It is believed by all who study Torah and the Prophets that our Messiah will appear on Yom Kippur to set up His Kingdom on earth. We must begin immediately to build His Temple and prepare the sacrifices in preparation of His soon appearing."

Adelson leaned back in his chair with an obvious revelation filling his face. He mustered all the composure he could as he ended the segment. The declaration of the Coming of Messiah had just aired on Channel 2 Haifa news. The Rabbi had no idea the controversy he would stir around the world with his proclamation.

Gabriella looked at Chris in disbelief. "You do realize that very statement will make every nation hate Israel even more. When the cornerstone is laid, all hell will break loose."

Chris was amazed how quickly he was beginning to understand how the prophetic pieces were fitting together. He realized it was not of his own ability that the revelation of the end of days was becoming so clear. It was a supernatural understanding.

It broke his spiritual heart knowing his people, Israel, did not see the truth. "It's so sad the rabbis don't realize the Messiah has already come," Chris flatly stated.

Gabriella sat silent for a moment in retrospect. "That's why we've been chosen, Chris." She took a deep breath before stating the obvious. "And that's why we will be hated by the Antichrist. He will use his evil forces to try to silence us from exposing the fact he is not God, and anyone who worships him and takes his mark will be lost forever. As the Professor put it...unredeemable." Her face turned somber and her voice lowered as if someone else was listening. "Those evil forces are the very ones Dr. Brotman's research exposed. The fallen angels are being released from the abyss to deceive the world. Only the elect, those of us with spiritual understanding, will not fall for the lies. It will be our mission to expose them and lead as many as will hear to eternal truth."

She picked up a letter from her father she had read the night before and began to read out loud:

Gabriella,

God has not cast away His people. In the final days, He will anoint and seal a great spiritual army of 144,000 chosen men and women (12,000 from each of the twelve tribes of Israel). They will witness to the whole house of Israel. As spoken by the Prophet Joel, "In the last days, God says, I will pour out my Spirit on all people. Your sons and daughters will prophesy".

Prophesy has two meanings, my daughter. It is to preach the truth and to know the future in advance. The Chosen witnesses will operate in both callings. I believe Yahweh brought Chris to us by divine appointment. You will not be alone during the years of great tribulation as you fulfill your destiny as one of The Chosen.

Chris struggled to stay composed. The police officer in him still dominated his reactions to emotional situations. "You would think Yahweh would call the Orthodox Jews, the ones that have studied and know the Holy Scriptures. Why would he choose me?"

"I felt the same way," Gabriella admitted. "As I was reading from the prophet Jeremiah, I found this verse: *The wise will be put to shame; they will be dismayed and trapped. Since they have rejected the word of the LORD, what kind of wisdom do they have?"*

Understanding filled Chris. He rose to his feet and began pacing back and forth. "They have had the Torah and the Prophets' writings in their hands all their lives. They have read, studied and searched God's Word; but they have never come to the knowledge of the truth, nor understood the prophecies of the Messiah. How sad." His voice cracked in spite of his efforts to keep emotional control.

"So very sad," she agreed, wondering how she would have a platform to proclaim the truth. She understood now Yeshua came to this sinful earth, died for the sins of man and rose again with victory over death. All you had to do was believe to be saved. But who would listen to her and where would she begin her ministry? She was already a hunted woman. To put herself on public display, where she was an open target, could end her witnessing before it even began.

"Today at sundown, Chris, I will join all of my people who are fasting and praying on the Day of Atonement. I am going to spend twenty-four hours in my bedroom in prayer and seeking the direction of Yahweh."

With great conviction of spirit Chris confirmed, "I will do the same."

Gabriella got up from the couch and crossed the cool, stone floor to where Chris had finally stopped pacing. She put her arms around him and laid her head on his chest. His arms of security encircled her. They had become souls with a divine mission.

In the background, the voice of Michael Adelson announced the interview with Rabbi Zimmerman would be replayed on primetime news during the holiest day of the year, the Day of Atonement.

WIN TV picked up the segment and in the days to come it was repeated over and over on news stations throughout the world. With anger and animosity, reports would vehemently declare Israel plans to rebuild their temple.

At sundown, the lodge bunker became a sacred place. The Day of Atonement had begun. Chris and Gabriella secluded themselves in their individual bedrooms for twenty-four hours observing Yahweh's holiest day of the year in fasting and prayer.

The following day as the sun was beginning to set on the early October evening, they emerged from their rooms each having experienced a private encounter with the Ruach HaKodesh, the Holy Spirit of Yahweh God. It was too personal, too intimate for mere words.

Chris knew the sound of the shofars at the temple mount would be echoing through the City of David as the Day of Atonement ended. He turned on the TV to witness the sacred event. The cameras were fixed and ready for all of Israel to view. The temple courtyard in Jerusalem was filled with Israelis standing amid the rubble swaying back and forth in prayer. Obviously missing was the Wailing Wall. Only a pile of demolished stones, with not one standing upon another, lay at the feet of those praying.

The crowd of Orthodox Jews held the *Tzitzits* of their *Tallit* in their left hand, holding them next to their heart as they repented of their sins against God for themselves, for their family, and for their nation. The wings of their prayer shawls swayed in the evening breezes often being caught by a whipping wind gust, pulling them into the air and appearing as the wings of eagles. It was a beautiful sight to observe. Chris tried to imagine the King of Kings bodily stepping into the scene at this holy convocation. The worship would then be fully on Him...Yeshua HaMashiach, Jesus the Messiah. He had no doubt whatsoever, in a few short years it would be reality.

Chris and Gabriella sat side by side on the couch with eyes glued to the TV screen as the cameras focused on the sun setting over the Mount of Olives. The last sliver of sunlight faded away and the shofars heralded with great pomp and circumstance signaling the ending of Yom Kippur, the Day of Atonement. Those gathered turned their prayers into dancing as music began and resounded throughout all of Jerusalem. The day of mourning was over and it was time to celebrate and prepare for the Feast of Tabernacles, the Season of Joy. Even with heavy hearts for the horrors of the Three Day War and those that had vanished, Israelis still found the strength to dance before the Lord in a sacrifice of praise.

Chris got up and pulled Gabriella to her feet swinging her around in the Horah Jewish Dance. For a moment, there was a pseudo notion of life being normal before reality quickly set back in.

CHAPTER 22

The time of dancing came to an immediate halt when a beeping sound was heard coming from the security system, alerting Gabriella and Chris someone was entering the lodge grounds.

They ran to the monitors. The now familiar black Suburban was ascending the long, winding driveway to the lodge entrance. Gabriella's heart was racing even though she knew they would never find them in the bunker.

Chris kept his eyes focused on the screens as the vehicle would pass one surveillance camera and be instantly picked up by the next one. The Suburban was never out of view as it slowly climbed the winding driveway. The motion lights were activated by the movement of the vehicle approaching the main entrance of the lodge. It came to a stop at the front door. Russo and Moretti exited, along with Detective Richards.

"I knew they'd be back soon. I didn't expect Richards though. I just wonder what they're up to." Chris' voice was filled with both perplexity and suspicion as his eyes moved to the next screen that monitored the main entrance from the inside of the lodge. The three men entered turning on the interior lights and closing the door securely behind them.

Detective Richards checked the downstairs while the two men went from room to room upstairs, searching for any signs of life. The securely hidden motion cameras automatically activated a digital recorder as they moved from area to area. Gabriella and Chris watched while the men searched every inch of the lodge. After a thorough investigation they were convinced there was no one on the premises.

They returned to the main area of the lodge anxious to get down to business. Richards sat down in the brown leather chair next to the fireplace, occupied by the Professor only days before. His face showed no expression. Chris could usually read him like a book but Richards' countenance was different from anything Chris had previously seen.

The two men sat across from Detective Richards with body language speaking loud and clear. They were sure the detective knew something he was not telling. There was an uncomfortable silence that hung in the air, waiting to be penetrated.

"Why have you brought me here?" Richards asked, staring directly into Russo's eyes.

Chris and Gabriella pulled their chairs a little closer to the monitors and anxiously watched the screen. Neither could have anticipated the conversation that was about to transpire.

"I've told you everything I know." Richards stated emphatically.

There was another uncomfortable period of silence before Russo replied. "Have you, detective? Really? There are too many missing pieces and someone has to be holding them."

"Well, it's *not* me." Richards stated with hostility. "You already know I only met them a few weeks ago after the Professor's accident."

Russo retorted in a gruff voice, "We don't need any attitude, Richards. We're just doing our job here. All we need is to find these people so we can get some answers and bring the matter to a close."

Richards knew exactly how the matter would be 'closed' if they were found.

Russo continued to push for information. "We know you brought them here so why no signs of anyone? Some might possibly have vanished with the others that are missing, but we know for a fact that Gabriella did not and neither did the police officer you assigned to her team. You told them to come back here didn't you, like we instructed?"

Detective Richards expression did not change. Chris then realized what was going on. The detective knew his precarious position and any emotional display would make it obvious that he was not on the side of the other two men.

"Yes, Russo, I did exactly as I was instructed," Richards stated matter of fact, again holding firm his composure. "I suppose Officer Harris suspected something and cleared out. Leaving his cell phone in his apartment was his sign he knew he was being followed. He has a sixth sense about him and I wouldn't be a bit surprised if he's taken the team into hiding and gone underground somewhere."

Chris and Gabriella both chuckled at the detective's choice of words. Chris smirked at the men on the surveillance screen and commented sarcastically. "Yes, I did...literally." He chuckled once more. "Well, Gabriella, anyway. The rest of the team went to higher ground." He looked at her and smiled.

Gabriella's heart warmed, thinking of the wonderful heavenly realm her loved ones were now citizens of. She whispered longingly beneath her breath, "Someday I'll be with them again." Chris reached over and gently squeezed her hand. Then as quickly he let it go focusing back on the men.

"If they found your phone, Chris, it means they went to your apartment. They were following us the entire time." She read his expression. "You knew they were, didn't you?"

He briefly nodded his head but stayed focused on the monitors. Moretti chimed into the conversation with Russo. "They were just here a few days ago. We know that for a fact so there should be some signs of life; food in the kitchen, personal belongings, something indicating they were recently here. Everything's gone, so that tells me they systematically left the premises. It wasn't a quick escape."

The detective offered further evidence they were no longer occupying the lodge and inwardly hoped that Chris had found a safe hiding place for the team. "We brought enough food and supplies to last at least a month. Seems obvious to me they've loaded up and moved out. I believe Officer Harris knew something was amiss. Maybe Gabriella's father had another hiding place you don't know about, but I don't have a clue where they would be." Chris and Gabriella knew for certain Richards did not know about the bunker.

Russo and Moretti both stared at Richards, trying their best to read his face and body language. Neither of them appeared totally convinced of his innocence.

"There is something very suspicious going on here." Moretti queried, continuing to suspect the mysterious circumstances. "How could they all get out, take all their supplies and get by our surveillance? Yet they obviously did and you have no clue, Richards?"

Again, Chris watched every detail of Detective Richards' face and body language, praying the detective could pull it off and make these thugs think he wanted to cooperate.

"I told you I don't know. I hadn't been in touch with Officer Harris since the day I brought them to the lodge. Within hours after they got here the war started. Then there were the vanishings and we lost communication until he showed up at my office a couple of days ago. I asked him about the team and he assured me everyone was okay. I thought they were all still here."

Gabriella looked at Chris and raised her eyebrows questioningly. Chris quickly answered, "Gabi, something inside warned me not to tell Richards the others were gone. I knew he wouldn't understand and my instincts told me to monitor every word I said when I was in his office. I suspected we were being watched or recorded, maybe both."

Gabriella nodded her head that she understood. "You weren't lying, Chris. They are more than okay."

The detective's next words brought their focus back to the monitor: "When Officer Harris asked me about his assignment, I made it clear he was to continue with his present assignment to stay at the lodge and keep everyone safe. Guess his sixth sense was working overtime since you said they weren't here last week when you checked the lodge for yourselves. He suspected something even before he came to my office and must have already made arrangements for their safety. I'd say he didn't know who to trust so he wasn't telling anyone anything. That's my guess, *but* I didn't help them and had no idea a move was taking place. They must have vacated the lodge when the war started and before you began surveillance."

Detective Richards tried to change the subject and glean some information of his own. "I'd like to know how, after all these years, you found out Gabe Russell was still alive. I tried my best to track down information on that mysterious box his daughter received. I thought there might have been some connection to the Professor's attempted murder, but everything was a dead end."

Chris glanced at Gabriella and confirmed: "Russo and Moretti do know about the box, but do they know it contains the information they're looking for? Hmmm...this web is weaving tighter and tighter."

Gabriella was fully aware the police mentality wheels were spinning in full motion. She remained quiet so he could concentrate as he continued to monitor the trio of men.

Russo lit a cigarette. Even without being near them, Gabriella knew the poignant smell that would be filling the room. He ran his hand across his bald head and laughed out loud.

"We got lucky on that one, detective." Russo willingly answered. "We've always had an agent at the University of Haifa keeping a watch on Gabriella's coming and goings; and on that Professor she worked for. We had to make sure she wasn't going to be a problem. Everything drifted along for years with no signs of her having any knowledge of her father's work. Not until his daughter came back from Saudi Arabia and the mysterious box showed up. We stepped our surveillance up a notch afterwards, making sure her father's research wasn't about to resurface at a very, well let's just say, inopportune time."

Chris leaned toward the monitor watching their body language closely. "Russo and Moretti don't know." He exclaimed. "Let's just pray Richards keeps his cool."

Chris sighed with relief as Richards said nothing whatsoever; no signs at all, not even a batting of the eye. Chris turned and looked into Gabe's bedroom where the black box was sitting on the stone floor next to the bed. The contents had been the source of decades of mystery and murder. The top intelligence agency in the world was searching for the information secretly held in that very box, which was now hidden in an underworld bunker which no one else knew existed.

Chris refocused on the men upstairs. Russo was watching Richards just as closely as Chris was as he continued explaining how they discovered Gabriella's father was still alive. It was obvious Russo's ploy was to willingly offer the information and in return Richards would be more cooperative.

Russo slightly leaned towards the detective closely observing his reactions. "One of our men followed Gabriella to a little coffee shop she often frequented near her apartment. Everything seemed normal until an old man, a Hasidic Jew, joined her. He had never been seen with her before."

Russo stopped and took another draw on the cigarette with his penetrating eyes still focused on Detective Richards. He exhaled slowly and coughed before he continued: "Our agent sat down at the table right next to them and pretended to be on his cell phone. Instead he was recording their conversation. The Jew was giving her some kind of warning that didn't make any sense, something weird about time and untime. We thought it might be some type of code so we did a voice profile on him and guess who turned up? Back from the dead after over a decade was good ole' Edward Gabe Russell."

After another long cigarette draw and slow exhale, he laughed again which ended in a prolonged deep cough. "Imagine our surprise when we found out he had been living in

Israel all these years under the assumed name of Eli Sheskin, a Hasidic Jew. In fact, living here at this very lodge. He's a sly old fox, that's for sure."

Gabriella grasped the arms of her chair and struggled to constrain her composure. She had been unknowingly sitting next to her father at that café, all the time believing, he was dead. Now she finds out she was being followed and recorded by only God knows who. She took a deep breath futilely trying to control her emotions while he continued the explanation of discovery.

"Well, what a stroke of luck that was for you," Richards calmly replied to Russo. "If Gabe had stayed here in his hideaway you may have never found him."

"Exactly so," he agreed. "It was just in time, actually. The 33rds and The Enlightened Ones are ready..." Russo realized he was saying too much and quickly changed the subject. "Detective, you've talked with Ugo Strozza. You know how important his mission is. We really *must* make sure everything is secure. Are we perfectly clear?"

Richards nodded his head affirming he understood. "How much longer?"

Russo got up and stretched. He looked around the room appreciating the comfort and seclusion. Then focused back on the detective. "Can't say for sure. I just know there's still much to do."

Chris leaned back in his chair totally confused. "What is Ugo Strozza up to?" he mused. "I've gotta know what's going on and who they're talking about."

Gabriella leaned closer to Chris for strength. Her voice was almost breathless as she muttered, "I know who The Enlightened Ones are, Chris."

Chris immediately turned to face her and gently clutched her shoulders. "Tell me everything you know."

She pulled away and rose to her feet, collecting and arranging her memories of the mystical night journeys. "I mentioned to you my astral travels with Arcturus, but I wasn't ready to explain then. Now I am."

She sat back down and grasped the arms of her leather chair in an effort to keep from shaking. "I know this is going to sound crazy, but hear me out. Arcturus told me The Enlightened Ones are chosen people of earth guided by our extraterrestrial brothers. These people are a very select metaphysical group who are preparing for the greatest event known to man. They believe the Enlightened Ones are here to save us from our own self destruction and prepare for the appearing of their celestial leader, the Ascended Master."

Gabriella's blue eyes misted over as she struggled to continue. "Arcturus told me I was chosen to be one of The Enlightened Ones. He convinced me I was one of their chosen. It's all for the greater good of the earth society, Arcturus told me. I believed him...hook, line and sinker. Now I know it's all part of the satanic plan. The paranormal world call him the Ascended Master, the one who will be the world leader. The Bible calls him the Antichrist; and amid total chaos, when it seems the earth is teetering on total destruction, he will appear."

Chris watched the color drain from her face as she allowed herself to continue to relive the evil encounters with Arcturus. "I was so deceived by the beauty of it all and I believed I was chosen by one of The Enlightened to lead others to the universal Akashic Knowledge. Had it not been for the prayers of the people who loved me, God only knows where I would be right now."

She took a deep breath and looked Chris directly in the eyes. "The point is, The Enlightened have been beguiled by demonic spirit guides who appear as friendly alien brothers. These evil spirits are totally deceiving their prey. They convince those they channel through into believing they have special powers and are chosen to help mankind. The people who have fallen into their spells truly believe they are preparing the way for their Ascended Master who will bring a utopian society to the earth."

Her voice became strong with conviction focusing on their present situation: "Ugo Strozza knows my father discovered the implant that would, in some form, be used by the leader of the New World Order. The IIIA as a whole may not be involved in preparing for the Ascended Master but it's apparent now the UN President is and he's a main player, too. He

170

must be one of The Enlightened and he's making sure nothing or no one gets in the way."

She took a deep breath and in an agonizing voice she exhaled, "God help us."

CHAPTER 23

———•◦•———

Gabriella and Chris continued to monitor every move of the three men in the lodge above them, not anticipating the turn of events about to transpire.

Russo and Moretti returned to the upstairs section of the lodge. The security cameras monitored every step as they moved from room to room. This time their purpose was totally different. Russo kept nodding his head and Moretti agreed; however, it was not immediately obvious what he was agreeing to. They opened closet doors and examined each bathroom adjacent to the bedrooms. They returned to the main level and continued their tour from room to room, giving close inspection to the kitchen and dining area.

They once again exited the back door of the lodge. The motion lights illuminated allowing full view of the stone walkway to the guest-house. After another walk-through of the cottage they surveyed the lodge grounds. Everywhere they walked the motion lights would activate. Never did Russo and Moretti suspect the security system was monitoring every movement. Gabriella's father was diligent in making sure no one would move anywhere on his property without him being alerted and able to record their activities. All cameras were completely obscure and undetectable.

Richards paced the floor inside while the two men were absent from the lodge, pondering why Russo and Moretti were retracing the previous inspected areas. When the two men returned to the lodge, Richards stopped his treading back and forth and halted next to the stone fireplace anticipating an explanation.

Russo continued gazing around the two-story living and dining area appreciating both the total privacy and beauty of the mountain structure. He retook his seat on the comfortable couch and leaned back lighting another cigarette.

"Detective, you said there's a security fence that completely surrounds the property? No entrance in or out, except the main gate, right?"

Detective Richards nodded his head in agreement.

Another draw from his cigarette and Russo stated emphatically, "Perfect".

"I agree," Moretti replied.

Detective Richards retained his non-expressive countenance but was mentally questioning what the two men were agreeing to, as were Chris and Gabriella, viewing from the secret bunker.

Moretti sat down and pulled a pen and notepad from his pocket. His gaudy diamond ring caught in the lamp light, sparkling as his right hand made notes.

Russo continued puffing on his cigarette and coughing as he exhaled. Chris was monitoring Richards' countenance for signs of irritation. He knew the detective was not the most patient of men when it came to wanting answers.

Gabriella watched Russo put his cigarette out in the glass ash tray used by the Professor for his mahogany pipe. She momentarily closed her eyes recalling the cherry tobacco smell that would fill the room when the research team occupied the lodge. She longed for those days again but begrudgingly accepted they would never be. Her attention was brought back to the men upstairs and her eyes flew wide open with the next words from Russo.

"Richards, we are going to suggest this lodge become the possession of the IIIA. We were to scout for a secluded place for private meetings with accommodations for an extended stay. What better place than a hidden mountain lodge on Mt. Hermon already constructed expressly for privacy and security; and right here where it all began. This just couldn't be any better. Seems Gabe Russell has provided us with exactly what we need and we'll get the rest of what we need from him, too. Have no doubt about that." Russo looked around the log structure once more and punctuated his decision. "Perfect."

In the bunker below, Gabriella and Chris both gasped in amazement.

Detective Richards nearly lost his composure. Pounding through his mind were thoughts of the team unsuspectingly returning to the lodge and being caught in Ugo Strossa's web. He knew he could not warn them even if he did know where they were. Everything he did and said was being scrutinized.

Moretti continued taking notes on supplies that would be needed. Russo pulled the cell phone from the case attached to his belt and prepared to take pictures. Once more he retraced his previous steps through each room taking pictures.

"Ugo and his 33rd hierarchy are going to love this place. It's absolutely perfect. Since Israel is now the world powerhouse, Ugo is going to be continually back and forth between here and Rome during The Final Phase. When he hears how close this place is to the 33.33 longitude and latitude, he will be extremely pleased. Yep, this is *perfect*." Russo clicked the send button and the pictures would soon be viewed by one of the evilest men on the face of the earth.

Chris muttered sarcastically to the monitor, "Okay, Russo. We got it, the lodge is perfect." Then he turned to Gabriella, not sure what reaction to expect.

She had not spoken a word. She was trying to process this bizarre turn of events. The men who wanted her father's research and who had already killed her mother to get it, would be frequenting her father's home above them. Only God knew who else would be joining them.

She couldn't stop the glib remark that escaped her lips. "So close and yet so far." She turned to Chris with a voice full of sarcasm. "They have no earthly idea the information they're desperately seeking is literally right beneath their feet."

"And they will never know," Chris spurted. "Do you have any idea why this location seems to be so important?"

"Yes, I know exactly why." She blurted. "That information was an intricate part of the Professor's research project. Actually, Mt. Hermon was pivotal to the project name, The Omega Watchers. According to The Book of Enoch, the 33.33/33.33 longitude and latitude, which is at the apex of Mt. Hermon, is a supernatural portal or a gateway to an alternate dimension. It's the precise location the fallen angels used to leave their Heavenly Realm and enter into the dimension of time."

Gabriella quoted from Jude 1:6: *"And the angels who did not keep their positions of authority but abandoned their proper dwelling--these he has kept in darkness, bound with everlasting chains for judgment on the great Day."*

Her voice reflected an ominous tone as she continued: "These fallen angels who entered earth's dimension through the Mt. Hermon portal will soon be released from the abyss for the end of days and ultimately their day of judgment."

She stared into the air and quoted from the Book of Revelation, Chapter 9: *"I saw a star that had fallen from the sky to the earth. The star was given the key to the shaft of the Abyss. When he opened the Abyss, smoke rose from it like the smoke from a gigantic furnace. And out of the smoke locusts came down on the earth They had as king over them the angel of the Abyss, whose name in Hebrew is Abaddon."*

She took a deep breath and looked directly into Chris' eyes. "The Professor made it distinctly clear the locusts are the fallen angels that have been chained until the end days." She stopped short of telling him her experience with Abaddon.

Chris leaned back on the leather chair, allowing the information to assimilate. "None of this is by accident, Gabi. I believe there's a divine plan in every detail of what's happening. We could never have orchestrated this. The path of our chosen calling has started right at our very door."

"But, Chris, some of the most demonic men on earth are going to be in my father's house directly above this bunker. I shudder to think..."

Chris wasn't deterred, "Gabi, think of all the information we'll be privy to and they will have no idea every word and deed is being heard and recorded."

"No matter how much we know, if we don't have a method of operation, what good will it be?"

Chris answered with certainty, "When the time is right the door will open."

The trio in the lodge was preparing to leave when Russo addressed Detective Richards with a dire warning. "No one, and I mean *no one,* is to know about this. Do you understand? The only reason you're in the circle at all is your connection to Gabe and his daughter. At some point, they'll try to contact you and you *will* let us know. Right?"

Detective Richards was usually the one that gave orders, not received them. Chris was well aware of what a challenge this was for him to stay calm.

"Yes, you've made yourself perfectly clear," he replied dryly. Astonishingly, he maintained perfect equanimity.

The three men exited the lodge, climbed into the black Suburban and were monitored by the cameras until they drove down the winding driveway, passed through the security gate, and pulled onto the highway leading back to Haifa. For the present time, Gabriella and Chris would have the lodge and grounds totally to themselves. Soon that would never be again.

Chris' head fell back against the top of his chair. He took a deep breath and slowly released the air from his lungs trying to relieve the tension in his body.

"Now, what?" Gabriella asked. "Do we just sit and wait for this evil entourage to arrive and take possession of my father's property?"

Chris took her hand and gently squeezed and released it. "There's really nothing else we can do, for now. Your father has done all the work for us, Gabi. This security system is amazing. We know the cameras work to the highest proficiency and our three visitors never suspected a thing. They won't be back tonight so I suggest we get a good night's sleep and regroup our thoughts in the morning."

"You're right as usual." She got up to leave and then she hesitated taking a long strand of hair in her hand. She began to slowly twirl the curl around in her fingers.

"What is it? What's wrong?" He could see a slight glimmer of tears that she was trying, unsuccessfully, to restrain.

She sat back down in the chair still facing the security monitors. She stared straight ahead for a few moments before she began sharing her innermost thoughts. "I told you about Arcturus. Now you know who Abaddon is. What I haven't told you is they are one in the same."

Chris grasped the arm of her chair and turned her to face him. He tilted her face upwards to look directly into his eyes and then took both of her hands in his. "Dear Lord, Gabi, tell me what you mean."

"I've only shared bits and pieces with you about my astral travels. It was just too agonizing to relive all the details. It still is but I have to tell you the ending of the supernatural journey."

Her eyes averted from his and she pulled her hands away clasping them together in her lap. Taking a deep breath, she released her painful memories. "I was only a step away from total convergence which I thought was becoming one with the universal powers. I've told you how those who loved me prayed feverishly for my deliverance from the demonic hold that possessed me. While I was caught in the world of untime, I could hear them praying. Their prayers became spiritual swords raining down from the heavens and the swords created a barrier between Arcturus and me. He was calling for me to cross over and I was being pulled by a force I could not control. Everything that had been so alluring and prepossessing instantly turned to horror as the swords became a barrier between good and evil. Spiritual truth was exposed and the beautiful Arcturus repatriated, revealing his true identity of wickedness and depravity beyond explanation. It was then..." Her voice halted. She was struggling to continue.

Chris once again took her hands. "You can tell me Gabi. What happened?"

She allowed her hands to rest in his. With her eyes focused downward avoiding eye contact, she labored to release the words. "Just before I was rescued by the prayers, the beautiful Arcturus morphed into a horrendous image screaming at me in a heinous voice beyond human imagination. He declared he was Abaddon, I had released him from the abyss and I would always belong to him."

She looked into Chris's eyes to ascertain if he thought her totally insane. She saw only compassion and concern.

"Why in the world would you believe *you* released him from the abyss, Gabi? You know that's not possible."

"Maybe it is possible." Her voice was quivering with an undertone of fear. "When we were exploring in a remote part of Saudi Arabia we found a virgin cave. The Bedouins warned us to stay away from the area, to not explore there. They said it was in the region known to be the entrance to the abyss, the gateway of Tartarus which is the underground chambers of the fallen angels." She once again looked Chris directly in the eyes. "We released *something* evil that day and it never left me, not until the prayers broke the stronghold during my supernatural sleep."

Chris rose to his feet and leaned against the wall. There was no room for his pacing back and forth; however, he didn't need much time to come to a conclusion on this matter.

He quickly sat back down as a spiritual understanding flooded his mind. He had never felt anything like it. He could feel The Presence enter the room, form his words and begin to speak through him. He again took both of her hands. "Don't you see this was a demonic deception? It's the oldest trick in the devil's playbook. Abaddon made you *think* you had released him and you believed the lie. That's the way Satan and his demonic forces operate. If they can control your mind and your thoughts, they can control you. The power of prayer released your mind to see the truth. When you discerned the evil, he tried one last time to recapture your thoughts and bring you back into his control. He is still trying to make you believe you released him from the abyss. You cannot let that happen!"

Chris laid his hand on top of her head. "Gabriella, remember the oil that flowed over you when The Prophet anointed you? You were sealed by Yeshua's Blood, the Blood of the Lamb. No demon, not even Satan himself, can pass through the Holy Anointing. You are chosen and nothing can touch you except that which Yahweh allows."

Gabriella's countenance changed and the fear melted away. A smile of peace crossed her face as a warm, liquid serenity wholly saturated her mind and body.

Chris pulled both of his hands away from her and a peculiar expression took possession of him. He was almost breathless when the words escaped his mouth. "Those were not my words. Gabi. It was like a voice inside of me bypassed my own thoughts and spoke through me. I've never had anything even close to that happen before." His face was filled with a mixture of perplexity and quietude.

Gabriella recalled the many occurrences of the Professor speaking supernatural words of wisdom and encouragement. She knew this was truly a gift from God. "We have just had our first encounter of how the Spirit of Yahweh can speak through us, Chris."She dropped her head into her hands realizing what a powerful tool the operation of the Holy Spirit would be. "In the days to come Yahweh's words will be our words."

They had crossed a spiritual threshold into a divine realm where The Chosen would be sealed in the end of days.

CHAPTER 24

The following afternoon supply trucks arrived at the lodge. Moretti was giving orders and a scurry of activity infiltrated every room. Items were being stocked in bathrooms, bedrooms, and the kitchen area. Chris closely monitored every move in the rooms above the bunker. He held his breath as the door to the pantry was opened and non-perishables brought in for storage. A man stocking the shelves was directly in front of the secret, hidden door leading down to the bunker. Chris slowly exhaled when the man exited the pantry and closed the door behind him totally unaware of the concealed chamber.

Gabriella joined Chris watching the precise way in which the intruders took possession of her father's lodge, organizing necessities and setting up what appeared to be some type of command center. "Obviously, they've done this before," she observed. "Every move seems calculated."

Chris nodded his head but made no comment. His eyes were glued to the monitors as he focused on the faces of each person on the premises. When the lodge met Moretti's expectations he gave orders the guesthouse was next.

Gabriella bit her lip in anger. These men were taking over and had no qualms whatsoever in doing so. "It's not right," she muttered between her clinched lips. "It's just not right."

"Nothing's right anymore." Chris' words were also edged with contempt for the intruders. "However, we're going to have a bird's eye view of whatever it is they're planning. I just can't put my finger on it yet but this is big...really big."

"I've seen enough," she spurted in disdain. "I'm going to read dad's letters. Watching this is too painful."

Chris raised his hand, not taking his eyes off the monitors, in a motion for her to go on. "I'm staying right here."

Gabriella exited the security room and settled in the couch with her father's letters and his Bible close at hand. There was an uneasiness in her body knowing evil men were so close, but there was a peace in her spirit which came only from her Heavenly Father. Before she began she whispered a prayer for spiritual direction. "I am yours, my Lord; guide me in the way I should go. Make my words your words and my thoughts your thoughts."

She picked up the next letter in the sequence in which her father had written them. It started with expressions of both love and regret:

My precious daughter,

It seems I cannot relieve my soul of the need to tell you over and over how much I love you and how I rue over the circumstances my research has created. Painful remorse echoes in my mind constantly as you lie there suspended between time and untime, because of me. I pray over and over that you can hear my voice and know how deeply I regret my decisions.

My only redemption from these sorrows of heart is giving you direction for the days coming upon the earth. As I have instructed over and over, you must heed my words, Gabriella. They will bring the light of truth in the darkness ahead and lead you to righteousness so we can once again be together.

I have already warned you to watch The Vatican. The Pope will set the stage for worldwide changes preparing the way for the one world religion. The highest position of The Roman Catholic Church will be occupied by The Black Pope, the one spoken of in the Book of Revelation as the False Prophet. This wolf in sheep's clothing will deceive the world with signs and wonders. He will even call fire down from heaven imitating the power of the prophet Elijah. All biblical truths of the Christian faith will be challenged and then altered as this evil man presents a new world-wide religion.

The False Prophet will introduce the Antichrist to an unsuspecting world. This is foretold in the Book of Revelation 13:16-17: "And he (the False Prophet) causes all, both small and great, rich and poor, free and bond, to receive a mark in their right hand or in their foreheads that no man might buy or sell, save he that had the mark or the name of the beast or the number of his name."

I truly believe the implant your mother and I discovered will be used in some form as the 'mark' on the hand or forehead identifying the worship of Satan incarnate. That is why a powerful group of evil men still seek my research and will do anything to obtain it. They believe if the truth is known too early, it will derail everything they have planned. I did not know until recently who these men are. When your mother was murdered, I thought the U.S. Government was behind it. As the years passed, I came to the knowledge it was not a single government or religion but some type of worldwide organization. Still I did not know exactly who nor did I understand the extreme power behind this group desperately seeking my research and discovery. Now I know.

The most powerful group on the face of the earth has select members from every government, every nation, and every religion. Together they are planning the New World Order. This group call themselves The 33rds. They do not realize obtaining my discovery does not matter anymore. The end of days has begun, prophecy will be fulfilled just as it is written, and nothing can change it. Yahweh is the conductor of every detail and all will go as He has spoken through the ancient prophets.

Gabriella dropped the letter in her lap and sat in amazement. Members of the most powerful, evil group on the face of the earth were setting up a command center in her father's lodge. The very ones who had her mother murdered. She and Chris would have access to everything they were planning. She knew this was *not* coincidence.

Taking a deep breath, she finished reading the words penned by her father:

If you do not awaken before we vanish, I pray you will be one of the elect and will proclaim truth to a deceived world.

Remember, you were always the best part of me. I am going to stop writing for a while and hold you in my arms while there is still time. Caleb is holding you now. We both love you beyond words.

Dad

Before sharing the information with Chris, Gabriella read through the letter one more time. She was savoring her father's words of affection and committing to her spirit his warnings. His letters had transformed into an emotional bridge between the past and the inevitable future allowing her to draw from the good times and prepare for the bad.

She sat quietly in meditation listening to her spiritual heart, knowing that is where the Spirit of God would speak to her. A still, quiet voice assured her Yahweh was in control and she had nothing to fear.

She was pushing herself from the sofa to join Chris when he entered the living room announcing the lodge was empty once again. "They've all left. Looks like everything is in place but I'm not sure for what...or who. Guess we'll know soon enough."

He settled in the recliner next to the couch where Gabriella sat with papers scattered. She handed him the letter from her father. He took the pages reading each word. It was obvious when he read the part about The 33rds. He took a deep, sharp breath and looked up at Gabriella without saying a word. He focused back on the letter, finished reading it, and laid it on the cedar end table that sat between them.

In a deep voice, he spoke with utter conviction: "This entire sequence of events has been a divine set-up, Gabi. When your father built this lodge, you working with Dr. Brotman, even when I was assigned to protect your team, it was all a divine plan."

She nodded in agreement. "God knows the end from the beginning." Gabriella's voice was steeped in certitude. "We were chosen from the beginning, Chris, for this day and this time. When John wrote about the 144,000 witnesses, Yahweh already knew who they would be. It's all divinely planned. He even knows the minute we will die...and how. Amazingly, I don't fear anymore. I know we have work to do and that day will not come until our work is done."

She reached for her father's letter and held it against her heart. "I think as the time of the harpazo approached my dad knew I wouldn't go with them. I believe he had a divine revelation of his own and God allowed him to know I was one of The Chosen."

She neatly placed the letter back in the stack and turned to look Chris in the eyes. "I also think dad somehow knew you would be with me and I wouldn't be left alone. We both had the choice of accepting salvation, and we both rejected it. It was our choice, but Yahweh knew what our choice would be; and still He has shown us mercy and grace."

Chris was obviously overcome with emotion so Gabriella quickly changed the subject. "Now, who are The 33rds? Apparently, their very name has a connection to Mt. Hermon?"

Chris pushed himself from the leather recliner, regaining his composure, and began his pacing back and forth. He began to weigh out the facts as he now knew them with the five police W's: "Who? Definitely Strozza and he will lead us to the rest. What? They are preparing for a one world government. When? Apparently very soon. Why? For the Ascended Master to set up his throne on earth."

Gabriella interrupted his dialogue and finished his officer rationale with the final W: "Where? At the place it all began, Mt. Hermon."

CHAPTER 25

Chris opened his laptop and inserted the flash drive he had downloaded at police headquarters. He was searching for any information available on Ugo Strozza, Russo, Moretti, and The 33rds. "I can't find anything of importance in these files, Gabi. The only one even mentioned is Strozza verifying he will be establishing and maintaining an IIIA office at Haifa headquarters for a length of time yet to be determined."

Gabriella was reorganizing her father's letters. She stopped to respond. "It seems these guys certainly know how to cover all their tracks."

Chris nodded and continued researching the downloaded files for any information he might have missed.

She turned on the television for current news updates while sorting into categories the letters she had read and those next in line to be read. She caught a glimpse of The Vatican on the TV screen and immediately focused, leaving the letters for a later time.

The young reporter, Katja Lody, stood in the sea of people gathered at St. Peter's Square. In a voice filled with a mixture of exhilaration and anticipation she reported to her viewers: "We are live in Vatican City where both our Holy Father and the President of the UN will be addressing the nations." She pointed her hand towards the balcony where the duo would soon appear. "I have been given no indication as to what the content of the message will be but I have been informed it is of international importance."

The live feed came in flawlessly as cameras scanned the expectant faces assembling at St. Peter's Square. Lody spoke as the cameras rolled: "As you can see behind me, tens of thousands have filled not only St. Peter's

Square but all of Vatican City. Men and women from all over Italy and surrounding nations have made a pilgrimage to The Vatican in search of answers from our Holy Father, Pope Romanus. The populace is longing for assurance of peace and hope from the leaders of both the political and the religious worlds."

The reporter's voice morphed into one of pain, mixed with compassion, as she struggled to continue: "Obviously absent from this sea of people are babies and small children. The world is still in a maelstrom of turmoil with no explanation of the vanishings. Rumors are they have been removed for posterity purposes in the midst of the war and desolation, to guarantee society will continue but who removed them and to where did the young go, along with millions of adults? We are all anxiously awaiting answers."

The attractive reporter turned and faced the papal balcony at the center of St. Peter's Basilica. The cameras panned the Cathedral as she gave a description of the holy structure to divert her audience from the somber situation and hold their attention while awaiting the appearance of the world leaders.

"The Roman Catholic church believes the Basilica to be the burial place of St. Peter, disciple of Jesus Christ and the first Pope. Built in 1506, the late Renaissance church located amid Vatican City was designed principally by Donato Bramante, Michelangelo, Carlo Maderno, and Gian Lorenzo Bernini. It remains one of the largest structures on earth and is considered by Catholics to be the holiest place in all of the world."

As the reporter pushed through the crowd, the cameras focused on individuals kneeling in prayer, pleading to the Holy Mother for answers and hope amid chaos and uncertainty. Hands were moving along the rosary beads worn by the faithful. Although the prayers were not audible, viewers could imagine the utterances of agony.

The camera refocused on the papal balcony and Lody continued her dissertation: "It is from this balcony, and only this balcony, that the elections of new Popes are announced and introduced to the world. From here The Infallible Pope delivers his *urbi et orbi* blessing. Justly, it is from this sacred place the UN President will address the nations of the world, endorsed by the Holy See."

As the camera zoomed in closer the reporter's voice could be heard behind the scenes. "The believers are hungry for answers. They are asking if there is any man who has the answers to the chaos that has engulfed us? Is there anyone who can bring peace and safety to mankind?"

Cameras panned the sorrowful faces of the masses as tears continued to stream in agony pleading with the Virgin Mary for a glimmer of hope in a world gone dark. With a jerk the camera immediately turned and focused back on the balcony. A mysterious hush settled over the thousands gathered when the Holy Father stepped from behind the curtain into sight and held his hands toward the heavens. An atmosphere of expectancy instantly filled the square. To the right of The Pope was the expected UN President poised to address the multitude and awaiting his introduction from His Holiness.

The Supreme Pontiff kept his hands raised and prayed in Latin the Sacred Heart Prayer of Peace, interceding for spiritual comfort for the grieving souls: "*Da, Domine, propitius pacem in diebus nostis, ut, ope misericordiae tuae adiuti, et a peccato simus semper liberi et ab omni perturbatione securi. Per Christum Dominum nostrum. Amen.*"

An echo was heard throughout the square as the multitude gathered cried out in unison, "Amen".

Scrolling on the bottom of the TV screen was the interpretation of the Latin prayer: "Graciously give peace, O Lord, in our days, that, being assisted by help of Thy mercy, we may ever be free from sin and safe from all disturbances. Through Christ our Lord. Amen."

The Pope's kind, loving voice was a blanket of hope covering the anguished souls. Expectancy began to move across the faces replacing the tears of distress. A synergy slowly and systematically filled the hearts of the faithful for the first time since the vanishings. His words offered hope of a new world of peace for all mankind.

Every ear in the sea of people was tuned to his voice which oozed with compassion. "My children, I speak comfort to your hearts today. There is hope in a world darkened with death and destruction. Amid the pain and suffering a ray of sunshine can break through if we will all join in unity. We must not let religious barriers and theology separate us any longer. We are all brothers and sisters born of this earth and as one family we can unite in one purpose, the purpose of peace and harmony among all. We must no longer look at religion, color, creed, or race; but we must take our brethren by the hand and walk together toward a new world."

The crowd erupted in applause and cheering as shouts of acclamation filled the square. The Holy Father extended his hands and waved toward his followers as they joined with him in a hopeful future. The cheering continued until The Pope motioned for silence. Once more, not a sound was heard among the vast throng.

"I have at my right hand the man who is seeking an answer for all humanity in a world that is self-destructing, UN President Sotoreo." His Holiness put his right arm around the shoulders of the UN President and with his left hand pointed towards the crowd, approving Sotoreo's awaited speech. Again, a surge of shouts and applause erupted.

The UN President took a step closer to the edge of the balcony to assume his position. The roar of voices silenced immediately.

In a strong, confident voice Sotoreo brought optimism for the future. "I come today in the name of peace. I have spoken with world leaders and we are endeavoring to unite together to find answers for the vanishings and to bring hope for all peoples. The only nation that refuses to comply is the nation of Israel."

Anger began to radiate through the square as a voice screamed, "Death to Israel! Death to Israel!" The chant quickly reverberated through St. Peter's Square and reverberated into Vatican City proper. Sotoreo allowed the antagonizing declaration to continue for several minutes, instilling within the hearts of the people a deeper hatred for the nation that was now the world powerhouse both economically and militarily.

When his anticipated level of vehemence had been reached, he held up his hands for silence. "I want to assure you, my friends, peace and unity will come in spite of Israel." The crowd was about to explode again, when he held up his hand signaling he wished to continue. "I cannot give you details now but we are diligently working towards a seven-year peace initiative for the entire world. These seven years will allow time to restore Mother Earth to what she was intended to be, not what mankind has created. We must prepare for future generations a world where there will be no more hunger or war. There will be no more anger due to bigotry, racial dissensions, differing religious views, and political stupidity. Everyone will share equally in all this beautiful earth offers. We will be of one mind and one spirit!"

The crowd erupted in applause and voices cheered in a hope for the future. Sotoreo lifted his hands and proclaimed: "There is The One that has the answers. He *will* lead us into a new age, the golden age of peace! He will usher in a time of international unity that has never existed on this earth. Soon he will appear. We must UNITE!"

As the voices of the multitude echoed, "Unite, Unite, Unite!", the camera zoomed in for a close-up of Sotoreo. He was holding his hands together in a triangle shape. Gabriella gasped. "Look, Chris, look at his ring! It's the same ring that Moretti wears. I would recognize it anywhere."

"You're right, Gabi. That's odd, very odd."

"The ring, the symbol...I know they mean something, Chris. I know they do." Gabriella's mind was churning trying to tie these ominous men together.

The Pope stepped closer to the EU President and took his hand. Clasping their hands together they raised them above their heads in their personal sign of unity.

The Holy Father gave a final shout to the evoked crowd: "I unite with President Sotoreo. If this planet is to survive, we all must *unite* in one religion where all roads lead to one god, one government, one world of peace for all mankind." A deafening roar echoed throughout Vatican City and resonated electronically to every nation viewing as Pope Romanus stated his closing words: "We anxiously await The One who will lead us; and I pray our Blessed Mother Mary gives a sign of approval."

As Pope Romanus' words echoed through the crowd, a cloud began to appear over The Vatican. A reverent hush covered the faithful as everyone stared at the sky. The cloud rolled taking a defining shape. Glitters of sunshine pierced through revealing an image forming in the midst of the cloud. Voices of amazement began to scream and cry out as an apparition of The Holy Mother hovered above Vatican City.

The TV cameras quickly focused on the cloud with the image plainly in view. For several minutes the apparition hovered in the sky with hands outstretched in blessing. The roar of the people was so overwhelming you could not have heard Lody even if she could have spoken.

As the image faded, cameras focused on the papal balcony for the Supreme Pontiff's reaction. He stood still with hands raised towards the image in the cloud. He seemed in no way surprised at the miraculous event. Sotoreo stood motionless.

The voice of the Holy Father rang in the ears of all who gathered for hope. "The Virgin Mary has heard our cry. She has appeared to us as a sign it is time to unite as one world and one people."

Some people were crying, some were in shock, while others were kneeling in prayer. Never had there been an appearing of The Holy Mother over Vatican City. The faithful who had gathered for hope had received their answer. It was time to follow the Holy Father and unite with the world.

Katja Lody resumed center stage of the camera. Her voice quivered as she struggled to speak. "I have no words to describe what we have just witnessed. The Virgin Mother Mary seemingly just appeared before thousands of witnesses to bless our Holy Father's instructions. Surely the world is on the threshold of a spiritual awakening. This is a historic day for the posterity of Mother Earth. I repeat the words of our Most Holy Infallible Father: one religion, one government, one world, and The One to lead us."

Gabriella collapsed against the back of the couch and stared at the television screen. It was beyond surreal to witness by television the supposed apparition and to hear the words spoken by Pope Romanus and the EU President.

Chris shook his head in unbelief. "This has to be a set-up, Gabi. Somehow they've been able to make that cloud appear to trick the people into believing this is the holy thing to do."

"The False Prophet will work signs and wonders to deceive the people into following the Antichrist; and my dad said he believed The Pope would be the False Prophet. It seems he has begun his deception with a miraculous sign. If I didn't know better, I would have believed him."

"It was amazing to watch," Chris agreed. "It'd be impossible to convince the people at Vatican Square this was not a divine encounter."

"I can't argue that point," she agreed. "You know when Sotoreo said The One, he was talking about will be the Ascended Master, the Antichrist. They're preparing the entire world to receive one man that will seemingly have all the answers for everything. They've even managed to have The Holy Mother put her stamp of approval on him. In a world of total pandemonium, The One will appear to be the savior of all mankind." She took a deep breath and quoted Professor Brotman, "Only the elect will not be deceived."

"And, it looks like he'll appear very soon," Chris replied dryly.

She pulled herself from the cushions and faced Chris. "Sotoreo just mentioned they are already devising a seven-year plan. When Israel signs it, the countdown of the final seven years has begun." She collapsed again into the pillows mentally reassessing the instructions in her father's letters.

After a few minutes of prophetic calculations, Gabriella sat straight up once again. "My father believes the war of Gog and Magog will take place before the final seven years, so that means even now Russia and Iran are planning a surprise attack. Hmmm, I wonder if Sotoreo knows that?" She mused the thought for a moment before finishing her observation. "He may even be in on it. Either way, Israel just *thinks* they are dwelling in peace and safety since they wiped out the immediate Muslim threat. Russia, Turkey, Iran and their cohorts will do anything to destroy Israel's control of military power and take possession of their wealth, especially the oil and gas. The Russian coalition will be defeated but Israel will be greatly weakened as a nation. Israel will be forced into the seven-year peace treaty."

Chris knew she was right. He also knew these prophecies would be fulfilled exactly as written and there was nothing they could do to stop it or change it.

WIN TV continued to repeat the address from The Vatican allowing all viewers a chance to hear the words of the two most powerful men on earth and to view over and over the apparition of The Virgin Mary. Israeli news did no replays. It was obvious the EU President was using this opportunity to incite further hatred against Israel and blame her for all the ills of the world; and do it with a so-called sign from heaven.

Channel 2 in Haifa instead was reporting news of The Return. Reporters were in Tel Aviv at the Exodus II Processing Center showing long lines of immigrants making Aliyah to their homeland. Entire families were coming from every nation of the earth.

Gabriella watched with a sense of prophetic peace. "How appropriate the second exodus is in progress just before the Feast of Tabernacles begins, Israel's Season of Joy." She assessed with a knowing smile.

Chris's voice was filled with humorous sarcasm. "Coincidence?"

A smile crossed Gabriella's face despite the world's chaos. Chris was right. No coincidence. It was all part of Yahweh's divine plan for Israel.

Gabriella focused back on the TV screen as news cameramen were allowed on the airport tarmac to film the reactions of those arriving in Israel. She watched with empathy as the descendants of Abraham, Isaac, and Jacob were exiting the airplanes. When their feet touched Israeli soil for the first time, the immigrants fell upon their faces and kissed the sacred ground, tears streaming down their faces. Some gathered in circles and began to dance while others raised their hands to the heavens in thankfulness. A receiving line of Israeli soldiers patiently waited at the terminal doors to direct the new arrivals to the processing center.

Gabriella was flooded with joy. Her birthright as a daughter of Zebulon dawned fully upon her as she watched her people coming to the land of their fathers, joining their ancestral brothers and sisters from all over the world. The Children of Israel were coming home.

Amid her joy, a foreboding was stirring deep inside. "Chris, Ezekiel described this very event in the chapter just before he prophesied the Gog and Magog war. She picked up her father's Bible and turned to Chapter 37 and read: *This is what the Sovereign Lord says: I will take the Israelites out of the nations where they have gone. I will gather them from all around and bring them back into their own land."* She looked up from the sacred writings and announced. "The Return is the final sign before all hell breaks loose and we are watching it in real time."

Acknowledging the obvious prophetic signs, they continued to watch the flood of people exiting the airplanes. "This is another prophecy happening before our eyes, *they will return on the wings of eagles,"* she commented as the news coverage cut to a commercial.

Gabriella felt a rush of both mental and physical exhaustion, admitting it had been an exhausting day. "I'm going to bed," she muttered trying to push herself to her feet.

Chris got up and extended a hand, pulling her from the couch. He gave her a quick hug and gently pushed her towards her bedroom door. "Night, Gabi."

She waved over her shoulder as she disappeared behind the closing door. Once alone, she retrieved Caleb's letters she kept secluded in the nightstand drawer. These were for her eyes only. She stretched on the bed with the lamplight shining on the words written by the love of her life:

My Gabriella,

I sit here watching you sleep, praying without ceasing you will awaken. If only I could rewind the past two weeks and live the days again, I would make sure you had no doubts...if only.

The one thing I would not change is submitting to the One True God, Yahweh, and His Son Yeshua. I could not deny His Presence which continually surrounded me when we prayed at the hospital when the Professor almost died; however, I do regret I had no words to reveal that truth to you. Every word I spoke in my efforts to explain turned into walls separating us. For the first time in my life, I was helpless. The physical strength I took pride in gave me no help. I admit I am an emotional wreck; but I will not give up my faith or succumb to spiritual weakness. I must believe somehow, someway you will also find this truth.

As I watch your beautiful face, I reminisce through the years remembering the wonderful times we had as best friends. You know now I always wanted it to be more and knew the day would eventually come when you realized I loved you more than life itself. Well, the day did come but our time was short lived. Do I regret it? NO! The few days we had, when we finally expressed our love, were worth a life time of waiting.

I continue to pray you open your beautiful blue eyes and see your father is still alive and sits with me by your side; we are here together, the two men that love you beyond words.

Always yours,
Caleb

Closing her eyes, she imagined being held in her father's loving embrace and feeling the safety of his arms she knew as a child. She whispered into the silence of the room, "So near and yet so far." She fought back anger arising in her. "All these years I have suffered the loneliness and emptiness of not having my father and the entire time he was alive and near me." Her mind could not totally wrap around that truth.

In frustration, she carefully laid the letter back in the bedside drawer, secluding it once again from view. She closed her eyes desiring sleep, but instead restlessness captured her. She would doze, feel Caleb's touches, hear his voice, and then abruptly awaken. She felt as though she was caught once again in time and untime, not being able to discern which part of her night was real and which was dreams.

When dozing, she could hear the Professor in the distance discussing the soon coming Russian led invasion, giving prophetic clarity as to what nations would be involved and what the outcome would be. Caleb and her father's voices, even the voices of Aaron, Faith, KJ, and Sandee were interjecting in to the conversation. She could not open her eyes but she could clearly hear their words as she lay lifeless. She tried to move her hand, to reach to them, but not a muscle would move.

Suddenly, she felt Caleb's familiar strong arms wrap around her pulling her from the bed and next to his chest. The voice she would recognize for all eternity whispered in her ears as he rocked her back and forth, "Wake up, Gabi, wake up."

Wake up she did...to an empty room.

CHAPTER 26

———•◦•◦•———

Gabriella faced reality as she opened her eyes to her bunker bedroom. There were no loving voices, no strong arms embracing her. She immediately shut her eyes, desperately trying to recapture the feeling of Caleb holding her. She longed to hear the soothing voice of her father but the room was quiet and still, totally void of those she loved.

She forced herself out of bed wondering what another day would bring. Chris was already up, coffee made, and watching the international news network. With coffee cup in hand, Gabriella joined him. He barely glanced up while motioning her to sit down beside him.

"What is *that*, Chris?" She was totally repulsed by the ceremony airing.

He kept his eyes glued to the TV screen. "That's the opening ceremony for CERN. They have named it The Awakening. I can't help but wonder what they're awakening with all this weird stuff."

Gabriella was very familiar with the underground Hadron collider in Switzerland and the ongoing CERN experiment. "I had no idea they were at the point of actually activating it. This project has been developing for decades. Scientists are looking for what they call the god particle. They think they can pierce through to an alternate dimension of existence. Crazy stuff," she commented taking another sip of hot liquid.

Her eyes were fixed on the bizarre, satanic style ceremony. A man representing the god Shiva was recreating the 'dance of destruction'. As he danced he entered a portal into an alternate dimension where he was engulfed by light. A dark figure slowly approached him from behind and began whispering in his ear. The dancing stopped. The man stood still listening. An evil smile captured his face.

"I don't understand what this pagan ceremony has to do with the purpose of CERN," Chris pondered. "I thought it was a scientific project." He continued to watch the nefarious ceremony and summed up the obvious. "Apparently not."

Gabriella set down her coffee and watched in amazement. The next words from the male reporter's commentary brought the satanic meaning into complete perspective. "CERN is built over the ancient ruins of the Temple of Apollyon, The Destroyer. It is for that reason CERN chose a god of destruction as their symbol." The reporter obviously struggled with his next words. "Also, it seems to aptly describe CERN's possible impact on the earth. If they create a portal to an alternate dimension, no one is sure what the effects will be. We are going live for a statement from the lead scientist at CERN's location near Geneva, Switzerland."

The television camera panned the seating area of the audience in attendance for this grand ceremony. There in the elite crowd of viewers were the EU President and the leaders of all the EU nations, among other dignitaries. Directly in the center sat UN President Sotoreo.

"From The Vatican yesterday to CERN today," Gabriella sarcastically stated. "From what is considered the holiest place on earth to what is now the epitome of evil."

A man dressed in a white ¾ length lab coat stood next to CERN's General Director. He was obviously uncomfortable with the media attention. He stepped to the microphone to update the world on their most recent experiment.

He took a breath and read from the scripted release: "Among our many experiments we have been testing the effects of antimatter behaving the same way as matter under the influence of gravity. We have been running tests and have made some major discoveries, proving antimatter is the mirror imagine of matter but with opposite electrical charges. To put it more in layman terms, we know gravity pulls matter down and conversely antimatter pulls matter up. At this time, I cannot give details as tests are still ongoing. However, as we go forward we will be giving further updates on the results and the effects." He turned and walked away from the camera refusing to answer any questions.

The General Director made vague comments about CERN being the threshold to the future of mankind while a large screen behind him continued replaying Shiva and the dance of destruction. As Shiva continued to dance a swirling wind began to move across the big screen creating the image of a portal.

The Director stated emphatically: "As the collider accelerates atomic particles faster than the speed of light, we are creating a gateway to previously unknown dimensions." As he continued with the ceremony, the big screen showed a simulated vortex being created by the collider. A portal opened in the middle of the vortex pulling undistinguishable matter through into this alternate dimension.

One could not deny the mesmerized look displayed on the faces of all the attendees. It was the same hypnotized look evident on all participating in the ceremony. Chris and Gabriella looked at each other with understanding but not saying a word.

The sound of the security buzzer interrupted them and Chris raced to the monitors followed by Gabriella. The familiar Suburban had come through the security gate followed by a long, black limousine.

"What in the world?" Gabriella exclaimed, then quickly quieted her voice even though she knew she could not be heard outside the bunker.

Slowly climbing the winding gravel road, the vehicles approached the entrance to the lodge. They were not surprised to see Russo and Moretti exit the Suburban; however, the man climbing from the limousine that followed them was a total shock. Ugo Strozza stood erect and gazed at his surroundings. A brief smile crossed his face, obviously giving his approval of the location chosen for their private meetings. He moved away from the limo door allowing the others accompanying him to also exit the vehicle. One by one unfamiliar faces emerged.

"Who are these guys?" Chris muttered under his breath.

Entering the lodge, the monitors followed every move the men made. Russo directed them to the large dining table where meetings would be held.

Gabriella sputtered in anger. "That's where our team met. How dare they just come in and take over?" She forced herself to control her animosity as they each took a place at the massive cedar table with Strozza at the head, the place that belonged to the Professor.

The men took computers from their briefcases and positioned themselves to take notes, just as her research team had done many times through the years. The godly Professor had been replaced at the head of the table by an evil entity.

"Look at their right hand, Chris." She leaned closer to the monitor screen trying to get a closer view. "They all have on that ring." Chris zoomed the monitor for a close-up of the ring. It was exactly the same as Moretti and Sotoreo wore: trapezoid shaped with a disjointed pyramid in the middle. In the center of the pyramid was the all-seeing eye.

"That ring means something. Maybe to some type of secret organization? It's similar to the hierarchy of the Free Masons, but not exact," Chris said. "Why didn't I know about this? Apparently, they are so secret they are under the radar of even law enforcement."

Moretti made coffee for the delegation and served the men in preparation for the meeting to begin. He and Russo sat to the side, obviously to be at the beck and call for anything this group would need.

Ugo Strozza walked to the window that offered a panoramic view of Mt. Hermon. He stared for a few minutes, uttering words incoherent to the two in the bunker below. It sounded like some type of chant and immediately Gabriella felt a presence of evil.

He returned to the head of the table, cleared his voice and addressed the delegation. All faces around the table focused on him. "Brothers of the 33rds, we know why we are here and to be so close to where it all began could not be a coincidence."

The men looked at each other with nefarious smiles of understanding before their leader continued: "As you know, our mission is to prepare events for The Appearing of our Ascended Master. We've been chosen for this high calling and we will use this undisclosed location as our command center. You will all stay here coordinating the events until the appointed time. I will be the liaison to our Cabal Pindar."

The men all nodded in agreement to their instructions before Strozza continued: "We will go over some of the most pressing issues and then you can settle into your rooms before we get down to business. Time is now of the essence."

Strozza turned on his computer screen and opened his file. As the information loaded he took a drink of coffee, turned his cell phone to vibrate, and cleared his throat to begin.

"We're all aware Israel is the stumbling block to our mission. That issue is being addressed and will be finally resolved. What we must do is coordinate all events necessary to initiate The Final Phase, using all media to reach and prepare mankind for the coming unity.

Strozza leaned back in his chair with a sardonic grin on his face. "The good news is the Final Phase will begin in just a few days. It will be a six-step process. Tomorrow's Land will now be known as a unity festival and is being moved to Italy in the countryside near Vatican City. It will be our biggest media challenge. You are already preparing to live-stream the event around the world. Afterwards, you will continue to loop the music through all media sources for days, hypnotizing and controlling the minds of the listeners. Humankind will never know what's really happening."

One of the unknown men held up his hand with a question and Strozza gave him permission to speak. "How many nations are participating in the Tomorrow's Land event? Our goal was to reach them all before The Final Phase began."

Strozza smiled knowing he had done his job well. "Our media center is still scheduling, but we expect all civilized nations will be live-streaming the Tomorrow's Land Unity Festival, except Israel of course. It will be promoted as the event that will bring the world together, finding hope after the international chaos. They have no idea..." He did not need to explain; the men around the table were all in one mind and one accord.

Chris grabbed his computer to find out about the Tomorrow's Land concert. "Wow," he gasped.

"What is it, Chris? I've never heard of it."

Chris quickly read aloud some of the article. "Tomorrow's Land is an annual electronic music festival in Belgium that's been going on for years. The last one was held back in the summer; before the war, when life seemed normal. It featured New Age music and a psychedelic theme with the CERN collider on their gigantic screens constantly spinning, seemingly opening a vortex to another world. The whole concert was live streamed to almost all civilized countries. Says here Israel had a gathering for the live stream, but it was a big flop. They had a very small attendance, plus all kinds of technical difficulties getting the sound and video. The article says Israel refuses to participate in the concerts in the future."

Gabriella smiled and with a voice of sarcasm stated: "Well, I wonder who caused the technical problems?" She knew Yahweh was protecting his people from the deception already beginning.

He turned the laptop screen so Gabi could see the video. The main stage screen of the concert was three stories high. In the middle of the screen was the image of CERN spinning, creating a portal. Over the portal in huge letters was the word 'UNITE'.

"Click on the audio, Chris." As soon as he touched "sound", new age music with a strange hypnotic beat came through the speakers. A mesmerizing woman's voice could be subtly heard in the background saying over and over, "The One will soon appear. He will bring us unity and love in tomorrow's land. The One will soon appear."

Gabi added, "The men upstairs are part of this deception. They were getting things in place from the very beginning of this event."

The bunker duo silenced as a new topic of discussion began in the lodge.

"One more question," the unknown man spoke again. "Will the supply meet the demand?"

Again, Strozza smiled. "The third strand implant has been perfected. The inventory will be ready as the supply is needed."

He pushed his chair back and stood up as a gesture to move to the most important issue at hand. "And now to the CERN Awakening announcement taking place in Switzerland. As we know, for decades this has been planned. Little did the TV viewers know a signal was being sent to The 33rds around the world...the time has come." He looked once again through the massive window with the view of the apex of Mt. Hermon. "Another portal has opened."

Clapping broke out among the brothers. In unison, they repeated a chant incoherent to the duo secretly listening. Gabriella looked at Chris and raised her eyebrows questioning if he understood. He simply responded with a shrug of the shoulders.

Strozza held up his hand and the chanting ceased. "You all know your assignments. Our interactive programs will allow you to organize and implement your individual tasks." He motioned towards Moretti and Russo. "Russo will show you to your rooms. After you've settled in, we will meet back for lunch and get to work. I will stay in the bedroom here on the main floor. The cottage behind us is reserved for the Pindar. He plans to arrive for the final planning tomorrow."

The men closed their laptops, left them in place on the table, and followed Russo to their rooms. Chris and Gabriella watched as the camera followed the men up the stairs and to the rooms once occupied by Professor Brotman's research team. Strozza would be using the Professor's personal quarters.

Gabriella swallowed hard. "This is unbelievable, Chris. They act like they own the place." She reflected for a moment and stated the obvious. "However, Yahweh isn't surprised by any of this."

Chris shook his head. "Nope, it's another divine direction. How else would we know what they're planning?"

She contemplated his words and understanding dawned crystal clear. Her voice was strong and certain as she prophesied her future: "The Chosen will know the great deception and declare The Truth."

CHAPTER 27

C hris continued to monitor the movements of the evil delegation in the lodge above them while Gabriella prepared lunch. The men unpacked their bags and settled in for what appeared to be an extended stay. Within the hour, they returned to the dining room where Moretti had their lunch ready. Strozza rejoined them and as they ate, verbal preparations of the work ahead of them began.

In the secret security room below, Gabriella and Chris ate their lunch while continuing their observation of the men.

Strozza updated his men on what to expect: "I'll be returning to Haifa first thing in the morning to meet the Pindar. He'll arrive at the airport at noon and we'll return here immediately to begin implementation. We only have days to get things in order. The clock is quickly ticking now." Strozza took the last bite of his sandwich and motioned for Moretti to remove his plate. The brothers followed his lead and pulled their computers forward to begin their individual assignments.

Chris could not determine any specifics. Apparently, their computers were interfaced as they feverishly worked. Periodically, they would take a break and discuss their progress but nothing was verbalized that explained to the two in the bunker what they were accomplishing.

Strozza arose from the table and stretched, allowing the other men to also take a needed break. Moretti brought fresh coffee while there was a lull in the computer activity.

"I've got my part all set," said a young man in his late 30's.

"Yeah, me too," said a slightly older man.

Strozza sat back down and sipped from the hot brew. "We're right on schedule. It's all jelling with perfection. Can't wait to get his reaction." A smile of expectation crossed Strozza's face. "Finally...."

The men all rejoined him at the table and chattered with disjointed sentences and unfamiliar terminology making no coherent sense to Gabriella and Chris.

After the men retired for the day, Gabriella and Chris compared their comments trying to piece together a clearer picture.

"Dad knew about the third strand," Gabriella pondered. "But, how does all this intertwine?" She quoted back the various elements mentioned: "CERN, Tomorrow's Land, The One, The Final Phase, The Appearing." There was a lull in the conversation as she mentally assessed the various pieces of the mysterious puzzle. She took a deep breath and exhaled in frustration. "I just can't see how it connects, but apparently we're supposed to figure it out."

Chris was pacing back and forth running his hand through his dark hair. "I've gone over it and over it in my mind. Maybe whoever is arriving tomorrow will be the missing piece. You go on to bed, Gabi, and get some rest. Everybody upstairs is asleep so nothing else will happen tonight. I've got a little research to do before I turn in."

"Okay." She quickly agreed, exhausted from the emotionally and mentally straining day. She closed the bedroom door behind her, thankful to have some time alone. She changed into her pajamas and crawled into the comfortable bed. She took the stack of Caleb's letters from the nightstand drawer. The sight of his handwriting made her heart leap with joy, which quickly turned to longing. She thought the passing days would become easier but instead she longed for him with greater passion.

Picking up the next letter, she prepared herself for the emotional roller coaster she knew would arrive with his words.

My Darling,

Sometimes I feel you can hear me when I speak to you. You give no outward indication but I can sense our soul connection. Our research team sits in your bedroom so they can be close to you while the Professor tells us of the things that are about to come upon the earth.

202

The Psalms 83 War is raging now, but we are safely hidden away in the bunker beneath the lodge. Both your dad and the Professor believe it will be over very quickly. They have spoken of the arrival of the Antichrist and believe preparations for his appearing are now taking place. They also believe whoever killed your mother and tried to kill Dr. Brotman will play a major part in the final world events and this world leader's arrival.

You know this is all new to me. As I sit here by your side they are explaining prophecy in detail. I know I cannot fully comprehend in the short time we have left everything they have learned over decades but I am gleaning all I can and the details are incredible. I sit beside you, hold your hand, and pray somehow you can hear their words. I know it would be a miracle, but I have come to believe all things are possible.

You have been asleep for almost 48 hours now. Dr. Nicholson says he will have to start an IV soon if you don't wake up. I watch you, my love, as you lay there in a world of your own. I wonder if you are at peace or if the paranormal world continues to hold you in a place you called 'untime'.

I pray continually you will return to us. The agony on your father's face is almost more than I can endure. Even though every decision he made was for your protection, he so deeply regrets not getting to explain to you why. He repeats over and over that he was wrong, hoping somehow you will hear. We both are heart-broken you left us without understanding.

I continue to pray you will return before it is too late. But, if not, as you read this letter never doubt my love again.

Eternally yours,
Caleb

She laid the letter next to her heart and closed her eyes, trying to visualize Caleb in the room with her. She knew the mind was a powerful force and she attempted to capture all the memories of their short time together after she allowed her love to finally surface. She shut out every thought, except for Caleb. She imagined his hand embracing hers and the tenderness of his voice whispering, "I love you". Her longing became so obsessive she actually could feel his arms wrapped around her and his hand pulling her head to his shoulder. It felt so real. She tried to force her eyes back open believing she could look into his face, but they would not budge.

A mystifying tranquility saturated her as she was captured by her dreams in which her soul again left her body and she was standing beside her bed watching the events taking place in her bunker bedroom. She could see herself lying on the bed with her father and Caleb by her side. Dr. Brotman, Sandee, Faith, Aaron, KJ, - they were all there. Caleb was holding her in his arms. Dr. Brotman was talking but she could not understand his words. Gradually, his voice increased in volume.

"CERN will soon open a portal to the abyss. The fallen angels now held in captivity will be released. Revelation 9 will be fulfilled." His words became louder and were saturated with fervor. "We must warn our people!"

The dream vision ended. She felt Caleb holding her, rocking her back and forth. "Wake up, Gabi, please wake up before it's too late."

And she did, again to her empty room and another day of her new reality.

Gabriella forced herself out of bed and into the day. She found Chris in the security room monitoring the activities in the lodge. One look told him her night had been less than restful. He motioned for her to join him and she settled into the black leather chair at his side. The delegation in the lodge was having breakfast and making small talk which allowed Chris and Gabriella time for personal discussion.

Chris turned her chair where she was forced to look at him. "Ok, Gabi, what gives?"

She looked down at the floor trying to conceal her agony. The emotions she thought were under control came surging like pounding waves through her entire being. Words of explanation just would not come. Chris took one of her hands, holding it firmly. He put his other hand under her chin lifting her face, forcing her to look at him. She managed to hold back the tears; however, she could not veil her feelings.

"What is it, Gabi? What's happened?"

She took a deep breath and steadied her voice. "When I go to sleep, it's like I'm in soul sleep again...flashbacks, I guess. It's as though I'm caught in untime again and hearing the conversations around me while sleeping, just like before every one I loved vanished. At one point, I was out of my body and saw everyone in my room. The Professor was giving dire warnings. Caleb was holding me and my dad was in the chair beside me."

"What kind of warnings?"

She looked directly into Chris' eyes and stated passionately: "He said CERN was going to open the abyss and release the fallen angels." She dropped her face and avoided his eyes.

He was silent for a moment and then gave his observation. "Do you think all these discussions in the lodge are wrapping into a scenario in your dreams? Yesterday Strozza was talking about CERN. It's been all over the news. Possibly reality is mixing with your feelings of the loss of your loved ones?"

He could see a slight relief cross her countenance. She leaned back in the chair and nodded. "That would make sense. Strange that I seldom dreamed until my cave experience in Saudi Arabia. Since then it's been nothing but dreams: all kinds of them, good and bad." She turned her chair towards the security monitors, forcing herself to face the unknown. She said more to herself than Chris, "But it felt so real."

He knew the comment was not meant for him and focused on the men above them. They were settling into their respective chairs ready to begin their implementation of The Final Phase.

Strozza took his place at the head and addressed the group. "I will be leaving for the airport shortly to meet our Pindar around noon. We should arrive back here at the lodge mid-afternoon. You must review every detail of your work beforehand."

The men simultaneously opened their computers ready to begin. "Let's review together the major points at hand. You each have your list to follow."

One by one Strozza went through tasks that had been completed. "The event is organized and the media will be live streaming Tomorrow's Land Festival to every nation with internet or satellite connections. This will prepare the minds for unity. Pope Romanus is standing ready to take the lead role in The Appearing. CERN has been activated. Once the vanishings have been explained we will have no problem in completing The Final Phase. Only Israel stands in our way; but not for long. The Russian bear and his cohorts plan to take care of Israel and then he *thinks* he can wipe us out, too. He has another *think* coming."

Strozza paused to laugh at his attempt at humor before pronouncing judgement upon the Russian President. "He is a traitor to the New World Order and he will be stopped."

The men in attendance again uttered the incoherent chant obviously declaring agreement with their leader. The very sound rang with satanic overtones.

One man voiced his concerns: "What if there's a revolt and some refuse to take the implant?"

Strozza's voice of total confidence took on a threatening dynamic. "We actually expect some to rebel, and we have planned accordingly. Once the Final Phase is fully implemented, any that refuse the implant will no longer be able to do any business transactions of any kind. The monetary system, financial records, medical records...every aspect of daily life will eventually be controlled by the implant. That means no buying or selling of anything, even food, unless they comply. Anyone that refuses will be eliminated. We will allow no one to stand in the way of the greater good." Strozza glanced towards the panoramic window where Mt. Hermon majestically stood and he smiled. "And we have already planned for that scenario also, if you know what I mean." The man nodded his head and asked no more questions.

Strozza's voice took on a slightly warmer tone as he complimented the delegation of men. "Brothers, you were chosen as the earth's brightest and most brilliant technological minds. I hope you realize the honor bestowed upon you to become one of The Enlightened."

The men looked at each other with faces full of pride. They knew they had done their jobs well and believed all would go just as planned. They were finally ready for their first meeting with the Cabal Pindar.

Strozza gave his last instructions before leaving for the airport. "Go over everything one more time. Don't leave a single detail without total scrutiny. When we return, we will have a final review before the next step begins."

Gabriella shuddered as she listened to the secret plans for a world coup being made. She knew the grave responsibility that came with the knowledge she and Chris were privy to. She now understood the Professor's words from her prior night's dream. It echoed over and over in her ear: "We must warn the people."

CHAPTER 28

After Strozza left for the airport the brothers were diligently at work. Moretti and Russo were readily available for any needs they might have. Chris continued to monitor the men even though they were deep in computer concentration. Gabriella prepared lunch while there was a lull in their conversations.

While they ate in the security room, Gabriella was in deep thought. She knew Chris was aware of her mood and was just waiting until she was ready to talk. She also knew, for whatever reason, they were divinely appointed partners in hearing this secret meeting and it would be best to just open her thoughts to him.

She swallowed the last bit of sandwich and cleared her throat. "I know you're probably right how all these events in the lodge, on the news, and in my father's letters are mixing together and forming my dreams; but I don't believe my dream last night was just based on that. I don't know if it's something I heard while I was soul sleeping and my subconscious is replaying, but I am certain these dreams have created a real urgency inside me. I know I've been chosen to warn my people. How? That's the big question." She hoped and prayed he would have some insight.

He did not immediately comment. He leaned back in his chair and stared into space mulling the current events over and over in his mind. "I wonder if Richards has any idea what's really going on? It's obvious he isn't in the inner circle, but just how much does he know about CERN and the other stuff? Sure wish I could talk to him privately. Just don't know how that could happen."

She knew he was not really asking her the question but was thinking out loud. "Maybe we'll know more after the Pindar, whoever that is, gets here," Gabriella commented as she picked up their plates to take them to the kitchen.

Chris opened his computer and commented: "I'm gonna go through the headquarter files again, see if I've missed something. Why don't you take a break? I'll let you know if there's movement upstairs." Chris knew Gabriella needed some time to herself.

She retraced her steps to the kitchen, quickly cleaned up from lunch, and retrieved her father's next letter to be read. She secluded herself in her bedroom and prepared her mind for the emotional response that came with both his familiar handwriting and the painful reminder he had been lovingly by her side only a few days prior.

Gabriella,

I struggle in how to explain to you with mere words what is about to come upon the earth. Satan in the form of human flesh will soon be unleashed and it will be like no other time in human history, the worst days ever known to mankind.

The enemy of my soul captured me for a time with deception as I researched extraterrestrial life. I thought the 'proof' existed that we were not alone in this vast universe and, as you know, I bought in to the entire lie. The world is about to do the same and they will have no idea that it is all a demonic deception to give place for Satan to reign upon the earth.

I stress to you again: watch The Vatican. I truly believe it is from that place the duplicity will emerge and saturate the earth. It is for this reason Yahweh will raise up voices crying out truth and many will be saved from the deception, coming to the knowledge of Yeshua, as I did.

In my quest for knowledge and understanding I traveled down many paths and I praise Yahweh those paths merged into one and eventually led me to Dr. Brotman. He revealed to me undeniable truth that I shared with you in the journal I left. If you had finished reading it before you arrived at the lodge you would have known the entity, which appeared to you as an angel of light, was a lying demon. Caleb has shared with me your night journeys and the paranormal world that captured you. It was very similar to the lies which held me captive until Yeshua delivered me. That was the truth I left you in my journal, but I cannot regress and think of what could have or might have been.

I feel time is running out. The Feast of Trumpets will end in only a matter of hours and the last trumpet will sound. I wonder if this will be the trumpet Paul wrote of in II Corinthians 15:52 – "...in the twinkling of an eye, at the last trumpet. For the trumpet will sound, the dead will be raised imperishable, and we will be changed."

If so, we that have accepted the blood atonement of Yeshua Jesus, will instantly take on immortality, be caught up with Him in the air, and forever be with The Lord. There is still time for you to awaken and be with us in that catching away. I pray it is so.

But if not, I must remind you of the most important elements of the days ahead...the great deception that is dawning. It is a time when men's hearts will fail them in fear of the things that are coming upon the earth. The only way to overcome is by the blood of The Lamb and by the word of your testimony; those that will love not their lives but are willing to die for their faith will receive eternal life. For the believer, death is only a doorway from this earthly life to the heavenly home with our Creator. Do not be afraid if that day comes. I will be waiting on the other side.

I love you, my little princess,
Dad

Gabriella closed her eyes visualizing her father sitting by her bedside penning the letter she held in her hand. Drowsiness overcame her and she fell into a deep sleep. When she opened her eyes again her father was sitting at her side with tears in his eyes. Suddenly he jumped up. "She's awake, my God, she's awake!"

She tried to sit up but her body would not move. Her eyes struggled to focus on the room around her. Caleb grabbed her in his arms. "Thank you, God. Thank you!"

She momentarily closed her eyes trying to better focus, but they would not reopen. She no longer felt Caleb's arms nor saw her father's tearful eyes. The room was now totally silent. She had no idea how long she had lain in limbo until the silence was broken.

"Wake up, Gabi, wake up." This time her eyes opened. However, it was to see Chris by her bedside.

"The limo just came through the gate."

She looked at the clock and realized she had been asleep most of the afternoon. Chris pulled her to her feet and made sure she was fully awake before he rushed back to the security room. "Hurry, Gabi."

Her adrenalin kicked in and she followed close behind him. There was no time now to relive or belabor the dream encounter. She sat down beside Chris and watched the monitors with great anticipation. The car had arrived at the entrance and the driver got out to open the door for the prestigious passengers.

Several men in black suits exited the vehicle, visually and electronically surveying the grounds and the buildings before the main occupant of the limo emerged.

Gabriella could hear Chris catch his breath. "I figured this might happen. Those men have RF detectors, specially designed to alert to an active security system. They're going to know they're being monitored. They can even pinpoint the area the frequencies are coming from."

Chris expected a panic response from Gabriella but instead she dropped her head, raised her hands and began to pray a Hebrew prayer of protection. She remembered Aaron and Faith praying the prayer when they were caught in an extremely dangerous storm just after leaving the ominous cave in Saudi Arabia. As the powerful words of prayer echoed in the security room, a supernatural peace infiltrated around them and through them.

The security guards covered the entire area and did not detect one radio frequency. Chris's face filled with amazement. "Gabi, we are seeing the supernatural hand of Father God's protection."

She took his hand and smiled with a glow on her face. "I know. This is just the beginning of what the days ahead will be like, Chris. We will have to depend on divine protection."

The guards returned to the limo and opened the door for the occupants to exit signaling the area was safe. The two in the bunker held their breath until the mystery of the Pindar was revealed. First Strozza exited. That was no surprise. However, Gabriella and Chris both gasped as the surreptitious man emerged into full view.

"Oh, my God." Gabriella could not hold back her shock.

Chris's expression exploded with ultimate surprise. "So, this is the Cabal Pindar. Who would have thought?"

UN President Sotoreo took a moment and stretched after exiting the limo. Then he did a 360 turn visually surveying his surroundings. It was apparent Strozza was awaiting the Pindar's approval. Sotoreo said something to Strozza in a voice too low for the cameras to pick up the audio. They both smiled as if they had a secret they were not willing to share.

Strozza and the UN President approached the entrance door to the lodge where they were met by Russo and Moretti. Sotoreo shook their hands as he crossed the threshold where another security monitor picked up the surveillance. Chris continued to be in amazement that none of the UN President's security guards were picking up warning of a surveillance system on the premises. He knew for a certainty it was a divine intervention.

Gabriella's long ponytail bounced back and forth as she shook her head in disbelief. "My father's property and they have just moved in and taken over, and that man is staying in my father's personal cottage. Well, it makes me so mad I could spit fire!"

Chris put his hand over hers trying to sooth her but did not take his eyes off the men upstairs. "If they were somewhere else, Gabi, we wouldn't know what's going on...now would we? Remember there's a divine plan at work here and we have to let it take its course."

She knew he was right but the anger still boiled inside her. "These evil men in my father's house makes me so..." She did not finish the sentence due to conversation beginning upstairs.

The men around the table all rose as Sotoreo entered the room. One by one Strozza introduced them to the Cabal Pindar. A mesmerized look crossed each face when the Pindar's hand interlocked with theirs. The duo in the bunker knew something supernatural was taking place, and it was not good. She looked closer at Moretti and Russo and noticed even their facial expressions changed.

"Did you see that? Their whole countenance changed when they shook hands with that man. What's happening, Chris? This is *really* strange."

"This entire scenario is strange, Gabi. From The Vatican one day, to CERN's Awakening Ceremony the next day, and then here to the lodge where we just *happen* to be able to watch their every move; it doesn't get any stranger than that," Chris responded in a voice unlike anything Gabriella had heard before. Was he piecing something together? She briefly glanced at him but his eyes were glued to the monitor.

The brothers stood at their places around the table until the Pindar motioned for them to be seated. Like robots they all methodically sat down and opened their computers in unison.

"Weird..." Chris muttered.

Sotoreo sat at the head chair previously occupied by Strozza. "No doubt the Pindar will be taking total control of matters going forward," Gabriella commented as they watched Strozza take his place at the UN President's right side.

Sotoreo looked deeply into the eyes of each man in the room. It appeared he was piercing into their souls affirming total allegiance to his agenda. After a few tense minutes, he smiled, satisfied there was total unity.

"I am going to freshen up before we begin our meeting. I trust you all have your work done and I cannot stress strongly enough the accuracy of every single detail. We are about to initiate The Final Phase." He smiled sardonically. "Everything on earth is about to experience a shift."

As Sotoreo arose to exit the room, he stopped suddenly. He looked in every direction. "Is there anyone here I have not been made aware of?" His eyes were piercing into Strozza's.

"No, Pindar. No one else, I assure you. Is something wrong?"

Sotoreo stood still and put his finger over his lips to assure the room would be totally silent. "I sense something."

No one moved, awaiting further instructions. Gabriella whispered, "Could he know we are here without seeing or hearing us?"

"There's no way, Gabi." Chris tried to reassure her; however, he was not so sure himself.

Gabriella took a deep breath and prayed again for protection. "Yeshua, I speak your blood covering and protection upon us. Hide us in the shadow of your wings that we will be safe in this place and accomplish Your will. I declare no weapon formed against us will prosper."

After she prayed, Sotoreo looked momentarily confused. He shook his head as if trying to get a clear communication of some kind. "Hmmm. I don't feel it now. Very odd." He stood still for a full minute with his eyes clenched. The room was as silent as the grave. He opened his eyes, looked around the room again and muttered under his breath.

Everyone relaxed, except the two in the bunker. Spiritual warfare was raging and Chris knew this was a battle he could not win in his own physical strength. No police training in the world could prepare him for what was ahead.

CHAPTER 29

————— •◦•◦• —————

Gabriella and Chris anxiously awaited the evening meeting. To avert their thoughts, they watched the WIN TV updates. They both thought it humorous the news was reporting the UN President had joined world leaders in an undisclosed location to determine the diplomatic steps into the future of the nations and their response to the powerhouse nation of Israel.

Chris chuckled out loud. "We could disclose that location really quick, but where's the world leaders? Just goes to show, you can't believe what you hear on the news."

Gabriella retorted quickly, "What if that's what Sotoreo wants people to believe? He can say the nations' leaders have met and come to decisions, but in the current world chaos who's going to really know? Instead he announces to the world what he and his evil cohorts have decided. People do believe the news reports and the news will report whatever the President tells them to."

Chris sat straight up in his chair. "Of course, Gabi, that makes total sense." He ran his hand through his thick hair and pondered the possibilities. "With everything in the world being such a mess people will be ready for some solutions, any solutions making their lives seem normal again. Strozza mentioned an explanation for the vanishings. If they can pull that off and get the world population to buy in to it, they will have set the stage to control whatever it is they're planning."

Gabriella agreed. "But there's still the Gog and Magog War that has to take place before the Antichrist confirms the 7-year covenant with Israel. This unity Strozza is talking about can't happen until after the war which will wipe out the remaining Muslim nations. It will also destroy Russia who is vying for world dominance since they took the United States out of the picture. According to Ezekiel's prophecy, Israel will suffer greatly but will realize they would have been totally destroyed had Yahweh God not delivered them. However, it will leave them weakened and vulnerable to a world leader negotiating a peace treaty. I'm just not seeing yet how this is going to play out."

She got up and paced the stone floor while prophetic scenarios played out in her mind. She settled on a conclusion and sat back down directly across from Chris, stating with a firm conviction: "After the Psalms 83 War, Israel expanded her borders to all the land promised to Abraham. This soon coming war lead by Russia, Turkey, and Iran is going to challenge again Israel's right to exist, especially since they now possess all the surrounding Muslim nations. We know Yahweh is going to intervene and the Gog and Magog war will be won supernaturally. Israel will not be able to take credit for winning through their military capabilities and will recognize that Yahweh is the only God and it was He who delivered them from destruction."

Chris nodded his head in agreement. "We've pretty much covered that already, Gabi."

"I know, but I see more clearly now." She spoke with new revelation. "This will begin a return to Israel's spiritual roots and create a determination to rebuild their temple, even signing a peace agreement with the new world leader to be able to do so. The new leader, who will be revealed later as the Antichrist, will confirm the covenant declaring the land taken in the Psalms 83 War belongs to Israel. The returning Tribes of Israel will be protected and allowed to migrate and homestead in the expanded State of Israel and this world leader will guarantee Israel's peace to rebuild their Temple. When Israel signs that agreement, the seven-year countdown to the return of Yeshua the Messiah to set up his kingdom on earth will have begun."

Chris sat silently trying to process the order of events Gabriella had laid out. It was obvious all the prophetic information her father had left her was beginning to form into a coherent picture. "That makes sense to me, Gabi. So, that would mean for Sotoreo to go forward with the world agenda, the God and Magog war has to take place first taking the Muslim nations and Russian power out of the picture."

They continued to discuss the prophetic events her father had detailed in his letters while they awaited the return of Sotoreo to the main lodge. They were mind mapping all kinds of possibilities as to what The Final Phase would be. Whatever it was, they both knew things in the world were about to change even more drastically than they already had.

In their discussions, neither Gabriella nor Chris voiced the ominous atmosphere which crept into the bunker after they suspected the Pindar had discerned their presence, but both were keenly aware.

"Chris, you know the spiritual battle has begun." Gabriella broke the reluctance to talk about the obvious. "The Antichrist isn't revealed yet, but his evil doers are definitely preparing the way. We'll constantly have to pray the blood of Yeshua over this bunker or Sotoreo will find us. We're not dealing with flesh and blood anymore; it's the powers of darkness, the demonic supernatural forces."

Chris had already accepted the fact his police training would help very little in the days ahead. He reluctantly admitted his feelings of inadequacy. "I thought I was here to protect you, Gabi. I thought that was Yahweh's plan in having me here, but I feel so useless against forces I can't combat physically."

She laid her head on his shoulder. "You are the brother I never had, Chris. I know I can depend on you no matter what we face. I do believe our Heavenly Father put us together, but He is letting us know our only hope is to totally depend on Him in the days ahead. He already knows what's coming and He won't leave us or forsake us. That's His promise."

Chris wrapped his arm around her shoulder. "I think I like being a big brother," he jested, trying to lighten the dismal atmosphere. He took a deep breath and his voice became husky, "You know I would give my life to protect you, Gabriella. You do know that...don't you?"

She nodded her head that was nestled in his shoulder. For just a moment the world seemed safe, until a beeping of the surveillance monitors signaled movement in the lodge. They quickly returned to the security room. The delegation of men was regrouping around the table.

Chris checked the recorders to make sure every movement and word in the lodge would be recorded for playback. Anticipation hung in the bunker air so dense they could hardly breathe. Chris took Gabriella's hand and did not let go until Sotoreo entered the room and took his position at the head of the table. Strozza took his place at the Pindar's right side. Moretti and Russo sat ready for whatever instructions they were given.

The brothers mechanically opened their computers and stared at Sotoreo. The mesmerized look possessing their faces when Sotoreo shook their hands still remained.

The UN President cleared his throat and addressed the group: "Brothers, as you know, in the last two days two major milestones in our mission have been reached. I believe the international address with The Pope has planted seeds of unity in the minds of the populace around the world. The media will play and replay my speech calling for unity. This will sublimely prepare listeners' minds for The Final Phase. When the miracle effects of the implant are revealed the population of the world will be begging to receive it. The entire process of converging the world and eliminating the opposition should only take a few short years after The Appearing of our Ascended Master. He will sit upon his earthly throne and be worshipped as the only god. At the time of worship the third strand and the convergence will be complete."

Gabriella gasped at his words. "Chris, that is what Arcturus was leading me to. This will sound wonderful to the people and it will be an amazing experience into a paranormal existence. It captured me completely and I was entering the convergence when the prayers broke the stronghold."

She gasped once again when realization fully dawned on her. "The Final Phase. That's it... the convergence!"

Chris immediately turned to face her. "Exactly what does that mean, Gabi?" His dark eyes penetrated hers trying to assess exactly with what they were dealing.

A look of pain crossed her face as she remembered being sucked into a pseudo beauty of demonic deception. "It means you sell your soul to Satan. There is no hope for redemption."

Chris leaned back in his chair mentally processing her revelation. "And the implant will play into this whole scheme of things?"

Gabriella nodded her head. "Exactly. It's all beginning to make sense. I can see now how so many people have already bought into this lie and sold their souls like I almost did. There are people all around the world from every arena of life who have already converged: political people, entertainers, some very rich and famous people. They converged for power, fame, beauty, wealth and got everything they were promised...in exchange for their soul. But the implant...that will be a totally different hook for deceiving people into converging."

Something clicked in Chris' mind that connected some of the dots. "That emblem on those rings they wear, the symbol of an eye. I've seen that being used in every avenue of entertainment, even in children's animated programs. They've already subconsciously been preparing our minds for years, haven't they?"

"I believe you're right. This isn't anything new, it's just entering the final phase...just as they call it."

Sotoreo's next words pulled their attention back to the lodge. "After leaving The Vatican I flew directly to Geneva for The Awakening ceremony of CERN." He looked around the table and smiled. "We all know what that means."

The men looked at each other, nodding and smiling as their Pindar continued: "We had our lead scientist at CERN make a statement to the international media explaining the on-going Hadron collider tests. He gave just enough information to prepare for us a scientific platform to explain the vanishings. In fact, that will be our next step, brothers. Once we have alleviated the concerns about the missing, the world will sigh with relief and we can move forward with unity."

Sotoreo read the faces of the men around the table and answered the unvoiced question. "No, the masses will never suspect the scientific explanation is a hoax, not with the supernatural revelations that will soon take place at CERN."

"Many will know the truth, you monster!" Gabriella blurted from the bunker. "Just like we do. We know where the vanished went and how they got there and no lie out of hell will change that truth."

"That's one of the reasons they will want to shut us up, Gabi." Chris interjected. "That and knowing the truth about the implant, the convergence, and who the Antichrist really is. Anyone who gets in their way will be targeted for elimination, especially The Chosen."

The prophetic knowledge Gabriella possessed was now creeping deep into her consciousness with a new reality. Seeing the face of the man who would initiate the tribulation of the end of days and hearing him plot his diabolical scheme birthed a verisimilitude so overwhelming she could hardly focus.

"Are you okay?" Chris observed.

She nodded she was, but she wasn't being totally honest. She felt light-headed and her vision blurred. Leaning back on the headrest of her chair she closed her eyes waiting for the dizziness to pass.

"Do you need something, Gabi? Anything I can do?"

She shook her head and muttered breathlessly, "I'll be fine."

Chris focused on the activity in the lodge, but also kept a watchful eye on Gabriella. He knew this was not normal. The men were discussing various electronic implementations that would be used for the next news release from CERN. He rechecked all the recording devices to make sure they were capturing every word for replay. Everything looked to be in order. He glanced at Gabriella and she appeared to be resting so he made no effort at conversation. His attention focused on the technical analysis of Sotoreo's plans.

Gabriella did not know if she was dreaming or experiencing something more mysterious. She felt her body being immersed in a liquid peace and her breathing pattern slowed but was in perfect rhythm. She was completely motionless. She heard voices all around her. The voices were not Chris', nor the voices from the lodge, but the loving voices which had vanished from her life. She tried to force her eyes open but to no avail. She felt a familiar strong hand close around hers. She recognized the texture of his skin...the roughness from years of climbing rocks and digging in caves. She knew it was Caleb and her whole being longed to rise to him and wrap her arms around his strong chest, to feel the safety of his loving embrace just one more time.

She briefly felt agony in not being able to respond to his touch, but was soothed by the gentleness of his hand embracing hers while the voices continued to swirl around her. Her father's voice stood out strong as he was encouraging the team. "We won't doubt. We will keep praying and believing. It's not too late."

In the distance, she could hear Faith and Aaron praying Hebrew prayers of deliverance and protection. She rested in the sounds of their voices and the liquid peace that continued to wash over her. She made one last concerted effort to squeeze Caleb's hand and she felt the muscles tighten in her fingers.

Caleb's voice rang out. "She moved! Her fingers moved!" She desperately tried again to squeeze, but no movement would come. He dropped her hand, clutched her shoulders and gently shook her. "Wake up, Gabi. Wake up."

She felt hands firmly on her shoulders continuing to gently shake her. Finally, she forced her eyes open. She was staring into Chris' dark brown eyes. "Wake up, Gabi, wake up."

CHAPTER 30

"Gabi, wake up." Chris's voice was filled with concern noticing the blood had drained from her face. "Are you alright?" He shook her one more time clutching her shoulders tighter.

Gabriella forced her eyes open and then immediately closed them again, desperately wanting to feel Caleb's hand around hers and hear the voice of her father. She was teetering on anger Chris had awakened her. She nodded her head affirming she was okay but kept her eyes closed in hopes the liquid peace would return. It was too late: reality had recaptured her.

Chris sensing her agitation, dropped his hands; he kept watch until color returned to her face and her breathing appeared normal. He did not say a word until her eyes opened.

He exhaled in immense relief. "I was really worried about you, Gabi. I thought you were just resting but then I noticed your facial color. When I tried to wake you, you didn't budge. Are you okay?"

She could see perplexity in his eyes and knew she had to be totally honest. It was just the two of them against the world and there could be no secrets. "I don't know how to explain what's happening, Chris. I suppose it's just my grief taking over my senses, but I keep having dreams of before the vanishings: I'm in my bed still in soul sleep and I can hear what's going on in the room around me." She took a deep breath and avoided Chris' eyes as she confessed the most intimate part. "In my dreams, I woke up before the vanishings had occurred. I could see all my loved ones rejoicing over my awakening. I felt Caleb's arms around me, looked into the eyes of my father and truly believed I had awakened before it was too late." The last words lingered longingly upon her lips.

Chris got up and pulled her to her feet. He wrapped his protective arms around her and held her until the emotions settled. He knew no words were necessary.

She could hear the men on the monitors discussing the technicalities needed as they moved forward with implementation. She reminded herself there were much greater things pressing and the past had to be just that...the past. She knew deep inside she could not change it, although her heart still longed for those she loved.

She straightened her shoulders and Chris released her. She looked up at him and forced a smile. "I know, Chris. I know it's just as you said. My emotions are playing out in my dreams and mixing with reality. I'll be fine. Really I will." She sat back down in her chair and forced her attention to the monitors.

"I'll go get some coffee, Gabi. All this technical stuff I can replay later. I'll have to listen to it several times anyway to make the notes I'll need."

She nodded and Chris exited the security room. She was not even going to pretend to understand all the media technicalities that would be used to achieve Sotoreo's end goal. She thought of KJ and wished he could advise them. He would understand every detail of their plans. This was definitely his forte.

A sigh escaped her lips as she voiced her frustration. "How quickly life can change."

"You got that right," Chris answered her, carrying in a tray of caramel coffee. The fragrance filled the security room with a soothing aroma. She smiled as she sipped the hot liquid and he noted she was her normal self again. He thought it best to let the situation drop and refocus on the meeting in the lodge.

Sotoreo stood and stretched. "You've done a wonderful job, brothers. I know you've worked long and hard, you are about to see your efforts come to fruition." He walked to the massive window with the majestic view of Mt. Hermon in the distance. "Amazing, isn't it? The top of that mountain is where it all began. Our extraterrestrial brothers chose to leave their quintessential, celestial realm and enter our dimension of time through that stargate portal." He paused and dramatically pointed to the top of Mt. Hermon. "The war between the heavenly forces has waged ever since but soon The One will appear and bring a new age of peace, old things will pass away and everything will be made new. We will become one with him, our Ascended Master, our AM."

He turned and faced the men in the room. "From the time man was placed on this earth our AM has watched us, often having our celestial brothers to teach us and guide us. We have not been good stewards of what was given to us. We have brought ourselves to the point of destruction despite all the wisdom made available by our AM. We are a world filled with greed, racial bias, religious hatred, and international division." He walked back to his chair and announced before he sat down: "That will all soon end."

The brothers again chanted in a language unknown to Gabriella and Chris, but it took no linguist to translate the evil overtones.

Gabriella's anger was boiling again. "Chris, we know what came through that portal at the top of Mt. Hermon and it *was not* caring celestial brothers. Sotoreo has completely distorted the truth."

"Isn't that what Satan does?" Chris was not asking a question, but rather making the point. "Distort the Word of Yahweh to confuse and deceive?"

"Of course, it is." She punctuated. "And did you hear what they call the Ascended Master? Our AM? Yahweh said His name is I AM. Satan is making every effort to replace Yahweh and deceive the world into thinking he is God! And these evil men are preparing the way." She grudgingly halted her rampage with Sotoreo's announcement.

"Now, brothers, we will plan the timing for our first step into the Final Phase."

The duo in the bunker both instinctively leaned towards the monitors. The air in the security room became filtrated with anticipation. Chris reached for Gabriella's hand and squeezed. "Here we go, Gabi."

"Let's begin." Sotoreo took his seat. "The Final Phase will be done in six steps. We will quickly go down the complete list of steps and I will give you specific details as each step is implemented:

Step One – Mystery of the Vanishings Solved

Step Two – Signs in the Heavens

Step Three – The Black Pope assumes his position

Step Four – Tomorrow's Land Unity Festival/The Third Strand Implant begins

Step Five – Eliminate Russia & Conquer Israel

Step Six – The Appearing

You will see the first matter on our agenda is dealing with the chaos the vanishings have created. The stratagem is complete and you have everything ready to release the breaking news on our World Intelligence Network and via the internet. You will control every media outlet worldwide and will air this event in real time replaying it over and over. This will begin the programming of minds, the first step into total convergence."

Sotoreo leaned back in his chair and chuckled. "We can thank the U.S. President for turning over control of the internet to the UN in 2016 just before he left office. Aren't we fortunate it was before their electric grid was destroyed." Cynicism was apparent in his voice and it was completely obvious he knew Russia planned to attack America. "Amazing how much devastation can be caused by an EMP attack, isn't it? So sad."

The knowing sarcasm in his voice left no room for any remorse whatsoever for the millions of Americans who were suffering and dying every day.

"The fact the U.S. President wanted to be our UN Secretary General had nothing to do with the internet control decision." He chuckled again and winked. "He had no idea the UN was planning, for the first time, to elect a World President to bring the nations into the New World Order."

Gabriella's heart was breaking for her people in America. Being born and raised there, it was almost unbelievable to know the country was literally crumbling to nothing. The most powerful country in the world was gone forever. She looked at Chris voicing her pain. "I know it had to be. America was standing in the way of the One World Government. Everything in the world is shifting for prophecy to be fulfilled." Her words were matter of fact; however, it did not help settle the sorrow. "I'm not at all surprised the president was in on the whole deal."

Their focus was brought back to the monitors when Sotoreo announced the timing of this event. "Tomorrow begins the Feast of Tabernacles in Israel. They call it the season of joy and celebrate for seven days. Well, since Israel is the only country that stands in the way of the New World Order, we will use their holy celebration time to announce to the world where all the vanished went. We will create some joy of our own." Again, he released the annoying chuckle. "I am fully aware there are many people that are declaring the vanishing event was Christians being taken by their god. It's time we offer the nations a more palatable explanation. This will be a major step in preparing the minds for unity."

Strozza, who had been totally silent, stood and began to applaud. The men around the table followed suit. Their Cabal Pindar accepted their accolades with pride, as a diabolical smile crossed his lips. For several minutes the clapping continued. Finally, Sotoreo held up his hand as a signal to cease. Simultaneously, the men seated.

"Tomorrow I will return to Geneva to be present for the so called scientific explanation of the vanishings. Step One will be completed. Afterwards, I will be meeting with world leaders to implement Step Two. The Final Phase is about to begin, brothers."

Immediately all the men in the room rose to their feet and began their chant in an unknown language. Chris and Gabriella jointly felt the evil atmosphere vibrating in the lodge and continued to pray the bunker would be filled only with the Presence of Yahweh's Holy Spirit.

Sotoreo shook hands with all the men and Chris noticed for the first time it was a very odd handshake. "Look, Gabi. Look at Sotoreo's hand. His four fingers are separated in the middle when their hands clasp."

Chris grabbed his computer and tried to Google '33rd handshake' or find a picture of the weird hand formation. Every link had been blocked. "I know that handshake is a sign of some kind. The information on the internet is definitely being controlled and it's going to make it even harder to get the information we need."

Sotoreo announced he would be retiring for the evening and would leave immediately at dawn. "I will stay in communication with Strozza. He will keep you posted on the timing of events. I will return before the second step begins." Moretti stood at the door ready to accompany him to the cottage. Before he exited he turned and raised his hand. Again, the four fingers were separated in the middle. He disappeared through the door.

Chris and Gabriella simultaneously collapsed back in their chairs. "I am exhausted," Chris admitted. "I feel like I've run a marathon."

"Me, too," she admitted. "I'm too tired to even eat. I'm going to shower and go to bed." Immediately, her thoughts turned to her dreams. Silently, she hoped Caleb and her father would join her there.

"I'm going to try to work a little longer." Chris commented. "I want to review the film and make sure I didn't miss anything."

She gave him a pat on the shoulder as she passed him to exit the room. "Night, Chris."

Shortly she was in snuggled in her bed. She felt she had no more closed her eyes when a voice called her name.

"Gabriella, heed my words."

She opened her eyes to a mist surrounding her. She was no longer in her bed, but instead standing at the Temple Mount in Jerusalem. The mist began to clear and she could see the destruction left after the bombing of the Wailing Wall. A figure of a man stood in the distance. He was beckoning her to approach him. She walked cautiously across the rubble of fallen stones, and as she drew near, his image came into focus. Her breath caught when she again was gazing into the eyes of Elijah the Prophet. She knelt before the prophet and closed her eyes as he laid his hands upon her head

"Daughter of Zebulon, one of The Chosen, the time is at hand. Prepare yourself. Pray much, for soon I will appear in the streets of Jerusalem. I will come to declare the great deception that is descending upon the land of Israel. The 144,000 chosen ones will take their place of ministry to preach truth to the 12 Tribes of Israel who have been scattered among the nations but are now returning to their promised land. The children of Israel rejected Yeshua their Messiah, the Son of Yahweh, and have turned to false gods. In mercy, He will again draw them unto Himself." She kept her eyes closed waiting for his next words. His hands lifted from her head and they were replaced by a warm thick liquid spilling into her hair. "You are anointed and chosen for such a time as this. Do not fear. The Lord is with you."

The flow of the liquid stopped and the voice ceased. Opening her eyes, she was in her bunker bedroom. She sat straight up in the bed looking for any signs of her night visitor. The room was dark; however, the glow of the nightlight illuminated the room enough to see there was no one with her.

She turned the lamp light on, surveying the room once again. It was totally silent, totally empty of any other presence. Plopping back on her pillow she kept her eyes wide open. Unable to rest, she got up and started towards the kitchen. As she opened her bedroom door she heard familiar voices. Sitting in the rocking chair by the media center was the Professor. He was surrounded by the research team and they were listening to him read the translations from the ancient writings.

"In the day of the great judgment, a day of terror and affliction as never seen by man, the fallen Watchers will be released from the chambers of the abyss. My two witnesses will return to proclaim truth against them. I will give power unto my two witnesses, and they shall prophesy a thousand two hundred and sixty days; and when they shall have finished their testimony, the beast that ascends out of the bottomless pit shall make war against them, and shall overcome them, and kill them. Their dead bodies shall lie in the street of the great city for three days and a half day."

This was what the Prophet Elijah was just telling her. He would soon appear as one of the two witnesses. Her ministry as one of The Chosen was about to begin.

She moved around her loved ones trying to get their attention, to let them know she was with them, but no one could see her. She waved her hand in front of their faces to no avail. She could hear every word but no one could hear her.

She stood by Caleb and tried to take his hand. Her hand moved through his and made no contact. "What's going on?" She cried out to her loved ones but no one heard her voice.

In desperation, she ran to her bedroom. The door was open and she saw her father sitting on the side of the bed holding her in his arms. She went to his side and watched him, longing to feel his embrace. The look in his eyes was deep love mixed with overwhelming sorrow.

She cried out in desperation. "Help me, Heavenly Father! Help me understand what's happening." Collapsing on the floor she laid her head on the side of the bed and continued to cry out in prayer. Throughout the night her agony became an intercessory prayer in a language she did not comprehend. She was fully aware the Holy Spirit was praying through her, knowing how to pray according to the will of the Father.

When morning came, she opened her eyes. The room was empty of voices. She pushed herself up to the side of her bed looking for her father in the chair beside her, knowing he would not be with her.

She raised her hand to push the long curls from her face. The prophet's anointing oil still saturated her hair.

CHAPTER 31

The usual morning smell of coffee filtered into Gabriella's bedroom. The sound of Chris moving around the kitchen penetrated her lonely silence. Reluctantly she climbed from bed, brushed her hair into a ponytail, and joined him.

Chris had perfected the ability to ascertain her moods before speaking. "Another rough night, huh?" His voice was compassionate and concerned.

She simply nodded her head and gave no details. He carried a tray of coffee and muffins to the table in front of the TV. Gabriella settled into the couch with her much-needed morning brew and turned the volume up.

"Seems all stations are focused on CERN this morning." Chris commented hoping to open a conversation. "We know what they plan to do today, we just don't know the details. Curious to see how they're gonna pull this off and really get the world to buy in to their explanation of the vanishings." He paused to see if she was ready for dialogue.

She did not immediately answer. She was not ready to relinquish the feelings of the presence of her loved ones. Her dreams felt so vibrantly real. So much so, she felt as if her loved ones were still in the bunker with them. Shaking her head to bring her thoughts back to reality, she broke her silence trying to focus on the task at hand. "Me, too," she finally commented.

Michael Adelson could be heard reporting in the Channel 2 newsroom in Haifa although the cameras were live in Geneva, Switzerland. The statue of the god Shiva posed in his dance of destruction was positioned behind the podium where the address to the nations was to originate. The director of CERN was in the background talking with the delegation of world leaders who attended The Awakening ceremony.

Adelson's voice was behind the scenes giving an overview of the day's planned agenda. "Leaders from many nations have remained in Geneva for this monumental announcement. UN President Sotoreo will be arriving back at CERN late this afternoon for the news conference scheduled for 6:00 PM, Israeli time. Ironically, it will be at the same time Israel begins The Feast of Tabernacles. Across our nation citizens have been preparing for this seven-day celebration. All of Israel will be rejoicing for the return of multiple thousands of our people from the hostile nations. It has been reported the mystery announcement will be cause for all nations to unite and celebrate. We shall see." There was definite skepticism in the reporter's voice.

"Looks like we have all day to see how this first step plays out," Chris commented, taking the last sip from his coffee cup. "I'm going to the security room and review some of the tape. There's been no activity in the lodge this morning but I'll let you know when something happens."

Gabriella poured another cup of the fragrant liquid before answering. "I'll be right here if you need me." With a wave of her hand she motioned him to go. She treasured some time to be alone. She muted the TV and rested her head on the back of the couch. Closing her eyes, she whispered prayers for strength and courage in the coming days. "Father, I know this is not going to be easy but I rest in your love and your protection." She continued to pray until her mind could no longer form cognitive words. At that point the Holy Spirit began to pray through her in groaning and moaning she did not understand. However, she felt wave after wave of tranquility flowing through her.

What seemed to Gabriella a very short time became several hours. Chris came back to the kitchen for lunch and found her kneeling on the floor with her face gazing upwards. Tears were streaming across her cheeks but the weeping did not overshadow the glow permeating her face. The Presence filled the room. He said nothing but quietly sat at the kitchen bar and bowed his head. Tranquility continued to flow through the bunker until the security buzzer sounded. The brothers had again assembled around the table. Chris helped Gabriella to her feet and they quickly returned to the security room.

Moretti was setting up the lunch buffet. As they waited for him to finish, small talk ensued. Disjointed words and phrases were spoken that made no sense to the two listening below them. Chris looked at Gabriella and shrugged his shoulders in confusion. She nodded her head in perplexed agreement.

Once the men finished their meal, they opened their computers and a flurry of activity and conversation began. Strozza sat at the head of the table formerly occupied by the Pindar. "Let's get this ball rolling, brothers."

"I'm in," one confirmed after several minutes of computer activity.

"Me, too," said another.

"Looks like you're all connected and ready to implement," Strozza confirmed, gazing at his computer screen. All communication links and domain sites are set up to be overridden simultaneously. Every TV network and radio station will be airing by satellite or landline from CERN so, on cue, all communication services will be electronically seized by us and an international emergency alarm signal will activate alerting anyone in the world connected to any media source to see, hear, and believe in real time."

Smiles crossed the faces of all the men and excited chatter filled the room.

Chris gasped. "I had no idea this was even possible."

"Does it mean what I think it does?" Gabriella questioned.

"It sure does," he mused. "This is the reason the UN pressed for total control of all satellite and internet communications. They've been planning this all along, just waiting for the right time to implement. Whatever they're about to reveal about the vanishings, the whole world will know at the same time. And, apparently, it's going to be extremely convincing."

Simultaneously, Chris and Gabriella collapsed into the back of their seats. They looked at each other with expressions of grave concern and yet knowing all these things must be. It was 3:00 PM. They still had three hours before the official start of The Feast of Tabernacles and the CERN announcement.

"I'm going to my room to pray, Chris. The battle is about to begin." She rose from her seat and leaned over from behind Chris's seat to give him a quick hug. "Let's get ready to go to war."

He reached up and briefly held her hand. "You go to war on your knees praying. I'm going to war by staying right here and learning every tactic of our enemy I possibly can." Chris dropped her hand to refocus on the monitors.

Gabriella went to her bedroom and focused on hearing the voice of Yahweh. She continued in intercessory prayer until Chris knocked on her door and told her it was time.

She was spiritually and emotionally ready for whatever would take place. They sat side by side on the couch waiting for the clock to strike 6:00 PM. Chris had his laptop open and on-line to see what would happen at the precise moment the men upstairs hacked in and overrode all domain sites.

Exactly to the second both the TV and computer screen went black. Within seconds both transmissions were showing the podium at CERN with the statue of Shiva, the god of destruction, directly behind it. It was a subtle sign of what was about to transpire.

Three men moved to the podium and took their positions. The CERN Director stood to the right of UN President Sotoreo as expected. What they did not expect was Pope Romanus standing on his left.

A gasp of shock escaped Gabriella's mouth. "What in the world is he doing there?" She exclaimed.

"And the plot thickens," Chris retorted. "Just like your father warned you...watch The Vatican."

Sotoreo stepped closer to the microphone. In a confident and commanding voice, he addressed the viewers around the civilized world. "My brothers and sisters, no matter what color, religion, race or creed, we are all family as we unite as one people of the world to bring hope and a peaceful future for all nations. We have survived the most horrendous war known to mankind. We have been left with the aftermath of the vanishing of multi-millions from every nation. Hearts have been broken and families are grieving for those who suddenly disappeared with no explanation of why or where. Today I bring you the answer!"

Chris and Gabriella could hear the gasps of both the reporters and world leaders sitting in the audience. It was obvious they had no knowledge of what was to be announced. Neither the CERN Director nor The Pope gave any expression of surprise. They knew exactly what was about to unfold.

Sotoreo stepped back and allowed the director to approach the array of microphones. He cleared his throat before he began. "CERN has been an on-going project since its inception in 1954. Decades of research and development coupled with numerous experiments, many of which ended in failure, have proven we actually know very little about our universe."

He cleared his throat. A slight sardonic smile crossed his face. "I am going to put this in layman's terms for the masses around the world to understand. Few people know CERN was the birthplace of the World Wide Web in 1990, then known as ENQUIRE. The project was for sharing information with researchers around the world. This has allowed us to make tremendous strides and discoveries through the years in quantum mechanics including, but not limited to, the discovery of the god particle; understanding dark matter and perfecting a linear electron-positron collider with enhanced targeted acceleration to increase the impact energy."

He looked at Sotoreo and was given the nod to continue. "Let me explain it this way. The CERN collider is composed of thousands of superconducting electromagnets which together are 800,000 times more powerful than the gravitational pull of earth. These magnets are used to accelerate atoms to near the speed of light through a 17-mile circular tube. The atoms are then slammed together thereby tearing them apart and releasing sub-atomic particles billionths of a millimeter in size that were bound within the original atoms. The properties, actions and reactions of these sub-atomic particles as they relate to gravity and anti-gravity is what we have been primarily studying. As a result of these experiments, we are also investigating disrupting the space-time continuum and entering dimensions beyond the four in which we live."

He allowed time for the full impact of that statement on the minds of the listeners before he continued. Chris looked at Gabriella. Neither had any idea where he was going with all the technical information most of which, so far, was common knowledge to anyone following current astrophysics and quantum science.

The director continued: "We know the human body generates vibrational frequencies which create an electrical force field, often referred to as the body's aura. In our research of gravity and anti-gravity, we discovered how the human body's frequencies react to these energy forces. Children are born with very low vibrational frequencies. As they grow some remain low, most develop to mid-range, and very few become extremely high frequencies. We have found that lower body vibrational frequencies significantly decrease the body's resistance to anti-gravitational forces, resulting in said body being in a very unstable molecular state."

The director paused briefly and took a deep breath before continuing. "We cannot explain why, but apparently as children grow and develop conservative, antiquated, and especially strong Christian faith beliefs, they maintain very low frequencies. We have been testing why these low frequency bodies do not intensify. It appears to be connected to lack of broader development of the human mind and spirit." Again, he paused allowing the statement to root deeply in the minds of every listener.

After a lengthy pause, he continued with the scientific explanation. "We have learned how to harness the body's aura energy frequencies and create what formerly was considered paranormal abilities. But this discovery came with an unexpected major consequence."

"Oh!" Gabriella exclaimed. "That's the very thing Arcturus told me. He beguiled me into believing I had extremely high vibrational frequencies that allowed me to enter the paranormal world and become one with the universe. Everything he told me was a deceiving lie. Now the CERN Director is using the same terminology. There has to be a connection, Chris." Her voice was pleading for an explanation.

She began to shake, remembering Arcturus's mystical countenance and the web of paranormal diversion she was caught in. Chris put his arm around her shoulders in support. "There's nothing for us to fear, Gabi. We know it's a deception. It's the rest of the world that's about to fall for it hook, line, and sinker. They're the ones that need to be very afraid."

Chris abruptly stopped as the director continued: "Today we share this historical announcement with all the world...what went wrong in our experiment and what we have discovered."

The CERN Director stepped back and Sotoreo stepped to the microphones. With a conquering smile and a commanding voice, he addressed the listeners around the world. "We will now reveal why and where the vanished have gone."

There was not a sound in the massive audience of dignitaries, world leaders, and reporters. All ears were tuned to the voice of the UN President. "Less than three weeks ago CERN performed a new anti-gravity experiment. The Hadron collider smashed highly accelerated spinning atoms together with enough force that for the first time, the subatomic particles exceeded the speed of light. This resulted in their penetration into another dimension which we have since discovered is part of an entire parallel paranormal universe. It has long been speculated by scientists at

CERN if they ever accomplished this objective there would be no way of predicting what the interactions would be."

An air of total suspense and expectation hovered over everyone under the sound of Sotoreo's voice. "The instant the fabric was breached there was a reaction between the gravity and anti-gravity contained in the two alternate dimensions. The resulting reaction caused a momentary disruption to the universal laws of physics as they applied to each dimension. This in turn triggered cataclysmic seismic and atmospheric disturbances here on earth resulting in low-vibrational human babies, children, and adults worldwide being transported by molecular frequency distortion from our dimension to the alternate dimension. The physical damage to the Earth was limited to the massive earthquakes we experienced."

Gasps of disbelief from the live attendees penetrated the airwaves. Newsrooms around the world tried to regain control of the audio portion of the viewing for commentaries, but it was impossible. The men sitting in the lodge maintained total control of cyberspace and landline communications so Sotoreo could finish his deceptive speech completing the first step of the Final Phase before they released control.

The UN President held up his hand demanding silence. Immediately, silence permeated the air. "Do not be alarmed by this! We believe those who have vanished are living safely in this alternate universe. There will be more details released shortly. Also, The Vatican will soon make an official statement regarding the vanishings."

Sotoreo looked at The Pope who smiled and held his hands to the heavens. He approached the podium for a short statement. "We are on the precipice of miraculous world changing events. What we have believed and been taught all our lives will be challenged, but truth will prevail. We are living in a time as never has been on this earth. The days ahead are going to be a journey into a new world as we unite across the earth as one people." The Pope waved to the audience and stepped back to join The CERN Director and the UN President. The three joined hands and raised them above their heads in a motion of triumph.

World leaders at the CERN event stood and began to cheer. "Unite, unite, unite!" During the celebration, the men in the lodge released cyberspace back to the domain holders.

Michael Adelson's face immediately appeared on the TV screen. An expression of total disbelief engulfed his features. He stammered, trying to find the right words for this totally unexpected announcement.

"Viewers, what can I say?" He took a deep breath and tried to steady his voice. "We knew some explanation for the vanishings was forthcoming and since it was suspected that Israel was somehow involved, I expected a totally different scenario. Now we hear

CERN scientists caused the vanishings. Do we know this for sure? They have proven nothing, but there's no doubt their explanation will be the truth accepted by the media and perpetrated across the world. I'm confident the Israeli government will not immediately be endorsing this announcement. This certainly has overshadowed The Feast of

Tabernacles that began at sundown."

Gabriella's face was filled with fury. "And Sotoreo planned it that way," she snapped at the TV screen.

Chris' mind was still spinning with this supposed revelation of the missing. "Do you think the world will buy into this, Gabi? This is a lie right out of the pits of hell."

She quoted from II Thessalonians 2: "*The coming of the lawless one will be in accordance with how Satan works. He will use all sorts of displays of power through signs and wonders that serve the lie; and all the ways that wickedness deceives those who are perishing. They perish because they refused to love the truth and so be saved. For this reason, God sends them a powerful delusion so that they will believe the lie.*"

CHAPTER 32

————— •◦•◦• —————

While a celebration of complete success for the first step of the Final Phase took place in the lodge above, an uncertain silence filled the bunker. Gabriella and Chris sat speechless and motionless as the full impact of the CERN announcement infused their minds.

The WIN Network continued to replay around the world the explanation for the vanishings. Cameras on all continents showed celebrations and rejoicing as people accepted the pseudo explanation of the vanished ones.

Katja Lody reappeared on the screen addressing her international audience. "I am live in Vatican Square where the faithful are in jubilant fête. They rejoice in knowing the vanishing was not as previously rumored. It was not Israel behind the disappearances of multi-millions, nor was it some sort of holier than thou spiritual event, leaving the rest of us to face the wrath of an angry God."

She began to move through the crowd. "I want to get the reactions of some of those gathered here." Katja approached an elderly celebrator. "Sir, would you tell our viewing audience your reaction to this amazing scientific discovery?" She held the microphone for him to speak.

The man spoke in English with a heavy Italian accent. "Hallelujah, what a day! I knew the fabricated reports of the missing being caught up by Jesus Christ had to be lie. I am a Christian. I believe in our Holy Mother, the Virgin Mary. I have confessed my many sins, prayed my rosary prayers and attended masses all my life. It was just a fabricated hoax, misinterpreting the Bible for people to say Jesus took his...so-called bride, the church. That is ridiculous." He pointed behind him to The Vatican. "The Pope is still here. Enough said."

Katja nodded in agreement and made her own personal notation. "If our Holy Father, the infallible leader of the Roman Catholic Church is not righteous, then none is righteous. If in fact Jesus had come for the church, The Holy Father would have been the first to go."

She continued to move through the crowd getting reactions. "All are in agreement," Katja reported with an arrogant attitude. "The fallacy of the vanishings or so called rapture of the church is just that…a fallacy. Science and religion have united and we are now entering a new world of truth. With the discovery of parallel universes containing anomalous dimensions, everything we have believed is about to be challenged. I will be covering live The Vatican's announcement on this momentous scientific discovery. The time will soon be announced. This is Katja Lody reporting from Vatican Square in Rome."

The WIN Network faded black momentarily, a sign the signals were being carefully controlled. The main WIN newsroom in Rome took over with commentaries and replays of the evening announcement.

Chris changed the station back to Channel 2 in Haifa. "Let's find out what's really going on," he commented with a voice edged in sarcasm towards the WIN reporter.

Adelson and Rabbi Zimmerman were in a heated discussion. The Rabbi was not believing for one minute the report of the missing being sucked into a parallel universe.

His voice was deep and stern as he commented. "Those of us that believe the Torah, the prophets, and the holy writings know this scientific explanation is some sort of deception. I have no idea what the UN, in cahoots with the Catholic Church is planning, but the outcome is not going to be good."

Adelson pushed for a deeper interpretation. "What is your opinion of the vanishings, Rabbi Zimmerman?"

The Rabbi's eyebrows narrowed and a look of certainty crossed his face. "A few weeks ago, my opinion would have been totally different from what it is today. I have had a divine revelation." He paused, took a deep breath and boldly announced: "Years ago, I studied the Christian view of what they call the *harpazo* or rapture of the church. I also studied the New Testament as a student of historical writings. I saw, in many ways, the writings to be connections to our Torah but slanted to the Christian view as they claimed Yeshua became the Passover Lamb of Israel. I was fully aware Yeshua lived and died claiming to be the Son of Adonai and He came to save the world. At that time, I considered it to be much like the Quran of the Muslim religion which also is a takeoff from the Torah; however, the Quran is a total mockery of the Holy Word. The Muslims make Allah the Supreme Being and do not acknowledge Adonai God at all."

The Rabbi cleared his throat and again took a deep breath. He leaned slightly toward Adelson as the next words shocked not only Michael Adelson but every listener to Channel 2.

"On the Day of Atonement, the day of the acceptable fast of the Lord, I was in my 25 hours of prayer and fasting as we are commanded in the Torah to do. I cried out to Adonai with an open heart, pleading to understand the things that were happening in our nation and in our world. In the last hour of the holiest day known to man, I opened my Tanakh to Isaiah 53. I would like to read this to you." The Rabbi paused, waiting for permission to continue.

Adelson nodded for him to proceed.

The Rabbi's voice slightly quivered as he read the prophetic words from Isaiah the prophet:

"Who has believed our message
and to whom has the arm of the LORD *been revealed?*
He grew up before him like a tender shoot,
and like a root out of dry ground.
He had no beauty or majesty to attract us to him,
nothing in his appearance that we should desire him.
He was despised and rejected by mankind,
a man of suffering, and familiar with pain.
Like one from whom people hide their faces
he was despised, and we held him in low esteem.
Surely he took up our pain
and bore our suffering,
yet we considered him punished by God,
stricken by him, and afflicted.
But he was pierced for our transgressions,
he was crushed for our iniquities;

the punishment that brought us peace was on him,
  and by his wounds we are healed.
We all, like sheep, have gone astray,
  each of us has turned to our own way;
and the LORD *has laid on him*
  the iniquity of us all.
He was oppressed and afflicted,
  yet he did not open his mouth;
he was led like a lamb to the slaughter,
  and as a sheep before its shearers is silent,
  so he did not open his mouth.
By oppression and judgment he was taken away.
  Yet who of his generation protested?
For he was cut off from the land of the living;
  for the transgression of my people he was punished.
He was assigned a grave with the wicked,
  and with the rich in his death,
though he had done no violence,
  nor was any deceit in his mouth.
Yet it was the LORD's *will to crush him and cause him to suffer,*
  and the LORD *makes his life an offering for sin."*

Tears were streaming down Rabbi Zimmerman's face. His entire countenance was glowing as he continued to speak. "This prophecy written 2700 years ago has been withheld from the understanding of our Jewish people. Blinders have been upon our eyes. I prayed they would be lifted from my eyes allowing me to see the truth...and they were. As the Day of Atonement ended, the Prophet Elijah appeared to me in a vision. He told me to heed the writing of Isaiah. The prophecy had already been fulfilled. He poured anointing oil over my head and told me I am among The Chosen to declare the truth to the lost tribes of Israel." The tears flowed down his face disappearing into his long gray beard. He waited for a response.

Adelson's face was questioning. It was obvious he had no idea the depth of meaning the rabbi was about to disclose. "What exactly does that mean, Rabbi?"

Boldly and without apology Rabbi Zimmerman stated: "Yeshua was and is the Son of Adonai. He is our Passover Lamb. I do believe there was a secret catching away of those who had accepted Yeshua as their blood atonement, the event the world is calling the vanishing. They did not go into some parallel universe discovered by CERN. Those that disappeared were caught up to be with Yeshua, the Son of the Yahweh the one true God, and forever they will be with The Lord. The Holy Word says believers were not appointed to the day of wrath. That is where we are on Adonai's calendar today, Michael. We are entering the day of wrath, the final judgment."

The Rabbi paused allowing a moment for his words to process. Then he continued with words of hope. "After the great tribulation upon the earth, Israel's eyes will be opened and Yeshua will return to Jerusalem and set up his earthly kingdom. I have been anointed to declare the truth to the Nation of Israel so they will not be deceived by this great deception being perpetrated upon the pagan nations. A one world demonic religion is beginning to consume the world. Israel must turn to Adonai for protection. We must not be caught in this web of satanic lies." He paused for a moment and made his final statement debunking the supposed scientific discovery. "There is no parallel universe where everything is wonderful. The dimension they have pierced into is the supernatural evil realm where demonic spirits dwell. A satanic attack is about to be unleashed upon earth like nothing the world has ever seen. Deceptions and lies on all levels are about to unfold. The fallen angels held in captivity until the day of judgment are about to be released from the abyss."

Adelson was speechless. This was like something out of a sci-fi movie. There was not a sound in the newsroom. No crew member was sure what to do. The cameras stayed focused on Adelson and the Rabbi, waiting for one of them to break the uncomfortable silence.

Rabbi Zimmerman's voice quivered as he admitted, "I know I have just put my life in jeopardy, but I have no fear for Adonai is with me." Then his voice instantly took on strength and exuberance. "Israel is now celebrating the Feast of Tabernacles. We celebrate despite a world in total chaos. For me personally, I am living in total joy. On the Day of Atonement, I was spiritually set free by the blood of the Lamb of Adonai God, Yeshua my Messiah."

The TV producer motioned for them to cut from the station's newsroom to silence the rabbi. Instantly, the cameras at the Temple Mount took over the news. A young reporter obviously was struggling to maintain his composure after reeling from the rabbi's words. He managed to gain verbal control and report on his surroundings. "Here at the Temple Mount thousands have gathered to celebrate The Feast of Tabernacles and the returning of our brothers and sisters from around the world. Many continue to mourn the loss of the Wailing Wall and declare it is time to rebuild the temple."

The camera panned the area for a visual of the people of Israel in celebration. TV viewers could hear in the reporter's background voices ringing in unison, "We will rebuild, we will rebuild." Those at the Temple Mount had not seen the news conference just held with the Rabbi Zimmerman. It was yet to be determined what the full impact of his words would have on the orthodox rabbis.

Gabriella broke the silence in the bunker. "The Prophet Elijah continues to anoint The Chosen."

Chris detected an overtone of dread in her voice. "Remember He will not leave nor forsake us, Gabi. You are chosen and nothing will happen to you except that which Yahweh permits."

"I know," she sighed. "It's not going to be easy even with God on our side." She remembered the scripture Professor Brotman had often quoted from Matthew 24. *"For then there will be great distress, unequaled from the beginning of the world until now--and never to be equaled again."*

She sighed again wondering why she had been chosen. "It makes sense a Rabbi respected by Israel would be among The Chosen. At least he has a platform for his voice to be heard. I have no earthly idea what I'm supposed to do."

Chris put his arm around her shoulder comforting her. "When the time comes, it won't be an earthly idea...it will be a heavenly leading, and you will know exactly what to do."

CHAPTER 33

Gabriella and Chris spent the remainder of the evening going back and forth from the WIN international news and Channel 2 Israeli News. WIN TV continued replaying the momentous revelation of where the vanished had gone. Most of the world accepted the scientific explanation without question. Israeli News continued to doubt the validity of the CERN announcement believing it was a ploy by the United Nations to gain world control.

Israeli News also replayed Rabbi Zimmerman's big reveal which was causing a major controversy among the Orthodox Jews. They were calling him a black sheep among the rabbis, a danger to the nation, a spiritual deception. They even wanted him arrested and tried by the Sanhedrin Court which had been reformed in preparation of the rebuilding of the Jewish Temple.

"This is crazy." Chris's irritated voice interjected between the news reports. "Something has to happen to get Israel's attention, Gabi. Something so big the blinders will fall from the eyes of God's chosen people."

She sat quietly for a moment mentally assessing the chain of prophetic events her father had left her. She stared at Chris with revelatory eyes. "You're right. There will be and it's one of the main pieces to the puzzle," she stated with unwavering conviction. "The event that will wake up Israel to hear the voice of The Chosen will be the Gog and Magog War. Don't you see, Chris? It makes total sense. When Yahweh dramatically and supernaturally protects us from destruction, our people will know it was the God of their fathers who delivered them. The voices of The Chosen will declare the truth and Israel will finally begin to open their spiritual eyes." She paused thinking about another main piece of the puzzle. "What will fully open all eyes, is when the Antichrist enters the rebuilt temple and declares himself as God. That's when all hell breaks loose...literally."

The bunker duo knew the prophetic time was at hand. The war Ezekiel prophesied 2500 years' prior, was soon to be. The Temple Institute was already planning to rebuild the temple. Nothing or no one could stop these events. For hours, the two secluded in the bunker discussed the possibilities of how these prophecies would play out, how Israel would respond, and how The Chosen's ministry would reach the nation of Israel.

Gabriella got up and stretched. "With all the possibilities for coming events, the only thing we know for sure is it *will* happen and all of our speculating will not change a thing. I'm too tired to even think about it anymore tonight. I'm going to bed, Chris."

He watched her cross the floor and disappear into her bedroom. "Sweet dreams, Gabi. Sleep well." And he prayed she would.

She closed the door behind her, changed into her pajamas and slipped between the cotton sheets. As was her nightly routine, she pulled Caleb's letters from her nightstand and read until she fell asleep. His words of eternal love echoed over and over in her soul like the never-ending waves of the seashore.

His written words became so powerful they overcame her senses. She could literally hear Caleb's voice whispering in her ear: *"Gabi, I believe you can hear me. Even though you cannot respond in words or movement, I still believe you hear every word and you will return to me before it's too late. Wherever your soul is, I'm calling you back to me with a love so deep it transcends the very essence of time and untime. I know it. I believe it. Somehow, someway, you hear me and know my love for you is eternal. Give me a sign, my love, any sign you hear my voice."*

Desperately, she tried to move, to speak, to give Caleb the sign he painfully desired, the sign she could hear his words. Nothing moved. She was frozen in time without any self-control. Her heart was breaking with desire to reach to him. Emotional pain welled inside her, pushing to the point of explosion. She could feel tears burning in her eyes. One lone tear escaped, caught in her long eyelashes, and cascaded down her cheek.

"Oh, my God!" Caleb's voice exclaimed. "She's still with us."

Gabriella heard the excited voice of her father moving closer to her. "Thank you, God, thank you." He grabbed her hand and clutched it to his face. She felt the roughness of his unshaved beard against her soft hand. His burning tears cascaded across her skin. "Open those beautiful blue eyes, my princess. Wake up, please wake up."

The voices of Dr. Brotman and the rest of the team surrounded her, all praying for another sign she was still with them. Another tear slid from her closed eyes. The voices surrounding her were rejoicing for the slightest of signs proving her soul was not lost forever.

She managed to force her eyes open, fully expecting to be surrounded by those she loved. Only the glow of the nightlight greeted her. The room was empty and void, just as her heart was.

She slid from between the sheets and knelt beside her bed. The rest of the night she spent in prayer, pleading for release from her prison of loss. Toward morning she finally slept, without dreams and without voices. When she awakened, she was lying on the floor.

She pulled herself to the bedside, closed her eyes, and tried futilely to recapture the voices of her loved ones. There were no voices, no rejoicing, no words of love, only the sound of silence. It had become her familiar morning companion.

She stretched back on the bed to rest, but sleep evaded her. "Oh well," she finally accepted the obvious, "I guess I'll be the one making the morning coffee."

As she entered the kitchen, she could hear the shower running and knew Chris was awake. Coffee made and muffins in the oven, she settled into the sofa prayerfully analyzing her dream encounters.

Shortly Chris joined her. "Morning, Gabi. How did you sleep?" One look at her and the question was answered.

"Very little but I think I've figured this out." Her voice was tempered with a definite resolve.

"Really?" He raised his eyebrows. "And what's the conclusion?"

She turned to face him. Her eyes were crystal clear but he could not help but notice the puffiness from the lack of sleep.

"My dreams are constantly going back to before the vanishings. Other than the dreams of The Prophet, they are all centered around Caleb, my father, and often the voices of the others that were in the bunker, too. I can hear them talking to me, feel them touching me. I'm sure I'm reliving what happened while they were still here, when I couldn't wake up. It feels real, Chris, because it is real! Do you understand what I'm saying? It must be so deeply branded into my subconscious that my extreme desire to be with them keeps the events, which took place in the bunker before the vanishings, replaying over and over during my sleep."

Chris did not respond immediately. He had already assessed her dreams were related to the feelings of her tremendous loss. He had not considered her subconscious mind was replaying the actual events occurring before her loved ones disappeared.

"After you wake up do you remember details, like what they've said and done? Or is it more of a blur?"

"I remember details. Every word, every touch." A smile crossed her face at the thought of her dream encounters. "In fact, my dreams feel like they are my true reality and then I wake up to this reality." Her smile quickly faded.

"Sorry, Gabi. I really am. I wish you didn't have to wake up to just me and the future we're facing. With all my heart, I do wish you could wake up and still be in the bunker surrounded by your loved ones and before the vanishings, before it was too late. I wish we both could and know what we know now."

She forced a smile, "If only."

Trying to push her dreams back into her subconscious and face her current reality, she turned on the TV for the latest updates.

WIN TV was reporting additional press releases would soon be forthcoming from CERN regarding the vanishing and the parallel universe. Also, The Vatican was preparing their official statement of CERN's unprecedented discovery and a full endorsement was expected from The Holy See. Israeli news continued to focus on the Rabbi Zimmerman controversy. The only reference to CERN and the vanishings was Israel was no longer suspected to be involved in the mysterious disappearances.

The security alarm signaled morning activity in the lodge. The bunker duo took their coffee and settled in their leather chairs to watch the follow-up meeting to the first step of The Final Phase. During their breakfast, there was a scurry of conversation. Strozza was applauding their cyber success. An attitude of major accomplishment was evident on the countenances of the brothers.

Strozza stood before the men and verbal accolades flowed from his mouth. "Without a single hitch, step one was implemented. From all reports, most of the world now believe they know where the vanished have gone, even though they have no idea what it means. The Christian scenario of a rapture has been completely nullified. We can now continue to step two. Sotoreo will not be rejoining us until after this next step. He is conferring with world leaders. He is confident, as I am, that you are ready to implement. We just need to recheck all systems and verify with him we are ready to go." The men opened their computers and activity began.

"Well, I wonder what's next in their countdown to the end playbook," Chris commented sarcastically.

As if he had heard the question, Strozza continued. "Tomorrow evening Pope Romanus will address the nations with The Vatican's official statement on the parallel universe. He will begin to prepare the world population for the revelation and spiritual awakening which will unite us all into one. I assume all cyber control is ready." He stated it more in the form of an expectation than a question.

"Yes, sir," was the reply.

Strozza chuckled and then voiced his thoughts out loud. "Very few people know Vatican City was built over the site of the ancient temple of Cybele, the virgin mother of the gods." A dubious smile spread across his fiendish face as he proudly announced: "Another portal is about to open, brothers."

The duo in the bunker knew exactly what to expect. The men around the table broke into their nefarious chant and continued until Strozza held up his hand.

Strozza was satisfied his point had been made and continued with the plans. "Immediately after The Pope's address, Tomorrow's Land Unity Festivals will begin in every civilized nation, drawing millennials across the planet together to experience the spirit of oneness. When we control the minds of the young, the final steps will easily ensue. Our AM will appear to bring order from the soon coming renewed chaos and the third strand will be the final step to a new world...unified in government, economy, and religion."

The familiar eerie chant began around the table in the lodge. Cold chills ran up and down Gabriella's spine as the sound of the evil voices invaded the security room. She clutched Chris' hand for support. He slightly squeezed, reassuring her they were safe; however, his eyes stayed focused on the monitors.

Strozza rose from his seat and walked to the panoramic window. The morning sun streamed across the majestic apex of Mt. Hermon creating a mystical backdrop. Strozza stared at the mountaintop and turned to address the brothers.

"The first portal through which our brothers came is within our view. Another portal will soon appear."

"This is just the beginning of what people will not believe even though it is the truth. But will believe a lie and be damned."

CHAPTER 34

T he bunker security room was silent as Chris and Gabriella listened to Strozza give the checklist for the end of days. The uncomfortable silence was broken by Chris. "Guess we have an outline on how this is gonna go down."

Gabriella nodded in agreement finding it difficult to articulate her disdain for the evil plan being devised. Her voice was shaking while she expressed the certainty of soon-to-be events. "The portal they are planning is exactly what The Omega Watchers project was all about, the return of the fallen angels."

She repeated the Professor's warnings: "Satan will appear as a star falling to the earth. He will then release the fallen angels from the abyss." She felt deep remorse remembering her reaction to his prophetic words. "When the Professor would tell us this I thought it was crazy. If what he described really happened, people would realize it was evil. I am getting a much clearer picture of how the deception could work now."

"Until I met you, I had no idea of any of this. That's the way most of the world is. Between the entertainment business and the ancient alien theories, most people's minds have been conditioned to all the sci-fi craziness and nothing will surprise them." Chris punctuated.

"You're absolutely right. It's been a mental set-up for decades preparing the minds for the great deception; and tomorrow night it all begins when the wolf in sheep's clothing will make his big announcement endorsing the parallel universe. The infallible Pope is about to rewrite what the Catholic Church believes." Her tone was filled with extreme sarcasm as she used the specious word infallible to describe the man who would be the False Prophet.

Their attention was drawn back to the lodge meeting by a hypnotic sound. "What is that?" Gabriella immediately recognized the mental influence of the mesmerizing sound.

"They seem to be running some kind of test." Chris answered fully fixated on the monitors.

Gabriella covered her ears. "I can't listen to that. That's pure evil."

The sound stopped. Strozza nodded giving his approval. "Perfect, absolutely perfect. When the music plays the spirit of unity will infiltrate the minds of the listeners. Immediately after The Pope's announcement the Tomorrow's Land seduction will begin."

The satanic chant of the brothers echoed through the lodge main area. Strozza raised his voice above the evil utterances. "We are at the dawn of a new day." He lifted his hand with his fingers parted in the middle. "Let the convergence begin!"

"I've got to get out of here." Gabriella swiftly exited the security room to escape the vile chants.

Chris muted the sound on the monitors and observed the activity only. Even though she was out of voice range, he commented. "I totally agree."

Chris spent the entire day monitoring the lodge. Gabriella read her father's letters, praying for wisdom to face the days ahead. Periodically she would turn on the TV for any new updates of world events. WIN TV's CERN news kept saturating the airwaves. The most anticipated event was The Pope's address to the world to be given the following day.

Channel 2 in Haifa belabored Rabbi Zimmerman's heretical announcement. The Sanhedrin continued to press for a trial of heresy against Zimmerman.

Gabriella whispered to the TV screen, "Hold on, Rabbi. You're not alone in knowing the truth. Israel's spiritual eyes will soon be opened and her ears will once again hear. Yahweh is raising up a mighty army whose sword will be the Word of God."

Gabriella returned to the security room to tell Chris an early goodnight. "If you need me, don't hesitate. I'm turning in early." As she turned to exit her father's bedroom, her eyes rested on the black box in the corner. She sat down on his bed and gently caressed the worn leather. She spoke as if the inanimate object could hear her warnings.

"Those evil men upstairs would give anything to find you. They've been chasing you all over the world and now you're literally right here under their feet and they have no idea." She looked up and Chris was watching her with a smile.

"Rather satisfying, isn't it? God sure works in mysterious ways." He came to the bedside and pulled her to her feet. Giving her a quick hug, he gently pushed her towards the door. "Go on to bed, Gabi. Get some rest."

With a forced smile, she disappeared. Settling in her bed, she had barely begun to read Caleb's next letter until she fell fast asleep. Immediately the familiar voice of her father could be heard. No muscle in her body would move but her hearing was perfect. Her mind was at full attention when her father used the word "secret" in his conversation with Caleb.

"In 1917 an apparition declaring to be the Virgin Mary appeared to three Portuguese children and revealed to them prophecies of the future. There have been hundreds of reports of Marian apparitions, but very few receive ecclesiastical approval by the Catholic Church. The Holy See declared the Portuguese appearing as the most important prophecies of the end of days given by the Holy Mother. It's referred to as the Three Secrets of Fatima."

Caleb interrupted her father asking, "Do you believe it's really Mary the Mother of Jesus in these apparitions?"

"No, Caleb, I definitely do not," her father responded vehemently. "When a person dies, their spirit cannot return. However, a demonic familiar spirit pretending to be that person can. These evil spirits possess great power and knowledge which people blindly believe and follow."

"You mean like Arcturus deceived Gabi?" Gabriella could hear the pain in Caleb's voice as he questioned her father.

"Exactly, Caleb. There are all sorts of paranormal deceptions taking place preparing the world for a major world-changing event, opening the supernatural door for the Antichrist. These apparitions of the Mother Mary will somehow play into the end time deception."

Gabriella felt the mattress on her bed slightly elevate as her father rose to his feet. She heard his footsteps cross the floor and fade away. After a few minutes, he returned to her bedside. She could hear him shuffling through papers and mumbling to himself. "I know I have it." The shuffling continued until finally he announced: "Yes, yes, here it is."

"The first two secrets of Fatima involved World War I and World War II and were very precise. However, the third secret was sealed and was not to be revealed until the time determined by The Vatican. Suspicions of what it contained grew and grew over the decades until the church was pressured into releasing the final secret. It was released in 2000 but fell far short of the prophetic mystery that had built around the infamous secret for decades. Many believe the complete prophecy has not yet been revealed. I believe there is more to be announced by The Vatican when the prophetic time is right."

Gabriella again heard the shuffle of papers and her father's voice announcing, "I'm going to read to you what was released."

His voice was reflective as he recited the Third Secret of Fatima as given by The Roman Catholic Church Holy See. "*At the left of Our Lady and a little above, we saw an Angel with a flaming sword in his left hand; flashing, it gave out flames that looked as though they would set the world on fire; but they died out in contact with the splendor that Our Lady radiated towards him from her right hand: pointing to the earth with his right hand, the Angel cried out in a loud voice: <u>Penance</u>, <u>Penance</u>, <u>Penance</u>!*"

Her father briefly paused. His voice was edged with perplexity. "This last sentence I'm going to read to you has been a real conundrum for me and for Dr. Brotman. We have spent hours speculating on the prophetic meaning and have come to no reasonable hypothesis. We both believe it will be some type of paranormal event that will happen and be a major part of the False Prophet's deception to declare the Antichrist."

In a perplexed voice, her father finished the Third Secret of Fatima: "And we saw in an immense light that is God: something similar to how people appear in a mirror when they pass in front of it."

Gabriella heard Caleb sigh in frustration. "There seems to be a limitless number of pieces in this puzzle of deception. It makes my head spin just thinking about it; and if Gabi is left behind, who is going to explain all this to her? How will she know what to believe?"

Even though Gabriella could not see Caleb, in her mind's eye she knew exactly his firm jaw that would be locked, his blue eyes squinted and the frustration that would cover his face. She had seen that same countenance many times when they were up against archeological mysteries. She longed to reach to him, to put her arms around his waist and lay her head on his shoulder. Desire burned within her to feel his strong arms hold her one more time and his words of love whispered in her ear. The familiar agony of soul washed over her and tears burned in her eyes. She tried to force the tears from her eyes as evidence she was with them. After several attempts, she felt the warm liquid escape and run down her cheek. She anxiously waited, knowing Caleb would once again see her tears as a sign she heard their voices.

"Gabi, wake up." She heard a familiar voice calling her name. Her eyes flew open fully expecting to see Caleb standing by her bed. Instead, Chris' face looked down upon her.

"Wake up, you have to see this." His voice was urgent. "Hurry," he called over his shoulder as he rushed backed to the security room.

Gabriella kicked the covers off and pushed the blonde curls from her eyes. Slipping into her house shoes she quickly joined Chris. His eyes were glued to the monitors as he motioned for her to sit down.

"You're not going to believe this, Gabi." His voice was raspy with a mixture of excitement and amazement. "I've been up most of the night watching these guys running their cyber tests for The Vatican's announcement. None of it made much sense until the last hour. Not only will The Pope endorse the CERN explanation for the vanishings, they are planning a much bigger event. The Enlightened Ones and The 33rds around the world will be chanting at the same time, calling up from the abyss the demonic familiar spirit of the Goddess Cybele. Remember Strozza talked about her last night? Only she will appear as the Virgin Mary. It's obvious they plan to use this event to convince the world a new age of religion with miraculous signs and wonders has dawned."

She sat motionless and speechless staring at the monitor as Chris continued: "From what I can tell from their conversations there's no doubt the spirit will appear and the men upstairs will make sure the whole world sees. I heard some of the sounds they will generate when the apparition appears and it will be spellbinding."

"This is so weird," she mused. "I was just dreaming of something kind of like this."

Chris turned his chair to face Gabriella. "What do you mean... like this?"

She shared with Chris everything her father had said concerning the Three Secrets of Fatima. "See what I mean, Chris? Those three children in Portugal saw a scene in the sky which they thought was the Virgin

Mary. She spoke to them and gave them prophecies which have already happened. Doesn't that sound a lot like what these men are planning for tonight, a Marian Apparition?"

He mentally processed her dream encounter. "It sounds too much like the same thing to be a coincidence. Perhaps the Holy Spirit was warning you, Gabi, allowing you to remember your dad's words." Chris briefly paused, "So you wouldn't be deceived."

"You're absolutely right; these are warnings." She echoed. With that resolve, the dreams became a blessing and not a source of pain.

The men on the monitors in the lodge took a break for breakfast and coffee. The bunker duo did the same. Breakfast was accompanied by WIN TV news and Channel 2 Israeli news. Both networks were devoting all coverage to The Pope's imminent announcement of The Vatican's response to CERN's scientific breakthrough.

Katja Lody's smiling face appeared on the WIN network. The backdrop was the familiar St. Peter's Square which continued to be filled with parishioners more hopeful now for a spiritual light in the world darkness.

The camera focused on the papal balcony at the center of St. Peter's Basilica from which Pope Romanus would address the world. The reporter's voice was filled with excitement awaiting the appearance of the Holy Father. "We are just hours away from The Vatican's response to the unprecedented CERN discovery. We will soon know if The Holy See embraces the announcement of a parallel universe. If so, how does this align with the holy scriptures and the traditional beliefs of the Roman Catholic Church?"

Lody waved her hand towards the massive gathering around her. "Tens of thousands are waiting in Vatican Square for the answer. Millions across the world will be gathered around their televisions, computers, cell phones...any media source available to finally have the answer we all desire. Just where did the vanished ones go and can they return?"

Gabriella temporarily muted the sound to address Lody's last comment. "Chris, this could be the catalyst to the appearance of the Antichrist. My dad told me to watch The Pope for answers."

Chris nodded his head as he answered, "We just need a few more details to fill in. I'm going back to the security room. Don't wanna miss anything."

Chris returned to the security room while Gabriella monitored the news. Rolling over and over through her mind was the final sentence of the third secret. "What could this possibly mean?" she asked herself as she quoted the prophecy out loud. *"And we saw in an immense light that is God: something similar to how people appear in a mirror when they pass in front of it."*

Numerous scenarios played out in her mind, but nothing seemed plausible. However, she realized whatever it was it would appear to be a spectacular, miraculous event with great signs and wonders...just as the biblical prophecies forewarned.

Mentally frustrated, she joined Chris in the security room. "Anything new?"

"They're performing the same tests over and over to assure no kinks develop at show time. I'll let you know if anything new comes up."

With some time to herself, she returned to the privacy of her bedroom to meditate and pray. Kneeling on the floor with her Bible in hand, she began praying for wisdom and discernment. Hours were spent in intercessory prayer as The Presence saturated the room. Late afternoon she opened her eyes to a bright light. The glow moved from a corner of the bedroom towards her taking the shape of a man as it grew closer. Instantly she knew The Prophet Elijah had returned to visit her. His eyes were piercing as he drew near. She tried to look away but her eyes were locked into his gaze.

"Daughter of Zebulon, the great deception begins. The wolf in sheep's clothing will lure the nations with signs and wonders preparing the way for the lawless one, the man of sin, who is the Antichrist. Do not be afraid for The Lord is with you." He held out his hand and touched her head. She closed her eyes awaiting his next words, but the room was silent. When her eyes reopened, Elijah had vanished. The only remaining sign of his visit was oil dripping from her forehead.

CHAPTER 35

Gabriella basked in The Presence filling her room until there was a knock on the door. "Are you awake, Gabi?"

She knew it was time. The great deception was about to begin. "Coming," she answered. She forced herself from the floor and momentarily sat on her bedside, allowing just a few more moments in the holy atmosphere.

When she opened the door to join Chris, he felt The Presence filtering from her bedroom. As she stepped closer he noticed the oil in her hair. It was obvious she had again been visited by The Prophet.

She sat down on the couch and motioned for him to sit beside her. She turned the TV to Israeli news knowing it would be unbiased. Michael Adelson was joined by numerous commentators, both religious and scientific.

Adelson was giving an overview of what to expect. "There is an estimated 150,000 people packed into St. Peter's Square with tens of thousands more throughout Vatican City. All reporters and cameramen on site are focused on the papal balcony awaiting the appearance of Pope Romanus. Immediately after The Vatican's response to CERN's announcement we will be back live in our Haifa newsroom."

The cameras in Vatican City took over the news feed panning the massive crowd gathered for the momentous occasion. A reverent hush filtrated the air as the faithful parishioners filled with unprecedented expectation silently prayed.

Gabriella broke the silence in the bunker. "All those people are waiting for the endorsement of their infallible leader. They will believe every word he says." She took a breath and exhaled slowly. "The great deception begins."

At that moment, the man dressed in white stepped from behind the veiled curtains and onto the sacred balcony. His linen robe swayed methodically in the fall evening breeze. The scene was hypnotizing as he raised his right hand towards the sea of people who were celebrating his appearance. Immediately a reverent hush consumed the atmosphere.

With a waiver in centuries of tradition Pope Romanus requested: "Instead of my prayers for you, faithful servants, I humbly ask you say a silent prayer for me." The Pontiff bowed his head allowing a minute of silence. Hands throughout the massive gathering moved up and down their personal rosary beads in intercession for their Holy Father.

With the backdrop of His Holiness with his hands raised to the heavens and the massive crowd in silent prayer, Katja Lody lowered her voice to address the viewing audience around the world: "I cannot begin to describe the air of expectancy that surrounds me. Since the CERN discovery of a parallel universe there has been much speculation on the spiritual impact to The Catholic Church. On the surface, it would seem to challenge all that has been held sacred since the Holy Mother's immaculate conception."

Lody turned back towards the balcony as Pope Romanus dropped his hands in a signal he was ready to speak. The news cameras zoomed in to capture every word of his unprecedented message.

"My precious sheep, it is with great excitement I bring to you The Holy See's response to CERN's unprecedented scientific discovery. I realize the grave concern regarding the possible contradictions of science and religious values we hold true and dear. CERN's announcement would seem to be a paradox to every religion on earth, not just the Catholic Church. However, faithful ones, instead of a contradiction I believe a scientific gateway has been discovered which will bring all religions to a common ground where in unity we can worship together. There will be many more scientific details forthcoming soon and together we will find our new road of peace and harmony into the future."

Not a sound could be heard through the prodigious crowd. The confusion generated by the parallel universe still controlled the minds of the people as The Pope continued his explanation. "The Holy See for decades has pursued a greater understanding of the universe from a scientific perspective. A select group of Catholic scientists have been overseers of this study both at our Vatican Observatory in Rome and the Mt. Graham International Observatory in the United States which houses the largest telescope on the planet. For many years, Dr. Consolmagno, the president of the Vatican Observatory Foundation, has written and made public reports on their findings. He has also continuously stated the possibility we are not alone in the universe."

A gasp of disbelief echoed throughout the crowd. Immediately, Pope Romanus held up his hand for silence and addressed their concerns. "Do not be alarmed: I am not announcing an alien civilization has been discovered. It is a spiritual truth greater than that and far beyond anything we could have imagined. This is the day of which the Prophet Daniel wrote, when there would be an explosion of knowledge." A smile crossed his face quieting the listeners.

He stepped a little closer to the edge of the balcony as if desiring to embrace each person individually. "Representatives from The Vatican along with scientists from our observatories have met with a delegation from CERN. After these extensive meetings, I will read to you The Vatican's official statement concerning the vanishings."

His aide stepped from behind the curtain and handed him the document, and he quickly disappeared. All ears were tuned to the words of His Holiness, believing their infallible Holy Father would only speak truth. He gazed out across the crowd and smiled offering a spirit of solace before reading their declaration.

Gabriella whispered to Chris, "This is it. Here we go." Chris took her hand and together they listened to the lies perpetrating the evil deception upon the world.

The Pope's voice was strong and unwavering. He spoke with authority captivating every listener. "The Holy See concurs with CERN's announcement on the vanishings. They endorse the scientific breakthrough believing it to be undeniable proof of the existence of a parallel universe. The Holy See believes millions of people who instantly and simultaneously disappeared have converged from the universe in which we live into this parallel universe where time does not exist. We believe science and religion have found a common denominator bringing the two together where we can understand the mysteries of death, eternal life and biblical truths. We pray the Virgin Mary will hear our prayers and give us confirmation."

The TV screen momentarily went black. "The brothers in the lodge have just taken control of cyberspace again," Chris confirmed. "Hang on, Gabi, evil is about to saturate the airwaves."

After the brief blackout, St. Peter's Square came back into view. The scene was the same. To the normal eye, it would be nothing of concern just a temporary media glitch.

The Pope's aide quickly stepped to the balcony retrieving the document, allowing His Holiness to once again lift his arms to the heavens. "Mother Mary, we pray you give us a sign." Arms were raised throughout Vatican City joining Pope Romanus' prayer for a heavenly sign. Expectation hung heavy with all eyes gazing into the air above the papal balcony.

At the same time around the world in hidden chambers of evil, The Enlightened Ones and The 33rds were chanting prayers to Lucifer. They were calling forth the familiar spirit of Cybele, the pagan mother of gods, to appear deceiving the masses into believing the Virgin Mary had come to bring her spiritual approval.

In a perfectly clear sunset sky over St. Peter's Basilica, a single black cloud began to form growing larger and darker. Inside the cloud a spinning spiral, hypnotic to the eyes, appeared with ring after ring of perfectly formed iridescent light. The circulation created a vortex with a hollow center, growing wider and wider. In the center appeared a gleaming light gradually taking human form. Then she appeared! Translucent shining garments flowed around her and a golden crown adorned her head. Her face shown as brilliant light which the human eye could not look upon.

An angel with a flaming sword in his right hand appeared to the left of the apparition. The angel pointed his sword towards the earth. In a loud voice hypnotically reverberating, the angel of light shouted: "Penance and unity!"

From the papal balcony, the Holy Father cried out: "Behold! Mother Mary, Queen of Heaven!"

Gasps of disbelief, cries of excitement, and shouts of praise rang throughout Vatican City. Thousands fell on their knees in worship, while thousands more leaped with joy. The cameramen were in shock struggling to maintain control of the news feed. Reporters were so shaken they lacked the words to report the events around them.

Immediately following the angel's declaration, the bewitching sound Gabriella and Chris heard being tested in the lodge echoed from the cloud and into the airwaves, reaching out around the world. It was synchronized high pitch sounds mixed with a subtle mesmeric beat, capturing the minds of multi-millions around the world. Step two of the deception was being perfectly implemented.

Gabriella covered her ears. "I can't listen to this. Help us, Father!" She cried out, discerning the evil web being cast upon the earth. She began to recite Psalms 91, declaring Yahweh's protection.

Chris took her hand. "The 33rds have certainly planned this to perfection," he admitted, continuing to watch every detail unfold.

All news cameras remained fixated on the images above Peter's Basilica. The mystifying sounds continued to reverberate from the pulsating vortex. Mother Mary with arms outstretched remained in the center of the spiraling circle of light; however, the hole in the heavens continued to grow larger with sounds of thunder and great flashes of lightening. The entire scene transformed into the appearance of what looked to be a gigantic mirror amid the circulating spiral of light. Reflecting in the mirror were the images of a multitude of people of all ages, all ethnic groups, adorned in shining robes.

The Holy Father cried out from the papal balcony. "Our Blessed Mother has shown us the vanished! They dwell now with her in the parallel universe."

The roar from the crowd became deafening. Never had there been such celebration in Vatican City. The scene in the sky began to fade as the vortex closed, but the rejoicing continued.

Gabriella gasped for air. "I understand now, Chris. The pieces are finally coming together. The Vatican's explanation for the vanishing is being perpetrated as the third secret of Fatima prophesied over one hundred years ago, supposedly by the Virgin Mary." She repeated the last part of the prophecy. "*And we saw in an immense light that is God: something similar to how people appear in a mirror when they pass in front of it.*"

"It makes perfect sense," Chris admitted. "Let's put the pieces together, Gabi. Since the true church has been raptured and the Muslim religion for the most part destroyed by the Psalms 83 War, the Catholic Church is now the main religion left on earth with over a billion members. They emphatically believe The Pope is infallible, he hears directly from God and every word he says is absolute truth. Right?" He waited for any discussion she might want to offer.

She nodded. "I'm with you so far. Go ahead," she encouraged him.

"From what your father and Dr. Brotman say, all prophetic signs point to The Pope as the False Prophet who, per the biblical prophecies, will work signs and great wonders. He will also be the one that introduces the Antichrist to the world. Right?"

Once again, she nodded for him to continue.

"It's only reasonable he will deceive the people by using what they already believe to be true. They are totally devoted to the Virgin Mary. Marian Apparitions are held sacred, as a holy sign to her followers."

Chris got up from the couch and began his contemplative pacing. "For a century, mysteries and prophetic speculation have surrounded the Third Secret of Fatima. Apparently, there is more to the long-awaited secret and it could be anything the False Prophet wants to use as the ideal gateway into the great deception. His sheep will blindly follow wherever he leads; and with working miracles, I can just imagine people of other religions or even no religion at all flocking to follow him, too."

Gabriella finished Chris's chain of thought. "And he will lead them to worship the Antichrist and take the mark of the beast."

Their eyes immediately were drawn back to the TV and the white figure on the papal balcony continuing to hold his hands toward the heavens. The celebratory atmosphere continued to engulf Vatican City.

"He must know, Chris. He must know what he's doing, the deception he's bringing on the earth." Gabriella felt anger rising in her. "How can he stand there in mock praise? He knows it's all a lie."

"Of course, he knows," Chris affirmed. "Lucifer knew what he was doing when he rebelled against God. The fallen angels knew what they were doing when they chose to leave their heavenly estate. When people choose to sin, they know what they're doing and do it anyway, never concerned about the end result."

The camera zoomed in on Pope Romanus as he motioned for the crowd to listen to his final words. Within seconds, silence once again prevailed. "Faithful ones, our Blessed Mother, The Queen of Heaven, has appeared to us this day with an angel of peace to bring unity to the earth and unity between the parallel universes as we step across the threshold into a new world of spiritual understanding. We are to prepare the way!"

Before he disappeared behind the curtain, he raised his hands one last time. It was ever so slight, but without a doubt his fingers were parted in the middle...just like Sotoreo.

The screen briefly went black. "We know what that means," Chris jeered heading for the security room. Gabriella was close behind. They were greeted by the sounds of exuberance filling the lodge above them.

Ugo Strozza was heartily congratulating the men on a job extremely well done. "Perfect, brothers, absolutely perfect! The rapture theory is destroyed. The second step to the Final Phase is complete. The Virgin Mother has set the stage for The Appearing. Let the convergence begin!

CHAPTER 36

The big screen TV in the lodge was being monitored by Strozza for any technical difficulties. However, Step Two was carried out with perfection. Now they awaited the news commentaries on the miraculous events at The Vatican. WIN TV in Rome was ablaze with replays of the Marian apparition.

Katja Lody addressed the international audience with breaking news: "The Holy See will immediately convene for an ecclesiastical endorsement of the Marian apparition and to seek revelatory guidance concerning the divine message given by the angel. The ecclesiastical authority does not doubt nor question Mother Mary's appearing, however an official endorsement must be documented. WIN TV here in Rome will be the first to report their declaration."

Applause came from the brothers upstairs. Pride for a job well done was evident in their faces. The 33rds were one giant step closer to completing their great commission.

Taking center screen of WIN TV in Rome was President Sotoreo prepared to call for unity and peace among the nations. "Today our world stands at the gateway of a new and exciting universal understanding. We have commonly believed science and religion were polar opposites. The Queen of Heaven with whom we cannot dispute has now negated that false assumption. She has allowed us a glimpse into the parallel universe in which she dwells along with the vanished. I cannot tell you if this is purgatory or heaven, there is still much to learn. We do know science discovered this universe. The Holy Mother, mother of all religions, confirmed it. The worlds of science and religion have merged into one preparing us for peace and unity on earth. The infallible Pope Romanus will be the mediator of information flow from CERN as it applies to the religious world. He will guide us through this transition time as all religions reassess the antiquated doctrines we have held as truth."

As Sotoreo continued to address the nations the scene behind him changed from the replay of Mother Mary's apparition to a video of rolling hills outside Rome. The countryside had been transformed into a festival celebration; full of young adults dancing to mesmerizing music while a giant screen of CERN's collider was spinning above them. An atmosphere of joy and harmony pulsated through the massive gathering. Many of the attendees held signs with one simple word boldly printed...UNITY.

Sotoreo challenged people from every nation and every spiritual belief to become part of the dawning of a new age. "Rome will be hosting a worldwide festival via the satellite and internet in celebration of world unity. I challenge you to move into this new age of peace by gathering together in parks, concert halls, open fields, anywhere you can meet to celebrate in unison our new hope for tomorrow. The concert will live stream from Italy. Join us as we electronically join hands across the continents to unite in mind and soul."

The cameras focused in on the live feed from the Italian countryside. The serenity of the green meadows filled with youthful exuberance gave a picture of hope for the future. The Tomorrow's Land music filtered through the airwaves. Subtly masqueraded into the melody was the same hypnotic sounds generated by the brothers into the Marian apparition.

The live coverage continued for several minutes showing swaying bodies in tune with the spellbinding beat. The massive screen continued to project the spinning of CERN's Hadron collider. Gradually the scene muted into a vortex of circular light beams with a glowing image radiating in the midst, obviously representing the Marian apparition. Slowly the visual returned to the spinning collider mentally unifying science and religion. The continual methodic movements of rotation with the backdrop of entrancing music seduced the soul and captured the mind.

Gabriella once again covered her ears from the evil sounds. "I can't listen to this. I'm going back to the living room to watch the Israeli news perspective. I'm sure it will be very different." She left Chris to monitor the men upstairs.

It was immediately evident that Channel 2 was not covering nor even talking about the Tomorrow's Land festival. Instead Adelson was hosting a new rabbi with his perspective on the Marian apparition and the parallel universe. Obviously absent from the newsroom was Rabbi Zimmerman. Gabriella whispered a prayer for him to hold strong to his conviction despite the spiritual attacks against him.

Adelson introduced Rabbi Adler, a director at the Temple Institute. "Rabbi, you are heading the committee for the rebuilding of Israel's temple. You are also convinced we are living in the days the Messiah will come to Jerusalem. We will discuss those important factors at a different time, but for now I would like to hear your Biblical view of what the world just witnessed at St. Peter's Basilica."

The Rabbi eagerly jumped in with his spiritual evaluation. "What we have witnessed over Vatican City would convince anyone a miraculous appearing has taken place, except for those who have studied Torah and know the deceptions of evil. We are forbidden to communicate with the dead. I do not know if it was a man created hoax or a satanic ritual, but either way a religious seduction of the nations is underway."

Adelson queried further: "Rabbi, where do you think this is leading?"

Rabbi Adler offered a prophetic scenario. "My supposition would be the purpose is to bring the nations in unity against Israel. Everyone knows Judaism does not believe in the Virgin Mary, the Mother of God. Catholics and protestant Christians hold the virgin birth belief in common, although Protestants have not worshipped Mary as Catholics have. Even Muslims hold Mary in high esteem as the Mother of Jesus, and Jesus being a great prophet. Queen Maya is believed by Buddhist to be the divine Mother and often associated with the Virgin Mother, going back to pagan connections to Mother Earth and ancient goddesses, such as Isis, Cybele, Gala, Diana, Ishtar...the list goes on in varying religions. This worship of Mary, a Virgin Mother and Queen of Heaven, could be one common ground for the major religions of the world to come together as one, which of course Judaism would have no part in. This would alienate us even more from the unity the UN is trying to bring to the nations."

Adelson's voice was doubtful. "It's hard to imagine the world following just one religion under any circumstances."

The Rabbi raised his eyebrows slightly. "Do you not believe people will follow miraculous signs and wonders appearing to be real? I believe that's exactly what this mystical appearance of The Mother of Heaven was all about." Sarcasm towards the devious plan was dripping from his lips. "This appears to me to be a universal ploy to accomplish that very objective."

Adelson apparently was beginning to see the bigger picture of probability. "How do you think the CERN discovery fits into the spiritual equation, Rabbi Adler?"

Again, he was poised and ready with a credible hypothesis. "Every religion believes there is a life hereafter, although they vary greatly in what it consists of. Perhaps the parallel universe will be the common ground for the heavenly plane, the eternal place of rest and peace. Supposedly the vanished are there now with Mother Mary, so perhaps they will claim all the departed dead are there also. This could be used as another step to unity. However this plays out, it will definitely be interesting to see the stratagem used for world control."

"Thank you, Rabbi. Your comments have been quite thought provoking; and I agree, it will be very interesting to see how this plays out."

Gabriella jumped to her feet and hurried to the security room anxious to share with Chris the Rabbi's perspectives. Chris had some news of his own to share.

"Gabi, I was just coming to get you. There's been some interesting conversation going on in the lodge." He motioned for her to sit down.

"You first," she said. "What is it?"

"The brothers have been watching the news reports and making comments along with the news. They've been filling in the blanks on what will happen next." It was all he could do to contain his excitement.

"What do you mean? Tell me every detail." She turned her chair to look full in Chris' face.

"I've got it all recorded so we can listen back, but I'll give you the gist of it. We know the Marian apparition was a satanic ploy. Well, now I know why and what their plans are!"

"Let me guess," she interrupted. "Mother Mary is about to make many appearances with the purpose of bringing together the one world religion?"

Chris looked puzzled. "How did you know that?"

Gabriella explained to him Rabbi Adler's hypothesis regarding both the Virgin Mother and the parallel universe. "I think he's right, Chris, and it will push Israel even farther out of any world unity."

"You're definitely right on that point," he agreed. "What they are planning will incorporate technology never seen before. If they can pull this off, the world will blindly follow. People will truly believe we have reached the Golden Age."

Their attention was drawn back to the lodge conversation when Strozza turned off the TV. "Sotoreo will be rejoining us tomorrow. The millennials will be organizing unity festivals and soon the main event in Italy will air. The next step after that will be the most precarious. We will have no cyber control, but the 33rds and world elitist have been maneuvering toward this end for decades. The world stage of nations is set. Israeli leaders think they are in control, but soon..."

Strozza paused and the brothers began their malevolent chant.

Gabriella voiced her fears. "What do you think that means? What are they planning?"

Chris repeated Strozza's words. "World stage of nations is set...you know what that sounds like, don't you, Gabi?"

She nodded her head. "The war of Gog and Magog. The next prophetic piece in the puzzle."

Strozza held up his hand and the evil men in the lodge ceased their chant. "I say we call it a day, brothers. Again, I congratulate you on a job well done."

The men prepared to retire for the evening. The lodge grew quiet as they disappeared up the steps. Russo and Moretti cleaned behind the men and prepared for the morning activities.

"I'm going to bed, too." Gabriella rose from her chair and patted Chris on the shoulder. "I suggest you do the same. You need some rest, my friend."

"Yeah," he admitted. "Looks like tomorrow Sotoreo will be back and the next round begins. This is moving much faster than I anticipated."

Gabriella gazed momentarily at the room of monitors and security equipment. "Still amazes me we have a front row seat to end time events. I'm sure my father had no idea his research would lead to this."

"I'm sure he didn't but Yahweh did." Chris gave her a brotherly hug of comfort as he quoted the Professor. "God knows the end from the beginning."

She kissed his cheek. "You're right. But it's still amazing to me God chose us. Makes no sense." She pulled away and exited the room. "See you in the morning. Sleep well."

Chris watched her disappear through the security room door and then exit her father's bedroom. Silently he prayed she would have a peaceful sleep.

Snuggled in her bed, she held Caleb's letters next to her heart. She closed her eyes and meditated on her dream encounters since the vanishings. She reopened her eyes to the dull glow of the nightlight. As her eyes focused, she saw Caleb sitting beside her bed with his face in his hands. His blonde thick hair hung down over his eyes. She reached out to him, but he was too far away to touch. Her arm fell back onto the bed beside her. She noticed the letters were no longer lying on her chest.

"Caleb," she whispered. She tried to keep her eyes open but heaviness prevailed.

As she closed her eyes his eyes opened. He pushed the blonde hair back from his face, a face filled with perplexity. He leaned towards Gabriella for a clearer view. Nothing appeared changed. He took her hand in his and closed his fingers tightly around hers.

"Gabi, can you hear me?" He moved closer to her, sitting on the side of her bed. With both hands, he gently cupped her face, leaned over and kissed her lips. The warmth of his mouth stirred emotions deep within her releasing an adrenalin force unlike anything she had ever experienced.

Breaking through the barriers of time and untime, she whispered again. "Caleb". Her eyes opened and she was looking directly into the eyes of the man she loved. "Caleb," she whispered again.

He took her into his arms and pulled her to his chest rocking back and forth. Tears were their language of love and spoke all that was needed. Clutched in each other's arms, Gabriella and Caleb transcended the corridors of time separating them. For a brief moment there was no other world, no before or after, no time or untime...only a realm where pure love defied all physics known to man.

CHAPTER 37

"Caleb," she whispered. The feel of his loving arms had vanished. Gabriella opened her eyes to the dim light of her empty room. Caleb's letters lay next to her heart. She laid his letters on her nightstand and sat upright.

"It was real, I know it was real," she muttered to herself. "There must have been a moment before the vanishing when I woke up just enough to look in Caleb's eyes and I was reliving that moment." She shook the long locks of her blonde hair hoping to clear her mind and remember something, anything. The only memories were from her dream encounters - nothing that even resembled reality.

She looked at the clock and sighed. It was only 3:00 AM and she was wide awake. Kicking the sheets off, she climbed out of bed, switched on the light, and got her father's Bible. Turning to Ezekiel 38 and 39 she again read the biblical account of the prophetic war of Gog and Magog. She shuffled through her father's notes searching for his list revealing the names of the modern-day nations the Gog and Magog prophecy was referring to and his subsequent personal commentary on how it would all play out.

"We will soon know if you're right, Dad," she muttered to the empty room. "If you are, Russia and the Muslim nations surviving the Psalms 83 War will make their move to destroy Israel and gain control before the UN implements their plan. It's obvious something will happen soon."

Gabriella sat in silence meditating on the myriad of events culminating so quickly. She slipped to the floor in a kneeling position desiring to be in The Presence. She closed her eyes and repeated over and over, "Holy is The

Lord, Holy is The Lord." Peace saturated her room as she worshipped. It was these times she spent alone in The Presence that would give her the strength to face the future without her loved ones.

She tried to push the memory of being in Caleb's arms to the back of her mind. Try as she may to find a rationale, there was no reasoning on how or why she was slipping from reality into the days before the vanishing and then back to reality.

"I feel as though I'm sliding from one reality to another with both existing at the same time. I think I have my own parallel universe," she sarcastically muttered to herself.

The smell of morning coffee filtered into her bedroom interrupting her emotional query. Another day beckoned with all the uncertainty of each preceding day. It was sure to be eventful with the return of Sotoreo. After a quick shower, she was ready to join Chris.

"Any news this morning?" She asked pouring a cup of coffee.

"No activity in the lodge so far, except for Russo and Moretti's breakfast preparations. They must find this awfully boring after chasing your father's mystery box around the world." Chris chuckled at how the two men had spent years in vain pursuit of the research which now lay just beneath their feet.

Gabriella shuddered remembering the recent encounter at police headquarters and again at the gas station. "Ironic, but scary. And the thing is, now is the time they need to make absolutely sure no one gets Dad's research."

"And you still think your father's discovery on the implant is a big part of what the 33rds are planning?"

She nodded her head in certainty. "Not a doubt in my mind and we'll know soon enough just how." She turned the TV on for new updates on world events. WIN TV continued with commentary on the Marian apparition interspersed with reports of Tomorrow's Land unity festivals being organized around the planet."

Katja Lody's smiling face reappeared on the screen. Behind her was a massive gathering of young people. "I'm coming to you live from the beautiful Italian countryside just outside the city of Rome. Behind me is ground zero for the Tomorrow's Land international festival which will livestream around our planet. From this location via satellite and internet the world will unite for the clarion call of peace on earth."

269

Lody approached a young lady just arriving at the festival. "Hello. We are live on WIN TV. May I ask you a question?"

"Sure," she agreed, smiling at the camera.

"Would you please tell our international audience where you're from and why you've come to the unity festival?"

"I am from Frascati, Italy and I have come to find truth. I've never been a spiritual person. There were so many different religions and none of them agreed, so I just agreed to believe in nothing. I had accepted this life was all there was, but with the discovery of the parallel universe everything I believed has changed."

Lody nodded her head. "Apparently, you are not alone in that quest," the reporter stated as the camera panned the exuberant scene of hopeful youth gathered for spiritual understanding.

The gigantic screen on the main stage repeatedly showed video footage of CERN's alternate universe and the Marian apparition. Subtly, in the background the transfixing sound of the hypnotic rhythm was seducing the young minds.

Lody made her closing comment from the Tomorrow's Land festival. "This afternoon there will be an announcement of a definite time for the world livestream event. All technical preparations are now underway and this momentous occasion is expected to be within the next few days. The rumor is everyone attending the festivals live, both here in Italy and around the world, will be given a microchip under their skin for identity purposes. This will be the first time such a device has been used."

"And so, the implant begins," Gabriella commented in a sardonic voice. "The millennials will be like sheep led to the slaughter. Everything is going to appear wonderful at first, but they're on the road to destruction."

"I'm sure the brothers will soon be hard at work making sure the big seduction goes off without a hitch. I'm anxious to hear what Sotoreo has to say about it when he gets here today." Chris went to the kitchen and refilled their coffee cups. "Speaking of the brothers, I'm going back to the security room. They should be gathering pretty soon."

Late afternoon, Sotoreo arrived at the lodge as scheduled. Strozza greeted him at the limo and they walked together back to the entry door. When Sotoreo crossed the threshold, an anomalous look crossed his face. He stopped in his tracks, looking in every direction.

"Is something wrong?" Strozza questioned.

Sotoreo stood frozen in the doorway. "I feel it again. I sense we are not alone."

Gabriella and Chris looked at each other with questioning eyes. Once again Gabriella began to pray for divine protection.

"Impossible, Pindar," Strozza assured him. "Our men have surveyed the area numerous times. There's no one here but us."

Sotoreo appeared skeptical but stepped into the foyer where the brothers met him. The expected celebratory handshakes and back slaps ensued.

"Great job." Their Cabal Pindar congratulated them. "We are one giant step closer to The Appearing."

Russo and Moretti had prepared an early dinner for the men. Around the table the atmosphere of celebration continued.

"Ok, guys," Chris complained from the bunker. "Let's get on with this. What's next?"

Ironically, at that moment Sotoreo held up his hand for silence around the table. "We need to get down to business, brothers. I had a meeting last night in Rome with the elite 33rds. We are all in agreement. We are in a race against time with the bear: Russia and her allies think they can destroy Israel and take control of her oil and natural gas through a surprise military attack, using secretly developed weapons. After Israel is destroyed, they plan to control the armies and wealth of the world. They already control what's left of the United States. There is no other military power left on earth that can stop them, if Israel is destroyed."

The Pindar got up from the table and walked to the window. The panoramic view of Mt. Hermon was fading into the twilight of the evening. Rays of dull sunlight streamed through the trees casting an ominous glow across the mountain range. There was not a sound to be heard in the lodge or the bunker below. Everyone was waiting to hear the Pindar's plan.

Sotoreo turned suddenly and he defiantly announced: "We will not allow this to happen. There is only one who will rule the world and we must prepare the way." He pulled his notes from his briefcase while Moretti cleared the table. "I'll give you an overview of our strategy. Timing and execution of every detail will be paramount."

The bunker duo instinctively and in unison leaned toward the monitors in anticipation. The men around the table were poised and ready to make the necessary notes for their individual assignments.

"We are ready to initiate Step Three. The Pope will address the world tomorrow announcing The Vatican's response to the parallel universe. The faithful of the Catholic Church will believe every word he says. The miraculous signs and wonders of the newly revealed truth will lure atheists and agnostics worldwide. Those of other religions will realize the Virgin Mother is the common denominator leading everyone to worship together. The infallible Holy Father will be the mediator between man and the Queen of Heaven."

Sotoreo momentarily paused and looked around the table. "You do understand the importance of timing?"

Strozza answered for the brothers. "They're ready, Pindar. All we need to know is when."

"Very good. Exact timing will be determined within the next few days. In the meantime, we monitor Russia's movement. Right now, Israel thinks no country would dare attack her. She truly believes she exists in total peace and safety. With precise timing, I believe the Russian coalition can be destroyed and Israel conquered. Judaism and the Hebrew teachings will be gone. There will be no religion left that will question the teachings of the unity. This leaves a clean slate for the new world order and the appearing of our AM, the eternal Ascended Master, to set up his kingdom on earth."

The men around the table began to chant, assuring their satanic allegiance to the planned agenda.

Sotoreo held up his hand, again requesting silence. "We are so close. This is the day our brothers throughout generations of time have worked for. This earth was stolen from our Ascended Master and his angels who have been held in captivity. The day of release is near and our AM will reign forever and ever."

The Cabal Pindar held up his hands in the familiar sign. The brothers around the table stood and joined him in celebration.

Gabriella and Chris knew all hell was about to break loose...literally.

CHAPTER 38

Sotoreo's words resonated in Gabriella's mind. "Chris, everything that evil man is planning is exactly what Arcturus told me was going to happen. Arcturus made it sound so wonderful: The Ascended Master will bring peace to the earth. There would be no more sickness or death. He will promise a utopian life and all people will need is to receive the implant to enter this golden age. I can see now how they're going to be deceived into believing the lies. Then all hell breaks loose...the fallen angels are released from the abyss."

Tears welled in Gabriella's eyes as she remembered how close she came to the convergence. "If it had not been for the prayers of my loved ones, I would already be one of them. A life without hope of redemption."

Chris took her hand. "But you didn't, Gabi. That's what matters. Their prayers reached beyond the boundaries of time and circumstances to save you. As a Chosen One, you will be doing the same thing."

"I know," she spoke in a voice barely audible. "It's just when I think of how close I came..."

The duo's attention was brought back to the monitors as the men reassembled around the lodge table. Sotoreo took his place of authority to continue discussing the implementation of Step Three. "Tonight, and continually until the event starts, WIN TV will be announcing to the world the date and time for the Tomorrow's Land Unity Festival."

You could see the excitement on the men's faces as their Cabal Pindar gave the details. "Friday, just four days from now, will be the end of the Jew's Feast of Tabernacles seven-day celebration. On the eighth day, they spend time in devout prayer seeking God for blessings for their nation.

They consider it a holy day and it begins at sunset on Friday which is also their holy Sabbath. A double holy, you might say." The diabolical look and sarcasm on Sotoreo's face was obvious. "That is when our festival will begin."

The evil chant in celebration began around the table with vile expressions on the men's faces. Apparently, they all knew the significance of this long-awaited day.

"Brothers, as the sun goes down on Friday evening you will be ready to livestream the festival. The world will hear the message of love and unity broadcast from ground zero in Italy, the first message coming from the parallel universe. Assemblies are being planned worldwide and all they need to do is connect to the internet or satellite feed to be part of souls uniting worldwide. If they cannot assemble, they can watch it on their computers, TV, or cell phone. Everyone can participate live in the greatest event ever to occur on this earth. This will be the beginning of the convergence.

Strozza jumped to his feet and the men all followed, chanting with exuberance. For several minutes the men celebrated the anticipated great success. Chris muted the monitors to keep the evil sounds away from the bunker. When the men finally took their seats, he readjusted the volume.

Sotoreo continued. "Tomorrow Step Three will be complete. The Pope will make an official declaration on The Vatican's biblical endorsement of the parallel universe. With the church's holy scriptures, he will convince the world this scientific discovery does not contradict any sacred writings. In fact, it is a fulfillment of prophecy. The Holy Father will also announce The Apostolic See's approval of the Marian apparition." The familiar sardonic smile crossed his face. His countenance projected extreme confidence that everything would go as The 33rds had planned.

The Pindar rose to his feet and stretched. "Brothers, I trust you for perfect execution of media in promoting the unity festival. The visuals, the music, every sight and sound coming from the Tomorrow's Land stage must be branded into the minds and souls of every person attending live or by live-stream. When we seduce the souls, we can conquer the world."

"Yes, Pindar," the voices rang in unison around the table.

"The last and most important thing before I retire for the evening. All who attend the live festival in Italy will be required to receive the implant as their festival pass. It will be promoted as an extremely small microchip for identity purposes and purchases only. A credit card will be downloaded on the implant, which will take the place of monetary exchanges. No form of currency or other credit cards will be accepted once they enter. We are promoting this with the news media so it will not be a surprise when attendees arrive. It will appear to be totally innocent; but the DNA of every person implanted will begin to change as the third strand starts to form. We can thank our celestial brothers for the knowledge." His expression changed from sardonic to pure malevolent. "Let the convergence begin!"

The Pindar raised his hand with fingers parted. The men stood and saluted back as Moretti led him out of the lodge and to his private quarters in the cottage.

In the bunker Gabriella was filled with emotional agony. "I see why the implant my father discovered was a major threat to them. If dad had exposed it, everything they were planning for the convergence could have been upset."

Chris laid his head on the back of the chair and gazed at the ceiling in deep thought as he mentally assessed the impact of the implant. "They say this is the first step towards the convergence. Apparently, it's going to be done over time, gradually seducing the world into taking the implant. As the recipients begin to show positive physical affects everyone will want one. It won't be forced on anyone."

Gabriella sat straight up in her chair. "Exactly, Chris. That's what I've been trying to tell you. My dad wrote in his journal about people with these implants and the amazing physical results. When he first found out about them, he thought the implants were done by an extraterrestrial civilization. He really believed they were testing the effects on humans."

Chris raised his head and looked Gabriella in the eyes. "And just where did the implants originate? Who are the celestial brothers? It's only been a few years since science began tests altering the DNA. Your dad discovered the implant decades ago."

"You may find my answer difficult to believe."

"I've found everything you've told me difficult to believe, Gabi. However, it's all playing out to be true. So, try me."

She avoided eye contact with Chris. Had she not lived what she was about to share, she would not believe it herself. She took a deep breath and let the truth flow. "I've shared bits and pieces of my Arcturus experience with you…my journey to the dark side. I have seen mysteries beyond man's imagination. Some call it the mysteries of the universe, but there are many paranormal titles for unexplained phenomenon. Among them are the celestial brothers. It's in that mystical place revelations can be given, knowledge no man on earth has discovered."

Gabriella took a moment reflecting on her father's journal entries. "It is what my dad thought was extraterrestrial knowledge imparted to earth humans. He believed it began at Roswell when the aliens or celestial brothers arrived, but Professor Brotman proved to him it has been happening since the fall of the angels when they gave forbidden knowledge to man. The fact is no matter how wonderful it appears, it's all satanic. It first appears beautiful but with a horrendous end. The DNA manipulation is not a new scientific discovery. It has been going on since Genesis 6 and it is what Yeshua said in Matthew 24 would happen again at the end of days. When the DNA God created in man is satanically altered, that person becomes unredeemable, just as mankind was before the flood."

The full impact bore down upon Chris. "All these people at the festival who are going to be implanted. Will it be too late for them?"

She weighed out the biblical prophecies before answering. "No, not yet. It will be the first step of seduction. Revelation 13 says they must worship the Antichrist and take his mark. Worship will be the essential step to completing the third strand. Then the convergence will be complete."

The duo sat silent in individual contemplation. The Antichrist scenario was playing out like a movie on the big screen and all they could do at this point was watch.

After several minutes, Chris patted her on the shoulder as he got up. "I need a mental break and some nourishment. I'm sure the brothers are going to be testing and retesting their programs for the big events." He moved toward the door motioning for her and then stopped. "The *brothers*? Do you think there's a connection there?"

She had not considered the possibility before. "It makes perfect sense now."

Gabi got up and followed him to the kitchen. She was deep in concentration as they prepared lunch. Over a bowl of soup, she shared her inner thoughts. "Dad first believed it was extraterrestrial entities that visited earth and brought the technology of the implant. Sadly, people would believe in aliens before they would believe in angels and demons. In fact, over half the people on this planet already are convinced they've seen some type of UFO. The world now believes in the parallel universe. How easy it will be to convince them our celestial brothers have been teleporting between universes for time immortal."

"It will be like something out of sci-fi movie," Chris interjected. "Young people will be sucked right in to the lie."

She nodded her head. "There will be tens of thousands of people, mostly millennials, at the festival. Can you imagine the impact when they realize their body is being transformed into perfection, and the implant technology came from a celestial being?"

It was more than Chris could comprehend. "I thought I'd faced every possible scenario in my years on the police force. But this, well, let's just say it's beyond my wildest imagination."

"As I read through my dad's journal and research papers, he had me convinced in extraterrestrial life. Being caught in Arcturus' dream world just cemented the deception. If I had just finished reading his journal I would have known the truth, the truth that would have set me free."

Chris could see her slipping back into the guilt and remorse. "Gabi, we have to keep our eyes on the world around us, not on the what ifs." He reached across the table and took her hand. "You know the truth now and that truth has set you free. And you're going to lead others to the truth, too. Focus on your calling."

"You're right." She dropped his hand and stood up. She walked to the couch and picked up her father's letters, holding them next to her heart. "I have to live in reality. These dreams of slipping back and forth, before and after the vanishings, make it so hard to let go."

Chris knew she needed some alone time. "I'm going back to the security room. Just let me know if you need me." He walked behind her and laid his hand on her shoulder before exiting the room. A simple touch spoke a volume of words.

She waited until he disappeared through the door before turning on WIN TV for international updates. As expected, the news was ablaze with anticipation of The Pope's address scheduled for the following day. In addition, promotions for Tomorrow's Land Unity Festival were already beginning, challenging the world to be part of the live event. There was even a short clip showing how live attendees at the festival would receive the microchip at registration for convenience. It all seemed so natural.

"No surprises here," she muttered to herself, changing the TV to Channel 2 News for Israeli updates. Instead of the familiar face of anchorman Adelson, cameras were live at the Tel Aviv Convention Center. The largest complex in Israel was now the processing center for The Return.

An attractive Israeli reporter stood in the massive entryway giving an overview of the Aliyah process. "Buses are bringing Aliyah immigrants from airports across Israel to this main processing center. Tens of thousands have already been cleared for Israeli citizenship and the daily arrivals are growing exponentially. Here it will be determined how they best can acclimate to Israeli society with their skills, education, languages, etc. Accommodations are being set up in the expanded territories and awaiting the return of our people scattered among the nations."

The young reporter gracefully moved toward a large map of the complex showing the layout of the entire center. "Upon arrival, they are directed to one of the eight indoor pavilions for processing to begin. Once they have been cleared, they continue to a 10,000-square foot canopied area where long lines of tables are set up with lab technicians taking blood samples for DNA testing. This will determine their lineage and tribe association."

Gabriella was thinking out loud, "This will also soon determine their DNA is pure from any third strand manipulations. Amazing how it is all coming together."

The reporter moved to the far right of the map pointing to the east section of the complex. "Our new Israeli citizens will then be directed to the outdoor pavilion where buffets of food are waiting before they began their transport to their new homes. This has been the largest humanitarian move ever undertaken by the Israeli Government and every detail has been planned to perfection."

Her big brown eyes misted with tears. "The lost sheep of Israel have come home." For several minutes the cameras showed the immigrants in the various areas of the convention center. The atmosphere throughout the massive complex was charged with excitement and hope. Many were singing songs of joy as they stood in the long lines.

"I am reminded of a holy scripture written by Isaiah the prophet." The reporter's voice echoed the joy resounding around her. *"Those the LORD has rescued will return. They will enter Zion with singing; everlasting joy will crown their heads. Gladness and joy will overtake them, and sorrow and sighing will flee away.*"

"This is Sarah Jacobs reporting. Back to you Michael."

The TV screen went to a split picture. Michael Adelson's face returned to half the screen and Sarah Jacobs was on the other. Many immigrants making Aliyah had gathered around her and were cheering as the segment came to an end.

"Thank you for that report, Sarah. It's exciting for all of us to see the tremendous success of The Return."

The attractive reporter smiled and waved at Adelson. She knew she could not be heard over the excitement that surrounded her. The screen went to a commercial break and Gabriella turned off the TV.

She collapsed against the back of the couch realizing how truly amazing it was to see ancient prophecies coming to life in real time. Then sadness penetrated her mood, as she wondered how many, if any, American Jews could make Aliyah with the electric grid down. Hurting for her people, she slid from her seat to her knees and interceded in prayer. After a time of intercession and exhausted from the long day, she fell asleep with her head resting on the couch.

When she awakened, she tried to open her eyes, but to no avail. Her head would not lift and her mouth could not speak. The familiar feeling of being frozen in time once again captured her. Voices surrounded her, but they were vague and incoherent. In vain, she tried to interpret the muddled sounds. At her point of total frustration, she felt a hand caress her head. That touch she knew without seeing or hearing. His fingers gently ran through her long blonde hair and rested on her shoulder. His voice was distinguishable but the words muted.

"Louder, Caleb," her soul was crying out. "I can't hear you." She knew her mental words could not reach him. His hand dropped from her shoulder. "Don't leave me, Caleb. Don't leave." She tried to force the words from her lips, but could not cross the boundary separating the two realities.

"I want to stay here with you, Caleb. I don't want to go back." She pushed her arms forward. "Hold me tight so I can't leave you." Her voice was pleading.

She felt arms wrap around her in a comforting hug. She clung to him, but she knew Caleb was gone. Momentarily she gently pushed Chris away.

"I'm sorry I'm not Caleb," Chris tried to comfort her. "I wish you could open your eyes and find yourself in his arms. I really do, Gabi."

"Me, too," she admitted. "What time is it, Chris?

"It's after midnight. Go on to bed. A big event's happening tomorrow and we have to be mentally sharp."

She kissed him on the cheek as he helped her up. "Good night," she mumbled.

Alone in her bed she faced her fear. "Is Caleb slipping away from me?"

CHAPTER 39

Gabriella was restless. She tossed and turned, desiring the deep sleep which allowed her to cross the threshold in time before the vanishings. It was useless.

She kicked the blankets off her legs and sat up. Retrieving Caleb's letters from the night stand, she poised herself for the familiar emotional roller coaster. There were only two unread letters. She purposely had saved them for a later time. Once they were read, there would be nothing more to look forward to. The letters were their continuing bond between time and untime.

She picked up his next letter in the sequence they were written. Holding it against her heart, she took a deep breath and slowly exhaled. She visualized Caleb sitting beside her before beginning to read. Each sentence was digested slowly savoring each word. At the end of the sentence, she would return and read it again before moving forward. In all the years she had known Caleb, she had not realized he was a true romantic at heart. His words were intimate and endearing, expressing both the depth of his love and his regret for failing her. Her soul ached to turn back time and relive her weeks before the vanishings. She closed her eyes reminiscing.

"At least I experienced love," she whispered to herself, "even if I did make a mess of it."

She turned his letter to the final page. Suddenly the writing changed. There appeared to have been an interlude in the time of writing. It was a different ink color and his perfectly formed cursive letters were now erratic and much larger, half cursive and half printed. It was the type of handwriting expected of one that was excited and written in haste.

Gabi, today for a moment you awakened! You looked into my eyes and smiled. I saw the expression of love on your face and knew you had forgiven me. I held you close and my hopes soared when you whispered my name. It has given me faith you are beginning your steps back to me. We have all prayed without ceasing you would awaken before it was too late. I believe this was a sign even though too quickly you were asleep again.

Gabriella kicked her legs high into the air and screamed with glee. "I knew it! It was real! There was a moment before the vanishings I woke up." She jumped out of bed and danced in circles. "Caleb knows I forgave him and still loved him."

A knock brought her to a dead stop. Chris pushed the door open. "Are you okay, Gabi?"

She ran to him and threw her arms around his neck. "It was real, Chris. It was real." She turned him loose and twirled in a circle. "I *did* wake up."

"What are you talking about?" He could make no sense of her jabbering and she certainly had never acted like this before.

She took his hand and pulled him to the chair beside her bed. Pushing him into the seat, she jumped in the middle of the bed and folded her legs beneath her. With eyes sparkling and joy oozing in her voice, she shared with Chris a portion of Caleb's letters. She handed it to him pointing to the paragraph about her awakening.

"Read this," she demanded with a smile of victory on her face.

Chris noted Caleb's change in writing from the previous paragraph. As a police officer, he was trained to detect any type of extreme changes in one's behavior. After reading the letter he did not doubt or question Gabriella had briefly awakened; however, he wondered why he was not told since he was in the bunker with the team the entire time.

He handed her the letter and smiled. "This confirms what we expected. You are not dreaming, Gabi, you are reliving your memories. I'm thankful you have this specific memory and, hopefully, you can turn loose of the pain now. He knows you forgave him." He got up and kissed the top of her head. "I'll leave you alone with Caleb," he whispered with sincere affection as he exited her bedroom.

Gabriella plopped her head back on the pillows and read Caleb's letter over and over until her eyes could no longer focus and she succumbed to sleep. When she opened her eyes again the smell of morning coffee filled the air. Her first thought was of the man she loved. She had expected the heavy burden of losing Caleb to be lifted, but quite the contrary. She was thinking how disappointed he must have been when he believed her brief awakening was a sign she was returning.

With a heavy heart, she climbed out of bed and dressed for another day and another step of the Final Phase.

Chris had breakfast prepared and waiting on the coffee table. He expected her to still be jubilant from her dream revelation, but one look revealed otherwise.

"Do you want to talk about it, Gabi?"

"Not now," she hesitantly answered.

He handed her a cup of coffee as she joined him to watch the handsome WIN TV reporter promoting the Tomorrow's Land event. He was challenging people worldwide to come together and be part of the livestream concert.

"This is a day that will change our lives forever," he declared with certainty. "Find a group, start a group, do whatever it takes to be with your fellow man as we unify to release the force of peace and love worldwide. We are opening the gateway to a new tomorrow's land." His play on words were very effective, capturing the minds of people looking for a way to escape an existence still filled with uncertainty.

A video promotion of the unity festival played for several minutes showing ground zero for the event. The music, the young people dancing and celebrating, the gigantic screens replaying CERN's opening ceremony, The Pope's clarion call for unity, and the Marian apparition – all were effectively capturing the imagination of viewers.

When the video ended, Katja Lody's smiling face appeared. She was standing on a hillside at the edge of the festival site. The monumental location for the event could be seen in the background. "In just four days the unity festival begins," she exclaimed. "The number of attendees for the live location is already growing rapidly. As you can see behind me there are tents and camping areas being set up by those arriving early. There will be days of celebration in anticipation of the main event

Katja pointed to an area to the east of her location. "There in the distance you can see the main gates for the festival entry being erected. Construction should be completed today. Tomorrow the registration booths will open and everyone here early will be able to obtain their official event pass. For the first time a new registration process will take place. An extremely small microchip will be injected under the skin in their hand downloaded with personal information which cannot be stolen or forged. They will need no other form of identity once they are registered. Vendors will be setting up all around the festival area and no one will be able to buy or sell without their implant. Purchases will be made by swiping a hand rather than using a card or money. We are truly entering a new era on many levels."

The camera refocused from the construction area back to the reporter. "I will be returning to Rome immediately to cover Pope Romanus' address to the nations this afternoon when he will give his spiritual analysis of the parallel universe. Also, he is expected to announce The Holy See has ceremoniously approved the Marian apparition. It is an exciting time in Italy and in our new world." Her smiling face disappeared from the screen as another commercial promotion for the Tomorrow's Land festival began to play.

"Hmmm," Gabriella grunted. "With all this TV coverage, they're going to have everyone convinced they need to be part of this big seduction."

"And that's the whole of the matter." Chris retorted. "After everything this world has experienced the last few weeks, people will still be swayed by whatever the media says."

He took his plate to the kitchen, poured another cup of coffee and headed for the security room. "The brothers will be gathering soon. I need to check the recorders before they get started."

"Okay, let me know when things get interesting." She waited until he was out of sight before picking up her father's stack of letters. She had read through them several times, but felt the urgency to read them again feeling she had missed something. Settling back in the couch, she skimmed page by page not sure what she was looking for. She read again the warning of the Black Pope prophesied by St. Malachy and saw nothing new. She continued page after page: the Abrahamic Covenant, Gog and Magog War, the rise of the Antichrist and his mark, the return of the lost tribes, rebuilding the temple - he had given detail by detail the events of the final days. It was so precise she believed she could have made a movie script from his notes. Then something caught her attention. She had read it several times before, but now with a new revelation:

Gabriella, as I have written these letters to you, I sat by your bed and read them aloud for you to hear. While you slept Caleb, the Professor, everyone in the bunker would sit around your bed and discuss what would happen in the days to come. We debated possible scenarios of how it would all play out. I have prayed our words would be branded in your subconscious so deeply you would feel the reality and understand what the future holds.

"Why didn't I realize this before?" She questioned. "All of the information in my dad's letters was already in my subconscious before the vanishings. While I was asleep, every detail was being verbally played out for me to hear. No wonder it was so easy for me to remember." She laid the letters back on the table and mentally relived the days since she awakened. "Everything has happened exactly as Dad said they would, detail by detail."

She was unaware Chris had entered the room and overheard her one-way conversation. "What has happened detail by detail, Gabi?"

Motioning for him to sit down, she picked up the last letter and read the paragraph in question. "Chris, were you in the room for the prophecy discussions before the vanishings?"

"No, I wasn't. I considered myself in the bunker only to protect your team and didn't interfere with their personal matters. Of course, some things I overhead simply because of the proximity." He hesitated before adding, "I sure wish now I had been."

"I wish you had been, too. Together we could have remembered so much more." Changing the subject, she moved to the day's pressing issue. "Is anything going on upstairs? Are they ready for the Pope's big lies?"

"Everything seems to be set for the cyberspace and satellite takeover. They're just rechecking all systems before show time. I'll keep monitoring just in case." He started to get up, but instead put his arm around her shoulders. "Are you okay? Is there anything I can do?"

"I'm fine," she spoke in an unconvincing tone. "Go back to the monitors. We don't want to take any chances of missing something this late in the game." He leaned his head briefly on top of hers and then was gone.

She read her father's letter one more time. "What am I missing?" She mulled his message over and over, feeling there was a mysterious link between time and untime hidden somewhere in his words.

CHAPTER 40

———— •◦•◦• ————

Gabriella continued reviewing her father's letters. She was certain there was a connection somewhere she was missing – a connection between her two realities. She was lost in her thoughts until Chris came bursting in.

"It's show time, Gabi." He grabbed the remote, tuned to WIN TV, and adjusted the volume. "Here we go."

The TV was showing a split screen with cameras focused on the massive crowd throughout St. Peter's square and the papal balcony where Pope Romanus would make his address to the nations. The sun was still bright over St. Peter's Basilica providing a luminous backdrop to the mystical scene. The voice of Katja Lody could be heard with a discourse of what to expect as they awaited the arrival of The Holy Father. The wait was very brief as he stepped from behind the veiled curtain. The late afternoon fall breezes caught in his white linen garment as he stepped to the edge of the concrete precipice. The microphones were tested and ready for his unprecedented treatise.

He cleared his voice and spoke with clarity: "Faithful Ones, since the creation of man there has never been a time as this. We stand at the threshold of new revelations as science and religion merge and open to us a new discernment of the Holy Scriptures. As I prayed for guidance in leading the sheep of the Holy Roman Church in this epoch-making time, I was led of the spirit to the prophecy of Isaiah the Prophet as he looked forward and saw this day. Isaiah 43:19 - *See, I am doing a new thing! Now it springs up; do you not perceive it?*"

A smile crossed his face and he held his hands over his head. "Behold, my children, all things are new! We must learn from the past as we walk into the future. We must leave behind hatred, racism, religiosity and all the things that separate mankind and allow pure love to spring up from the wells of our souls. We all serve the same creator and we must find common ground and come together in unity."

Cries of affirmation were ringing throughout Vatican City. Hanging in the air was a numinous expectancy like nothing mankind had experienced.

"There are many Holy Scriptures telling us of the heavens, but we never understood the meaning. Not until science revealed to us the alternate dimensions of time and space. In his sacred writings, St. Paul told us he had visited an alternate dimension. II Corinthians 12 - *I know a man in Christ who was caught up to the third heaven. I was caught up to paradise and heard inexpressible things, things no one is permitted to tell. After that I demonstrated my powers among you with signs, wonders and miracles."*

The Pope took no break before giving additional scriptures for proof. "In II Kings, Elijah was taken in a chariot of fire and never died; in Genesis, we read Enoch was a man of such purity God took him and he did not feel the sting of death; even Jesus was caught up in a cloud as his disciples watched his ascension, and He promised that in like manner He would return. And most importantly, our Queen of Heaven, the Virgin Mary had her Assumption of both body and soul when her mission on earth was complete." He paused briefly to allow the full impact of his intent. "What we have referred to throughout the ages as heaven we had not really understood, not until now. Our universe has existed side by side with an eternal perfect universe which will be our guide to the golden age. Elijah, Enoch, Jesus and Mary – they all demonstrated the Path of The Ascension to this celestial plane of perfection. They embody the highest aspects of divine love, a radiant love which permeates all space and matter and in which death is not required."

A gasp could be heard among the people when this new revelation was given, which was immediately followed by applause and cheers of joy. Momentarily The Black Pope motioned for silence. A hush settled across the masses as he continued: "The Apostolic See has whole heartedly endorsed the Marian apparition. They have reminded us through the years The Queen of Heaven has appeared many times weeping with sorrow for the sins of her children and the pain saturating her Immaculate Heart.

We have seen her warnings, but did not heed them. She has come at this appointed time to guide us into this new age of which Isaiah spoke of."

Again, roars of celebration penetrated the reverent hush. The Pope allowed it to continue for several minutes. "It is with immense excitement that I now share with you the part of The Third Secret of Fatima withheld by The Holy See. They awaited the time in which this prophecy would be fulfilled to announce it to the world as proof the Queen of Heaven is our guide into the future." His voice grew louder and with great elation he announced: "Faithful Ones, this is the time."

Cameras focused on the crowd while Pope Romanus waited for his words to fully register. Looks of bewilderment and amazement had captured the faces. Not even the sound of breathing could be heard as the crowd awaited the prophecy given by the Marian Apparition over one hundred years prior.

A scroll was handed to The Pope from behind the curtain. He unrolled it and stepped closer to the microphone. "I will read first the portion already made public in the year 2000 by His Holiness Pope John Paul II:

> *"At the left of Our Lady and a little above, we saw an Angel with a flaming sword in his left hand; flashing, it gave out flames that looked as though they would set the world on fire; but they died out in contact with the splendor that Our Lady radiated towards him from her right hand: pointing to the earth with his right hand, the Angel cried out in a loud voice: <u>Penance, Penance, Penance</u>! And we saw in an immense light that is God something similar to how people appear in a mirror when they pass in front of it."*

The infallible Pope gave a short dissertation on the meaning of the first part of the message the apparition had brought: "Our Holy Mother of Heaven and Earth warned us to repent of our sins. The immense light represents the love which emanates from her and from the consummate parallel universe of her assumption. The mirror of light is love and harmony, the cohesive powers of the universes. As we pass in front of the light it reveals whom we truly are inside with our darkest secrets and hidden sins. As we see our failures, penance and love prepares us for the golden age of love and unity."

He looked out over the great mass of followers and smiled. "Our Mother Mary has a message for this day, Faithful Ones." His voice was like a tender father oozing words of love to his children as the final message of the Holy Mother from the Third Secret of Fatima rolled from his lips. The Mother of God our Queen of Heaven declares:

> "All authority has been given to me to lead you into under-
> standing and wisdom. Whoever makes himself willingly
> obedient unto the law of love and unity, has perfected life
> and together perfected this earth to prepare for the return of
> my son. My children, my little humble children, I appeal to
> you as your Mother, go forward on foot, knock on the doors;
> bring the light of love and unity to your brothers and sis-
> ters. Prepare the way! For as the angel told the disciples at
> my son's ascension, He will come back in the same way you
> have seen him go into heaven."

The Holy Father bowed his head and raised his hand in prayer: "Behold, as we stand before you, Queen of Heaven, before your Immaculate Heart, we desire together with the whole Church to unite ourselves with the consecration of love. The power of this consecration is for all people, tongues and nations as we unite as one, Amen."

As he concluded his prayer, the same miracle affirming the Marian apparition in Fatima, Portugal in 1917 repeated...the sun began to dance. The sun appeared as a pale, opaque sphere, entirely surrounded by a luminous circle. A very light cloud in front of it allowed the Faithful to look without the slightest bother to the eyes. The opaque sphere moved outward and backward, spinning from left to right and vice versa. Within the sphere, you could see movements with total clarity. As the sun danced, a vortex again appeared over Vatican City; in the center, it was spinning and enlarging. Shimmering, shooting lights encircled the Holy Mother as she emerged once again; this time with a smile of approval upon her face."

Gabriella jumped to her feet, pounding the cool stone floor. "It's a lie! It's all a pre-fabricated lie!"

Chris just shook his head. He had no words to describe his total disdain.

CHAPTER 41

G abriella and Chris rushed to the security room for the post-Papal comments. The sounds of evil chants were vibrating the airwaves. It was obvious that satanic praises were being offered for the mystical appearance of the Queen of Heaven and the supernatural dancing sun.

Sotoreo had remained at the lodge to monitor firsthand the brothers in action making sure every moment of step three was captured and aired worldwide. Now the most important media event of the Final Phase, so far, was only three days away and perfection had to be insured.

The UN President was congratulating the men with great accolades. "The spirit of Cybele, the Mother Goddess, reappeared right on time and very convincingly as the Virgin Mother. We have accomplished our objective. Pope Romanus is now the world's spiritual mediator and the Virgin Mary our spirit guide into the future. The dancing sun was the perfect miraculous sign from heaven to seal the deal...or to state it rightly, the sign from the parallel universe."

Gabriella interrupted from the bunker: "To state it rightly would be from the satanic universe." Her voice was shivering in animosity. "They have this deception right where they want it, even the elect would be deceived if it were possible. That Bible verse is truly coming to fruition."

"Who wouldn't believe a dancing sun?" Chris interjected. "People just automatically follow miraculous signs believing it's all good, never realizing Satan works miracles too."

"When, Chris? When do I start declaring the truth as one of The Chosen? I can't do anything from the prison of this bunker. I want people to know this is all a horrible demonic trap preparing for the Antichrist."

"For everything there is a time," he answered in a soothing voice. She was amazed at the spiritual understanding so quickly developing within him. She knew he was right but patience was not her best virtue.

She leaned back in her chair, folded her arms and grunted. "I'm tired of waiting. I want to do *something*."

"Patience, Gabi, patience. Yahweh is still in control."

She realized she needed Chris' voice of reason, wondering what she would have done had she been left in the bunker totally alone. She finally admitted, "Yes, He is still in control."

The next words from the lodge brought them back to full attention. Sotoreo had taken his place at the head of the table with the brothers in their respective seats. The celebration was over and it was back to planning the next step. His strong voice dominated the atmosphere: "The seclusion of the lodge has proven to be the perfect place for our mission. No one would suspect within the borders of Israel the media overrides are taking place."

A victorious smile covered the Pindar's face. "We expect to have a special visitor to our location tomorrow, The Pope himself." He hesitated and his smile was quickly replaced with a look of conquest. "He is meeting with the Israeli President in two days and will secretly visit with us beforehand to firm up some final details. I plan to stay here until after the unity festival and step four are both completed."

"The Black Pope?" Gabriella gasped. "Here?" It was beyond her comprehension.

"Well, well. Isn't this interesting?" Chris murmured. "We're about to get a front row seat to plans for the biggest spiritual deception ever known to man."

She shook her head in disbelief. "Of all the places in the world, my dad's lodge is headquarters for planning these evil events. This seems like a horrible dream...all these prophetic events...playing out right here before my very eyes..." Her head began to swim and dizziness came over her. The room went dark as she slumped back in her seat with her body feeling weightless.

Chris was engrossed in the lodge conversations and totally unaware of her condition. She tried to lift her hand and motion to him, but she could not move. Her eyes closed.

When she reopened her eyes, she was in her bed surrounded by her loved ones. They were all chattering at the same time and she had difficulty understanding anything being said. Among the babblings, she discerned some words and phrases: "The Black Pope, Queen of Heaven, rebuilding the temple, Gog and Magog, CERN." All the prophetic topics her father had written about were surrounding and closing in on her in a verbal onslaught. She looked from one face to the next. They were all staring at her with pleading expressions, their voices growing louder. "Listen, Gabi, listen."

"Stop!" She screamed, closing her eyes.

"Stop what?" Chris questioned in a puzzled voice.

Reopening her eyes, she was next to Chris in the security room. The voices were silent. The faces had disappeared. She shivered as strength gradually refilled her body.

Chris turned to face her. "Stop what, Gabi? Are you okay?" She did not answer but his eyes told her he knew. "Can I get you anything? Is there anything I can do?"

"No, thanks." She laid her head back and waited until the weakness totally passed, but she refused to close her eyes. Any one of those voices would have been endearing, but all of them together vehemently warning her was mentally overwhelming. She was beginning to question her emotional state. Maybe the bunker seclusion was having psychological affects she had not realized. Whatever it was, she knew something had to give.

She tried to force herself to listen to the conversations in the lodge as they reviewed plans for the upcoming festival but it was useless. "Doesn't seem to be anything new so I'm going to watch the news. It'll be interesting to see if Israeli News is covering The Vatican event."

She settled into the couch and turned on the TV, pushing the prophetic warnings temporarily from her thoughts. Channel 2 cameras were at the Temple Mount covering The Temple Institute's monumental event of laying the cornerstone to the new temple. Crowds were gathered celebrating; some were dancing, some singing and many had faces bowed with *tallitot* covering their heads praying for protection to rebuild their place of worship. To Gabriella's surprise a camera focused in on the face of Rabbi

Zimmerman. Aware he was a rabbi, the reporter asked his opinion of the historic event, having no idea this rabbi had a special message.

Zimmerman smiled and was of perfect composure as he addressed the nation of Israel with live feed which could not be edited. "Children of Jacob, the laying of this cornerstone heralds the most prophetic event of our day - the second coming of the Messiah. He came 2000 years ago as the suffering servant, Messiah ben Joseph; and will return soon as the King of Kings and Lord of Lords, Messiah ben David."

It was obvious the reporter had not yet discerned the Messianic content of the rabbi's message. Zimmerman was going to hit it with both barrels as long as the cameras were rolling. "Hear me, Oh Israel, there is salvation through the blood atonement of Yeshua, the son of the Living God, the Lamb slain from the foundations of the earth. By no other name can man be saved."

The reporter realized the anti-orthodox Jewish message and tried to interrupt. The rabbi continued to declare the Good News of salvation through the blood of Yeshua Ha-Mashiach, Jesus the Messiah. The reporter motioned for the cameraman to turn the feed off, but it would not disconnect and the message of salvation continued to saturate the airwaves until the Haifa newsroom internally disconnected from the live feed.

"Good for you, Rabbi Zimmerman!" Gabriella exclaimed. "Shout it from the rooftops and let the world know who is really Lord of Lords." Her voice turned to sorrow with the next words: "I'm stuck in this bunker and can't tell anyone." Agony poured afresh through her soul.

"What's going on?" Chris asked as he entered the kitchen area. "I could hear you over the monitors."

She relayed to him Zimmerman's declaration. "The big news of the day in Israel is not the Marian apparition or the dancing sun, they have laid the cornerstone for the new temple. The prophetic clock is ticking, Chris."

"Don't you think the timing is strange?" He questioned, joining her on the couch. "They lay the cornerstone two days before Pope Romanus is scheduled to meet with Israel's President? Seems like an act of defiance to me."

"I think The Temple Institute is definitely marking their territory," she agreed. "Professor Brotman told me years ago, The Vatican owns a huge amount of Israeli land. They have taken over land in Israel for centuries and leased it back to churches, homes and businesses. Ownership of the

Temple Mount has been in dispute for decades and The Vatican has tried to claim that territory, too. However, with Israel's new status of world dominance, everything has changed."

Then it dawned on her. "Step five of The Final Phase is to conquer Israel. Then the whole satanic lot of them plans to take over the land of the Abrahamic Covenant. However, the ancient prophets wrote when Israel is back in their homeland they would never be removed again. The Pindar's plan to take over Israel is going to get hijacked." Her voice took on a revelatory tone, "That's when something will happen to force a peace agreement between Israel and the Antichrist and when Israel will rebuild their temple. It has to be rebuilt for the Antichrist to sit in the Holy of Holies and declare himself as God..."

For several minutes, no words were spoken. Then Gabriella dryly stated: "And that is when the world will worship him and the third strand will be complete. Everyone with the third strand will have the DNA of Satan and will be damned for eternity."

Again, the room was silent. Each was captured by their individual thoughts.

Gabriella broke the silence and pushed herself from the couch. "I'm going to bed and try to get some rest. It should be a very interesting day tomorrow." She crossed the stone floor and paused at her bedroom door. "Who would have dreamed The Black Pope would be here in my dad's lodge?" She shook her long blonde curls in amazement and closed the door.

She turned off the light and settled into the bed, questioning if she really wanted rest or to relive time before the vanishings. She closed her eyes and pulled the comforter under her chin. The room was silent. Only the nightlight lit the room. She turned from side to side, restless and sleepless. Frustrated, she opened her eyes to the dim light. Gradually her eyes focused. Sleeping in the recliner close beside her was Caleb. His head was leaned back, his feet elevated, and his left hand lay on the bed next to her. She reached over and took his hand. His hand closed around hers but he did not awaken.

In the living room, she could hear voices. Professor Brotman's voice was growing in volume. "The apparitions of Mary and The Black Pope's demonic miracles will deceive the nations. Then the Antichrist will appear in the clouds. He will come in like manner as Jesus ascended into heaven. He will claim to be The Messiah. Because of the miracles, signs and wonders, the people will believe and be deceived. Only the elect will not be deceived."

She tried to get out of bed, to go to her friends and tell them it was already happening. Everything the Professor was telling them was true; but no other muscles would move, only her hand around Caleb's. She could feel sleep capturing her and gently squeezed his hand. She desperately desired to let him know she was awake. His eyes opened and he leaned toward the bed. She closed her eyes and waited for his lips to touch hers. The touch never came. She reopened her eyes. Caleb had disappeared and the voice of the Professor was silenced.

She closed her eyes, passionately hoping to feel Caleb's embrace and pierce the veil between time and untime.

CHAPTER 42

———◆•◆•◆———

G abriella looked at the clock: it was 7:00 AM. Today The Black Pope would arrive. The anticipation was too great to relax so she jumped out of bed, quickly dressed and joined Chris.

"Gonna be a big couple of days, Gabi," he commented. "Channel 2 is reporting tomorrow's meeting between the Israeli President and Pope Romanus. Seems everyone is very curious as to what this is all about." Chris handed her a mug of coffee. "No one is stirring in the lodge this morning. We have a little time before the action begins. Were you able to sleep?"

She sipped the hot brew and rested her head on the couch, debating if she should tell Chris about her night's encounter with Caleb. She decided it better not to do so. "If you can call tossing and turning restful. There's just too much happening for my mind to rest...day or night."

Their attention was drawn to the TV when Rabbi Adler made another appearance with News Anchor Adelson who was questioning him on the temple cornerstone.

The rabbi's face was filled with joy. "This is the greatest event since Israel was reborn as a nation. This means our Messiah will soon appear. When the temple is complete, He will arrive. It has been almost 2000 years since our temple was destroyed and today we see prophecy being fulfilled." The joy in his face drained with his next comment. "But it will not be without major obstacles. The Vatican insists they control the Temple Mount."

Adelson nodded in agreement. "I have no doubt this will be addressed in the meeting tomorrow between our President and Pope Romanus."

Adler quickly agreed and continued his exposé: "Russia and her cohorts want our riches, the Roman Catholic Church wants our holy sites, and the UN wants to control our nation. We have become a burdensome stone to all the world."

"He is right about that," Gabriella injected. "The Zechariah 12:3 prophecy is fulfilled."

The security system signaled activity and the duo scrambled to the monitors. Russo and Moretti were preparing brunch for the men with much pomp and circumstance. The brothers were starting to gather for coffee and excited morning chatter. It was with great anticipation everyone, both in the lodge and in the bunker below, awaited Pope Romanus' arrival.

Strozza shortly joined the men with an outline of what the day would hold. "His Holiness flew into Israel last night. He will be arriving here shortly. We will review with him plans for step four before Sotoreo and I have a private meeting with him in the cottage."

Chris' eyes automatically went to the monitors of the cottage interior. "I better run tests to make sure the video and audio are ready for that meeting."

Gabriella knew he was talking more to himself than to her. "I'll make some more coffee and let you work." She exited the security room, allowing him space and quiet time to be prepared for what would soon prove to be the most elucidative of all information they had heretofore been privy to.

Shortly before noon, the black limousine pulled through the gated entrance with security SUVs both in front and behind the limo. Gabriella and Chris watched the monitors as the three vehicles came up the curvy, gravel road to the entrance of the lodge. There stood Sotoreo in the front of the delegation that would welcome The Black Pope. Directly behind him stood Strozza, Moretti, and Russo. The brothers waited at the door.

The security team exited first, affirming the area was secure. The man apparently in charge of security stepped to the limo door and opened it, helping The Black Pope to exit. First to be seen was the long, white robe. As he stood up, Romanus' face came into view.

Gabriella unwittingly shuddered. "The vilest man on the planet is now on my father's private property. This is a nightmare."

Sotoreo took his hand, kneeling and kissing the ring on his finger. He introduced the three men behind him which followed the etiquette set forth by their Pindar. The brothers followed suit. Sotoreo opened the massive wood double door to the lodge entryway allowing His Holiness to enter first, followed closely by his bodyguards and then by the lodge occupants. The security team surrounded the lodge premises.

When The Black Pope entered the lodge, he paused. He looked directly at Sotoreo. "Pindar, are you positively sure this place is secure? I am detecting a strange vibration."

The bunker duo once again felt the threat of being detected. Gabriella prayed for supernatural angelic protection from the evil forces and immediately the familiar Presence of The Lord filtered through the security room and they both relaxed. "We're okay," she assured Chris.

Sotoreo confirmed all was well. "We have surveyed the area completely, inch by inch. There is no one else here. I felt it, also, when I first arrived. I believe it is from the many years of this building being inhabited by those Messianic Jews. It has left a negative vibration."

Romanus closed his eyes trying to determine the nature of the unwanted vibrations. He held his hand up for silence. Momentarily he dropped his hand. "Perhaps you are right." He looked around the lodge and announced: "I'm ready for a tour of this magnificent structure."

Pope Romanus was highly impressed with the command center choice. He stopped at the window displaying the panoramic view of Mt. Hermon. For several minutes, he gazed as in a trance muttering abstruse phrases. Eerily the noon sun illuminated the apex of Mt. Hermon and filtered through the huge window, framing the profile of The Black Pope in an ominous glow. He stood as if frozen in the esoteric sunlight.

"That's just plain weird," Chris muttered. Gabriella was awestruck, unable to speak.

For several minutes the sun continued to bask upon The Unholy Father, then the shining rays slowly withdrew. He turned with a nefarious expression and addressed the men: "I am honored to be here, in this location." He pointed to the top of Mt. Hermon. "On that mountain top it all began. It was the first portal of entry for our brothers who are being held in captivity."

The vile chanting erupted and continued until Romanus held up his hand for silence. With a diabolical smile, he ceremoniously announced: "Soon they will be released."

Gabriella felt as if a sledgehammer had hit her stomach. She struggled to get the words to her lips. "The Omega Watchers, Chris. That's what he's talking about. The release of the fallen angels held in captivity until the end days."

Chris slumped back in his chair. "We knew this was coming, but to hear this evil man announce it is too surreal."

Gabriella dropped her head in her hands, shaking her long curls. "For over a decade I listened to Professor Brotman explain this would happen. You know our team worked with him on ancient archeological proof verifying the writings of the biblical prophets. And when we finally found it, the team all vanished. It was too late. Now in real time, this man considered to be the most holy man on earth is calling the fallen angels his brothers. God help us!" She continued to shake her head in unbelief. "What's even worse...he is right here in my father's lodge where the Professor and my team would review and discuss research for hours on end. This is a nightmare."

Gabriella and Chris tried to push their raging emotions to the side and concentrate on the lodge conversations. Romanus congratulated the men on their tremendous cyber abilities and briefly discussed the upcoming unity festival, giving his assurance the brothers would make sure all would go as planned.

After brunch and polite conversation, The Black Pope, Sotoreo, and Strozza held a private meeting in the cottage. Chris had the monitors ready to follow every movement and record every word.

The quaint structure was rustic, cozy and inviting. Gabriella's father had updated the conveniences but left it much as it was when the property was purchased to preserve the nostalgia. The three men settled in chairs surrounding the stone fireplace. The bodyguards remained outside the door. This conversation was to be heard only by these three men.

Gabriella sighed deeply. "I haven't told you this, Chris, but dad wrote in the last letter contained in his research box that I was conceived in that cottage when he and mom were here in Israel on sabbatical. It's the same cottage they rented while living here for a year. That's the reason he bought this property and personally lived there instead of in the massive lodge he built for our team's private getaways. He wrote when he was in the cottage he felt close to both Momma and me even though we were no longer in his life."

Chris looked at her in disbelief. "And you are just now telling me this?"

"It was too personal, a timeless secret between just me and my dad. It made no difference to what our mission is."

He felt convicted of his reaction. "You're right, I'm sorry. You have no reason to share with me the intimate details of your life. I do feel honored you did though." He took her hand and gently squeezed. "You're very special to me, Gabi, and I would do anything for you. I would protect you with my very life."

"I know," she whispered. She did not know how prophetic his words were.

They focused their attention back to the monitors displaying the activity in the cottage. Moretti had brought a tray of coffee from the lodge and quickly departed. The three most powerful men on earth were alone and ready to begin the final plans which Gabriella and Chris would soon have privy to.

Sotoreo began the conversation with discussion on the upcoming festival and the beginning of the implants. He explained how the music would be hypnotic and capture the minds of listeners.

"The messages through music will be hypnotic. And," Sotoreo looked directly at The Black Pope, "your video address along with another appearance from our Queen of Heaven will be the crowing points of seduction. The world will soon be ready to welcome our Ascended Master."

Romanus smiled and nodded. "For millenniums, our brothers have been preparing for the time our AM would reign upon this earth. I am honored to be the mediator heralding his coming. Tomorrow when I meet with the Israeli President I will make sure plans for rebuilding his temple are escalated. The Temple Institute believes they are rebuilding for their Messiah." He chuckled at the thought. "Little do they know."

Strozza questioned the bargaining powers The Vatican would use. "How can you be so sure they'll cooperate with you?"

Again, Romanus smiled. This time it was obvious he had a well-kept bargaining secret. "We have enough to bring them begging at our door." The Pindar obviously also knew the mystery; however, Strozza was very much in the dark.

Ugo Strozza's gaze was piercing. "Well? Is someone going to let me in on the mystery? I am the World Intelligence Director, you know." He tried to force a laugh, but it was obvious he was irritated.

Pope Romanus' voice transformed into an extremely serious tone. The jesting was behind and the business was now serious. He put down his coffee cup and straightened in his chair, leaning towards Strozza. "I am going to give you a history lesson, my brother. One that has been lost both to The Church and to the world as a whole over two millenniums of time; but this hidden knowledge has not been lost to the hierarchy of the Knights Templar who have held and protected the secret treasures."

Strozza leaned forward in anticipation. "Treasures?"

"Yes, *great* treasures." The Pope punctuated. "In 70 AD the Roman General Titus conquered Jerusalem which included the destruction of Israel's Temple. As part of the spoils of war, all the temple treasures were taken back to Rome. Everything the Jewish Priests needed for their sacrifices and worship became the possession of the Emperor."

Pope Romanus took a sip from his cup and carefully replaced it on the table before continuing: "As the Empire of Rome fell and The Roman Catholic Church became the dominating power of Europe, all spoils of war became the property of The Roman Diocese. The Jew's temple treasures were safely hidden in the catacombs below The Vatican and closely guarded through the centuries by The 33rd Knights Templar. The treasures are still there today. Very few know of their existence. You can imagine what Israel would be willing to give - or do - for their return."

Strozza slumped back in his chair and momentarily gazed at the fire before answering. "I would imagine they would give or do anything."

"Exactly." Pope Romanus folded his arms in victory.

Sotoreo had been silent through the conversation but reiterated the most important factor. "Israel *will* rebuild their temple. Their priceless temple vessels will be returned to them. BUT! Our AM will take possession and sit upon the throne in the Holy of Holies..."

The Black Pope finished his sentence, "and the whole world will worship him."

Strozza thought as an Elite 33rd he knew all the secrets; obviously, he did not. He pondered for a moment wondering if he should ask. Then he pressed further: "One more question. Does The Vatican also have possession of the Ark of the Covenant? Was that taken with the other temple treasures?"

The Pope's face changed from victorious to frustrated. "The Ark of the Covenant was not in the temple during the 70 AD destruction. In fact,

The Ark had been removed and hidden sometime before 598 BC when Nebuchadnezzar invaded Jerusalem and destroyed Solomon's Temple. The King took the temple treasures to Babylon but the Ark of the Covenant was never found. All the temple treasures were returned to Israel under King Cyrus almost a century later. The Ark remained hidden and was never in the second temple. The Holy of Holies in the second temple sat empty for over 400 years, until it's destruction."

The Pope smiled as he revealed the deception upon the Jewish people. "For centuries, the Jewish people believed The Ark of the Covenant was in their rebuilt temple abiding in the Holy of Holies where their High Priest atoned for their sins. Only the High Priest could enter the Holy of Holies and he alone knew the truth."

The now familiar malevolent smile curved The Black Pope's lips. "I believe the tribe of Levi knows the location of The Ark and plans to restore it to the rebuilt temple. However, it will not be needed. When the temple is rebuilt the rightful one will sit upon the throne in the Holy of Holies... our Ascended Master, our AM!"

In the bunker Gabriella and Chris sat in amazement. They both knew the bargaining value of the temple treasures and Israel's determination to rebuild their temple. "More pieces to the prophetic puzzle, Chris." Gabriella contemplated. "They plan for Israel to rebuild the temple for them while they are implanting people in preparation for their Ascended Master. When the time is right, the UN will somehow manipulate Russia to attack Israel, knowing Israel can wipe out both Russia and the Muslim nations joined with her. However, the attacks will leave Israel weakened and in threat of a UN takeover which will open peace negotiations."

Chris got up and began pacing back and forth in the security room summing up the obvious: "The new world leader will arrive pretending to be a friend to Israel. He will confirm the Abrahamic Covenant guaranteeing peace and allowing Israel to keep the expanded territories. Then using the temple treasures as a bargaining tool, the seven-year peace treaty will be signed assuring Israel will be protected to rebuild the temple."

Gabriella took a deep breath, exhaled slowly and stated reluctantly. "Then in the middle of the peace agreement the Antichrist just waltzes in to the Holy of Holies, sits down and proclaims himself as god. The world will already have the implant and as each person worships the False Messiah, who is Satan incarnate, the third strand is complete."

Chris sat down in his chair with a thump. "Only the elect will be saved: those who have hidden the Word of Yahweh in their hearts, refused to worship the False Messiah and will not receive his mark."

CHAPTER 43

The trio of men continued their plans for the Final Phase in the cottage behind the lodge. Chris was recording every word.

The meeting ended with Sotoreo reviewing plans for step four, the Tomorrow's Land Unity Festival. "In three days, the implants begin. Once the implementations are complete and our AM appears, the brothers will shut down the internet, satellite feeds, cell phones...all forms of communication. Our AM will then activate the implants which will be the new source of *all* communications and business transactions with a password issued only to those in allegiance to him. It will be three sequences of six; six numbers, six symbols, and six letters -- 666." He laughed out loud at the planned deception. "Each person will have a unique password which will be their international identity. Without it, survival will be almost impossible. In fact, we will make sure of it."

Pope Romanus stood up and looked out the cottage window which displayed a magnificent view of Mt. Hermon. The sun was going down, casting ominous shadows across the Golan Heights. His voice was just as arcane as the view as he uttered the words, "And when we promise them perfect health, youth and a life without death...," he turned and faced his companions, "who would deny themselves the utopian life?"

The three men all held up their hands with fingers parted and chanted a satanic praise. With their evil plans complete the UN President, the Cabal Pindar and The Black Pope made the short journey back to the lodge where The Pope made his departure to Jerusalem. The security monitors followed the trio of vehicles until they exited the gated entrance and disappeared.

"Well, that explains a lot." Gabriella commented. "I've heard every possible scenario of the mysterious 666 Antichrist mark, all of which made no sense at all, until now. Unless people are warned, they will have no idea what's happening. We must tell them, Chris. Somehow we have to tell them!"

He put his arm around her shoulder trying to comfort her, but it was obvious she was too irate. She pulled away and excused herself. "I'm going to my room. I need some time for all of this to process." She briefly hugged him so he would know her emotions were not aimed at him. Then she was gone.

Chris stayed in the security room to monitor the lodge conversations in case anything new developed. He knew she needed her alone time.

Gabriella collapsed on her bed and buried her face in the pillows. She cried out in prayer: "Oh, God, how much longer? I need to warn my people." She spent hours in supplication until her strength had drained and a fatigued sleep captured her. When she opened her eyes, The Prophet was standing by her bedside. She slipped to the floor and bowed before him waiting for his words of wisdom and warmth of the anointing oil upon her head.

"Daughter of Zebulon, you have proven yourself faithful and submitted to your calling as a Chosen One, no matter the cost. You have been given a prophetic glimpse into the future and you know the traps being laid by the vile ones. Daughter, you are being prepared to be a voice of truth crying to your people Israel. Do not be confused by the turn your life is about to take. It is part of the divine plan."

The Prophet touched her forehead and she felt the warmth of the oil. "I will not fear," she vowed to him.

She spent the next three days in prayer and fasting for her people Israel. She was questioning what major change was about to occur in her life. She anticipated the evil that would be released from the unity festival, but did not feel that was what The Prophet meant. Was she going to lose Chris and be on her own? Was he warning her so she would not fear? She shuddered at the very thought of not having Chris beside her, and she knew this visitation was not one she could share with him.

Through the three nights, she continued to hear the voices of her loved ones pleading with her to wake up. She could hear her father as he sat by her bed and read his prophetic letters out loud to her. When she would awaken in the mornings, her room would be empty of both sound and presence. She felt drained as though sleep never came.

Finally, the day of the Tomorrow's Land Unity Festival arrived. At sundown, the vile seduction would begin. At the exact time, Israel began *Shemini Atzeret*, the holy eighth day ending the Feast of Tabernacles. The evil trio had planned this specific day to begin the convergence.

The brothers in the lodge were at the height of activity making sure all media would be perfect. Chris was monitoring their every move, while Gabriella watched WIN TV and the preparations for the opening ceremony. Tens of thousands were already at the festival site and had received their implants. The camera zoomed in on the registration process showing attendees celebrating as they were being microchipped. One group of festival attendees held up their implanted hands in front of the camera, proudly displaying the small red spots where the chips had been inserted.

Spellbinding music was already saturating the air. The day would be full of pagan rituals performed all around the festival countryside, releasing demonic spirits from the dark dimension. By the time sunset arrived, Gabriella felt she had been inundated with wickedness. Consistently through the day she prayed for the protection of the Holy Spirit.

Chris joined her as the sun started to set. Before the festival began they prayed together, pleading the blood of Yeshua over their minds knowing evil was going to permeate the airwaves. Together they watched the gigantic screen in the Italian countryside swirl with magnificent colors. Fireworks were exploding around the screen. The spinning colors morphed into the Hadron Collider at CERN. It continued the soporific rotation with hypnotic music vibrating and echoing through the festival area. All minds were seductively being brought into a mesmeric control.

The swirling collider became a vortex of gyrating lights in the midst of which appeared The Queen of Heaven. "Come with me," she beckoned. "Gaze into the alternate dimensions of time and space." Behind her was a place more beautiful than words could describe - mountains with waterfalls cascading through brilliant colors and flowers of unspeakable beauty with hues not known to planet earth.

Gabriella caught her breath. "Summerland," she whispered.

"What?" Chris questioned. "What's Summerland?"

"Arcturus took me there in one of our mystical night journeys. He said it was the higher plane of rest for those who had passed over. A place where souls reflect on their earthly deeds and then return for karma balance to eventually reach perfection. It's all part of the deception into believing there is no heaven and hell."

Chris' voice was edgy when he replied. "I have to admit, it is really convincing."

She shot him a questioning look. "Chris!"

"Not that I mean I am falling for it," he assured her. "But for those not knowing the truth, well, I can see how captivating this is."

The seductive scenes continued to vibrate from the giant screens. All around the world groups were gathered to watch the festival in unison and all feeling the mind-altering effects.

As The Queen of Heaven faded into the vortex, her voice cried out, "Behold, my son!" Appearing beside her was a brilliant, shining image clothed in white robes and sitting upon a white horse. The vortex closed and both vanished.

The screen went dark. All music ceased. Only a hypnotizing drumbeat could be heard. On the big screen a silhouette appeared. The entrancing beat continued as The Black Pope emerged from the silhouette. In a magnetizing voice, he addressed the world: "My little sheep, I am your Shepherd as we cross the threshold into a new world. Tonight, we have had another glimpse into the parallel universe which we have known as heaven."

The crowd roared in excitement until Pope Romanus held up his hand for silence. "The Virgin Mary has chosen me to be the mediator between the two universes and prepare for the coming of the one who will be the embodiment of love and unity...her son. All religions across the planet have revered The Holy Mother of Earth. We have called her by different names, but we all know her. She is our salvation, and in her we come together, laying aside all religiosity standing between us. As we unite we open the portal between the universes allowing our Master to come and our Holy Mother to pardon us and lead us to perfection."

The Black Pope held his hands above his head and cried out: "Unity of all mankind!"

Reverberating through the countryside was the thunderous voices of tens of thousands. "Unity! Unity! Unity!"

Celebration continued all though the night. The entire festival had become a love fest of hugs. Attendees greeted each other, displaying acceptance of everyone regardless of race or religion. The giant screens replayed over and over the spinning of the CERN collider, the message from The Queen of Heaven, and the brief appearance of her son. In the background, the music continued to seduce the minds of every listener.

"I've had enough," Gabriella stated. "We know their plan, we know what they've started and we know what the outcome will be. The stage has been set for the false messiah to descend from the alternate universe bringing peace to all the earth. Yeshua Jesus went up in the clouds and disappeared into the heavens. He said he would return the same way. However, the false messiah will come first, pretending to be the son of Mary the savior of the world."

"And the world will be amazed and worship him." Chris continued her thought, turning off the TV. "You're right, Gabi, everything is now in place."

They sat silent, hand in hand. Both felt they were at a junction in the road, but neither was sure where it was taking them.

CHAPTER 44

⬛━━━◆◆◆◆━━━⬛

C hris and Gabriella returned to the security room to watch the reaction of the brothers to the 'successful" unity festival. As expected, a huge celebration was taking place. The Cabal Pindar was basking in the glory of the convergence genesis.

"We are on the home stretch now, brothers." His voice was on the edge of euphoria. "Nothing can stop us now!" He was about to sit down in the Professor's chair by the fireplace when he came to an abrupt stop. He closed his eyes and put his hands over his ears. For several moments, he did not move. He dropped his hands and his eyes shot open, darting all around the area.

"What's going on?" Gabriella whispered.

"I have no idea," Chris answered in a husky voice, but his police instincts told him something was not right. They waited with bated breath.

Fury filled Sotoreo's eyes. "There is a hostile presence in this place. I can feel it!"

Russo and Moretti jumped to attention and drew their guns. "Where, Pindar? Where?"

He closed his eyes again in deep meditation then pointed towards the kitchen. "There," he instructed. Moretti and Russo ran to the kitchen while the brothers followed close behind. The room was empty. The men looked at their Pindar, questioning.

Immediately Chris inserted a flash drive in the security computer and began to download all the files from the monitors. Gabriella could see the impatience in Chris' eyes as he watched both the monitor and the percentage of download. She was holding her breath praying the secret pantry door would not be found.

Sotoreo walked to the kitchen and again closed his eyes and covered his ears, as if waiting for telepathic instructions. Without opening his eyes, he moved towards the pantry.

"Oh God, Oh God," Gabriella begin to cry. "He's going to find us. What do we do, Chris?"

The download was complete. He thrust the flash drive in her left hand. "Run, Gabi. Go through the storage room and into the cave. Close the secret door and wait for me. I'll try to barricade the door from inside to give us a little time to get through the cave and to the Jeep." He pushed her towards the door. "If I'm not there in a few minutes, go without me. Whatever you do, don't let go of the flash drive."

"No, Chris! I won't leave without you. Where would I go? You'll get out, I know you will. Hurry! I'll wait for you."

"If I don't get to you, Gabi, go to Detective Richards. He'll be the safest person for you. Give him the flash drive."

"You'll make it, Chris." You *have to* make it, she thought. Gabriella turned and ran toward the kitchen, through the pantry and opened the hidden door leading to the cave. She kept her fist clenched protecting the flash drive as she fumbled for flashlights. Exiting into the cave she knew the evil men had found the secret pantry door to the bunker - she heard footsteps rushing down the wooden stairway. Loud voices were muting as the cave door was closing behind her. The sound of gunshots filled the bunker before the secret passageway clicked closed and silence filled the cave.

"NO!" She was about to scream, but put her hand over her mouth to silence her own words. "Help me, God, what do I do?" Gabriella started to run for safety. It was hard to see in the muted light and she kept stumbling over fallen rocks. Briefly hesitating, she listened for sounds behind her. The cave was as silent as the grave. Gabriella knew they had not found the hidden exit in the bunker storage room.

She held the flashlight in front of her making her way through the tunnel. She paused one more time, desperately hoping to hear Chris' voice calling to her and praying he somehow made it out alive. An eerie silence filled the cave and panic gripped her. She began to run with all of her strength. She was almost to the cave exit when her toe caught under a rock. Losing her balance, she fell forward. A sharp pain shot through her head and everything went black.

When Gabriella opened her eyes, she was back in her bunker bedroom and Detective Richards was standing over her.

"He's dead, isn't he?" She mumbled, barely able to speak from weakness.

"Who's dead?" Richards asked.

"Chris, of course. They killed him. I thought they would kill me, too."

"Who killed him?" The detective's voice was filled with confusion.

"She's hallucinating." A strange voice said. "She's been drifting in and out for days. Sometimes she knows she's here and other times her mind tells her she's living a totally different life.

Gabriella was too weak to keep her eyes open. Half awake and half asleep, she was unable to discern reality from dreams. The voices of all those she loved surrounded her; even Chris' voice was in the mix. "I must be dreaming," she thought. "This can't be real."

Gabriella tried to force her eyes open but the light was too painful. She listened to the sounds of the room in an effort to separate the worlds of truth and memory.

"I think Gabi will be alright now," the strange voice spoke again. "She just needs rest and nutrition."

The familiar hand gently clasped her right hand and pulled it to his face. "I knew she would be. I knew it! Thank God, it's not too late."

Her soft hand closed around his. "I thought you were gone forever," she managed to whisper.

"I told you I would never leave you." His tender voice cut deep into her soul.

"I know, but..." her voice faded in weakness. Again, Gabriella tried to open her eyes but the light was too bright and she could not focus.

The voice of Detective Richards filled the room: "This area is secure and safe now. There is nothing to worry about. The world is in chaos after the war but Israel has not only won the war, but also conquered all the nations surrounding her. The whole world has changed while you've been secluded in this bunker."

Her mind was spinning as she was thinking to herself. "What was he talking about? Of course, they knew the world had changed. Chris had talked to Detective Richards when they went to police headquarters. Why is everything so confused?" Her mind was spinning and head pounding as she tried to bring coherency to the conversations.

Detective Richards continued with instructions: "It's safe to leave the bunker now. You can take Gabriella to a hospital, if needed."

"No." She managed to push the words from her mouth. "Those evil men are looking for me."

"Her mind is playing tricks on her again," the unfamiliar voice of Dr. Nicholson stated. "I really don't know where she is mentally, but as I studied similar cases the hallucinations are usually influenced by what a person hears around them while in a comatose state. In their minds, they slide back and forth from one reality to another."

"Gabi, wake up. Can you look at me?" The loving voice was again encouraging her to open her eyes. Her surroundings, the conversations - Gabriella was in complete perplexity. What she was hearing, could it be real? Her heart was begging for it to be true but her previous reality was tempering her joy.

Finally, her eyes focused. "Dad!" She looked to the right side of the bed to the familiar hand holding hers. "Caleb!" She closed her eyes one more time, opening them to a world of dubiety.

Gabriella's father leaned over the bed and wrapped her in his arms. His voice was shaking, overcome with emotion. "Thank you, Yahweh, *thank you*! I have looked in the beautiful blue eyes of my daughter one more time." For Gabriella, it was a dream come true - to feel her father's embrace just one more time.

Reluctantly her father released her allowing Caleb to take Gabriella in his strong arms. She rested her head on his chest and whispered the words he had prayed to hear, "I love you, Caleb. I always have, I always will."

All of Gabriella's loved ones surrounded her bed. Rejoicing through tears were Professor Brotman, Aaron, Faith, Sandee and KJ.

The voice of The Prophet rang in her ears: *Daughter of Zebulon, you have been given a prophetic glimpse into the future and you know the traps being laid by the vile ones. Daughter, you are being prepared to be a voice of truth crying to your people Israel. Do not be confused by the turn your life is about to take. It is part of the divine plan.*

Standing in the doorway she could see Officer Chris Harris staring into her eyes with a knowing smile. Her left hand remained clinched. The flash drive was still firmly in her possession.

Her only conclusion...time and untime had merged.